Praise for Wayne Johnston and

𝒜 WORLD ELSEWHERE

#1 NATIONAL BESTSELLER
Winner of the Writers' Trust Engel/Findley Award
Nominated for the Scotiabank Giller Prize
A *Globe and Mail* Best Book
A Chapters/Indigo Best Book

"A brilliant and accomplished writer."　　　　　　Annie Proulx

"Wayne Johnston spins wonderful stories; he is a gather-you-round-and-I-will-enchant-you raconteur. . . . Johnston's fiction is subtle, his passion understated, his humour underpinned by tragedy. All of his work, superbly written, is a powerful combination of insight, talent and revelation. It is made to endure."
　　　　　　Writers' Trust Engel/Findley Award jury citation

"Fans of . . . *The Colony of Unrequited Dreams* will love this one."
　　　　　　The Telegram

"*A World Elsewhere* marks perhaps his greatest achievement in conveying the emotional state and psychology of tackling one's past and culture."
　　　　　　Telegraph-Journal

"Wayne Johnston is a wondrous writer—of rich, irresistibly readable prose. He possesses a deft intelligence and a rare sense of what's truly interesting to tell about life."　　　　　　Richard Ford

"Why I love reading Wayne Johnston: . . . [his] stories have characters who move in and take up permanent residence."　　　　　　Mary Walsh

"Biting wit and brilliant puns. . . . Worth the attention of anyone who delights in Johnston's imagination and the riches of the English language."
　　　　　　Ottawa Citizen

"His books are beautifully written, among the funniest I've ever read, yet somehow at the same time among the most poignant and moving."

Annie Dillard

"Riveting, muscular prose carries spellbound readers along."

Quill & Quire

"A literary giant who has god-given talent." Will Ferguson

"Always engrossing and moves swiftly forward. . . . All the characters are fascinating and complex and the plot offers plenty of surprises."

Here (New Brunswick)

"A masterful storyteller with larger-than-life characters who imprint themselves on your consciousness. . . . An intricate yarn."

The Sun Times (Owen Sound)

"Compelling. . . . Characteristic of a Johnston novel is playful language and word play. . . . Reminiscent of P. G. Wodehouse, James Joyce and G. K. Chesterton." *Scotia Today*

"Johnston has strong descriptive talents. His depiction of Vanderland is masterful." *The London Free Press*

"Written with Johnston's accustomed verve and humour."

National Post

"I've said many times that Canadian novelists are too obsessed with the past and ought to get with the urban present, but I'm fine if Wayne Johnston sticks to his period pieces. His fictionalized stories . . . are gripping portrayals of ambition." *NOW* (Toronto)

A WORLD ELSEWHERE

A WORLD ELSEWHERE

WAYNE JOHNSTON

Vintage Canada

St. Charles Manor

Jane
Claire

VINTAGE CANADA EDITION, 2012

Published in Canada by Vintage Canada, a division of Random House of Canada Limited, Toronto, in 2012. Originally published in hardcover in Canada by Alfred A. Knopf Canada, a division of Random House of Canada Limited, in 2011. Distributed by Random House of Canada Limited.

Vintage Canada with colophon is a registered trademark.

www.randomhouse.ca

This book is a work of fiction. Names, characters, places and incidents either are the product of the author's imagination or are used fictitiously.

Library and Archives Canada Cataloguing in Publication

Johnston, Wayne
A world elsewhere / Wayne Johnston.

ISBN 978-0-307-39991-5

I. Title.

PS8569.O3918W67 2012   C813'.54   C2011-902231-1

Text and cover design by Terri Nimmo

Image credits: (figures on beach) © Michael Trevillion, (porthole) © P. Eoche/Stock Image/Getty Images

Printed and bound in the United States of America

2 4 6 8 9 7 5 3 1

In loving memory of my Mom and Dad:
Jennie Johnston and Arthur Johnston.

Author's Note

I WAS INSPIRED TO WRITE *A World Elsewhere* after a series of extended visits to the most fabled palace of the Gilded Age, Biltmore, which took hold of my imagination. The young George Washington Vanderbilt II built his massive house, instantly world famous, not in or near New York or Rhode Island, but in the wilderness of North Carolina in the late 1800s, and I have attempted to recreate its eccentric, enigmatic grandeur in my novel. Many, if not all, its structural details will be recognized by visitors today. Biltmore still stands essentially as it was originally created by two of the greatest architects of its time, Richard Morris Hunt, who died just months after its completion, and Frederick Law Olmsted, who also designed Central Park in Manhattan. It is now a self-supporting tourist estate run by George Vanderbilt's great-grandson, William Amherst Cecil.

I have drawn on the historical existence of George Vanderbilt, his ancestors, his wife, Edith, and their only child, their daughter, Cornelia, but none of them are models for their counterparts in *A World Elsewhere*: the actions, words and thoughts of these counterparts are not those of the Vanderbilts but are fictions. However, since Biltmore would not have existed without George Vanderbilt, I believe it would have been disingenuous of me to wholly alter the family surname of my characters. I have borrowed from a great writer who was also inspired by the Vanderbilts, and called my family "the Vanderluydens," after the Vanderbilt-like Van der Luydens of Edith Wharton's novel *The Age of Innocence*. Edith Wharton was a friend of George Vanderbilt, as was Henry James. Both of them visited him and appear as characters in *A World Elsewhere* as guests at Vanderland, the Biltmore-like house of my book.

A WORLD ELSEWHERE

Dark Marsh Road

LANDISH DRUKEN LIVED in the two-room attic of a house near the end of Dark Marsh Road that was in no way remindful of any other place he'd ever lived. A mile away, in a twelve-room house, his father lived alone.

Under the terms of what Landish called the Sartorial Charter, his father had let him keep his clothes but had otherwise disowned him. When he was too hungry and sober to sleep, he walked the edge of the marsh in the dark, smoking the last of his cigars, following the road to where it narrowed to a path that led into the woods.

He had gone to Princeton, where father-made men spent father-made fortunes. Now they were back home, learning the modern form of alchemy, the transmutation of sums of money into greater sums of money. He'd told them that this was, at best, all they would ever accomplish. "Whereas," he'd said, "I will write a book that will put in their places everyone who has ever lived. It may take me as long as a month, but I will not falter."

It was five years since he'd made the boast and he'd yet to write a word that he could resist the urge to burn.

He'd had but one real friend at Princeton, Padgett Vanderluyden, who went by Van. They'd met while Landish was sitting on one of the benches that ran along both sides of the path that led from the centre of the quad to the steps of Nassau Hall, smoking a cigar under a gauntlet of oak trees from which a steady shower of leaves fell despite the lack of wind. Van had sat down beside him.

Landish's first impressions had been vague ones—pale, thin, elegantly dressed. He turned and saw his benchmate in profile: a pale, unblemished face, the sort of vein-marbled temples Landish had always associated with fragility and even weakness in men. Removing a cigarette case from inside his coat, the young man opened it and offered it to Landish until he noticed his cigar. His hands shook so badly he almost dropped the case.

"You've chosen the only occupied bench on the quad," Landish said.

The fellow held his cigarette between his third and fourth fingers, pressing his whole palm against his face as he inhaled. His body shook and his lips trembled though the day was unseasonably warm. Landish wondered if he might be ill.

"I'm Padgett Vanderluyden," he said as he looked away from Landish. "Van, I like to be called. And you are Landish Druken. I hope you don't like to go by 'Lan.' That wouldn't do. Van and Lan." He attempted to laugh but wound up coughing smoke out through his nose and mouth.

Landish, the back-of-beyonder who scored unaccountably high grades in all his courses but was not, and was never to be, affiliated with any of the clubs, had been sought out by a Vanderluyden. *Vanderluyden.* Landish felt like demanding that the fellow prove it by presenting his credentials.

But then Van made the first of several odd admissions: he had stayed up half the night rehearsing what he would say to Landish.

"I didn't want to come unarmed. But I've forgotten everything that I rehearsed."

"You stayed up all night preparing to meet me?"

"Yes, I did."

"It was smart of you to choose a battle of wits. If you'd used your hands, you might not be nearly so gracious, or conscious, in defeat."

"You see? How am I supposed to answer that?"

Van's voice quavered so badly that Landish felt a tinge of regret for having spoken to him as he had. He extended his hand and Van shook it.

Van next told him that his sister, Vivvie, had died just shy of the age of two. "I had a breakdown over it. I'm thought by everyone, including my father, to be inherently given to breaking down. My father once told me that I would be presumed guilty until I was pronounced dead. Here you are now conspicuously sharing a bench with me in front of witnesses."

"Guilty of what? Witnesses to what?"

Van told him he was joking.

"Well, at least you acknowledge having parents. Most of the fellows here never speak of whatever predecess pool they crawled out of."

"All night I tried and could not come up with one line as good as that. I am not only not quick-witted—I have no wit at all."

"You're very forthright," Landish said. "Sometimes it takes more nerve to be forthright than to be wittily ironic. I keep people at a distance with my wit and wind up in solitude—that is not always as splendid as it seems."

Van smiled and blushed.

Noticing his embarrassed expression, Landish was again about to amend his remark when he noticed a man sitting on a bench on the opposite side of the walkway, six benches along perhaps. He sat side on, smoking a cigarette, staring at them. Not even when Landish's eyes met his did he look away. He wore an overcoat and gloves and his hat lay on the bench beside him. He seemed to squint appraisingly at Landish.

Even now, on Dark Marsh Road, eighteen months since Princeton, Landish found himself looking over his shoulder, especially at night, to see if he was being followed by Van's bodyguard, Mr. Trull. "I don't need a bodyguard," Van had said. "But my father wants people to think I do. Mr. Trull used to be a Pinkerton."

Mr. Trull, who carried two pistols, stayed out of eavesdropping range but followed Van and Landish everywhere, unselfconsciously conspicuous, a cigarette-smoking sentinel, staring at the ground. Landish imagined him running towards them, a pistol in each hand.

Van had declared himself. How odd. *I want us to be friends.* Landish knew that he would have graduated Princeton without ever having made a friend if such a declaration had had to come from him. For most of his time at Princeton, he had thought he would remember their meeting as one of the great events of his life.

The closest thing to work Van had ever done was ride a horse. He said he was a good rider and asked what sort of rider Landish was. Landish said he would let him know as soon as he found out.

Landish sat alone, in silence, in the taverns of St. John's, spending the hundred dollars in "compensation" that had recently arrived from Van. Other than that word typed on a piece of paper, there had been no note of explanation, nothing but the money. He had thought of— and then thought better of—sending it back.

He drank and considered the bargain he had made with his father: send me to Princeton for four years and I will return and give you the balance of my life. The real terms of the bargain were: send me to Princeton so that, for four years, I can pretend that I am not the son of a sealing captain, pretend the man who paid my way does not exist, and I will come back and follow in your footsteps, low though my opinion be of where they lead. Four years of hoping against hope that something will come up so that I don't have to do for a living what the father I'm ashamed of did to pay my way through Princeton.

When Landish told his father that he wished to be a novelist instead of the skipper of a sealing ship, his father said that a novel was about people who never lived and all the things they never did.

Captain Druken had first taken his son with him to the hunt when Landish was twelve. Landish had sailed on the *Gilbert* many times by then. Short trips, mostly in the summer. His father began to teach him about the sea long before he stepped on a boat. Landish's maiden voyage was in a dory that the boy rowed out to the *Gilbert*. He still remembered how it felt, an inch or two of wood between the water and his feet. It was like standing on a sea-surrounded seesaw.

He'd never been swimming. His father had forbidden it. He said that knowing how to swim would do him no good if he fell into what he called "real water." It would only make him less afraid of it and someday that might lead to carelessness and mean his death.

"The water is your enemy," he said. "It has things you want that you will have to take from it by force. It will give you nothing and no matter how little you take from it, it wants nothing in exchange except your life."

When Landish finished high school, he had come to imagine for himself a life other than the one that he was born to.

"You were born with sea legs," his father said. "You can't go against your nature. You can walk the *Gilbert* in rough weather day or night as well as any sailor. And make your way across the ice as well as any sealer. I didn't teach you that. It can't be taught. I've seen you in a storm of freezing spray, your hands bare so that you could better feel the wheel, your knuckles blood red from the cold. And look at you. The size of you. You could stand eye to eye with any horse. Hands and fists as big as mine. As broad across the shoulders as the doorway of a church. A head so big it should be on a statue. You need a chair for each half of your arse. And you think you were bred for writing books?"

Landish couldn't help but like Van who, minutes after they met, had confessed that he was widely regarded as a "dud."

"My father thinks I'm one," he said.

Who better than the richest man in the world to spy out a dud among his children?

But Van said he was going to surprise everyone by doing something "big" with his life.

Landish had doubted it. He guessed that not every graduate from Princeton would practise the modern form of alchemy. It was true of some that the more generations removed they were from the source of their wealth, the less able and inclined they became to increase or maintain that wealth. Landish called it the Law of Layabout Descendants.

Van said he was going to build, "cause to be built," a great house in North Carolina.

Landish told him that, when he was nine, he had caused a campfire to be built and then caused it to be lit.

Van said, "I discovered the site of the house in 1887. The excavations are completed. I plan to live there, alone if I have to, far enough from Manhattan to forget the place. It may sound morbid, but I have to wait for my inheritance to begin the main work."

It was 1893. Van was building Vanderland now. Landish had read about it in a week-old edition of the *New York Times*. The Carolina Castle, it was called in the article. There had been a picture of Van reclining on the forest floor at the feet of a team of famous architects and engineers. Van, his elder by several years, looking his age at last.

Landish bought drinks for those of his tavern mates who were not afraid to ask him to. They must have thought he was spending Druken money, that his father had relented.

By the time Landish's story had made it back from Princeton to St. John's, there were many versions of it, in all of which he had cheated, not to help a friend but to keep from flunking out.

The full four years at Princeton and he came away with nothing, people said. The Druken who imagined he was born to a better fate than captain of a sealing ship. After so many Drukens went scot-free for greater crimes, their name was ruined because it was proved that the family's first intellectual, the would-be man of letters and refinement, had *cheated on a test*. The shame was that so many Drukens had died of old age in warm beds before the boy that brought them down was even born.

"You have been played for a fool," his father said. "Come back to the world in which you count for something. It doesn't bother *me* that you didn't graduate. It doesn't bother me *why* you didn't. If cheating at school is the worst thing you ever do, you'll be the first saint in the family. I gave you your four years. You said that you would give me the balance of your life."

But Landish told him he would never set foot on a sealing ship again.

"So it doesn't matter that you cheated your own father. It only matters that some rich man cheated you. Because I deserve to be cheated and you don't?" His father was right. That was how Landish had squared it with his conscience. A necessary transgression by a son against his ignoble father to achieve a noble end—which might never be achieved. But he could make amends only by relenting to a life that would destroy him.

Even had he been inclined to look for one, he could not have found a job aboard a ship or on the waterfront. Neither his father's associates nor his enemies would have anything to do with him. His father was the last Druken who could afford not to care what people thought of him.

He applied to every newspaper in the city for a job. He sent in samples of his writing and they sent them back.

He found employment in a beggars-can't-be-choosers kind of school. One day he went there drunk and fell asleep. He woke up to find that all his students had left, his classroom was dark and empty, and a note of dismissal was pinned to the pocket of his coat.

Van had told him of the rhyme which other boys used to chant when they saw him: "Padgy Porgie, pudding and pie / Killed the girl who made him cry / When the boys came out to play / Padgy Porgie ran away."

"*Killed?*" Landish said.

"One of the rumours is that I so hated my infant sister for supplanting me as the baby of the family that I did away with her and that it was all hushed up by my father. It's absurd, but there you are."

There you are. The under-built, slender-built Vanderluyden who his father said could not look their lowest servant in the eye, the dud with the long, pale, slender fingers that bent back to touch his wrists, was said to have killed his sister out of spite.

When Van's father died, he left Van six million dollars, as well as stocks and properties worth about four million. Each of his three older brothers got ten times as much.

Ten million. Henry Vanderluyden's notion of disownment.

"I get it after I graduate. I will sink all of it into Vanderland if I have to."

"I should marry for money," Landish said. "No worries then about making a living as a writer. Matrimoney."

"My mother married for it."

"Your grandfather made a name for himself. Your father bought one."

"As I suppose I shall have to someday."

In the attic on Dark Marsh Road, Landish calculated that had *he* been thus disowned, he could have given his landlord a seven-hundred-and-fifty-trillion-year advancement on the rent.

Though Van had all his life been mocked and hectored by his father, his death left Van so dejected that Landish thought he might fall ill. One day, as they passed a haberdashery, he pointed and said:

"Full fathom five thy father lies/those are pants that were his size." He was ridiculously pleased when Van, finally, could not suppress a smile.

In the middle of his junior year in the spring of 1890, Landish moved out of his dorm room and into Van's house in town. They were inspired by Tennyson's poem "The Lotus Eaters" to call the hilltop house and its spacious grounds Lotus Land. Van insisted on paying all the rent for a house that was bigger than the Drukens'.

"You could fit this house into one room at Vanderland," Van said.

"Is the idea of building this Vanderland all that keeps you going?"

"Isn't that enough? The greatest house in the world?"

They each had a storey of the three-storey house, Van the upper one, Landish the middle. Mr. Trull lived in three rooms on the ground floor. He had his own entrance and there was no connecting passage between his rooms and theirs. "He keeps an eye and ear out in case I leave, I suppose," Van said. "I doubt he ever really sleeps."

Van chose as his bedroom the one at the opposite end of the house from Landish's so that, he said, he wouldn't be kept awake all night by the footsteps of "a stomping insomniac who can't compose a word without roaring it out loud."

"And then I burn the words," Landish said. "So far, I haven't left a single word of my book unburned."

"You really are writing a book? I thought you were kidding and just reading your assignments out loud. What's the book about?"

"I can tell you it will be a novel. I know little more than that about it myself."

"You speak so often of Newfoundland, I'm maddened by your infatuation with the place. It's just your childhood you miss, not Newfoundland," he'd say. "Your childhood when everyone was nice to you, when you had no enemies and there was no one who was out to bring you down."

"Perhaps," he'd say, and then start in about Newfoundland again.

He told Van that he remembered the smell of ripening crab-apples borne up by the wind from the street below his house in late September.

The shadow of a cloud moving over the patchwork colours of the mown fields in the fall. The white-capped waves on the harbour before a storm, the water all racing one way like that of a river as if the whole wind-driven harbour were moving on to somewhere else. The stream whose water was so cold and clear that, in defiance of his mother who warned him that he'd catch his death, he took off his clothes and lay in it on his back, all of his face immersed but for his nose as he looked up through the water at the sky. He remembered how good his skin felt when he put his clothes back on. How the air smelled of rain long before the rain began. Lightning so far away it seemed to make no thunder lit up from within the clouds above the Petty Harbour hills.

On Dark Marsh Road, as at Princeton, Landish wrote every night, and every night burned what he wrote because it wasn't good enough.

In the attic, he composed his sentences out loud, drummed out their rhythm on the floor with his boot heels while his neighbours shouted protests from below. At the end of the evening he reread each page before he fed it to the fire. He remembered Van watching him do so, shaking his head in wonderment.

Landish watched as, from the top windows of Lotus Land, Van trained his binoculars on Princeton, a general scanning from a carefully chosen vantage the movements and new developments in the enemy's encampment.

"We have the tactical advantage of high ground," Landish said, "and even though we are greatly outnumbered, we will bring down a great many before they overtake the house." Van ignored him, looking down the slope of Prospect Avenue for hours, sighing loudly with—Landish wasn't sure—exasperation, impatience, disapproval.

"What are you hoping to see, Van?" Landish said, but Van ignored him. He looked like a child who was pretending to disdain a group that had arbitrarily excluded him, turned him away with derisive taunts and mockery.

"You can be part of it all any time you like," Landish said, "whereas I came here *expecting* to be shunned."

Van smiled. "I like to watch it from afar," he said. "The laughable vanity fair of the world. All that frantic toing-and-froing on the quad."

Van hadn't liked it when Landish brought back to the house women whom he referred to as "fair ladies." He required Landish to give him advance notice of his intentions to bring them home and vacated the house, staying away hours longer than he needed to and afterwards brooding in silence for days. There was also a middle-aged wealthy woman known among the students as the "trolling trollop" whose carriage with its tinted windows made the rounds of Princeton once a week. Landish was one of many sheepish-looking undergraduates who hastily climbed into it. "Methinks she doth divest too much," he said to Van.

Van said that, as a Vanderluyden, he could not take the chance of "availing" himself and thereby bringing upon America's most famous family who knew what sort of infamy.

They took English literature together, and upon going to class one day their professor told them he was glad to see that "the infamous twosome had come out from the cozy confines of their tryst."

His words were much quoted, their meaning lost on no one.

It came to seem that the real purpose of their coming to Princeton was to establish Lotus Land, to live there and entice visitors from the university. They made it known that there would be salons at Lotus Land on Thursday nights.

The president of Princeton had just declared that alcohol was the prime evil of the day. At the first Thursday salon, Landish raised a glass of cognac to the room at Lotus Land and said: "Leave us not without libation, and de-liver us, prime evil."

Looking about his two-room, marsh-overlooking attic, Landish could not help but long for the days when, once a week, four discreetly armed men who rode in the backs of coaches that drove up to Lotus Land word-lessly delivered cases of wine, cognac, cheese, grapes, smoked meats, bread, caviar, cigarettes, cigars—the Bare Excessities, he called them.

The men and the goods arrived by a Vanderluyden train from Manhattan. The men were Norwegian—the Four Norsemen of the Metropolis. The most exclusive eating club at Princeton was The Ivy, referred to simply as "Ivy." Landish called it "Scurvy."

"Not my best," he said, "but I just can't stop myself."

Now, in the darkness of his attic, he could not credit that there were such things as "eating clubs" anywhere on earth. Eighteen months and two thousand miles away from Princeton, "Hunger Clubs" seemed less far-fetched.

He had called Lotus Land the Gobble and Guzzle Club. If someone had admonished him not to take it all for granted because, unlike those of his fellow students, his days of ease were numbered, he would not have listened. He'd known he had to think of the future and told him-self he would, he *would*, but not just yet.

Even now, it suited him to leave unasked, "What next?"

When they heard of the board that was being served nightly at Lotus Land, ever more students came by, some of them deserters from the eating clubs. They were fledgling writers who proved, Landish said, that "the art of drivelry" was not dead. Landish asked that a vote be taken as to which of two names the new group should go by: The Knights of the Round Table; or The Knights Who, in Full Armour, Jostling Noisily for Room, Sit Side by Side on a Very Long Sofa. He named one student Sir Mountable, another one Sir Osis and another one Sir Vile.

Van didn't drink at the salons. He ate very little. He had no work to read aloud, not having written anything in his life but school assign-ments. He merely watched and smiled while Landish held court, and he only drank with Landish. No one said they minded that Van didn't drink with them, even as they refused to abstain.

"I'm a plodder," he had often said. "I envy you. The words come pouring out just when you need them."

"You're fair to middling," Landish told him. "But you could be middling if you applied yourself."

"I'm so damn mediocre. I have no talent, Landish. None. I inherited a lot of money from my father but not much in the way of a mind."

"Imagine," Landish said, "if you could acquire the minds of geniuses and leave them to your sons. You would still have been shortchanged. 'To my oldest son, I leave the mind of Shakespeare. To my second oldest, I leave the mind of Milton. To my third, the mind of Tennyson. To my youngest son, I leave the mind of Sir John Suckling."

After the others left, Landish and Van would sit side by side, slumped in their chairs in the living hall at Lotus Land, puffing on cigars, blowing plumes of smoke towards the ceiling, glasses of cognac warming in their hands, while Landish made anagrams of their last names.

So it had been for Landish not so long ago—cognac sipped in front of roaring fires, nightly engorgement on the finest of foods, wit-appreciating dinner guests, the unstinting friendship and generosity of a wealthy young man who worshipped him.

In St. John's, he glanced at his reflection in windows, his moss-like mass of hair, what was left of the clothes that had been made by Van's tailor who came to Princeton from Manhattan and pronounced Landish "unimprovable" but, at Van's insistence, did his best.

Whenever Landish saw a woman pushing an infant in a pram along the streets of St. John's, he thought of Van's sister, Vivvie, who had drowned at the Vanderluyden country estate when she was eighteen months old.

Her nurse had been walking on the dock with Vivvie in her arms. Van happened to be the only other person there. Nurse stumbled.

When Vivvie fell into the water, Nurse was still holding the blanket that she had been wrapped in. The child went under very fast. Van dove in to save her, but the water was so dark that he mistook a sunken piece of wood for his sister and was clutching it against his chest when he shot up to the surface.

His family, his father especially, blamed him for her death.

After telling him of Vivvie, Van stood, his face in his hands. Landish stood as well, uncertain what to say or do. Van threw his arms around Landish and pressed his head against his chest. He held on to him as if to keep *himself* from drowning, his fingers clawing Landish's back. Landish hugged him, patted him. He tried to ease himself away, but Van clung tightly to him, sobbing, his fingers digging into his back. Their embrace lasted until the tears stopped and Van, his breathing back to normal, clapped Landish on both shoulders, stepped away, and turned to face the fire.

"I'm sorry," said Landish. "But *you've* nothing to be sorry for. Absolutely nothing."

"Now you will think that I'm—that way. Others think I am."

"I don't," Landish said, unable to summon up a less perfunctory denial.

"Really," Van said. "I'm not. It's Vivvie that makes me seem to be many things I'm not. Don't put any store by what other people say about me. When you belong to a certain kind of family, people like to think the worst about you. You of all people should understand. The only difference between the Vanderluydens and the Drukens is one of scale."

"Perhaps."

"You, with all your women—you're an exoneration of what many people think to be my nature."

There were nights, still, when Landish lay sleepless on his bunk in the silent house on Dark Marsh Road, picturing Vivvie sinking, drifting slowly down, her dress buoyed up around her face, her arms above her head. Nothing so made him wish that he and Van had never parted as the image of that little girl in the mud-darkened water, her brother just inches away, flailing about in panic.

They *had* been friends. How their friendship ended did not change that. Thick and Thin, Landish had called them. Prince Ton and Prince Ounce.

"I would never do such things," his father told him when Landish repeated to him what he had overheard boys say at school. "Never mind what people say. They need someone of a lesser rank than God to blame. Nothing short of my death could satisfy them that I did everything I could to save my crew. I won't die just to keep up appearances. All survivors are suspected of surviving at the expense of the dead, of forever keeping to themselves some awful secret."

He believed his father until he acquired enough knowledge from him to see for himself the truth behind his father's reputation. He challenged his father then, who acted as if Landish hadn't spoken, as if each "mishap" at sea or on the ice had been unforeseeable, inscrutably caused, the doings of some whimsy of the elements, against which Landish was too green to know it was pointless to bemoan or rail.

Eventually he realized one day, by his father's manner, his expression and his tone of voice, that he was waiting for it to dawn on him that things would remain the same with or without the blessing of Landish Druken. Later that night, he looked at his father, at his face that, even as he slept, seemed to register every second of the life that he had led, every accusation, spoken or unspoken, made against him, every spit or slur that had followed the mention of his name.

He would not be the first idealist to learn the knack of squaring his conscience with a way of life that in his youth he thought could be reformed. There was an intricate set of necessarily imperfect rules that were followed the world over except by fools who, in the course of their foredoomed and lonely insurrections, were destroyed.

His father was the first sealing skipper in the world to bring back one million seals from the hunt. *Million.* The word was everywhere in Newfoundland. The Board of Trade threw a dinner for Captain Abram Druken. One thousand flipper pies were served.

"Million Abram" received the award of the Blue Ensign from the Governor. A gold medal from a prominent merchant. The OBE— the Order of the British Empire from Buckingham Palace. A "white-coat hat," which his father called "the laurel wreath of sealers."

As a child, crouching down by his parents' bed, Landish had reached underneath, taken hold of the small wooden trunk, and as gingerly as if it held explosives, eased it out.

"The lock is just for decoration," his father had said. He held the sides of the top of the chest with his fingers and slowly, ceremoniously, much as the Governor must have done at the official presentation, raised the lid.

The first thing he noticed was the red velvet lining the inside of the chest, then the hat that was supposedly made from the very fur of the millionth seal. A baby seal. The purest white that he had ever seen.

The first to bring home one million seals. *Bring home.* It made it sound as if the seals were dead when his father found them and all he did was bring them back.

Every night, even if there was not so much as a breeze by day, the wind came up like something brought on by the darkness. It blew in through one side of the attic on Dark Marsh Road and out the other with a screeching whistle. Landish heard what he called the droning in the wires several streets away.

He stood at the attic's porthole, its only window, and looked out past the marsh, across the rooftops and chimneys of the city, to the Narrows. It was mid-October. He thought about the words "the fall." No others would do for how things seemed, for the tantalizing transformation that was taking place, the slow, sad fall of all things into winter. It seemed to him that "the fall" was shot through *with* the fall and in part made it what it was and caused him to feel about it as he did.

Everything was falling, failing. Night was falling faster, the light fading faster from the fields. Time by day passed faster and by night seemed not to pass at all. He turned the attic lights on sooner, but not before something like a dusky silence filled the two rooms. It was as if some old regime of time was falling and a new regime was near.

It had been this "feeling" of the fall that first made him want to write.

He wrote more than he ever had at Princeton.

It was so bad he wished that he could burn it twice.

In his and Van's final year at Princeton, more and more students began to vie for an invitation to the Lotus Land literary salons. Van was the gatekeeper. He chose not only outcasts, the previously unpopular, the "unaffiliates," but also young men whose fathers were almost as rich as his, some of them deserters from the usual eating clubs, The Ivy as well as The Cottage and The Cap and Gown.

Landish assigned more nicknames:

There were three brothers who were known as Pliny the Elder, Pliny the Younger and Pliny the Tiny. There were the Duke of Unwellington, Le Marquis de Malarkey, the Duke of Buxomberg and Sorethumberland.

Landish's authority was sometimes challenged, most often by way of allusions to his having no "name." He would pretend to take it in good humour. When he felt most wounded, he deferred the taking of revenge, storing up witticisms until he was able to give far worse than he'd got, so destroying his would-be rival that the fellow either dropped out of the Druken circle or hung on as a sullen, silent member, a chastising sight to others with a mind to challenge Landish. And he sang along when they started up "What shall we do with a Druken sealer?" which they usually did late at night when all were drunk.

Landish defended Van when the others mocked him for writing "Vanderbilge." Landish called him "VanPun" and wrote puns for him which Van passed off at the salons as his own. He continued to do his best to be seen as something of an *enfant terrible* and Van managed to look as though he wrote the lines that Landish merely delivered, standing at his shoulder, not smiling, impassively savouring what his mouthpiece said. They put many a nose out of joint, Landish noting that Van could do so without much regard for the consequences.

One night, even as he was laughing at his own cleverness, Landish was told that he and Van were being called sodomites by their professors.

Landish sometimes took out of his attic closet his box of Princeton compositions, the only writing of his he had not burned. They— mainly Landish—wrote a *roman à clef* musical under the pseudonyms Filbert and Mulligan, which they called *Nutstewyou*. It was a great hit among those who were not the models for their characters. Among the ragged sheets and scrolls of paper, he found the main creation of the Umbrage Players, which had been called *Who Consumed Keats?*

It began with a corpulent character named Stilton who was at work on an "epicurean poem" called "Parodies Lost." Stilton, around whom everyone holds their nose, tells the audience that his purpose is to justify "the weight of man to God." The characters were all major English poets and were all portrayed as corpulent with enormous bellies and backsides. Alfred Lord Tennyson became Well-fed Lard Venison. Coleridge and Wordsworth were the hybrid Cramyouwell Curdsworth. Shelley, groaning and clutching his belly, spent the entire play writing "Ode to the Worst Wind." A rotund, burstingly buxom Mary Shelley was carried onstage by Frankenstein. A caricature of

Rudyard Kipling, Rhubarb Nibbling, nibbled on shoots of rhubarb and every so often roared, "My gun comes up like thunder/On the bed where 'Manda lays." Ne'er Hard Unmanly Hopkins danced about, lisp/singing "It seems I've sprung rhythm."

The play stirred most of the audience to protest, especially the professors who shouted "ENOUGH" and "TOO MUCH."

Soon nailed to trees on the quad were copies of an unsigned rhyme called "The Ballad of Lotus Land."

Van can't well
Or moderately well.
In the Vanderluyden Bordello
They say the poor fellow
Can't even manage at all.
Can it be that poor Van
Is in need of a man?
They conferred in the hall:
"I've seen this quite oft,
We'll get him aloft."
"Just wait till it rises
They come in all sizes,
Though not many come when they're soft."
"Begging your pardon
They're bringing the Bard in.
He's saying, 'This time he won't fail.'
He's in the Garden
Trying to harden
And make of Van's Moby a whale."

"It seems that I've started rumours by trying not to," Van said. "It seems that one is presumed to be that way unless one consorts with prostitutes."

"Never mind," Landish said. "I'll write and plaster all over Princeton a rhyme called 'The Enormous Endowments of the Vanderluydens.'"

"It would only make things worse," Van said, "no matter how clever it was. I should never have come to Princeton. I should have kept on with my tutors in New York, where I was dogged by so many rumours I hardly took notice when a new one came along." Van paused. "Do you think it odd to grieve for one's sister, Landish, even if one's grief goes on for years?"

"No," Landish said. "But Vanderland will not bring your sister back."

"It is not in the lunatic hope of resurrecting the dead—"

"I'm sorry," Landish said, "but it seems to me that you are suffering more from guilt than grief, guilt due to the unwarranted accusations of your family."

"You don't understand. And it will be years before Vanderland is completed in Carolina. I shall have to live in New York until then. At least in the winter. I despise New York."

Van put his hands on Landish's shoulders.

"Don't go home, Landish. Come to New York and then to Vanderland with me. I won't be able to measure up without you. I will fail just as all the people in my life expect me to."

There had been tears in his eyes. It was Landish's turn to feel guilty. His wit had merely emboldened their enemies to attack the one of them who was defenceless. But, unsure of how to answer, he told Van that he would think about his invitation.

He began to think about graduating from Princeton, the end of the reign of the Umbrage Players, the end of Druken and his Circle, his leadership of both, the dismantlement, abandonment of Lotus Land. He wondered if he might somehow be able to linger on in the town of Princeton, perhaps convince other members of the Players and the Circle to do so and cull the most interesting of the new students for their Thursday salons. But without Lotus Land, without Van's seemingly self-replenishing board of food and drink and cognac and cigars and the settees and sofas on which they lounged about—without all of this, none of it would work.

Yet, though Van many times repeated his entreaty that Landish come to Vanderland, Landish said no.

"I've been dreading the end of Lotus Land as much as you have," Van said. "The two of us going our separate ways, you to as remote and wild a place as Newfoundland. At my invitation, famous writers and other artists will be staying at Vanderland for months, perhaps years. You could be the presiding wit of Vanderland. We could still have our salons."

"Me? Me, the presiding wit of a room full of world-famous writers. What do you plan to do, make it a condition of their stay at Vanderland that they pretend to take me seriously? I can just imagine what a figure of fun I would come to be among the artists of Vanderland. The ascots' mascot. The writer who burns his every word. I would have no *credentials*, Van. All of this—Lotus Land, the Umbrage Players, Druken and his Circle—it can't just be relocated to Vanderland. Not even the Vanderluyden fortune can prolong this time in our lives."

"You don't understand what sort of place Vanderland will be. I'll invite whomever I want to stay there, whomever *you* want. I'll consult with you. If you don't feel at ease among one group, we can simply find another."

"Another group. Made up of lesser minds whose presiding wit I could be."

"You've made such a promising beginning, Landish. Please don't squander it. Don't tell me that, after making your escape from it, you are going to return to some back-of-beyond place where no one has ever done or ever will do anything worth remembering, anything that will endure. I'm offering you what every writer dreams of, freedom from the nuisance of some body-and-soul-draining, penny-earning occupation. Even Shakespeare needed a patron whose praises he sang in sycophantic sonnets."

"I'm not Shakespeare. Though they called me the Bard in that broadsheet."

"Forget that. Forget them. Vanderland will not be some hermit's hut. Those of us who live there will want for nothing. But it will be so self-sufficient there will simply be no need to go elsewhere. It will be a sanctuary, but a vast one. Think of it as being enclosed by a mesh that will admit only what little there is of true value in the world and filter out the rest."

"I would never be at home in some Carolina mansion."

Van had begun to suffer a decline. He had always struggled to get even passing grades, but was soon unable to put pen to paper.

"Vanderluyden or not, I have to at least *seem* to be a student, if only to guarantee that I get my inheritance."

So Landish wrote Van's essays, mimicking his style. That is, he underwrote them, for he knew it wouldn't do for a C student to suddenly start getting A grades. Landish wrote them. Van copied them out in his handwriting and submitted them.

Van returned to Lotus Land frantic one afternoon, saying that he had made a dreadful mistake, submitting the wrong essay, one that bore his name but was, as his professor noticed, in the handwriting of Landish.

So they were caught, Van and Landish.

But Van would be allowed to graduate and his cheating would be kept a secret—whereas Landish, for whose comeuppance his professors had long hoped and prayed, would be expelled.

"Come to Vanderland with me, Landish," Van said. "You need never go home. You can be my lifelong guest. A couple of years in New York and then you can help me finish overseeing the building of Vanderland. You can write your books and we'll raise our families there. No one will know what took place at Princeton. Anyone who does know won't dare say a word. This house, this world that I'm constructing, could be yours as much as mine. As soon as you set eyes on it, you'll understand."

But Landish told him that he couldn't conceive of living anywhere but among the only people he knew well enough to write about.

Landish walked the length of Dark Marsh Road. He didn't turn back where the path met the woods. He ran until the path so narrowed that branches lashed his face and brought to his eyes tears that wouldn't stop. He looked up at the sky in which there was so bright a moon he couldn't see the stars.

Landish had only to gather his things from Vanderland and catch the Vanderluyden-owned train to New York, from which he would sail on a Vanderluyden ship to Newfoundland.

He lingered for a few days, throughout which Van apologized and refused to go to class. Van said it was unfair that Landish be expelled. "But I must warn you not to publicize the truth, or you and yours will be sued penniless, or worse, by my brothers."

"It had never crossed my mind to ask you to do anything but stay silent on the matter," Landish said.

"Isn't it better that one of us survives than that both of us be destroyed?" Van said.

"I don't think of myself as having been destroyed."

"I didn't mean destroyed," Van said. "Of course you haven't been destroyed. It's just that you have nothing to return to. Unless you agree to captain the *Gilbert* for the rest of your life. Which I know how loath you are to do."

"What would you do in my circumstances?" Landish said.

"I would go with my friend to Vanderland. Please reconsider."

"I can't simply enlist in someone else's dreams and discard my own. Nor can I put into words how much I will miss you."

"I refuse to say goodbye to you. I will write to you every day asking you, begging you to change your mind. It will never be too late for you to change it. We will one day be reunited at Vanderland. I am certain of it."

"You make Vanderland sound like some sort of afterlife."

"As you know," Van said, "I as yet have no real money of my own. But I will see to it soon that you are fully compensated should you incur any losses because of your expulsion from Princeton from now until you accept my invitation, which I predict you will do once you are back in Newfoundland and see what not accepting it would mean."

Landish told him he needed no compensation for helping a friend, but Van insisted.

"I'll never forget, Landish," he said. "Never, as long as I live, will I forget the sacrifice that you made for me."

"I'll never forget you, either," Landish told him. "Nor the day we met, the day that you approached me on the quad."

On the day before Landish left Princeton, he met on the street a student who had applied for admission to Lotus Land and been rejected.

"You have Vanderluyden to thank for what's been done to you," the fellow said. "He approached some professors about devising a scheme to get you expelled. I don't know why."

At first Landish took it to be nothing but a spiteful lie. But he walked about the streets of the town, trying to convince himself that the fellow was foolhardy enough to tell such a lie about a Vanderluyden.

He ran back to Lotus Land. Van was in the front room, standing, arms folded, in front of the fire.

"Why did you *do* this?" Landish said, advancing on Van, who backed away and began to cry.

"How else could I keep you in my life?"

"You ruined me so that I would have no choice but to go with you?"

"I had to try *something* or else I would never have set eyes on you again."

"Nor *will* you," Landish said. "Nor hear from me again."

"You're no better. You've known for years that you'd betray your father."

"Yes. For which I deserve to be disowned. As I will be."

Mr. Trull walked into the room as casually as if he always had the freedom of the whole house. Dressed for the outdoors in an overcoat and hat, he slowly withdrew a pistol from the pocket of his coat and pointed it at Landish.

"We'll be leaving now, you and me," Mr. Trull said. "I'll take you to the station and you won't say a word or give me any trouble while we're waiting for the train."

Van began to make his way from the room. He stopped in the doorway and rubbed his nose with his sleeve. "It would have worked, Landish," he said. "If only you'd said yes."

Landish might never have known he'd been betrayed if he'd said yes after "they" were caught. Would their friendship have been a sham even if Landish didn't know what Van had done and Van believed that he had done no wrong?

He thought so.

But he would not be living in an attic now, counting what remained of his "compensation," with no clue what he would do when it ran out.

The Attic

L ANDISH WOKE AND SAT on the edge of the bed in the darkness, trying to decide, his feet on the floor, his hands on the mattress. He could make his way to Cluding Deacon through the snow, demand to be let in no matter the time, go from room to room, bed to bed if need be, looking for her baby boy, reading her letters aloud if he had to, though he doubted it would come to that, it being unlikely that they would say no to the first person of *any* name who had gone there with what he had in mind.

He sat on the edge of the bed for hours, then lay down again. He tried to reason it out. With whom would the boy be better off, him or them? He couldn't name a child who had prospered because of or in spite of the place called Cluding Deacon. But what chance of prospering would a charge of his have? They knew better than he did how to care for a child's most basic needs. With them, the boy would at least have comradeship, even if it was no more than company in misery.

He would be alone with Landish, and Landish himself had every reason to expect to be alone. But there was Cluding Deacon's reputation. Better the boy suffer who knew what number of lesser torments than the ones that were rampant at that place.

He mulled it over night after night in this manner and found that he could make as good an argument for taking the boy from the orphanage as for ignoring the letters the boy's mother had written to him demanding that Landish take responsibility for him. And then there was the matter of what Landish wanted. He thought first of his book. He didn't even know yet what it would be about, but the "feeling" of fall, which he could summon up in any season, convinced him that the book would follow on the writing of an acceptable first page, the subject of which would only announce itself as he was in the act of putting pen to paper. The boy would surely be an impediment to the book's completion, given that without the boy he had yet to write even a sentence that he could stand. So he obsessively argued both sides of the question but came no closer to an answer.

She said that she was halfway gone herself, as good as lost, so she was writing to him while she was still able to. She said Landish would bring upon himself God's eternal shame if he didn't take Deacon from the orphanage and raise him as his own. She said her husband had made a lot of money for Landish's father that should be spent on *her* baby, not just on Landish, whose father was to blame for her husband's death two years before. Landish wrote back to her that it was only to satisfy his father's wishes that he was still the skipper of his own clothes.

She replied that she would soon be "in the place from which no one knows the way back home." He was astonished by the eloquence of her letters.

I am only sorry that I let him live, have let him think for so long that he would go unpunished for his crimes. I should have gone to his house with my husband's gun the day the Gilbert came back without him.

I am guilty, but only of every breath I could have prevented him from drawing, every moment I let him live after I heard on the street that, far from bringing my husband safely home, he had not even brought his body back to me. He never spoke a word of consolation or regret to me.

For some time now, I have been silent in a silent world,
often spoken to but never speaking. I "hear" but nothing touches
me. Things that once made sound have for some time made none,
though I have never stopped expecting this to change, never stopped
anticipating sounds that never came, sounds of collisions, voices,
vehicles, the striking of hammers and the blowing of whistles, the
sounds of footsteps and the galloping of horses, the shrill pitch
of the wind.

It has for long seemed that the world was buried deep in snow or
lay submerged beneath the fathoms of a sea that muffled every sound.
Perhaps because I have been for so long not quite fully alive I have
no fear of death, no feelings at all about it in fact. I will do nothing
to hurry near the day of my death but will merely await it with my
customary patience.

An inscrutable universe had, by foisting the riddle upon him, offered
him the chance to change two lives. The boy knew nothing about it
and likely never would if Landish declined him. So Landish decided
it was no one's choice but his.

Birth is a bundle of joy.
Death is a dwindle of joy.

He heard the answer. No impetus, no volition inclined his will
towards the boy except the word which, though it woke him, was
beyond recall.

He went there early in the morning and brought the boy back to
the attic. The boy went to sleep in a place he would never see again
and woke up in one he had never seen before.

"Welcome to the attic," Landish said to the face that peered out at him
from a bundle of blankets. "It is ever a hovel and no place like home."

There were two rooms, a kitchen to which the stairs led and a bedroom you could only reach by way of the kitchen; no windows except for a kind of wooden-shuttered porthole in the bedroom. It always seemed like nighttime in the attic, especially in the kitchen, where the lamps were lit at noon the same as they were long after sunset. There was a black iron stove with a single damper so Landish could heat only one pot at a time; a wooden table that wobbled no matter what you put beneath its legs; two wooden chairs whose legs were enwrapped with reams of twine; a sink with a long faucet that at one end looped like a cane. Ice-cold water dripped unceasingly from it and barely reached a trickle when you turned the tap.

The attic in the summer was so hot you couldn't breathe, and the wind in the winter blew right through the walls. The candles flickered when it gusted and guttered when it roared and you could catch your death unless you slept with your head beneath the blankets.

The boy's name was Deacon. They had told him so at the orphanage and said they couldn't account for the coincidence, the boy having the same name as their institution. Deacon's father was known in St. John's as "Carson of the *Gilbert*," legendary for his heroism and the manner of his death.

Landish had known Carson but not well. They had never had a conversation. First mate of the *Gilbert*, and the only man who knew the ice as well as Captain Abram Druken did. Francis Carson, who would not under any circumstances abandon the men and boys of his watch. Captain Druken had sent them out from the *Gilbert* when all hands could tell that a blizzard was imminent. They lost their way in the storm and, despite Carson's advice to return and his ministrations, lay down to die. Had he left them to their lonely deaths, he would almost certainly have saved himself because he was stronger than them and had twice before survived a night outside on the ice. He'd have seen his wife again and seen their baby born. But he couldn't bear to leave his men. The best first mates were as loath to leave the men in their care as a captain was to leave a sinking ship. And so he stayed with them. And a piece of the ice pan on which the watch of men were huddled broke off and Carson drifted away, though the men of the watch—for all of whose deaths Captain Druken would also have been responsible because he had discontinued the search for them too quickly so as not to lose time hunting seals—were saved by the captain of another ship. Not even when drunk and at his most vainglorious did Landish fancy he might someday be as good a man as Carson of the *Gilbert*. A chastening life. A chastening death.

He was the opposite of sole survivor. Carson alone was left behind. He may have written something in case his body or effects were found, last words that were never read. Last words to his wife, first and last words to the child who was not yet born. He wouldn't have burned the words he wrote, wouldn't have cared how they'd be judged. He may have spoken aloud to his wife and unborn child, to others, to himself. The sole lost soul. There should be a word for all saved but one.

He alone had not come home. Deacon's mother must have thought a lot about that. Why hers but no other woman's husband? Why him but no other men? An inscrutably arbitrary death—or had God spied out some secret sin in Carson of the *Gilbert* that now would be forever secret? A young, pregnant widow pondering the motives of the universe. No doubt she would have blamed herself, however absurdly disproportionate to her "sins" her punishment was.

Captain Druken lives on in a warm house, but also alone, surrounded not by family and friends but by the effects of a life spent at the hunt. Alone though his son is but a mile away, while his neighbours, whose houses he has never been inside of and who have never been inside of his, wonder how much that is said about the man is true. Survived by his son and his ship. Landish wouldn't be surprised if he scuttled the *Gilbert* so that no one else could be her skipper. Still, he wrote to his father, asking him to help the boy, assured him that he would not spend on himself one cent of any money that his father gave him. There was no reply.

Landish discovered that, if he spoke to him long enough, Deacon, though he couldn't understand a word, would fall asleep. Landish called his bedtime soliloquies "tranquiloquies." The tranquiloquies kept Landish from getting too lonely.

Landish wrote, and read aloud to Deacon:

Like other children who come from the orphanage, Deacon did. It is called an orphanage because children of orphan age live there. Up to twelve. Grown-ups can pick you, but like a snot they won't. No one in Cluding Deacon got picked. The longest one was Kenneth. Fifteen. A favourite but a burden on the colony.

It was heave ho, out you go. You had your chance, now make the best of it. And if you do nothing else, never forget who was here for you when what you needed most was a good kick in the arse. Don't come back to us with your bed between your legs and some boy named Lloyd curled up inside of it.

Dead. Survived by his wits and many friends. The boys of Cluding Deacon, in their thirties and their forties now, many of them men, gather in their first and one true home, to meet in the place where those years of his life that were spent indoors pre-pared Kenneth so well for the other two.

There was a rule at Cluding Deacon that no boy could be picked by a young unmarried man unless a young unmarried man willing to part with fifty dollars asked if he could pick a boy.

At last, a young unmarried man availed himself of this long-standing exception to the rule. He chose a one-year-old boy whose last name was Carson. His real first name was unknown at Cluding Deacon, so the man called him Deacon after half of the orphanage because he was so small. The man, whose name was Landish Druken, liked the sound of Deacon Carson Druken.

The much-cherished but yet-to-be-enacted ritual called "Let Us All Delight in the Good Fortune of a Boy Who Has Been Picked Instead of Us" was at last enacted, after which the boy was hustled from Cluding Deacon by his new guardian, who was himself cele-brated by the many older boys he might have picked but didn't.

Landish looked at the boy.

"I ransomed you, but you were no bargain. I didn't pay a king's ransom or even a prince's. Fifty dollars. The going price, they said. They told me I could ask around but they couldn't guarantee you wouldn't be snapped up while I was gone."

It wasn't easy for a man who was an only child and had never known a human being younger than himself to raise a boy. Landish wondered if Deacon Carson Druken cried too much. It seemed to him that it was not unreasonable to expect that, over the course of a month, the average child would stop crying at least once, even if only to catch its breath.

Deacon Carson Druken cried when he was hungry. He cried when he was eating. He cried when he was finished eating. He cried when Landish picked him up. He cried when Landish put him down. The urge to pee made him cry. The satisfaction of the urge to pee made him cry. He cried before, during and after a bath. Tears seeped from Deacon Carson Druken's eyes while he was sleeping.

He cried so much that Landish worried he would die of thirst.

Landish tried to write while Deacon cried. He paid fair ladies who were used to being paid for something else to watch over Deacon while he went out for a walk, for a drink. He thought about spending time in the attic with a fair lady who did exactly what she was used to being paid for doing. He looked at the boy and thought against it.

Seemingly for no reason, Deacon Carson Druken ceased to cry.

The boy looked at him as if there was nothing Landish could tell him that he hadn't heard before.

Man and boy slept.

"This is your homo supine period," Landish said to Deacon. "All you do is lie on your back."

Then came homo suprone when he lay on his belly *and* his back.

Then came homo repine when he sat up, spat up, crawled and bawled and Landish repined for the days when he was cribbed.

Then came "the great uprising" when Deacon stood up.

Then what Landish called his "first pittance of an utterance," a "word" that seemingly had neither vowels nor consonants.

No others followed for a while. A long while. It seemed that the boy's first pittance of an utterance would be his first and only one. Landish could see that the boy understood him when he spoke. He didn't doubt that the boy was able to speak. He had seemed about to many times. Landish wondered what he was waiting for, this boy who was now almost three.

Landish made up many stories for Deacon. There was one about "a boy who lived inside a hollow iceberg, a great palatial shell of ice, through the walls of which the sun sometimes shone so brightly the boy had to cover his eyes to keep from being blinded. The boy was called the 'bergy boy' and lived alone in the Palacier. He was ravenice for licorice, the gathering of which was very dangerice in the cavern-ice Palacier . . ."

The time came when Landish thought Deacon was old enough to hear how he and Landish had come to be together. He told him how his father died, of his mother's letters, of Cluding Deacon and the fifty dollars that he gave the orphanage in exchange for Deacon.

At last Deacon spoke his first words. A torrent of words by the time he was barely four. He asked Landish to repeat the true story about his parents and about how he and Landish came to be in the attic. He nodded as Landish spoke. He said that, because he'd never met his parents, he wasn't all that sad that they were gone. Landish said he might be sad about it one day. He might hate Captain Druken. But Deacon shook his head.

Where was I before I was born?

The same place I was.

What's it called?

The Womb of Time.

What do you do there?

You wait.

Who picked us?

God did.

Why?

God only knows.

What's God like?

I don't know.

Who picked Him?

I don't know.

What's *this* place called?

The world. You go from the Womb of Time into the womb of your mother and from there into the world. The world leads to the *Tomb* of Time, the place from which no one knows the way back home. From the Womb of Time to the Tomb of Time. Life.

What happens in the Tomb of Time?

Only Lazarus and Christ went there and came back. They never said what it was like.

Landish told him that you passed from the Womb of Time into what he called your birth "Murk," which was the interval between your "commencement screech" and the first moment of your life that you remembered. No two Murks were of the same duration. Some lasted eighteen months, others twice or even three times that. No one really knew what went on in your mind throughout the Murk, what caused it or what its purpose was. While you were in the Murk you learned things that you remembered when you left, but you did not remember learning them. Your caretakers could tell that you were learning and remembering and years later told you what you did and what you looked like, but you had to take their word for it.

They may have photographed your body while your mind was in the Murk. They may have kept a diary and let you read it. But none of it rang a bell. Your actions and appearances as recorded and recalled by others while you were in the Murk consisted mostly of mis-remembrance, embellishment and outright fiction. You emerged from the Murk knowing the names of things. It was not possible, even in retrospect, to tell where the Murk left off and your memory began. You didn't burst from the Murk. You left it gradually. Memory didn't dawn on you. It came and went, came and went, the Murk breaking, then re-forming, memory like the sun behind a threadbare cloud. The Murk lifted until you could nearly see through it, but then closed in again. And so it went, a seesaw flux of memory and Murk, a fast succession of eclipses from which some light as weak as that of soon-to-vanish stars survived.

You emerged from the Murk and then life as you would remember it began: the stages of life that were known as "hoods." Childhood, boyhood, manhood, fatherhood, many more including some you had no way of naming yet. Oldhood comes next to last . . .

Deacon imagined a procession of hooded figures approaching him in single file, each one shorter than the one behind it, all faceless except for the first, which bore *his* face.

. . . Over time, some hoods, especially the early ones, dropped out of the procession, and some walked side by side with others until the final hood went by. The final hood. The largest of the hooded figures. The nameless one, abandoned by the others, left by them to walk alone into the Tomb of Time.

"What are you in?" Deacon said. Landish thought of saying father-hood, but said manhood instead. Deacon nodded.

Landish told him that Deacon's father had fallen short of fatherhood by ninety days. From the procession of his life, fatherhood had been removed, and with it all the others but for the one that had no name.

"You're in your childhood," Landish said again, and smiled. Wildhood, he thought, but could not imagine Deacon running wild. Orphanhood. Happyhood, judging by his eyes and the smile that almost never left his face.

Landish also told Deacon about Just Mist—the realm of things that at one time were possible but had never happened. The actual course of events threaded its way through Just Mist by way of sudden turns, double-backs and circles. Just Mist was full of phantom, nearly lived lives, such as the one Deacon would have had if not for his father's death.

Landish's father had hoped he would have a family that would grow into the Druken house, but Landish, by the time his mother died when he was eight, was still the only child. He and his mother were often alone in the house. Her name was Genevieve. She always wrote it Gen of Eve.

She said she made up "Landish" so he would never have to share his name with someone else. But she gave him a middle initial, B, and never told him what it stood for. She said it was good to be the one and only Landish but also "good to be a B." He asked her what she meant but she told him that maybe one day he would understand. She told his father that his last name was a mixed blessing. Other boys were about as likely to play with a Druken as to pick on one. At school, he'd be ignored. If she taught him at home, they could keep each other company. But Captain Druken said that too much time with his mother would make him a sissy.

So she had been alone a lot. She read while Landish was at school. When he got home, they made forts and castles with her books. She told him stories about a baby who slept in Sir Walter's Cot. She helped him read some pages out loud. He pronounced mutinous "muttonous."

His mother said, "Good luck to any skipper cursed with a muttonous crew." She never spoke of God or Heaven. She told him she had no idea where she'd come from and none where she was going. She died of a cold that just kept getting worse. She slipped so suddenly into her final fever that her last words to him were "I'll see you in the morning, sweetheart."

Gen of Eve. The rest of her was in Just Mist. He still couldn't stand how much it hurt to think that she was gone.

Her marriage to Captain Druken had come about by some arrangement of which Landish no longer remembered the details. She came from a sealing family like the Drukens. She had a brother who left school when he was twelve. No sisters. Her father and brother died when their ship sank in a storm, her mother some years later of pneumonia. She said she'd never minded being matched with a man who, like her father and her brother, would almost always be away. She used to say that the ship was his, the house was hers. She could have had servants but didn't want them.

"It will just be me here soon enough. Himself will want you all to Himself." Landish told her he would rather be with her. "We'll see," she said. "The house or the ship. Which will it be for Landish?"

His father couldn't stand coming ashore. Houselife. Captain Druken slept on the *Gilbert* even when it was docked in St. John's. He visited his own house like an invited guest, had dinner, then went back to the ship. He would let himself in and Landish's mother would take his hat and coat and hang them in the vestibule, and help him on with his coat when he got up from the table and said that it was time to go. At dinner, he spoke almost exclusively to Landish.

She said the *Gilbert* was his home away from her. It doubled as a coastal supply vessel and even as a passenger ship for those who had no alternative or could afford no better, so he was almost always away. They attended Sunday service with him, and the two of them went when he was away because Captain Druken said it would look bad if they didn't.

Landish's mother said she got "looks" from men who thought she must be lonely with a capital L. But she said that looks were all that a woman neglected by a Druken had to fear. "Or hope for," she'd once said beneath her breath.

"I'll go mad here when you're gone," she said to Landish. She stamped his face and head all over with kisses until he laughed and pretended that he wanted her to stop.

"Who does Landish love?" she'd ask out of the blue, at dinner when his father was away, when they went out for walks. "You," he'd say. Or else he'd tease her and say he didn't know. He'd hold out until she pretended she was crying.

"I love *you*," he'd shout.

Who does Landish love? No one else had ever said they loved him. Not even Van. He hadn't heard it or said it since her death.

She had taken up pencil sketching while she was pregnant with Landish. Later, she scrolled up all her drawings—mostly St. John's streetscapes—tied them with ribbon at both ends and in the middle, and piled them in her closet. There were dozens of them but she said she didn't think anything she drew was worth framing or displaying in the house or elsewhere. She dismissed every one of her sketches as "hideous." He thought her actions similar to what he did with his writing. But she hadn't destroyed her sketches, only hidden them. Captain Druken might have destroyed them by now. All of them but one.

The one thing other than his clothes that he managed to remove from his father's house as he was leaving it for the last time was a three-feet-by-two-feet sketch that his mother had drawn of herself.

"GEN OF EVE and LANDISH" she had printed below the drawing in large letters, meaning that Landish was "in" the picture as well. "Can't you see yourself inside my belly?" she asked.

Inside the paper itself, he'd liked to think when he was younger. A secret, in spite of the title. She must have added "and LANDISH" after he was born, there being no way, when she drew the sketch, that she could have known the gender or name of the child she carried. So Landish called the sketch what she must first have called it, simply *Gen of Eve*.

The sketch matched—and had probably influenced—his memory of her. She was sitting with her arms on the arms of a chair. She was not smiling but looked playfully skeptical of the notion that she was worth depiction. A long angular face, thin but wide lips, prominent cheekbones, dark hair—and wide, dark eyes.

Gen of Eve was undated and was signed, in the bottom right-hand corner, "Gen of Eve Marcot," Marcot being her maiden name, one of French origin that was pronounced "market" in St. John's. Why she had not used her married name he wasn't sure, unless it was that the sketch was part of the house, which was "hers," as opposed to the *Gilbert*, which was "his," her husband's.

Deacon liked it. Landish was in Gen of Eve. He was in Genevieve when she drew Gen of Eve. He was there but you couldn't make him out. Like a ghost. You couldn't tell by Gen of Eve. Her belly wasn't big. You could tell she was keeping a secret but you couldn't guess what it was. Deacon wouldn't have guessed if Landish hadn't told him. Landish told him the story of the wooden horse. No one knew the Greeks were in it. Landish looked at Gen of Eve for a long time. He shook his head. A smile came and went. He said it was the one and only image of his mother. His lips moved when he touched it with his hand, but Deacon couldn't hear the words. He wiped his eyes with the back of his hand.

Landish would unroll the portrait on the table when the table was clean and uncluttered, and otherwise unroll it on the floor. He'd weigh it down at the corners with beach rocks, and hold the lantern while Deacon walked, and sometimes crawled, around the sketch, appraising it from every angle. In the lamp-and-lantern-lit attic, they stood over the image of his mother. It was an eerie light and an eerie manner in which to view the sketch of Gen of Eve and Landish. They might as well have been examining a just-discovered sketch of uncertain age and provenance that depicted a stranger.

When it was on the table, he took Deacon in his arms, lowering his face towards the portrait when the boy asked him to go closer. "She was good at drawing," Deacon said. As Landish looked at her, he wondered what she'd make of what his life had come to.

"Genevieve drew Gen of Eve," Deacon said. "Is that what your mother looked like?"

"Just like that."

"She's nice. She died. She's in the Tomb of Time with *my* mother and father."

He couldn't afford to put a frame around it and have it encased in glass. If he tacked it to the wall, the smoke from the lamps and lanterns and the fireplace would blacken it with soot and it would warp, curl up in the middle, on the sides. In no time, Gen of Eve would be unrecognizable. He wasn't sure he'd have put it on the wall even if he could afford to have it framed. His mother hadn't wanted anyone but him to see it.

Their attic was in an old house.

The house was built on a slope but stood alone, no prop house on either side. It was a rectangle tilted on its short side. It was narrow and shallow and pointlessly tall, the ceilings abnormally high for a house of that size except in the attic, where the ceiling was the height that you'd expect. Landish guessed that the house was more than three times as high as it was wide. It was portioned into three levels, all accessed by the original stairs so that you could not reach the second level without passing briefly through the first, nor the attic without passing through the first and second.

The attic was the best level of the three, Landish said, because Deacon had plenty of headroom and they had no intruders. Landish said he would rather walk around bent over than have his neighbours tramping through his house. It was better than being sandwiched between or living under everyone.

Deacon could fit his head through the porthole window, but Landish could only fit his arm. They had to take turns looking out because the window was so small. They could see the marsh and beyond it the harbour, the Narrows and the Brow. They were north of Barter's Hill at the end of Dark Marsh Road.

Luckily, the ceiling of the attic wasn't high enough for Landish to carry Deacon on his shoulders. He refused to crawl, would not let Deacon ride him like a horse. He declared the hour before tub time to be toddle time. "A toddler is supposed to toddle," he said, but Deacon wouldn't walk just for the sake of walking, so he had him march about the attic with a stick resting on his shoulder like a gun.

"What's the biggest man you could carry on your shoulders?"

"I don't know."

"How old will I be when you can't carry me anymore?"

"How old will *you* be?"

There was a curfew of ten o'clock so that the lower tenants could lock their doors. There was an old couple on the first floor who were called the Barnables.

They rarely glimpsed the Barnables because of how hastily they fled the kitchen when they heard Landish and Deacon at the door or coming down the stairs. Landish and Deacon heard the scraping of the kitchen chairs and hurried footsteps. Sometimes they opened the door to see a small table set for two, steam rising from food and cups of tea, slices of half-eaten buttered bread, chairs askew. Other times, a meal in mid-preparation spat or bubbled on the stove, or the kitchen was unlit and empty, the first floor silent. Deacon wished the man and woman didn't have to run and hide because of him. He thought of the old couple standing in some other room, waiting to hear the closing of the door upstairs, then coming out to resume their silent supper.

There was a man named Hogan on the second floor. Landish knew that Hogan would have liked nothing more than to have a silent ceiling, but he saw in his eyes that he would never complain to a man the size of Landish, who, to top it all off, was a Druken, a member of a family that no one with a mote of sense would ever cross.

Hogan had been suffering from an apparently symptom-free complaint since his youth, and got by on a combination of what he called "top-ups"—some kind of disability pittance, rent relief and food vouchers.

There was a closet where they did their "business." A bucket with a board on top, a round hole in the board and sawdust that you poured into the hole when you were finished. Each night Landish put the bucket on the path beside the road. The Night Soil wagon took the bucket and replaced it with another one. The business buckets.

Landish dealt with Hogan's buckets. Hogan left his business bucket on the stairs outside his kitchen every night. They would have been there forever if Landish hadn't dealt with them.

"You should mind your own business," Landish told him. "I shouldn't have to mind it for you. Never mind your 'condition.' What *is* your condition? No one's ever seen any sign of it."

Hogan snitched on his neighbours to the landlord, the nuns who came to visit him, the man who came by with his food vouchers, the 'Stab, and other authorities whom he collectively referred to as the Clout. Landish sometimes felt sorry for Hogan and just as often was sickened by the sight of him.

Hogan wore long underwear with pants but without a shirt, his white top always buttoned to the neck, a pair of suspenders hanging loose about his waist. He smiled at Deacon in a way that made Deacon smile back even though he didn't want to.

He was always in the kitchen when they came and went. They opened his door one day to see him racing to the stove lest they close the door at the bottom of the stairs and pass through his kitchen without his having seen them. Landish told him his socks would last longer if he simply put his bed beside the stove.

Hogan muttered something under his breath about Mr. Nobleman, their landlord, whom Landish simply called "the nobleman."

"What was that?" Landish said, but Hogan turned away.

The nobleman sometimes wrote letters warning Landish what would happen in the event of more complaints. The letters always enraged Landish. He said that one day, the nobleman would find out what came of slipping letters under doors in the middle of the night. He wrote letters to the nobleman that ended up in the stove with the nobleman's once he had read them aloud:

"Should you, as you say in your letter, have no recourse but to evict howsoever many tenants now occupy the premises known as the attic, I will have none but to evict howsoever many living daylights now occupy the premises known as the nobleman."

Later, Landish opened the attic door, went downstairs and hammered on Hogan's door, shouting "kitchen snitch."

"Tell the nobleman you live below a den of thieves," he shouted. "Tell the Clout I taught Deacon how to pick the smallest pocket. Tell the nuns they'd better keep us both in front of them when they come to visit, unless they want to see their rosaries in the window of a pawnshop."

"Landish, come upstairs," Deacon whispered. "If Hogan tells the nobleman, we might be sacked." Landish did as Deacon said but clomped on the steps as loudly as he could.

He bundled up the boy and took him down to the harbour to see the *Gilbert* once when his father was in Harbour Grace.

"If you add up the weeks, I spent almost three years on that ship," he said. He and his father had not spoken since Landish had left Princeton in 1891. He had seen his father since his disownment but only from a distance and by chance.

Landish said that among the men for whose deaths Captain Druken was blamed was Deacon's father, Carson of the *Gilbert*. Deacon, his nose running from the cold, stared at Landish. "It might not have been your father's fault," Deacon said, but Landish said it was.

Landish told the boy everything he knew about the Carsons.

"You were born three months after your father was lost at the seal hunt. Your mother died less than a year later. She held out hope for months that he'd be found alive. 'He is still out there,' she wrote to me, 'and he may yet come home.'" But he came home only in her dreams. Cruelly joyous dreams which she struggled not to wake from, in which he simply showed up at her door as if no time had passed since she had last seen him.

"She's in my Murk."

"That's right."

"But mostly in the Tomb of Time."

Landish said that Deacon was a "gauntlet," a smaller version of a "gaunt," which was a gaunt-looking grown-up. He said that *he* was a "brawnt" and so was Deacon's father. He said Deacon's mother had been a "plumpling."

"So there's no accounting for you," Landish said. "I hope you won't be a gauntlet much longer, but you'll never be a brawnt. 'Ungaunted' might be all that we can hope for."

A wing of a Cornish hen should have done Deacon for a week, though Landish had yet to encounter the amount of food that would do him for a day. The boy was always flushed from hunger. His body didn't so much digest food as destroy it in the blast furnace of his belly.

Landish told the boy that even though Deacon Carson Druken had three names, he had the appetite of a boy with many more, so he called him by twelve names: Deacon Carson Bacon Touton Onion Mutton Capon Chicken Lemon Melon Cinnamon Druken. But that didn't work. So Landish took Deacon Carson Druken to a puniatrist, a doctor who specialized in "robusting" puny babies. But Deacon did not robust in spite of all the doctor did. The doctor told Landish not to worry because the boy would probably "spontaneously robust" when he was older. He said that cases of spontaneous robustion were not as rare as most people thought.

"Deaconian measures are called for," Landish said. He explained to Deacon that he was named after Deaco, who was the brother of Draco, the first legislator of ancient Greece who imposed, and wrote down for the first time, the laws of Athens. Punishment for the smallest crimes was severe, he said, usually death. But under the less stringent, less exacting Deaconian system, Deaco granted an instant pardon to anyone who misbehaved. Then he granted universal pardons in advance and therefore made it impossible to break the law. Not even Draco had been able to accomplish this.

But Landish—though he joked about it with Deacon—knew that there was something wrong with the boy, not an illness per se but a seemingly innate weakness of body that nothing, so far, could rid him of, something at the very core of him that could not stand up against the world. Landish wondered if the grief that Deacon's mother had endured during the last months of her pregnancy had so weakened her body that it also weakened her soon-to-be-born child. Perhaps the grief itself had somehow seeped into Deacon while he was in the womb, into his very bones where it still resided, an enervating agent for which no one could find the antidote.

There was a library called the Athenaeum in which Landish had spent much time as a boy. Not long ago, it had been damaged in the fire that destroyed much of the city. It had been partially restored and Landish took the boy there some afternoons. They could not afford the small subscription fee but the librarian let in them in anyway, telling him she had fond memories of watching him with his face pressed to within inches of books that he could barely lift. Landish told Deacon her name was Library Ann—even though Ann was not her name. He said that she worked for the rights of the poor and encouraged the poor to vote. The poor, he told him, were known as the Scruff. The Clout were on the top and the Scruff were on the bottom. He said Library Ann was a scruffragette.

Library Ann said almost no one went there anymore because it smelled too smoky from when they had the fire and people were afraid it would collapse. But it didn't smell as smoky as the attic and it wasn't as dark. Library Ann told Deacon that Landish had spent a lot of his life there before he went to Princeton, and he was the most unlikely looking bookworm she had ever seen. His voice echoed even when he whispered. But he had been her best customer. Now he and Deacon were almost her only customers and she was very afraid her beloved Athenaeum's days were numbered because it wasn't safe. She said they would have nowhere to store the books, so when the time came they could have their pick.

They went in the afternoons and sat side by side at a long, bare table. Using books that were smudged with soot and had little holes burned into them, Landish taught Deacon how to read. They skipped printing and went straight to writing words. They did arithmetic. In the winter months it was warmer than the attic. Sometimes he sat beside Landish and slept, curled or slumped in his chair, while Landish read—though he was restless even as he read, surrounded by shelves of unburned books written by writers who, often against odds greater than the ones he faced, had succeeded. "The Athenaeum's books burned by accident," Landish told Library Ann. "I burn my book on purpose."

But one afternoon the doors were locked, a notice, pinned to the wall, stating that the condemned building was about to be torn down. They banged and heard a key turning in the lock. Library Ann peered around the door at them. Her eyes were red and she dabbed them with a handkerchief as she pulled Landish and Deacon hastily inside. She told Landish they could take as many books as they could cram into the wooden wheelbarrow she had put beside the steps.

Landish pushed the barrow up the hill. I look like a book peddler, he said. They stood the books on the floor along the wall. They had to lie on their bellies to see the names. In a library, he told Deacon, the shelves of books are called the "stacks." And we have a Smokestack. You'll have the Attic School from now on.

�֍

A priest who gave Communion to shut-ins came by with the nuns who were nurses too on Sunday afternoons to visit Hogan. Sometimes, Landish and Deacon were passing through Hogan's kitchen when they arrived. The priest wore his vestments, the hems of which the two nuns carried as they trailed behind him. The holy vessel that contained the Host was covered in white cloth whose purpose Deacon fancied was to keep something warm until Hogan ate it. Deacon said he could tell that the priest was pretty high up in the Clout.

"That boy was baptized in the Catholic Church," the older of the two nuns said one time. "There is the matter of his religious instruction and his preparation for the sacraments."

"The Drukens are Anglicans, Father," Landish said, "as I believe you know."

"Mr. Druken may raise the boy as he sees fit," Landish was very surprised to hear the priest say.

"Yes, Father," the older nun said.

Landish and Deacon had left, Landish gently guiding Deacon by the back of his head with his hand.

Captain Druken had made it known throughout St. John's that he had stipulated in his will that his estate, when he died, would be divided equally between the Churches of the city, doled out to them in annual stipends. Landish assumed that the priest was concerned that the stipends of the Catholic Church might be withheld if he took an interest in Deacon's upbringing.

But the nuns began to come upstairs to check on the boy, who, they said, was dressed no better than the boys who all but lived outdoors. When Landish told them that Deacon's face was bruised from the latest surprise hug he had staged on his leg, the older nun said it would be a shame if the boy's face had got that way from the very hand that held his own.

The nuns asked Landish a lot of questions when Deacon was in the other room, and Deacon a lot of questions when Landish was in the other room.

When Landish spoke with the nuns who were nurses too, he was always sober and unLandishly polite, so time after time they went away, but each time seeming more reluctant than before. Landish feared that one day the nuns who were nurses too would tell him they had come to take the boy. He wasn't sure what he should do.

He tried again to find a job, but scarce to the point of non-existence were employers who were unaware of both the Sartorial Charter and his reputation, the latter best summed up by one of the bishops who said he would rather choose his teachers from among God-fearing grade-school dropouts than from among men who, though they had gone to Princeton, lived like Landish.

Though Landish grew used to having Deacon on his shoulders, he tried everything he could to convince the boy to walk more often, short of punishing him or threatening to punish him or even getting angry with him, none of which he could bear to do. He had nothing he could bribe him with.

"It's better up high," Deacon said. When he was tired, he would rest his head sideways on Landish's, entwine his arms up to the elbows in his hair, and go to sleep.

They walked for hours because there was not much else to do.

They wandered one night into the better neighbourhoods where there was electric lighting.

"Their lights go out every time there's a storm of wind," Landish said. "Then they have to use what we use in the attic."

Deacon nodded.

"My father's house has electric lights," Landish said. "We got electricity long before I went to Princeton."

"You don't have it now."

"No."

"But you wish you did."

"Not really."

"Are electric lights nicer?"

"You don't have to keep them lit like you do with oil and coal and wood and candlesticks. Less work. Cleaner. They don't have any smell."

"But smoke smells nice."

"That's right."

Landish told him that electricity ran through the wires that were strung from pole to pole along the streets, and from the poles to the houses.

They heard the wires humming when the wind was calm.

Electricity ran like water did through pipes, Landish said. It flowed.

There were no poles or wires or even gas lamps on Dark Marsh Road.

One day Landish told him that a woman named Lucy would mind him for a while. Landish said that he was going for a walk with Lucy's sister. Landish went down the stairs when Lucy was coming up. They didn't say hello or look at each other. Landish was gone for an hour. Lucy had a wooden ballerina spinning top, painted white and red. They sat on the floor and the ballerina spun back and forth between them, one hand on her head, one arm stretched out. Lucy lay back on the floor and fell asleep until she heard Landish's footsteps on the stairs. Sometimes Lucy's sister, Irene, minded Deacon. She spun the ballerina too, but she talked more than Lucy and smoothed back Deacon's hair.

The "compensation" from Van was long gone. It seemed clear that, despite Van's promise, no further compensation would arrive. Landish vowed that he would hold out as long as he could before accepting top-ups. That summer, by charging less than anyone else, he managed to find piecework here and there, digging holes for fence posts, clearing and burning brush. He was often paid in food from the gardens of his employers. He made mash from blight-blackened potatoes and called it "spudding." Mimicking Deacon's pronunciation, he called his rabbit recipe "rabid stew." He made it from rabbits that he snared at the end of Dark Marsh Road. He made "turnip your nose." He also made "homophone soup," which was yellow pea.

He made cabbage à deux, shredding the cabbage and mixing it with thrice-soaked, thrice-baked, hard-boiled beans. It was one of Deacon's favourites. They went outside and walked for a long time after eating it, "venting their gustations," Landish said, which Deacon said was just a fancy way of saying farts.

"I'm not sitting on your shoulders," Deacon said. He said a dose of Landish was ten times worse than a dose of Deacon.

"The flatulent are petulant," Landish said. He could get the boy to walk more often if he could stand to eat cabbage à deux more often.

They had veg-edibles and Dark Marsh Fish. France's bacon, henglish eggs. Cod au cretin. Black Forest Cram. Dark Marsh Toad. The traditional Easter Rooster.

But Landish got fewer jobs as winter came on.

"We're down to the vestiges," Landish said.

Landish milked goats and cows that belonged to others who let them roam to graze on whatever they could find. Deacon didn't like it when Landish milked other people's cows. "Well, you can't unmilk a cow," Landish said, "so you might as well drink up." He gathered up the eggs of wayward hens whose legs bore the bands of their owners. "Just-laid eggs from unlaid hens."

When the boy had a stomach ache from lack of food, Landish would lie beside him on the bed and rub his back and belly. The boy was paler than the newly perished. Landish pretended to eat so that Deacon could have more. He went to bed hungry and, unable to sleep, made up food puns: The Merchant of Venison. Broth fresh from the brothel. A sacrificial lamb was a mutton for punishment.

Would the winter never end? Season desist.

He should write Van and tell him they had dined tonight on Sham Chowder, Lack of Lamb, Crazed Ham and Duck à Mirage. Steam of Mushroom Soup and Perish Jubilee.

Landish remembered the food they had when he was growing up, the holiday feasts. His father, who lived in the house once Gen of Eve was gone, spread a good board: imported fruits and vegetables, brightly coloured, many of them from the tropics, smoked meats, cheeses, jams and sauces, all manner of bread and cream-crammed pastries. He remembered the apparition on the Druken board of whole pineapples, coconuts, wreaths of grapes, bananas in layered bunches of fifty or sixty, brightly coloured and oddly shaped marrows. The board was as important a decoration as the Christmas tree and much of it was merely admired, never eaten.

Deacon asked Landish how you got inside your mother from the Womb of Time, and how you got from her womb to the world.

Landish told him about Dick and the happy couple. Deacon asked him what the happy couple did. Landish said they had no choice but to live in wedded bliss.

He answered all of Deacon's questions. Deacon laughed until he coughed. Landish swore that it was true. He added that he wondered if he should have waited until Deacon was older because at his age he might get it all mixed up. He said he had known men who were still confused about it when they died of old age.

"You'll see. But not until you're older. If your parents hadn't done it, you'd be purely hypothetical."

"What's that?"

"An idea in Just Mist."

Landish looked at him. If the boy were purely hypothetical, he wouldn't weigh much less than he did now.

Deacon looked inside his underwear and laughed again.

"It grows on you," Landish said. "I hope to God that something does."

Deacon knew when he was joking, so he knew that it was true. The father he had never met. The mother he could not remember. When he was hypothetical.

The "contribution," Landish called what a father did. Deacon was not old enough to make a contribution. Landish said he wasn't sure how many *he* had made but he was almost certain that none of them had worked.

If Deacon's father hadn't made a contribution, Deacon would still be waiting in the Womb of Time. More waited there forever than ever had or ever would be born.

Landish tried to see and feel what Deacon did. He tried to remember when he himself was fresh from the Murk.

Deacon seemed to see only what was good in others. He delighted in watching others enjoy themselves as if he were one of them, as if their fine clothing and conveyances, their large houses with their lavish furnishings were not things that he lacked, or was excluded from or deprived of, but were glittering spectacles in which all who merely witnessed them could share. He waved at everyone, even those he knew would not wave back. To him, everyone seemed equally deserving of attention.

Even the story of his father's death had not inclined him against Captain Druken. The point of the narrative might simply have been to relate a series of events that the two men had been equally unable to avoid, the allotment of blame being the prerogative of no one and nothing.

Landish tried to leave unposed the question of how he would get along without the boy if he had to. But he thought and dreamt about it. He woke from dreams and, finding himself alone in bed, roared out Deacon's name.

"Here I am," said Deacon, who'd been sleeping on the floor. Landish gathered him up into a hug and walked about the attic with him, saying "I thought you were gone. I dreamt that you were just a dream. I dreamt there never was a Deacon and that I lived alone."

"I'm here," Deacon said.

"Pull on my ears to make sure," Landish said.

Deacon pulled on his ears until Landish said he was convinced.

When the boy was asleep, Landish would walk about the middle of the attic, the only part in which he could stand up straight and fully stretch out both his arms. At night, when he'd been drinking, he thought about the early lives of famous writers—Dostoevsky standing at the foot of an open grave, waiting to be shot, his death sentence commuted at the last second by the emperor to seven years' hard labour in Siberia. It would take more than an emperor to convince a firing squad of Newfoundlanders that a man named Druken should be allowed to live. And they would think it a strange form of punishment that consisted of seven years of regular employment.

Having children hadn't kept Charles Dickens from becoming a writer. Paid by the word. How lucky for his wife and ten children that he didn't choose to be a poet. There would have been fewer copies of his books in the stores than there were of him around the house. He imagined Dickens the poet trying each week to build a readership. Cliffhanger endings. Leaving his readers to wonder which word he would use to rhyme with "doldrum" in the next instalment.

Tolstoy had sense enough to wait until he had his fill of one kind of life before moving on to another. A womanizing bachelor, drinker and decadent layabout for almost twenty years, he married, stopped drinking, became affrontingly industrious and began to rail against those whose careers as womanizing bachelors, drinkers and decadent layabouts had just begun. A world-famous writer whose fame would endure forever even if he never wrote another word, he realized and began to preach the virtues of obscurity, unable to find fellowship except in the company of writers who, having despaired of ever getting published, had given up writing.

He had recently written of the emptiness of all pursuits, declared himself outraged by any man who upon reaching his allotment of three score and ten continued to fend off death by consuming food and drink, but he was over seventy and very much alive.

Landish would lay a page flat on the embers and watch it ignite, scorching outward from the middle, curling up at the corners. He wondered if it was just a pose, this burning of everything he wrote. The great, uncompromising artist who accepted nothing less from himself than perfection. He took the pages he wrote and reread each one before he fed it to the fire. Everything he wrote struck him as a failed, forced imitation of something he had read. Sometimes, somehow without his noticing until he was reviewing what he'd written, phrases, even whole sentences from his favourite writers made it into his night's work.

What would have been the point of keeping the pages, storing them in some ever-growing pile, the accumulated futility of years, there, very there every time he pushed another heap beneath the bed or made room for another in the closet? It would be hard to convince himself that they were not the measure of how much of his life he had so far wasted.

Perhaps he was all too typical a Druken, his nature inimical to creation, suited only for destruction.

"What's your book about?"

"I'll tell you when it's finished."

"A secret."

"Not really. Just for now."

"You should read your book to me."

"I will when it's finished."

"When will that be?"

"I don't know. It's hard to put people into words."

While Landish was writing, Deacon would stare at him. Landish would look up and Deacon would look away.

Landish didn't notice anything while he was trying to put people into words. Maybe he could hear them in his head. "Characters," Landish called them. Landish could hear them but Deacon couldn't. Deacon wasn't a character. Landish didn't notice Deacon. He acted as if Deacon wasn't there. Landish shielded his face with his hand. He hunched over the table. He pressed down with his pen so hard that Deacon heard the writing from his bed. The table shook. Landish whispered as if he was talking to the people in his book. Deacon thought they must be more fun to spend time with than a runt like him. It bothered Landish when Deacon moved or made a sound. He looked at Deacon like he was about to shout at him but all he did was sigh and shake his head.

When Landish took a break from writing, he put a blank piece of paper on top of the pile of paper and a beach rock the size of his fist on top of that. That meant that he wasn't done for the night, just taking a break. He would read for a while, or nap, or sit and stare into the fire. The rock was to keep the papers in place. Landish told Deacon that he was also to think of the rock as a lock. He asked him to promise not to move the rock and Deacon promised. He made him promise with his left hand on the rock and his right hand held up like in court.

"The book is not your rival," Landish said, and explained what "rival" meant. Still, Deacon would look at the pile of paper on his desk and feel the urge to burn it in the fireplace. Other times, when he watched Landish feed page after page into the fire, he was glad. But then he felt bad for Landish, and thought how sad and angry he'd be if *Deacon* burned his book. It was Landish's book. No one else was allowed to burn it. Deacon even felt sorry for the people in the book who Landish said would "go down in mystery." But the next night he would be tempted again by the sight of the pile of paper on the table.

"It's about my father," Landish said. "I haven't even made up a new name for him yet. That's all I'm going to tell you."

But then he said it was about the adventures of Captain Druken, who lived in an attic in a city where no one lived except in attics and the sealers at the seal hunt all lived in one big attic on the ship and the Governor lived in the attic of Government House and the Queen lived in the attic of Buckingham Palace and had to walk through two hundred kitchens to get to *her* kitchen.

Landish always looked at the map before he started work on his book.

He told Deacon the map stood for the world, the way the world might look if you could see it from halfway to the moon, which was too high up for birds. There was nothing halfway to the moon but empty space, nothing to stand on while you looked down at the world. A round map called a globe was even better. Landish grew up in a house that had a globe in every room, but he said that even one was too expensive now.

A place on the map that was called the key explained the dots. Five dots in descending size. It showed one kind of line that stood for railroads. There was a broken line that connected ports of call.

But there were no lines of any kind on Newfoundland. There were no lakes, rivers or mountains. It was featureless but for its name, which was spelled out in three words instead of one. The map was made in England.

There was no dot for St. John's on the map. No dot about it. Not dot-worthy. A place of nil repute. The island bore nothing but the name of Newfoundland, as if every inch of it was just like every other inch.

"Surely they could spare one dot for here," Landish shouted.

"Shhhhh," Deacon said.

"I'm sorry, Deacon," Landish said. "I am besotted with dots."

He said he had never read or even heard of a book set in a place that didn't rate a single dot.

Deacon said, "St. John's might get a dot if you wrote a book about it."

Landish said he might be right, but St. John's should have a dot, book or not. And what chance did a book written in and about a dot-unworthy place have against all the books from places such as London and New York that had the biggest dots of all?

Deacon wished he could make Landish go to bed, but sometimes everything he said only seemed to make him worse, make him talk louder and stride back and forth with his boots still on, the hobnails scratching up the floor that wasn't theirs.

He told Landish that no one cared about the dots, but Landish shook his head. He said most Newfoundlanders had never seen dot-acknowledged places such as New York and London. That's why they didn't care about the dots. But dots were important to people who lived in places that were deemed worthy of dots.

"I don't care about the dots," Deacon said. "I don't mind if we stay here forever."

"You will mind, though," Landish said. "Here we are poor and it won't get better, and that will matter more as you get older. Anyone can be an unread writer. Any fool can burn the fragments of a never-to-be-finished book."

Landish stayed up late, drinking, decks awash with grog when he was done.

Deacon heard Hogan in the kitchen down below. Hogan would tell the nobleman, who would write a letter and push it underneath the door when he and Landish were asleep.

Landish's father went to the place from which no one knows the way back home. Was found dead in his house on a snowy day by his house-keeper, his arms on the armrests of a chair that faced the front-room window that was so thickly coated with frost and snow the room was as dark at noon as it would have been at twilight.

"You're an orphan, too, now," Deacon said.

"A brace of orphans," Landish said.

The *Gilbert* would soon be someone else's, though her new owners would not be allowed to change the name. It would be sold by the Churches to the highest bidder. To Landish, his father left the laurel wreath of sealers: the white sealskin hat.

On condition that they not hire Landish as a teacher or otherwise pay him for services he might be qualified or willing to perform, the Churches got the ship, the house and all its contents, and the money. Landish got the white fur hat.

And the Churches sold it all to the nobleman, who not only kept many of Captain Druken's things but left them exactly where they were, visible through the windows. Landish pictured the Druken house looking exactly as it had when he was last inside it, the nobleman roaming the rooms like some pale simulacrum of his father.

Landish sat in the attic with the hat on his lap for part of every day for two weeks after Captain Druken died.

He thought of Deacon's father and he thought of Deacon's mother. Outside, snow was falling. He heard the crunching sound of boots on snow packed hard by other boots. Carson was three months missing when the boy was born, his wife a widow when she gave birth to her first and only child. The boy was in the womb while his father lay in a place of ice so far from shore there was no shore, the sky a flat black wafer at whose rim a perfect pale of light remained until the sun came up again.

What was the message of his father's gift? *Why should I care what you think of me when I am so highly thought of by the world that has already cast you out?* He hadn't so much bequeathed him the hat as he had shoved it in his face. Looking at the box, he fancied that the answer was literally contained within it, a note of explanation from his father sewn into the lining of the hat or that of the box. He felt like ripping box and hat apart just to satisfy himself that they held no secrets. *It doesn't matter if you destroy it, burn it, sell it, lose it, give it or throw it away. It will ever be an affront to you.* He could not in this manner decipher the meaning of the hat, for how would he know, who would tell him, which conjecture was the one? It might take nothing less than the decipherment of his father to puzzle out the meaning of the hat, nothing less than the completion of his book.

He remembered again how his father's face looked in repose. There was still the hint of the face of a man who in his youth might have been like Landish and had once had put to him by his own father the question the hat might be meant to pose to Landish: what do you want and what are you willing to do to get it and how much of what you could have are you truly willing to renounce in the name of virtue?

He tried in vain to convince himself he didn't care why his father wanted him to have the hat. Didn't care what kind of final gesture of contempt or last attempt to change his mind it was meant to be.

Perhaps his father meant to tell him that he was all too typical a Druken, his nature inimical to creation, suited for destruction, the only thing that distinguished him from *them* being the self-abhorrence that he mistook as proof that his basic nature was unlike theirs. His father and the others had not lamented or made excuses for their natures. All the self-abhorrence he could muster would not redeem him if he simply lacked the gumption to *act* according to whom and what he was. What would he have done if his father had not disowned him, if he had left everything to him, attaching no conditions to the inheritance of his estate, the *Gilbert* included?

He wouldn't have renounced his father's fortune, though he knew it to have been immorally acquired. He wouldn't have scuttled the *Gilbert.* He would have sold it to another sealing skipper or some wealthy merchant, someone who had provoked almost as much dark talk as his father had. He would have accepted his inheritance with the sincere intention of doing something more worthwhile with it than simply enlarging it by any means for which he could escape all blame. He would have convinced himself that, even tended by a Druken, a foul tree need not blossom forth in a foul manner. Would that have made him a better man than Abram Druken or merely an opportunistic hypocrite? It might be that the answer to such questions lay nowhere but in his book.

Landish brought out the sealskin hat and Deacon smoothed it with his hand. "It's soft," he said. "Is that what a seal feels like?"

"It's something like what a pup feels like," Landish said. "Their white coats are not as long as this. This hair is woven together."

Landish looked at the hat. Perhaps his father was taunting him. Do something with your life that rivals what I did with mine. Measure up to me. Win the laurel wreath of *something*. But that wasn't quite it because writing didn't measure up to sealing in his father's estimation. Nothing did. Writers were ineffectuals who came close to not counting at all. His father might merely have been daring him to decline the hat. Tempt fate by declining it.

There appeared in a local paper:

IN MARCH OF EIGHTEEN NINETY-FIVE
The news rings out from every bell:
The *Gilbert*'s dead with God survive
While Captain Druken burns in hell.

Landish decided that it was time to take Deacon to see the Crosses.

He knew that Deacon's mother was buried in a boulder-strewn Catholic cemetery called Mount Carmel, but he had never been there. All he knew was that the graves (one empty) of Deacon's parents were marked with wooden crosses. The graveyard was on the windward side of the Brow, across the Waterford, up the hill from the top of which you could just see the lighthouse at Cape Spear.

Landish climbed the Brow with Deacon on his shoulders, pausing to rest from time to time.

"We're really far from the attic now, hey?" Deacon said when they were halfway up the hill.

"Really far."

"Are we still in St. John's?"

"Not really," Landish said.

"Where are we?"

"Nowhere—smack in the middle of it. You talk, I'm out of breath."

They walked until they reached the road that led to nowhere but the cemetery, and then they were offered a ride the rest of the way by others driving carts piled with tools, paint, tar and other things they needed to repair the gravesites.

At first, Deacon was scared at the thought of his mother and other people being underground. He imagined them all lying on their backs with their hands folded on their stomachs as he and Landish did sometimes. He didn't want to think about what Landish said were their "remains." Landish said that he had never seen remains. Most people hadn't—not after the remains were buried. He had seen animals when there was nothing left but bones, but people were in boxes with their clothes on, so they didn't look like that.

Two small white wooden crosses about three feet high stood side by side, one for her and one for Deacon's father. There were no inscriptions aside from their names, just the dates of birth and death for her, and for him the date of his birth and the date that he was "lost at sea," burned into the wood by what Landish guessed was pitch.

Landish recited a verse he had composed the night before.

"His date of birth by none forgot/His date of death recorded not/So think his way from death to birth/A timeless time upon this earth."

The cross bore his father's name, but his father wasn't there. His remains were in the ocean. Landish said it was too late to find them now. They wouldn't turn up.

"This is where my mother is," Deacon said, pointing at the ground in front of the cross on the left. "This is where they put her." Landish knew that, like him, Deacon had no idea who "they" were.

"Her head is here and her feet are there," Deacon said.

"That's right," Landish said.

"There's no one buried there," Deacon said, pointing at the other grave.

"No," Landish said, "but it's good to have a cross for him beside your mother's."

Deacon nodded. Landish remembered the words of the woman the boy could not remember, the woman who for months had written to him. He remembered well the face of the man Deacon had never met and had no picture of. He felt guilty at the knowledge of whose fault it was that he was gone. He wondered if, even as a powerless, unknowing apprentice to his father, he had ever been the smallest bit to blame for some man's death.

Landish borrowed an axe to hammer the crosses deeper into the rocky ground. He and Deacon propped them up with stones, and Landish, with some borrowed twine, anchored them to pegs that he made from branches that he cut and notched. They had picked wildflowers on the way to the cemetery and they placed them at the feet of the crosses.

Landish had been able to think of little he could say to prepare the boy for the visit. He had guessed that there would be no stone or marble monuments to Deacon's parents, but he hadn't been prepared for the makeshift, wooden, weathered crosses, or the sight of plots that for more than three years had been left untended.

He didn't pray or say words over the graves as he and Deacon stood there looking down. He wasn't sure that Deacon knew that such things were ever done. He let the boy have his say and left it at that.

It was dark by the time they got back to the attic.

"Let's go see *your* parents' graves next," Deacon said.

Landish had not been among the hundreds who attended his father's funeral and he hadn't gone to see where he was buried.

"All right," Landish said.

The gravesite was cared for by a man who was paid from a fund set up by Captain Druken before his death. The stone marking his mother's grave had been removed to make way for a mausoleum that was about the size of a tool shed. The mausoleum contained the remains of Captain and Mrs. Druken. Abram and Genevieve. There was a sealed metal door that had no handle. Though Landish had never been inside it, he had been told that his parents lay in two marble coffins supported by a granite catafalque. The family name was spelled out above the door.

The mausoleum was surrounded by lesser Druken monuments that relative to most others in the graveyard were quite large and ornate: trumpeting or sword-wielding angels crouching atop head-stones, tall stone crosses, schooner-shaped stones, markers fashioned after figureheads, bas-reliefs of ships, sealing captains in uniform, seals like family totems lying peacefully asleep on the graves of children. Seals instead of lambs.

But the mausoleum was the centrepiece of this largest-ever gather-ing of Drukens, this Tomb of Time reunion on whose invitation list his name had once appeared, but from which it had been struck, though any sons whom he might have in lawful matrimony who made sealing their profession would be welcome, according to his father's executor.

Captain Druken wasn't underground or underwater, just indoors. Deacon knocked on the door, then tried to push it open. He knew of houses that were not much bigger and they were made of wood and looked as if they would fall down in a gust of wind. Deacon couldn't imagine anything that would knock the mausoleum down.

It was all there, in the cemetery, the history of the Druken line, spelled out in epitaphs, inscriptions, chronologies, necrologies. The oldest grave that of a second mate, 1722. The first first mate, the first captain. Some of them lost at sea. "At repose within these walls lie Captain Abram Druken who died in the seventy-sixth year of his age and beside him his beloved wife, Genevieve, who died in the forty-second year of her age. 'And all that handle the oar, the mariners, and all the pilots of the sea shall come down from their ships, they shall stand upon the land.' Ezekiel 27:29."

Looking at the mausoleum, Landish could not help but think of the two wind-tilted wooden crosses.

His father had set aside more for the mausoleum than Landish had so far spent on Deacon.

"Why did they put them in a house?"

"It's called a mausoleum. Some people think that it's better than being buried. But you can't have windows. They'd get broken and people could see in."

"They might have been afraid of being buried."

"A mausoleum stands out more than a grave," Landish said. "You notice it more. That's what he wanted."

"It's pretty small," Deacon said, looking at it as though he pitied its occupants, or even the house itself.

"Small for a house," Landish said, thinking of the one he'd grown up in and had shown Deacon several times, though they'd never gone near it. "Two dead people don't need a lot of room."

Deacon referred to it as "the little stone house." He was not comparing it to the other monuments in the graveyard but to the other houses in the city, as if the hut-like stone house was the measure of the pitiful penury in which the Drukens had lived and died, the name Druken seeming to Landish to evoke for Deacon a humbly indigent couple whom everyone felt sorry for because they had nothing to their name but their little windowless house on the grounds of a graveyard.

He asked Deacon what he thought about leaving Newfoundland.

"Are you going too?" Deacon said, wondering if Landish was sending him away but determined not to cry.

"Of course I'm going too," he said.

"Where?"

"I don't know. Away from here. Somewhere else."

Deacon looked around him at the attic.

"When will we go?"

"I don't know. As soon as we can."

He told Deacon it would be their secret. He mustn't tell anyone, especially the nuns who were nurses too. He told Deacon not to even *look* like they were leaving soon.

"I'm going to write to Van, asking for his help," Landish said. He had told Deacon nothing about Van but that he had been his best friend at Princeton.

"Van will help us," Deacon said.

"Maybe. It's worth a try. He paid for *everything* at Lotus Land. I wonder how he feels about me now."

"He misses you."

Landish told Deacon about Van's sister, Vivvie.

Deacon imagined Van trying to find his sister, patting the bottom of the lake the way Deacon patted the floor when the room was dark and he couldn't find his shoes. But Van's little sister was in the dark *and* underwater. Deacon had never been underwater, not all of him at once. The washtub wasn't big enough. He could sit or kneel in it, sit back on his heels. His head didn't fit under except when Landish held him by the feet and dunked him, but even then most of him wasn't in the water. Deacon thought about Vivvie, all of her underwater, so far under it was dark and her brother couldn't find her. It would be hard to find someone so small. Her wet clothes weighed her down, dragged her down, Landish said. Her little shoes, her stockings, her dress with all the ruffles, even her hair which was so much longer than a boy's. Van went down to the bottom of the lake and came up with a piece of wood that he thought was Vivvie.

"Van is from the Land of Plenty," Landish told Deacon. "We are from the Land of Scanty."

"Van will help us," Deacon repeated.

Dear Van:

I told you when we parted that you would never hear from me again. Nothing short of needing your help to save a child's life would make me change my mind.

I have in my care a four-year-old boy who, because of my father, has no parents, a bright, sweet boy whom I love as much as any father-by-blood has ever loved his son.

We are near penniless. We live in a two-room attic and often do not have enough to eat. I fear that, soon, certain well-meaning but deluded people may decide that the boy would be better off without me.

I don't want him to wind up back in one of the city's denominational orphanages. Abominational, they should be called. He would be raised by clergy who believe that the best education for a boy is one that is beaten into him.

In these orphanages, it is widely believed, the taking of liberties, physical and otherwise, is commonplace. Such an upbringing would be more than you or I could have borne as children, and this boy, Deacon, has even fewer reserves of strength than other boys his age.

Even if he were healthy, it is likely that, as I am unmarried and not perceived as being, in every sense, a moral exemplar, the courts might take him from me. But I will do all that I can, legal and otherwise, to prevent it.

Should you agree to my proposal, I could earn my keep by tutoring the children of the servants at Vanderland, or by any other means that you propose.

I hope you will see fit to send funds for our transportation to Vanderland, which you may deduct from my wages under such terms as

you see fit. If you do, we will then set out from Newfoundland before
any person so inclined has the opportunity to lay claim to Deacon.

I believe that, given all that has transpired between us, and all the
material means and powers of benign force that you possess, I am not
asking for too great a favour. Van, I write in memory of the friendship
we once had and—who knows—perhaps might have again . . .

Two months later, Landish received a brief reply in an envelope
addressed to him in handwriting that he was certain wasn't Van's.
There was no return address, nor any opening or closing salutations
in the letter:

I regret that the circumstances of the past make it necessary that we
never correspond or meet or otherwise communicate again.

"Van won't help us," Landish told Deacon.
"But he's your friend."
Landish shrugged.
Deacon gave his leg a reassuring hug.
"I don't know why I hoped he would. I didn't tell you this before,
but he got me sacked from Princeton and I renounced him for all time.
Perhaps I shouldn't have. I don't say that just because we need him
now. It's a terrible thing to consign someone to the outer darkness of
your life forever. I should have known that, having been thus consigned
by my father who can never change his mind now, never offer an apol-
ogy or ask forgiveness. Perhaps it's not too late for me. Perhaps I
should write to him again and tell him how I truly feel."

My Dearest Friend:

I know that your motives for doing what you did at Princeton were
not malignant. I knew it then, but was so confused and hurt, so angry

and hateful-hearted that I could think of nothing but revenge, which I had but one means of exacting from a Vanderluyden. Your actions were wrong-headed, meddlesome—and treacherous, I thought, but I no longer think so.

We were both naive in our different ways. Given your upbringing, how could you have understood how much harm your hoax would do to me? The reversal of a fortune like yours is inconceivable, impossible—and therefore, such a profound reversal of fortune and fate as I have suffered may have been inconceivable to you—as may the possibility that, even when the alternative to it was all but nothing, I would turn my back on the life my father sought to impose on me.

I am sorry for having said what I hope will not be the last words I ever speak to you, for disowning you as if consigning you to non-existence, an act of greater hubris than any you committed.

I feel better from just having written this letter. I want you to know that, even should you not change your mind about my request, even if I should never hear from you again, I will remember you fondly and cherish the time we spent at Lotus Land. I wish you well.

Yours truly,

Landish Druken

Three months later, a letter from Van arrived:

. . . It is unlike you to have burdened yourself with a beggar boy, especially as, by doing so, you've made a beggar of yourself, all out of stubbornness, pride and spite. You're doing penance for a crime you had no hand in. You cut off your nose to spite your face—renounced your inheritance to spite your father because he wanted you to be what all fathers want their sons to be, his successor.

Much has changed since the moment you vowed that I would never hear from you again. I moved into Vanderland on Christmas Day, 1895.

At Princeton, when you and I lived at Lotus Land, I more or less offered you co-proprietorship of Vanderland. I spoke of us raising our families at Vanderland. I have begun my family, and you, in the oddest manner imaginable, have begun yours. I have a wife, and a daughter who is about the age of the boy you bought as if from a shop his mother pawned him to.

You are in desperate circumstances, a state for which I am sorry but not responsible. It has taken me a long time to reconcile myself to the fact that you, my long-hoped-for, long-yearned-for life mate, are gone for good.

Hours, days, weeks that I should have spent with my team of architects and engineers I spent instead walking the barely begun roads and paths of the estate, wondering if there remained any point to Vanderland, if I might not just as well abandon what was now the dream of many.

Leave it, I told myself, leave the razed landscape, the heaping piles of stones and timber, mounds of stumps and miles of tangled roots, leave it as a monument to failed conviction and the bafflement of imagination.

I eventually reacquired my belief in Vanderland, reminding myself that I was wholly alone when I first decided to give over my life to the raising up of my utopia, the most distinguished private residence on earth, far from the hurried, frenzied, riotous advance of Manhattan and the other cities of the North.

So then, to answer your request: I have become accustomed to your absence from my life. Neither of us are who we were when I proposed that you follow me to Vanderland. Your presence now would upset my peace of mind, my hard-won equanimity. I would fret about what might have been, what would have been, but which now can never be.

I could simply give you some money, enough to allow you to start afresh elsewhere. But I doubt that you could start afresh even were you not weighted down by that millstone of a child. You would ask for more money. You would never stop asking. And your letters alone would remind me of you and might cause me to fret in the very manner that you being here in person would do.

We have hurt each other too deeply ever to reconcile. It is too late, Landish. You made a vow and must keep it from now on. You must make good on your promise that I would never hear from you again . . .

Landish began another letter to Van:

. . . Your letter finds us ensconced at Whileaway, which, as you may know, is modelled after the famous Attic on the Seine, perhaps the most architecturally distinctive one-room dwelling in the world, though worthy of at least a tip of the hat are Mudd Hutt Haus on the Rhine and Hovelhaven of East Anglia.

You once wrote, "What man can claim to be civilized who doesn't have a second residence?" How right you were we didn't know until we began to winter in one room and summer in the other, our beloved Idlehours, which each September we must take our leave of to return to the irksome minutiae, the hustle bustle and congestion of "real life" in the adjoining room.

You need not have gone to the trouble of writing in such detail of your safari and "the most magnificent beasts" whose heads you now have mounted on your wall to one as accustomed as I am to the thrill of bringing down a rabbit.

As for hobbies, yes, of course, a man must have them, all work and no pay, etc. My avocation is the acquisition of knowledge. I have read that horses are your avocation. To tell you the truth, I read so much about horses that I have no time to ride, race, breed, hunt with or avoid being trampled by them, or run over in the street by the conveyances they pull. In truth, I have yet to pull myself away from reading about horses long enough to look into the purchasing of one, or to consider the question of how to get it up the stairs or decide which of our two rooms would best double as a stable.

But how few they must be who, from reading about them, know horses as I do, know, for instance, that to horses the avocado is fatally toxic. When they were all but conquered, the Aztecs walked out against the conquistadors with nothing in their hands but avocados . . .

"I don't expect we'll hear from Van again," Landish told Deacon.

Landish drank and began to sing.

"Shhhh," Deacon said. "Hogan will tell. The 'Stab will soon be here. They'll take me back to Cluding Deacon. They'll take you off to jail."

Landish nodded. He could hear Hogan down below, walking about as though ransacking his rooms in search of something that would make the singing stop. But then Landish stamped his feet and began to sing again, banging his fists on the table.

Deacon threw his arms around his leg.

"My dear old friend from my dear old days at Princeton. My pal. He said no. I'm glad."

"You don't sound glad," Deacon said.

"Well, I am."

"You hate your father. I hate mine too."

"No, no," Landish said. "Never say that you hate your father, Deacon. Never. He was a great man. Remember the story of Carson of the *Gilbert*. Never forget it."

"Because it's true?"

"That's right."

Carson, long gone before he slid into the sea. Warm and peaceful at the frozen end. Alone but not lonely. Unafraid. Untroubled. No reason to doubt that he would soon see her again. And soon after that their child. A boy perhaps. Perhaps a girl. He would have felt for certain that everyone at home and all the men of his watch were safe and warm like him. No one to look out for now. No reason not to close his eyes. Dark. A pale of light around the rim. *Zodiacal*. Light from a sun long set, now shining elsewhere. He would not have known the word.

"My next crossing of the Gulf will be the final one for me. The first for you. But the ninth and last for me."

"Why?"

"I'm not coming back. If I ever get away from here, I'm never coming back."

"I'm not either."

"The first and last crossing for you then."

"What will where we go be like?"

"I don't know. Nicer than here."

But they didn't go, because they couldn't.

The nuns came by more often. They took Deacon aside and asked him if he liked Landish and did Landish treat him well. They took Landish aside and said that he and Deacon could not go on like this forever. Anyway, he had to go to school. If their situation didn't soon improve, measures would be taken.

Landish called the two nuns Nun One and Nun Too Soon: Landish said she'd become a nun when someone told her to and she was too young to know she could say no. He said that Nun One was in charge. The other nun was nice. Her face and hands were always red. Landish said she had an after-bath complexion and could have been Deacon's not-much-older sister. She never piped up except when Nun One told her to. She smiled at the floor.

Nun Too Soon brought him clothes that were donated to the Church. She carried a bag of them over her shoulder up the stairs and sorted through it while Nun One was talking to Landish. She found him shirts and trousers that fit. Nun One said they were from boys who were younger, but bigger, than him. Hand-me-ups, Landish called them. Nun Too Soon smiled at Deacon as he tried on the shirts and trousers.

He knew that he must somehow keep the boy away from school. He told the nuns who were nurses too of his Princeton education, going along with their pretence that they never knew he had been to Princeton and didn't know it was his father who had given to their Church the money that was buying food for them instead of for the boy whose circumstances so concerned them.

Landish told them he could go on teaching the boy at home, being better educated than anyone in any school who taught the lower forms. Just for a few more years at least, he said, knowing that Nun One would not abide the dragging on forever of this or any other manner of defiance.

He told them without invoking his last name that the boy would not survive a month, let alone a year, at school. He told them he was far too small, small in a way that no amount of food would fix, helpless in a way that other boys could smell, in a way that would have drawn them to pick on him even if he were twice their size.

"It's true," Nun One said. "I wouldn't give him a fighting chance against a girl half his age."

Nun One allowed that overcrowding was a problem, there being too few schools, so they would let him teach the boy at home until a place for him became available—a place for him to sit or stand, she might as well have said. Landish thought of Deacon cast adrift in such a place, the parentless, adopted son of a Druken who no longer had immunity, a powerless Druken who had no wealth to wield against the fathers of his classmates, the last of a line whose legendary wrath they could now avenge without fear of being blacklisted by the Drukens, and so turned away from every door.

The nuns who were nurses too began to give them a small amount of money each time they came to visit. They told Landish they would hear about it if he spent it on anything but food. Just before they gave Landish the money envelope, Nun One recited a prayer:

For every Bane there is a Blessing
For every Wound a Dressing
For every Malady and Misery a Cure.

On one occasion, Landish replied:

But I think it, Sister, worth confessing—
For it's us you are assessing—
That it's you we find the hardest to endure.

"I'm sure, Mr. Druken," she said, "that you would find it no burden to do without your stipend for a month. But I think the boy would find it burdensome. Tell me, were you thinking of the boy or only of yourself when you made up that hurtful verse? Here is your stipend. I hope you'll be more cordial the next time we stop by. You're very clever, Mr. Druken, and you're only in your twenties, but unless you turn it to some better use, your cleverness may outlive this little boy. You haven't been poor long enough to truly understand what it means to be poor. But this child has lived in poverty since he was born."

Landish knew she was right, knew that he'd not only been hurtful but selfish and reckless to mock Nun One who held Deacon's fate in her hands.

A man they nicknamed the "wealth inspector," of whom Hogan often spoke and who Landish thought meant well, began, at the behest of the nuns, to come by once a month to give them food vouchers and to see if the contents of the attic matched the list of their possessions, which he held in front of him on a clipboard as he walked about, ticking off each item with a pencil. He enumerated every object in the attic as if preparing for an auction. The table and two chairs. The bed. A few dishes and some cutlery. A few books. Gen of Eve and Captain Druken's hat. Two washtubs.

His job was to make sure that those to whom he gave vouchers that could be redeemed for food at certain stores had no secret sources of income. Landish told Deacon that some wealth inspectors would quibble over the smallest gift. They would count the number of trout you caught and dock you accordingly. Or the number of blueberries you still had strength enough to pick.

But *their* wealth inspector never quibbled. He always made the same joke, pretending that Deacon was an item on his list, opposite whose name there was a box in which he put an X.

· "Just the one Deacon, same as last month?" he would say. "Good. No Deacon deduction then."

He sometimes gave Deacon a large candy called a peppermint knob.

He measured off a wedge of vouchers from the roll he carried in his coat.

They were required to allow him—or else forfeit their right to vouchers—to search through closets, cupboards, under beds, through bed linen, dresser drawers. He could do anything that might turn up what he referred to as "excess."

It was always roughly a month between visits, but they never knew for certain when the wealth inspector might arrive. As soon as you leave, Landish told him, we start roasting legs of lamb that we have hidden beneath the floorboards in the house.

"Mine is a thankless job," the wealth inspector said, "but one that I cannot afford to lose. You never give me any trouble, Mr. Druken, but some others, let me tell you."

So he did. He told Landish of the others while Deacon sat and listened to them talk. "What I see is what you have," he said. "I never doubt it but I must go through the motions of making sure. This attic poses no great challenge to a man of my profession."

"What with it being so uncluttered," Landish said, "and having only one porthole we can throw things out of when we hear you coming up the stairs."

"I know you like to joke with me," the wealth inspector said. "I enjoy it, it helps me keep perspective, and I have always done right by the two of you. Truth be told to no one but you and me and the boy, I have sometimes allotted you an extra voucher or two."

Landish, well able to imagine the treatment that he received in certain houses—the threats and offers of God only knew what sorts of bribes, the avowals of revenge and of nighttime visits to his house, whose address would have been widely known—felt grateful to him. He wore a wedding ring, no doubt had children of his own of whom he never spoke.

Landish suspected that no other wealth inspector would omit from his list as valuable an item as Captain Druken's hat. But their inspector said it should stay in the family of the man whose great accomplishment it symbolized.

Deacon liked the hat. It was the only new-looking thing they owned. The fur was like snow that never melted and was never spoiled. The wooden box shone like the polished tops of tables he had seen in the windows of a store on Water Street when they walked to the west end to watch the trains come and go. He could see himself in the golden clasps that gleamed like the doorknobs of some houses they passed when they went out for a walk.

Deacon knew that the hat stood for something and that Landish liked it more than he let on. The hat stood for first, best, perfect. It looked nice and felt nice. It reminded Deacon of a pet dog he had seen a lady holding in her arms in a carriage that went by them on the road the day they went to see the Crosses.

That winter, they felt so pent up in the attic that they went out in the daytime even in the worst of storms, Deacon astride his neck and hunkered down behind his head like a jockey as Landish barged, waisted, chested on through drifts he couldn't see and Deacon shouted things he couldn't hear. Once a storm stopped, the snow was quickly spoiled by walkers and horses and carriages. For a while the snow in the streets looked like mashed potatoes and gravy, but even that never lasted long. The streets got worse, all churned up by wheels and hooves, and what the horses, cows and goats—the "dungsters," Landish called them—left behind from their behinds.

Landish told Deacon he was lucky. He didn't have to walk in it, and his nose was further from the smell of it than other noses were, including Landish's.

"To the manure born," Landish said. "Ordure will out."

When they got home, Landish cleaned his boots as best he could before he went indoors. And then he had to climb up to the attic, boots in hand, his socks stuffed in his boots, his bare feet sticking to someone else's stairs and floors while Deacon walked noisily ahead of him in boots as clean and dry as they were when he went out.

When it snowed heavily, Landish was hired as one of the Snowmen, the brigade who were paid to shovel snow from the streets. Landish didn't have a shovel, but he was hired because of the rate at which he shovelled snow, about twice as fast as anyone else. They gave him a shovel, and gave Deacon a spade that was used for digging in confined spaces. A back-breakingly short spade, unless you were the size of Deacon. The other Snowmen didn't mind Deacon. They joked about how they might shovel him by accident and throw him up on someone's roof. Deacon picked at the snow with his spade while the men worked around him. Landish looked back now and then to make sure he was keeping up, and was not too cold or tired or getting in the way.

The Snowmen appeared in streets all over the city once the word went out that men were needed. No one was guaranteed a job. You could have shovelled the streets a hundred times before, but if you were late getting out you might not get hired. Each Snowman was given a piece of paper signed by one of the foremen that showed the exact time that the piece of paper had changed hands. When you brought it back to the foreman, he calculated how long you had been working, how much money or how many food vouchers you were due.

It wasn't necessarily true that the bigger the storm, the more money you made, because big storms brought out what Landish called the Snowpokes, who did almost no work and only came out because they wanted to be part of Something Big.

Flailing shovels were everywhere as the Snowmen loaded wheelbarrows and horse-hauled carts with snow or simply threw it to one side.

"We can't have a boy in the middle of that," one foreman said, and told Landish that unless he did something about the boy, he would have to give up his shovel and another man would take his place.

"We'll make sure nothing happens to the boy," the oldest of the Snowmen said, but the foreman said no.

Landish told Deacon to shovel doorsteps and stay off the streets. Deacon did as Landish said. Most of the time someone came out when he was done and gave him a piece of candy. A man gave him a steaming damper dog, a bun of pan-fried dough smothered in molasses that he quickly ate before it could get cold. He looked up from eating to see Landish smiling at him from among the Snowmen. His hands were cold and sticky when he put his mitts back on.

He became tired and cold more quickly when he shovelled by himself. Landish told him not to wait until his feet and hands hurt to say that he was cold. When he thought that Landish wasn't looking, he put his hands in his armpits and stamped his feet. But Landish always saw him and came running and hoisted him on his shoulders. "Time to call it a day," Landish said.

He gave the foreman back his shovel and took his pay in coins or vouchers. There was always what Landish called a shovel deduction. Less two vouchers for the shovel. Deacon hated it when, because of him, they had to go home early and Landish made less pay. But he couldn't help stamping his feet once they got cold and wet. Landish would put him straight in the tub when they got home and examine his fingers and toes.

"You lasted longer than some of the men," Landish said.

"I can stay here in the attic next time," Deacon said. "Then you can shovel as long as everyone else."

"No, I'm not leaving you alone. Especially not at night."

"I won't do anything wrong," Deacon said. "You used to leave me alone with Lucy and Irene."

"I know, but I shouldn't have. Something might happen downstairs. Or the nuns might come and find you by yourself."

"What might happen?"

"You never know, that's the thing, you never know. Something."

"A fire?"

"Maybe, or something no one can prevent or name. I don't know what. I just don't want you alone in the attic out here on Dark Marsh Road. If there's one thing we'll never run out of, it's snowstorms. So I can come in early when you get too cold."

But the following month went by without a flake of snow.

"I never thought I'd miss it," Landish said, who had taken to gazing out the porthole in search of any sign that the weather might be turning hard. It did nothing but rain for a month. And then it turned much too cold for snow.

Landish had no gun, but some men gave him seabirds until, because they had so little ammunition left, they told him they could spare no more.

They walked past stores in which rabbits, though they were out of season, hung upside down in doorways. They passed a window showing apples piled in rows a dozen deep. When Deacon wasn't looking, Landish stole two sweet oranges and some sugar-dusted cherries. He made a dessert for the boy, surprising him with a dish of orange wedges sprinkled with chopped cherries.

Soon, because of ice, no supply ships could reach the island. No fishing boats could leave it. Every port was cut off from every other.

The wealth inspector still came by, giving out fewer vouchers because the stores were running low on some supplies.

They tried to fish in nearby ponds. Landish didn't have an ice auger and the ice was too thick for his axe. It was the same with the pools on the smallest brooks. The axe struck mud at the bottom of one hole.

Over the more distant, larger streams there formed shells of ice through which you could barely hear the tantalizing sound of running water.

Landish fished in the streams as he had when he was a boy, with a bamboo pole, a length of twine and one single-barbed, barely baited hook, baited with almost anything depending on how cold it was. There were patches of open ground, but he couldn't break them with his axe to look for worms, so he had to fish with the eyes of trout he had caught the day before.

One day, though the footing was treacherous, Landish walked out onto a river and hacked his way to water. He told Deacon to stay back.

He had just dropped in a hook when the ice gave way beneath him. He went all the way under, briefly, then bobbed up in the hole he'd made. He heard himself breathing like a whelping seal. His heart made a mad bid to escape, battering the walls and floor and ceiling of his chest. He thrashed his way to shore, planks and squares of ice falling from his shoulders, his hair and clothing matted to him.

Deacon had thought Landish was gone. Engulfed. But Landish came up from the river like he lived beneath the ice.

Landish scrambled up the riverbank. Putting his hands on his hips and bending over, he breathed like Deacon did when he ran so fast he scorched his throat. He looked up at the sky and dribbled water from his lips.

"Landish."

"We have to get home fast."

Landish hoisted Deacon on his shoulders and began to run. His clothing froze, stiffened, rubbed against his skin. He reached one hand inside his hair and squeezed his ears until they burned. On the tip of his nose there was a frozen drop of blood.

"You all right, Deacon?" Landish said through clenched teeth.

"I can run."

"No, you can't keep up. It's faster like this."

Landish's voice sounded like it did when Deacon drummed on his back with his fists.

"Fell in, did ya?" Hogan said. He was wearing a coat with the fur-fringed hood pulled up. Deacon couldn't see his face even when Landish put him on the floor.

"He went right under," Deacon said. "He went way down and came back up."

"I haven't got the stove lit," Hogan said. "I'll light it later on when it gets dark. I can't spare no coal. I'm lyin' dressed like this beneath the blankets."

Landish lurched from side to side as he climbed the stairs. In the attic, he slipped out of his coat and let it fall on the floor behind him. The coat was coated. It stood up by itself, taller than Deacon who pushed it over because he didn't like the way it looked.

"My follicles are icicles," Landish said.

He clawed at his beard. His hair made a clicking sound when he shook his head. He took off his pants and fumbled with the buttons of his shirt. His collar had left a welt around his neck, his trousers another one around his waist.

He'd never fallen through the ice before, never been in winter water, salt or fresh.

Landish said his balls were in his belly and would stay in hibernation until May. There was ice in the hair above Dick and the happy couple, the former the size of a grub, and the latter like a single, purple plum.

"My toes are froze," he said. He examined them for signs of frostbite. His big toes were rimmed with white, as were all his fingertips. White was better than red. He should never have ventured so far from home in cold like this. It could just as easily have been the boy.

They had two wooden tubs, the small one for Deacon, a larger one for Landish, barely big enough for him to sit in with his knees up around his chin. Landish, his hands a palsied pair of claws, his head a

Medusa of icicles, half filled his wooden tub with water heated on the stove. He splashed his torso. He hugged himself to keep from shaking.

"You're like this," Deacon said, nodding his head and clacking his teeth as he spoke.

Landish cursed himself for having tried a stream that large so far from home.

He knew from his time on the *Gilbert* that he should be stretched out in a longer, deeper tub with nothing but his head above the water, which someone helping him should be keeping hot, and that upon emerging from the tub he should be rubbed with reeking blubber, made to drink mulled rum and mummified in heavy blankets.

Using his hand brush and his back brush, Landish scoured his skin as hard as he could stand it.

"You're making yourself redder," Deacon said.

"Good."

"How long can a fish hold its breath?"

"Fish breathe with their gills."

"How long can you?"

"I don't know."

"I thought you were a goner."

"Did you know the way home?"

Deacon shook his head.

He had taken the boy too far into the woods, a couple of hours of daylight left. He had told no one where they were going. The boy would have perished too. They would have found Landish in the water and Deacon in the woods.

"Ask me more questions about fish," Landish said.

"Why?"

"More questions."

No, fish didn't have ears, so they must be deaf. Did fish have noses? Maybe. He would closely examine the nose of his next fish. He wasn't sure how fish did their pee. Or where. Somewhere private. That wasn't where all the water came from, but yes it would be funny if it was. Yes, that might be why the ocean was so salty.

He had never seen a fish chewing food or throwing up.

Fish had no lashes, so they never blinked.

He gripped the edges of the tub, meaning to climb out, but nothing happened. He tried again and rose up streaming water. The room spun. If he overturned the tub, the water would run downstairs into Hogan's kitchen, and Hogan would report it to the nobleman.

A fine ending for the Druken line, his father would have said. A child's death, not a man's. Nothing but a swimming hole named after him. The hole where Druken drowned. That wouldn't get you the OBE or a dinner from the Board of Trade. He shook his head and counted his fingers. His eyes looked like they did when he was angry. Landish tried to clench his teeth. He splashed water on Deacon but didn't laugh or say he was sorry. He closed his eyes, then opened them as if he'd heard a noise.

He got dressed and quickly heated for the boy a bowl of turr stew from the last seabird of the larder.

"Are you having any?" Deacon said.

Landish said he didn't feel like eating.

"What does the ice look like from underneath?" Deacon said.

He managed to say it was probably like when you took the pie crust off to see the other side. He heard the boy say he had never done that because he had never had a pie. He heard himself promising him a pie so that he could see what the under-ice was like. He said he thought he needed a nap. If he had been stronger to begin with—but he had eaten even less than usual every day for ten days.

He told Deacon he was going to climb into bed for a while. Deacon said it wasn't bedtime yet. Just for a bit, Landish said, to get warm, just until the shaking stops. He said he wouldn't go to sleep. Deacon could climb in with him if he wanted to, but he didn't feel up to reading to him from a book or telling him a story. As he tumbled onto the bed, he heard Deacon say something about the kitchen.

❈

Landish kicked the blankets off, thinking they were snow.

He folded his arms and drew his knees up to his chest. He wondered where the others were. They knew as well as he did what to do when you were lost and couldn't find your way back to your ship.

But they were young and not as strong as he.

It was one thing to know you mustn't run, another to resist the urge. Foolish things made perfect sense. Lighten yourself of everything that made it hard to run, encumbrances such as coats and boots. Shed your clothes so you could breathe. He knew he should be on his feet. His father said that if you fell you must get up, you must. Don't sacrifice yourself for nothing. Don't die just so that another man won't have to die alone. Don't die just to keep him company. Each man goes by himself to the place from which no one knows the way back home. Even the young, the weak, the blameless and the kind of heart. Don't be like Carson of the *Gilbert* who stayed with his men even though they were already goners and he could have saved himself.

Deacon said his name and clapped his hands close to his face, but Landish never moved. He seemed unaware of him though his eyes were open and going slowly from side to side like they did when he thought so much he couldn't sleep.

His undershirt, long johns, face and hair were as wet as when he came out of the river. But now they were wet with sweat. There was a yellow halo of it on his pillow. His face was red like when he dug holes in July. Deacon tried the window, but it wouldn't budge. He thought of telling Hogan that Landish wasn't right, but he had promised Landish he would never leave the attic by himself. And the nobleman might come or the nuns who were nurses too, so he threw some water on the fire and stabbed it with the poker until the coals went out.

He turned the lantern down until the flame was blue. His shadow stretched across the floor and halfway up the wall. He was afraid to turn his back on it. It scared him when he moved.

He put on his hat and coat and boots, took a chair from the kitchen and set it by the bed. He sat and looked at Landish.

When Landish shivered and clacked his teeth, he covered him with blankets that Landish pulled tight around him until he began to sweat again and threw them off.

At times, it sounded like he was speaking to someone. He spoke, waited, spoke again, but Deacon couldn't understand a word.

You saw what wasn't there. You looked straight through what was.

A man stood over him. He shook his head and walked away.

Now there were a man, a woman and a boy. What were a woman and a boy doing on the *Gilbert*? They must have fooled his father.

The boy sat on the man's shoulders, the woman linked arms with the man. The three of them looked down at him.

The man said: "We can't just leave him here."

But the woman said the sun was setting and the boy was sick.

"He's a goner, like the others," the woman said. "There's no point holding hands with goners. Let them hold each other's hands."

He filled a cup with water and brought it to the bed. "Sit up," he said. "Please, Landish, sit up. Have some water."

But Landish lay there, eyes darting about even as he smiled, too canny to be fooled by a voice that offered water.

Deacon went closer, held the cup to his lips, and tilted it slightly until some drops spilled out, ran down his chin onto his throat.

"Landish, wake up," he shouted, and shook him by the arm.

Landish swung his arm and the back of his hand caught the peak of Deacon's cap. He dropped to his hands and knees, grabbed his hat and crawled away from the bed. Landish rolled onto his side, his back to Deacon.

He moved closer to the bed but out of range of Landish in case he rolled onto his back and swung out his arm again. He looked at Landish and the massive shadow of him on the wall.

He lay down on the floor beside the bed.

There were no blankets. He'd been sleeping as he did on the warmest summer nights, covered by nothing but his long johns. He listened for the sound of horses' hooves, but heard none. Evening, he guessed, unless today was Sunday.

Deacon was asleep on the floor. A kitchen chair that bore an empty lantern faced the bed. He could tell by the light at the porthole window that it was either early morning or early evening. It was so cold in the attic that he could see his breath. Long plumes of it each time he exhaled. Deacon lay on his side, dressed for the outdoors. Landish tried to rouse him. The boy woke momentarily but shook his head and curled up tighter as he always did when Landish came to wake him in the morning.

Landish sat up, swung his legs out over the bed and onto the floor. He picked up Deacon and barely managed to stand.

He laid Deacon in the bed and covered him with blankets. He removed his hat and boots but otherwise left him as he was. He put on his own clothes and went out to the kitchen.

Only minutes later, the boy came up behind him in the kitchen and wrapped his arms around him in a leg hug. Landish crouched down and gave him a hug, and upon standing became so dizzy that he lurched across the room. He caught himself from falling by grabbing the back of a chair.

"I'm not all better yet," he said. He asked Deacon if it was Thursday, but Deacon shook his head and said he thought it was Friday but it might be Saturday. He said the last time he had eaten was when he finished the stew that Landish had made. The boy looked as if he had fought an illness of his own for the past two days and nights. Landish found some potatoes and fried them up with a block of fatback. He ate as much as he could stand to, then went downstairs, where Hogan told him it was Friday.

"I've been sick," he said. Hogan looked at him as if he had last seen him lurching up the stairs with a bottle in his hand.

Landish remembered almost nothing of the past two days, far less than the boy did and would forever carry with him. He thought of the empty chair that faced the bed when he woke up. He could think of no illness against which the boy would have a chance.

"Where are you going?" Deacon said.

"Out."

"Where? You said you wouldn't leave me here by myself, especially at night."

"Just this once, all right?"

He wouldn't be long, he said, maybe an hour at the most, and all Deacon had to do was stay put and wait.

"Will you be gone a long time?" Deacon asked.

"Don't leave the attic," Landish said. "Don't go near the lanterns or the fireplace or the stove, all right?"

Deacon knew by heart the things he mustn't do. He didn't even nod his head while Landish spoke. Landish wouldn't look him in the eye. It was like he was talking to someone else over Deacon's shoulder.

"I won't be long," Landish said. "I have to go where boys are not allowed so I can get some things we need, all right?"

Landish didn't care that Deacon knew that none of it was true. "You might be asleep when I get back, so leave the door unbolted," was the last thing he said before he closed the door and went downstairs.

Deacon threw a few coals on the fire, more because Landish told

him not to than because he was cold. He felt like going down the stairs
as far as Hogan's kitchen, knowing that Hogan would tell Landish if he
did. If Landish's book were on the table now, he'd throw it in the fireplace. Landish thought he couldn't reach the closet shelf, but he could
if he used his own bamboo fishing pole. He could get the sealskin hat
and burn that too. He could burn Gen of Eve and he could burn the
vouchers. He could get past Hogan if he wanted to.

He stared at the fire for a while. He bolted the door and went to
bed instead.

He woke to the sound of Landish banging on the door and shouting,
"Let me in." He ran across the kitchen and stood at the door. Landish
sang "London Bridge" in a voice so loud Deacon covered his ears.

He let Landish in. Landish was decks awash.

"My fair lady," Landish sang.

"Go to bed," the boy said.

"I told you not to bolt the door," Landish said.

He sat down at the table, all but knocking the chair over. Deacon
sat in front of the fire. He drank grog from green bottles and poured
Deacon a glass of cold lemonade from a bottle so he could join the
party. Deacon didn't decline it even though he thought he should.

Landish sang "London Bridge," but he changed some words.

"Landish Druken's falling down, falling down, falling down, Landish
Druken's falling down, my bare lady. Take the key and lock him up . . .
Bone so strong will last so long, last so long . . ."

Landish laughed as he sang and laughed even harder when he
looked at Deacon.

"He disapproves of man fun," Landish said. "He thinks that boy fun
is better even if you're not a boy. Deacon fun is good, but Landish
fun is bad. See the way he looks at me. Like he really is a deacon."

"Who are you talking to?" Deacon said.

Landish laughed.

"What's man fun?" Deacon said.

Landish told him he was sorry, and he looked like he was, for a while. He poured Deacon another glass of lemonade. Landish sang "London Bridge." He made up more new words. Deacon sipped his lemonade.

He sang another song, "Mary Had a Little Lamb," just like "London Bridge." Landish slumped onto the table with his head between his arms.

"Mark me, Deacon," he muttered. "I have with an angel been abed. That's what man fun is."

"Dick and the happy couple?" Deacon said. He finished his lemonade.

"That's right. Just like I told you."

"Did you make a contribution?"

Landish laughed.

"You might bring another baby home," Deacon said.

"No," Landish said.

"Maybe a girl."

"NO."

Deacon started to cry. He said Landish was worse than Hogan, who was nothing but a lazy busybody, and so what that he was always in the kitchen when they were going up and down the stairs, he didn't wake them up or beat on their door in the middle of the night. He said the Barnables on the first floor liked Hogan more than Landish because they were afraid of Landish. They hid because anyone with any sense would keep their distance from a Druken who was drunk. How would Landish like it if Hogan went out and came back singing songs? Landish didn't care if Deacon stayed awake all night. He was worse than Captain Druken. Deacon went without his dinner because Landish couldn't stand to go without a drink. What would his mother say if she could see him now, if she knew she'd left her boy with a sorry excuse?

Landish, his head on the table, seemed to be asleep.

Deacon did what Landish sometimes did when he was decks awash. He went downstairs and punched and kicked at Hogan's door and said the whore who had him was ashamed to call him hers. He said it was high time he lugged his own business bucket out to Dark Marsh Road.

He shouted, "Don't complain to Mr. Nobleman if you know what's good for you."

He kept hitting Hogan's door until Landish came and carried him upstairs and drew the bolt.

Landish told him not to follow his example. Then he went to the bedroom.

Deacon took a swallow of grog. The bottle was almost full. The grog spilled down his chin onto his shirt. He coughed and spit. His throat felt like it did when he was sick. He smashed the bottle in the fireplace. The fire roared up and out into the room, almost reaching Deacon, who fell back just in time onto the floor. The fire sounded like the wind.

Landish came out and looked at him. He said he could have burned himself. He could have burned the attic to the ground. The smoke might leave soot marks on the walls that he would have to pay for. He went back to the bedroom. He came out again and roared, "Farewell and adieu to ye mannish ladies."

"Are you listening, Hogan?" he shouted as he opened the door. "The boy told you what he thinks of you. And what he thinks of me."

"Oh, I see," Deacon heard Hogan say. He heard the slamming of the downstairs door and then Landish slammed the attic door.

"You should sit down," Deacon said, getting up off the floor. "Here's your grog. You drink your grog and we'll sing songs."

Landish declined at first and went on about a girl, saying she was harder-looking than the witches from *Macbeth*. But he sat down and in silence finished all the grog while Deacon watched.

"Go to bed," Deacon said, knowing that if he cried, Landish would start up again.

Landish went to bed and Deacon went in when he heard him snoring and lay down on the floor beside the bed. He held his pillow against his chest and fell asleep.

❖

In the morning, Deacon had a headache and his stomach hurt. He sat at the table and waited for Landish to join him. Landish came out.

"I spent the rent," he said. "Every cent of it. I'm sorry, Deacon. I was feeling bad and then I went and made things worse. I'll work it out with the nobleman. I'll pay him more than twice as much next month. Pay no attention to me when I'm decks awash. I don't mean it when I say mean things. Did I say mean things last night?"

Deacon shook his head.

"I shouldn't have gone out," Landish said. "I'll never leave you on your own again, I promise."

Deacon nodded.

"That's good. I don't drink very often, do I?"

"No."

"But when I do, I drink too much."

Two days later, two men showed up at the attic. Landish heard footsteps on the stairs and a knock at the door, on which no one but the nuns and the wealth inspector had knocked in all the time they lived there. They were big men, almost as big as Landish. They looked and smelled like they'd been drinking. He could see they didn't like what they were doing but that they would see it through to whatever end he chose.

"This is from Mr. Nobleman," one of them said, handing him an unsealed envelope. Landish read the note inside.

"Evicted as of five o'clock?" he said. "Three hours from now?"

"Mr. Nobleman says he owns everything here except your clothes. He says pack up and go. The sheriff will be here at five o'clock."

Deacon stood beside Landish and looked up at the men who acted as if he wasn't there.

"The boy," Landish said.

"Mr. Nobleman says you can stay for a year in exchange for the hat. No rent for a year. In exchange for the hat."

Landish put his hand on Deacon's head as Deacon hugged his leg.

"I have a contract here that you can sign. Or you can leave today."

He heard the boy say, "No, Landish."

"We always knew we would have to sell the hat," he said.

Landish wasn't sure what the hat was worth. As much as someone was willing to pay for it. If he had time to make it known it was for sale, he might get more, maybe a lot more, than one year in the attic. Three hours. Any buyer would see how desperate he was. He might get less than the nobleman was offering. He could hold out past three hours, survive eviction from the attic, but the boy—where would they stay, what would he do with Deacon, until the hat was sold? Winter wasn't over yet. It wouldn't be warm enough to sleep outside until July or later. There were places you could go, but Landish vowed that Deacon would never know what they were like. And what if no one wanted the hat at any price, the hat that Captain Druken bought with blood?

"Let me see the contract," Landish said. The man reached inside the pocket of his coat, took out a single sheet of paper and handed it to him.

"'Should there be further instances of noise-making and misbehaviour after hours,'" Landish read aloud, "'the tenants will be evicted and the proprietor shall retain ownership of the hat.'" If he gave the nobleman the hat, they might be evicted anyway, a day, a week, a month from now. He was betting that Landish would be unable to hold out for a year without a drink.

"I'll get the hat," Landish said. "Don't set foot inside this room."

"No, Landish," Deacon said.

Landish went to the bedroom, took the hat box from the closet shelf and went back to the kitchen, where Deacon was now sitting at the table, still looking at the men who were staring awkwardly at the floor.

Landish looked at the man who'd given him the contract. "This is theft, pure and simple. Your boss as good as broke into my home and stole this straight out of my bedroom closet. Feel free to tell him I said so." Laying it on the hat box, he signed the contract. He handed over both.

He slammed the door, went back to the bedroom and lay down. "No rent for a year, Deacon," Landish said. "We'll save most of what I make and maybe this time next year we'll have enough to go away."

Six days later, Landish received in the mail from Van two first-class tickets from St. John's to New York, two first-class train tickets to Ashton, North Carolina, the nearest town to Vanderland, and a small amount of money for expenses. There was no note from Van, none of any kind from anyone.

"He has answered me at last," Landish said. "For all he knows, we no longer need his help. He doesn't know for certain that we are still alive. How strange, after all this time. Tickets, instead of money to buy tickets that he thinks I would have spent on something else. The whole thing a booze ruse for all he knows."

Landish told the nuns who were nurses too that he and Deacon would be leaving for the mainland soon. He showed them the tickets but said nothing about the money, having told Deacon not to mention it to anyone, especially the wealth inspector, who might have to count it as an asset and withhold its worth in vouchers.

"So you're leaving," Nun One said. Deacon nodded. "We'll remember you in our prayers. Will you be so kind as to remember us in yours?" Deacon nodded again.

"Many have left," she said, and for a moment touched his cheek. "But few have ever felt at home again. You will miss this place no matter if your fortunes rise. Do you believe me?"

Deacon nodded.

She smiled and made no attempt to stop a tear from trailing down her cheek.

Nun Too Soon, who had come with her usual bag of clothes, gave him two shirts and two pairs of trousers. "They'll fit," she said. "I know your size now. Just as you're leaving." She leaned forward and kissed him on the cheek.

"America?" the wealth inspector said. "I have a sister in Boston. She left when I was Deacon's age. I don't remember her. I have nieces and nephews that I've never seen. Don't even know their names. I haven't heard from her in years."

He told Landish that he knew about "the business with the hat."

"Just six days ago. I think I can get it back."

"Even if you don't, it's not nearly as dear a price as some have paid to make the rent."

He gave them two dilapidated carpet bags. Landish packed them with their few clothes and put the sketch of Gen of Eve in one of them on top of a selection of Deacon's favourite books from the Smokestack. He wasn't sure that Deacon understood what going away meant. He showed him on the map.

"What will we do there?"

"I'm not sure, but I think we'll live someplace nicer than the attic."

"Your friend picked us," Deacon said.

"Yes."

"How many people did my mother write to?"

"I don't know. Just me. Maybe. I don't know."

"I don't want to go to school," Deacon said.

"You won't go unless you want to."

"Unless I want to?"

"Right."

He climbed the steps of the nobleman's house, the steps he had climbed countless times when he lived there and the house was still his father's. He rang the doorbell, but no one came. He knocked on the middle panel of the door, which was made of frosted glass. The lace curtains of the downstairs rooms were drawn and the lights were off. He went down the steps and surveyed the upper storey. The curtains on the windows of what used to be his room swayed from side to side.

"Mr. Nobleman," he roared. He roared it three more times. The casement windows of his room opened outward.

"What do you want, Mr. Druken?" a voice shouted back. Landish couldn't see him.

"A word with you."

"Concerning what?"

"Unexpected developments. If I'd known, I would have kept the hat." Landish waited. "The boy and I will be leaving soon. We're booked on a ship that leaves for the mainland in a month. I can pay you for that month and the past week and then you can rent our rooms to someone else. Then we would be square if you gave me back my father's hat."

"It's my hat, Mr. Druken. I have a contract that says so."

"But it's only been a week," Landish said. "If I'd known. I received a letter from a friend six days after I gave you the hat. A man named Vanderluyden. I believe you know the name. Everything is different now."

"Except that I still own the hat. I've been more than fair to you, Mr. Druken. Other landlords would have evicted you long ago. You are not required by our contract to occupy the premises. Vacate them if you want. I will make arrangements with other tenants. You will have no legal claim on what they pay me if you forfeit."

Landish strode up the steps and pounded on the door. "It wouldn't take me long to convince you I'm right. And I'm as sober as a judge."

"As sober as the judge you'll have to face if you lay a hand on me. We have a contract, Mr. Druken. One that will stand up in court. If you force your way onto these premises and lay a finger on me or my wife, I will have you arrested."

"Your contract might stand up in court, but you won't," Landish shouted up. "You'll be on your back in bed when you appear before the judge."

He walked down the steps, by which time many of the people who had once been his neighbours were gaping at him from their windows.

From inside what had been his father's house, the disembodied voice of a man to whom he had been paying money for six years for the right to occupy an attic on Dark Marsh Road had told him that the manner in which his father's hat, his entire inheritance, had been taken from him had been fair and legal. Perhaps it was. Legal at least. It was not just losing the hat but how he had lost it and to whom that played on his mind. Landish couldn't help feeling that the loss of the hat bore out some prediction of his father, that Captain Druken had given him the hat in the expectation that he would prove to be unworthy of it.

So when he and Deacon went out walking, Landish made a point of going close enough to his old street to see his house, but he didn't walk along that street or go so close to it as to risk being seen by the nobleman or his neighbours.

"Why do we always stop here?" Deacon asked.

"It's a good place to rest," Landish said. "There's a good view from here."

It was out of the question to break in while the house was occupied. He vowed that he would do no one any harm. He would not so much as startle someone. He would only enter an empty house and therefore had to know for certain when it would be empty.

After four weeks spent watching the house, Landish noticed that the nobleman and his wife, who had no servants, went out about seven every Tuesday. They walked down the hill to the stable where they boarded their horse and carriage, then drove on from there to Water Street where, turning left, they passed from sight. At what time they were in the habit of returning home he didn't know, never having seen them return despite having several times risked drawing attention to himself and watched the house for half an hour after they left. So he should have at least that long.

He would only be taking as much from the nobleman as the nobleman had taken from him and Deacon. In fact the nobleman had taken what they could not afford to do without, their fallback. So he had taken much more than Landish would take back, infinitely more.

At night, in the attic, he tried to think it through. Landish still had the set of keys that his father had forgotten to ask for when he banned him from the house. He didn't know if the nobleman had changed the locks. Whether he used the keys to enter the house and to lock it behind him when he left or whether he broke in through a pane of glass in the back door, he would be the first person the nobleman would suspect. But they wouldn't find the keys on his person or property, wouldn't find them at all, because he would dispose of them on his way back to the attic, throw them in one of the sinkholes on the edge of Dark Marsh Road.

He would search the house, put the hat in a potato sack and leave without so much as looking at anything else.

Leaving the attic, he would have to get past Hogan, and again on the way back in.

If he was lucky, the Tuesday he chose would be a windy one and whatever sounds he made would be masked by those of the wind and the trees.

Landish had a hunch about where in the house the hat was located. He doubted the nobleman would keep it in the attic, which was full of dust and mould. There was no basement or cellar. The problem was that if the nobleman had put it inside a lockable piece of furniture such as a sideboard or a wardrobe or a study desk, it might take hours to find. Landish knew that he could smash his way into almost anything, but the noise he made might be overheard by neighbours or passersby, or drown out any sound of the nobleman coming up the steps.

He went to bed but didn't close his eyes. Deacon said he couldn't sleep until Landish closed his eyes, so Landish turned and faced the wall. He thought of the box, its inner walls upholstered like a casket's. What would he do with the box from the time he took it to the time the ship departed?

If he was caught, caught in the act while still in the house, or caught in possession of the hat, he would go to prison for a term that he would likely not survive. He would never see the boy again. The boy would go to Cluding Deacon and never leave alive. But though he dwelt for hours every day on the folly of stealing from the nobleman, he dwelt as much or more on the unfairness of having to forsake the hat to such a man, to leave Newfoundland without it and never set eyes on it again, leave it in the house and hands of a man who would never have to answer for the crime of getting rich by extorting money from the poor.

His father had done worse things to get the hat than the nobleman had. In which case, why not renounce the hat, be satisfied that it had found just the home and owner it deserved? But even as he thought these and many other things, he went on devising plans.

"Where are you going, Landish?" Deacon said.

Landish said there were still a few more arrangements that needed to be made before they left. "I just want to say goodbye to some grown-ups you don't know."

"Fair ladies."

"No. Just some men I haven't seen since my last trip on the *Gilbert*. No more questions, now, all right?"

Deacon stared at him. He thought Landish wasn't going to the taverns. But he was making things up. He looked as scared as he had the day he nearly drowned. Landish knelt in front of him and hugged him until Deacon's feet came off the floor. Deacon thought about not hugging back, just hanging there. But he hugged him and Landish kissed his neck.

Landish stood up. "I won't be long," he said. "Lock the bolt this time." Landish closed the door behind him. It sounded like he ran downstairs. Deacon wondered if Hogan would have time to reach the kitchen first. Then he heard Landish say, "I don't want to see you in this kitchen when I get back tonight or when we come and go tomorrow. If you know what's good for you, this will be the last time I ever see your face." Deacon slid the bolt closed.

This was a strange way to be occupied on the night before you left your lifelong home for good. One last stroll about the town for old times' sake it should have been, with Deacon on his shoulders. And after that a fret-free night, not one of waiting for the sound of footsteps on the stairs.

He took a route that brought him to the street just west of the nobleman's. He walked down the tree-lined alleyway that ran between the nobleman's house and his uphill neighbour's. The nobleman's house was dark but for the front porch light.

He unlatched the gate that opened onto the side of the house and stepped into the yard. He went round to the back door, took the ring of keys from his pocket and climbed the steps.

He tried the key. It turned. The nobleman had left *everything* the same, even the locks. The door creaked when he opened it, exactly as it had throughout his childhood. He went through the porch and into the kitchen. The front porch light, the street lights, the lights from neighbouring houses allowed him to see just enough to keep from knocking into something.

He made his way through the kitchen, certain the hat would not be there. In the front room he saw the piano that his mother used to play. He glanced at the Druken china cabinet, dining room table, buffet and sideboard.

He went upstairs to the master bedroom, his parents' room in which he had not set foot since his mother died, noted the armoire from the landing, but bypassed it in favour of the closet in which it was so dark he had to feel his way about. He started with the upper shelf, just inside the door.

He knew the instant he touched it that he had found the hat box. The nobleman mimicked both father and son. He had put the box where Landish had put it in the attic, where the two men who came for it must have told him Landish kept it—on the shelf in his bedroom closet.

He slid it off the shelf. He left the closet and laid the box on the bed, eased it open just enough to satisfy himself that the hat was inside, then closed it.

The box now held in front of him like an about-to-be-presented birthday cake, he left the room and went downstairs, where he paused, allowed himself a moment to imagine his father sitting in what had been his chair, which seemed not to have been moved an inch from its place before the fire. The scale model of the *Gilbert* stood where it always had, in the centre of the mantelpiece.

He made his way down the hallway to the kitchen, the porch, the porch door. He put the box beneath one arm and with his free hand turned the knob. He nudged the door with his shoulder and stepped outside.

A cat ran up the steps and into the house.

He removed the key from his pocket and locked the door.

He heard what he thought were raindrops on the box until he realized that beads of sweat were falling from his forehead. He removed the potato sack from inside his shirt, put the box inside it, knotted the sack, slung it over his shoulder, and walked without haste down the pathway of his father's garden toward the gate.

Deacon heard Landish ascend the lower stairs, then Hogan's. Landish didn't pause in Hogan's kitchen, didn't say a word as he passed through and climbed up to the attic door. Deacon unbolted the door and then returned to his chair at the table.

"There, you see, back in no time." Deacon looked at him. He was flushed and sweaty. He looked like he was decks awash, but Deacon couldn't smell the grog. He didn't have anything in his hands.

"Did you say goodbye to everyone?" Landish said nothing. He sat at the table, on the other side from Deacon.

"Did you take the hat?" Deacon said.

"Yes," Landish said. "I was lucky. It wasn't hard to find. We mustn't say a word to anyone."

"Where is it? Did you hide it?"

"I'll tell you when we're home free."

No one could prove that he took the hat. No one would find it. As long as the wealth inspector did his part.

The wealth inspector had the hat and was going to hold it for him until he wrote to him from Vanderland. He had tried to talk him out of stealing it back but when he saw that Landish was going to steal it with his help or not, he told him he would help him, not for his sake but for Deacon's. They agreed that if Landish were caught, he wouldn't say a word about the wealth inspector; if he hadn't met the wealth inspector when and where they planned to exchange the hat, the wealth inspector would simply have gone home.

Still, the nobleman might soon arrive with the police or, worse, the men he sent before. In either case, what a scene might then play out before the boy.

"If someone comes to ask us questions, tell them I went out tonight. Don't lie about that, because Hogan knows that I went out. So do the Barnables. Tell them you're not sure how long I was gone or else you'll sound like I've been coaching you. Don't say anything unless you have to. We might be long gone by the time the nobleman even notices the hat is missing. But we're not home free."

Deacon nodded.

Deacon knew they would think about the hat all night. They wouldn't sleep. They would jump at every sound, even when they knew that it was Hogan. Sometimes, when tomorrow was the day you thought would never come, it was nice when you couldn't get to sleep. The Big Day, Landish always called it. There had been many big days, but none like the one that was almost here at last.

In the morning, Landish couldn't keep still. The ship's departure time was hours away. They went out for a long walk. Coming back, as they neared the last turn on Dark Marsh Road, Landish saw the nobleman's carriage, parked, the nobleman seated up front, reins and whip in hand.

"Remember what I told you," Landish said, squeezing Deacon's hand.

Deacon had never seen the nobleman. He looked smaller and older than he'd imagined. The coats of his two black horses shone in the morning sunlight. They had feathers on their foreheads.

"The cat was in when we returned home," the nobleman said. "That's how we discovered that our house was broken into. Think about that, Mr. Druken."

"What do you want from us?" Landish said.

"I searched the attic," the nobleman said, "even though I doubted you'd be fool enough to hide it there."

"You entered my premises without my permission?"

"I came to call, as landlords are allowed to do. You were out. I had a key. I locked the door behind me when I left. Everything is exactly as it was. I did everything as you did it. Almost."

"What were you looking for?" Landish said.

"I wouldn't be surprised if you stole it and destroyed it out of spite. Is that what happened, boy? Did Mr. Druken steal my hat and burn it in the fireplace? Or dispose of it somewhere, along with the keys to my house? Did you help him steal my hat last night?"

"A man of your means should know better than to leave his doors unlocked," Landish said.

"You cannot break into my house at night, creep about from room to room, rummage through my private things, make off with something from the very closet of my bedroom and expect to get away with it. I will have my satisfaction one way or the other."

"Let's go inside, Deacon."

"You'll be back. It won't take long for you to wear out your welcome. And you, boy, are now apprenticed to a cheat, a liar *and* a thief."

The Ship

T HEY BOARDED THE SHIP early in the evening, gaped at by the
others who were boarding, recognized by most of them judging
by how frequently he heard them say their names. Even as the seal hunt
was getting under way, Landish Druken was leaving for New York with
the son of the man his father murdered.

They stood at the rail, waiting while the crew made their final
preparations. Deacon felt the shudder of the ship as the engines started
up and churned the water white along the side. A gap between the
dock and the ship began to form. Deacon thought it was so wide that
even with a running start, Landish would have landed in the water.
And the people on the dock would have had to fish him out, and
Deacon would have had no choice but to cross the Gulf alone and
Landish none but to turn and walk away.

Having all his life seen the sea from St. John's, Deacon was now
seeing St. John's from the sea. Everything was backwards. He saw
things that had been hidden from him all his life, the sea-facing side of
the lighthouse at Fort Amherst, the great bay that, mimicking the harbour, lay behind the Brow. Mesmerized, he all but pitched forward
through the rails into the sea.

Walking on the ship was like trying to walk on the bed in the attic while Landish bounced the mattress with both hands.

They cleared the Narrows. The ship turned. He saw the sealing of the cleft between the headlands. It seemed that they had departed just in time, just as they were shutting up the harbour for the night. The rigging was traced out by lantern lights like the one that Landish hung in the window in the attic when it was dark enough outside to see the stars.

To their left was a battery of cannons in front of a lighthouse.

"The English put them there," Landish said, "so they could blow the smithereens out of the French. They took turns blowing the smithereens out of each other. When the smoke cleared, the English had more smithereens left, so they got Newfoundland."

The cliffs to their right were too steep and sheer to support anything but small, gnarled trees whose roots were fastened to the rock like vines.

"Well," said a man standing near them at the railing, "at least we don't live in *this* place."

Landish told him he had never understood why some people were cheered by the notion that however bad was their lot, someone else's lot was even worse. "By that reasoning," he said, "we should all be content to live anywhere but Hell." He smiled. The man and woman moved further down the rail.

Deacon could see other lights along the coast but not bunched up like in St. John's—small clusters, lone lights further down, and one so dim that he wondered if the man who lit it even knew there was a city on the far side of the hill.

A couple of hours into the voyage, Landish overheard a passenger talking to a steward. "They look like they escaped from steerage. He must have robbed someone. How else could he afford first class? God knows what we'll be infected with because of them. Tell the captain I would like to have a word with him."

The boy, now almost seven, had never been in a vehicle of any kind. Landish was the closest he had come, Landish who conveyed him on his shoulders more often than he led him by the hand.

He had never walked on a frozen lake or river.

He had never gone swimming or skating.

Except at tub time, Deacon Carson Druken had never been immersed in water.

He had never been to sea or in any kind of boat.

Their cabin was five times bigger than the attic, maybe ten. It had six portholes, not just one. Landish said the names of some things but he sounded like he wasn't sure. There were several tables, but none were like the table in the attic. Landish smiled at how astonished and confused Deacon looked. It saddened him to think what the boy had grown accustomed to, what he thought was normal and didn't know was even possible.

"This is first class," said Landish. "Steerage is worst class. And second class is in between. Enjoy first class while you can. They might put us in steerage once we get to where we're going."

Landish said the passengers in steerage slept below the waterline. At night, the skylights and hatches and other points of access to the walking decks were shut. There were no portholes because you couldn't take the risk that they would give way in collisions or in storms.

He saw the look on Deacon's face. "It won't be steerage," he said, "but it might be second class."

"That's better than the attic."

Deacon asked Landish what you would see through an underwater porthole if they did have underwater portholes. Landish said that, in the daytime, especially if it was sunny, you'd see fish and long strands of seaweed floating by like bunting. The sun would shine through the water in shafts like it did through glass. In shallow water, you might see the ocean floor. In a storm, the sand on the ocean floor would be stirred up by the waves like the snow was by the wind. An underwater blizzard.

Deacon asked Landish what you would see at night through an underwater porthole. He said that if the lights were on, you would see your own reflection in the glass, just like they did now when they looked out through their own portholes. Deacon asked what the passengers in steerage would see if there were windows. He imagined: their noses pressed against the glass, hands flanking their faces as, in mimicry of their curiosity, an underwater-dwelling host of look-alikes peered in.

He looked at the boy who, judging by his expression, was imagining something that would keep him up all night. Faces still pressed against the outside glass after all the lights had been turned out and the unsuspecting passengers had gone to bed. The windowless, sub-surface confinement of the passengers in steerage after dark, separated only by the hull from water they couldn't see and would only feel and hear if the hull gave way.

The never-seen-by-human-eyes bottom of the mid-Atlantic had been the habitation of Deacon's father for ninety days while the boy was in his mother's womb and more than two thousand since he was born. His father borne about by the same storms that stirred up the sand like clouds of desert dust.

The Gulf was the space between two things. Neither here nor there. A great gap. In this case, the sea. In other cases, empty space. That which engulfs. To be engulfed was to be swallowed up.

"My father was engulfed."

At first by snow. And then by darkness. By fear. By sleep, deep and warm and treacherous. And finally by water.

"Maybe," Landish replied.

"Will the boat pass over where my father was engulfed?"

"No, it goes the other way. You know. Jonah was engulfed. It was dark inside the whale. The wolf engulfed Red Riding Hood. But both Jonah and the girl got out."

Deacon had never seen a bathtub that wasn't round or made of wood. This tub was like a bed with walls. It made a funny, tinny sound when he struck it with his hand. "Porcelain," Landish said. "Like the toilet and the sink." Landish had to show him how they worked. Cold water came when you turned one tap, hot water when you turned the other. And when he pulled the chain, water rushed into the bowl as if the ship had sprung a leak. Deacon thought the bowl would overflow but smiled up at Landish when the water went back down.

His pillow was so soft and deep it closed around his head, enfolding it completely as a pan of dough would do. He had to exchange it for a cushion.

He had never slept in as cozy a bed as the ones in the cabin——or sat in as cozy a chair as the one that he needed Landish's help to climb into. He had never seen a chandelier except from the street.

"What's it like on a sealing ship?"

"You wouldn't like the *Gilbert*. You wouldn't want to cross the Gulf on her."

"Why?"

"It's a lot like the attic, but worse. These cups and plates and bowls are known as Chinaware. They made such things first in China. The ones we had on the *Gilbert* are known as Everyware."

Landish told him that on this ship, the men in charge of engines had what were known as "engine ears," which meant that they were deaf from the noise the engines made. Also there were pursers who made sure that no one's purse was stolen. There were men called stewards who were in charge of serving stew. And other men called porters who were in charge of serving port. "I'll give you my stew if you give me your port," Landish said, but Deacon shook his head.

After they put your port in front of you, Landish told him, they performed what was called the "port bow," and then you performed it and they went away. Landish demonstrated the port bow, one arm across his stomach. He had Deacon try it. "Lower," Landish said. Deacon tried again. Landish told him they would practise every day until he got it right.

Landish told Deacon there was another bow that was performed on the observation decks at night. To signal to the other passengers that you had grown bored with looking at the stars, you performed what was known as the "star-bored bow," then said good night and went downstairs. While doing or acknowledging the star-bored bow, you kept both arms at your sides and, your head upright, bent forward slightly from the waist. They practised the star-bored bow until Landish was satisfied that Deacon understood the subtle difference between the acknowledgement of the bow and the bow itself. The meaning of the former was: As I have yet to reach your degree of boredom with the stars, I will stay up top until I do, but do join me for a drink should we meet again downstairs before lights out.

And, Landish said, there were petty officers, short, unhelpful men who were in charge of petty passengers and their complaints. The chief petty officer, the least helpful and shortest of them all, dealt exclusively with the least gracious and shortest of the passengers.

"It might take you a while to find your sea legs," Landish told him. "It means to learn how to walk straight even when the ship is going up and down or from side to side. I've got mine, but I don't think I could keep you on my shoulders in bad weather. You never lose your sea legs once you find them."

Sea legs. He looked at the boy's legs. As thin at the thighs as in the calves. Two hollow reeds interrupted by two knobby knees. He watched as Deacon tried to find his sea legs. He wobbled and swayed. He took a couple of steps with one hand against the wall like some convalescent infant. He ran towards Landish as if Landish was at the bottom of a hill so steep that to walk down it was impossible. He took dead aim at Landish and dove face first into his arms.

There were two bedrooms in their cabin. Each room and each bed were big enough for both of them, so one bedroom went unused. It simply sat there as unchanging as a photograph from one day to the next.

Deacon thought a bathrobe was a kind of coat. The smallest was too big for him and the biggest one too small for Landish. Deacon wore his anyway. Sometimes it became entangled in his feet and he fell down. Or it trailed on the floor behind him like a bridal gown.

Everything was bright and looked brand new. Like when the snow stopped and the sun came out. Except this was indoors and it wasn't cold. He saw himself reflected in the walls.

Side by side in bed beneath the blankets, Landish and Deacon sang: "We'll sleep and we'll snore like two Newfoundlanders/We'll sleep and we'll snore on bed and pillow/Unless there's a woman between us two bunkers/And then to his own bed young Deacon must go."

"What woman?"

"She's hypothetical."

"An idea in Just Mist?"

"Right. But it's better than antithetical. If she was that, she wouldn't like me."

He watched Deacon absorbing the new word.

"If you married her, would she be my mother?"

"Stepmother. One step down from mother. But I'm not getting married."

"Not even to her?"

"There *is* no her. Hypothetical means I've never heard of her and she's never heard of me. We don't know each other's names. She might not exist."

"She could fit in the bed between us."

"She could. But then we'd have no privacy."

"Then she could sleep in the other bed."

"I mean her and me, not you and me."

Landish sang: "We'll rant and we'll roar like two Newfoundlanders/We'll rant and we'll roar on bed and pillow/One hand on her bottom and one on her sunkers/It's straight through her channel to Toslow I'll go."

"I'll be David and you be Goliath."

"All right. I'll go lieth down."

At first, it looked as if they would have an easy crossing of the Gulf. The sea was calm. The air was warm and there was not much fog. No one in first class was sick. Landish put Deacon on his shoulders and went out on the deck when they had it to themselves. It was windy. Deacon scanned the sea for ice while he held his hat in place. Landish thought about the *Gilbert* and the men whose skipper he could have been, men who even now were on the ice, for the hunt was under way.

He hoped the weather would hold until they reached New York. But something about the water and the sky and the motion of the ship betokened otherwise. He smelled something of it in what little wind there was. He had wakened the previous night as he used to on the *Gilbert* when something that was lost even on his father, something in advance of all the instruments and for which there seemed to be no name, told him that far away, in some as yet unknowable direction, some botherance that would swell to provocation had begun.

Icebergs. Each spring, a strange fleet of white, unmanned, unnamed vessels was launched from Greenland for no purpose but to drift south on the current to the east of Labrador until they ran aground or melted in the warm Gulf Stream below Cape Race, a fleet of ever-shrinking, shape-shifting vessels on its first and only voyage. Some of them, even if they were one-tenth as large as when they started out, made the largest of ships look like pilot boats. They followed an impossible-to-alter course. It was pointless to argue with their assumption that they had the right-of-way. They could not be reasoned with, bullied, reprimanded or confined to port. Even Captain Druken would look up in silence as a tower of ice went gliding past the *Gilbert*, his one consolation being that the iceberg would be short-lived and would soon pass from existence, uncommemorated, unrecorded. There was no iceberg registry. There was no iceberg lore that some skippers knew better than others. No matter how many you had seen or how much damage you had seen one do, each one seemed anomalous, unprecedented, the first of its kind, the sensible response to which was awe.

On their ship bound for New York, an iceberg was spotted off to the southeast, ten miles away perhaps. A gale whose effects they could have avoided by continuing southwest was on the rise. Landish was surprised to hear some passengers say that the skipper meant to go as close to the iceberg as he safely could so that those in first class, many of whom had never seen an iceberg, could get a good look at it.

"I hope he's taking into account how quickly that thing is coming towards us," Landish said as he and Deacon joined the others at the rail. Those within earshot dismissively looked Landish up and down and went back to gazing at the iceberg through binoculars.

"Every two miles we go decreases the distance between us and it by four," he said. "It's not as if the iceberg dropped anchor."

"I wish that someone would tell that fellow to be quiet," a woman to his left said loudly.

"Your husband looks sensibly disinclined to grant your wish," Landish told her.

They neared a bank of clouds with shrouds of rain hanging from them. The iceberg loomed up so suddenly beside the ship it seemed to have been carried to them by a single wave. It looked like a gondola towering over them, a spire at each end, between them a deck that Landish guessed was a hundred feet high which meant that the iceberg drew nine hundred feet of water.

"The captain should start turning away *now*," Landish said. But the ship drew closer to the iceberg and sheets of rain swept across the deck as the passengers scattered to their cabins. Landish carried Deacon to their cabin in his arms. Deacon stood on a sofa below an open east-facing porthole and Landish knelt behind him. Landish felt the ship begin to turn, fighting against the sub-swell made by the deep draw of the ice.

Deacon asked if the *Gilbert* ever sprang a leak. There were always small leaks in the *Gilbert*, Landish said, but the ship had never sprung a big one. He had never thought the ship would sink. Deacon asked what was the most scared he ever was and Landish said he wasn't sure but it was a lot more scared than he was right now.

"Don't be afraid," Landish said. "The skipper knows what to do. Never mind what I said up top. That was just a joke."

The ship and the iceberg seemed to be linked, a dual vessel with some underwater mooring strung between them that for now was keeping them a constant distance apart but which might buckle or snap at any moment, allowing the iceberg to be swelled by a wave that would drag it across the ship, dredge through the decks and cleave the hull in half.

The iceberg tilted like a buoy, gushing water from a puncture in its hull.

The iceberg was much bigger than the ship—a white mountain that rose up on the waves like a piece of cork, rose up until they couldn't see the sky, only ice. Other times, when they looked up, all they saw was water, black as slate. Anything on it or in it was nothing when you matched it with the sea, even this iceberg that Landish knew might topple over, tumble down and smash the ship to pieces.

The iceberg made a rumbling sound. They couldn't hear anything else, not even the wind. It was like the loudest thunder with no silence in between the claps. They didn't hear but only felt it when a wave hit the ship.

A lantern-wielding steward came to their cabin and said that all portholes were to be closed and all passengers confined to quarters. He gave Landish a coil of rope and told him to lash himself and the boy to something he thought would not give way. Landish tied the rope to a table that was fixed to the floor. He and Deacon got beneath the table. Landish sat him between his legs and tied the rope round both of them. He took him in his arms and told him he would not let go.

"Hold on, Deacon," Landish said. When the steward left, the cabin was pitch-dark.

Surely this could not be how they ended, bound to a table in the cabin of a passenger ship, no more in control of their fates than the chairs and tables that were fastened to the floor.

Landish tried to tell what was happening from the sounds he heard. It seemed that a giant saw was slicing through the metal of the hull, rasping, screeching, the rivets of the keel popping one by one.

"DEACON," Landish shouted. He felt the word in his throat but couldn't hear it. He wished he could free his arms so he could cover the boy's ears with his hands. The *Gilbert* would long since have been battered to pieces. Landish waited for the feel of water gushing in, the sudden jolt of cold.

The commotion stopped so suddenly that Landish was convinced the ship had gone under, out of range of the storm-stirred surface of the sea. But he felt the rolling pitch of the waves and realized that the ship was once again contending with nothing but the storm. The sound of the wind and wind-blown sheets of rain returned. Cheers of relief could suddenly be heard from the other cabins, and laughter as if at how foolish their fears had been. Landish had heard such laughter before from sealers who for hours had been riding out a storm below deck in grim silence.

"Deacon?" Landish said.

"It's pretty dark," Deacon said. He sounded as out of breath as if he had pitched in with the crew to save the ship.

The steward with the lantern came and helped them release themselves from their ropes.

Deacon hugged Landish around the waist and Landish pressed the boy's head against his stomach. "That was something, wasn't it?" he said.

Deacon nodded and closed his eyes, still out of breath. "I thought we were goners," he said. "I wish we were back in the attic."

"That was the worst of it. The storm is nearly done."

"That's good." A whisper into his stomach.

"You didn't get sick. I bet that a lot of people a lot older than you got sick."

"It makes me hungry when the ship goes up and down. But not sick."

Deacon, still trying to catch his breath, began to cry.

"Landish . . . I . . . want . . . to . . . go . . . home . . . I'm scared."

Landish sat on the sofa and took the boy in his arms. Deacon buried his face in the crook of Landish's arm, his own arms hanging limp.

"Were we almost in the Tomb of Time?" Deacon said.

"No." Landish held him close. "We didn't even get hurt, did we?"

"No," Deacon said through hiccupping sobs as tears ran down his cheeks.

Landish said the Tomb of Time would not be dark and loud. There would be no wind. The snow and rain would fall straight down. Fog would never spoil a summer day. There would be no peril on the sea. The lost would not be *lost* but found and brought back home. No more crosses would mark the empty graves of forever-unrecovered souls like Carson of the *Gilbert*. It would be as warm as a church, but they wouldn't get kicked out for talking. They wouldn't have to sing or pretend to pay attention to the priest.

You wouldn't need to be strapped in to keep from being hurt. It was quiet. No one was scared. No one was mean. You always had enough to eat and drink. No one was ever sick. No one was alone or had to go away. You were reunited with the ones you missed, the ones you thought you'd never see again, the ones you couldn't remember because they left when you were in the Murk, and the ones who left when you were in the Womb of Time. No one goes away forever. Everyone comes back. No one holds a grudge or has regrets or has cause for using words like "forgiveness" and "revenge." It is a place of reconciliation absolute.

❊

For whom the swell rolls.

The ship was left in the bobbing rubble of the iceberg, bits of ice the size of barrels in a heaving sea of slush. Deacon and Landish saw sailors dodging chunks of ice that slid back and forth across the deck. They looked out across the sea and Landish said: "Many waters cannot quench it. Nor can it be drowned by floods."

Deacon asked him what "it" was.

"Love," Landish said.

It must seem to the boy, more now than in years to come, thought Landish, that we have always been together, that I have not only been at hand since the moment he was born but somehow was the agent of his birth, perhaps even that my life began with his, he being unable to conceive of a time when our lives were not yet joined. So I must not forget what he cannot remember or has never known. I must remember that the odds are always heavily against things being as they are, that it was by the dodging of innumerable alternatives that we came to be together, and it will only be by the dodging of many more that we will stay that way. I am not his father. He is not my son. He is my charge. I am his protector. I must not allow my love of him and his of me to lull me into lapses of remembrance. Things seem to him as they one time seemed to me, but I never had such faith as him. He may never lose it. He may never change no matter what is done to him, no matter what he sees.

Everything that in St. John's Landish had said was too expensive you merely had to ask for on the ship. Deacon didn't have to worry that Landish would come home awash with grog and tell him he had spent the rent. Deacon ate as frequently as Landish drank.

"Our respective appetites cannot be slaked," said Landish as he watched Deacon clean his plate. Beef, pork, veal, lamb, all of it awash with butter, gravy, rich sauces made with cream and eggs, great heapings of colourful desserts, meals that Landish couldn't bear the sight of when he was decks awash, disappeared into the boy as if he would not be full until he had consumed at a single sitting the equal of every morsel he had missed since he was born.

Their table was just inside the entrance to the dining room. Landish sat facing the wall to the left of the door. Deacon sat facing the diners. Many people smiled at Deacon, but no one smiled at Landish. Landish knew that the passengers who boarded in St. John's had told the others who he was and how the boy had come to be his charge. He knew they were speculating on the purpose of their journey to New York.

Van might not have foreseen, though Landish had, the sight that they would make in the dining room and elsewhere in first class, the commotion they would cause just by sitting at a table that was set aside for them, wearing, over their tattered clothes, jackets pressed upon them by the stewards.

Most of the non-Newfoundland passengers were Americans returning home from Europe. One night, Landish got drunk at dinner. He stood and loudly proposed a toast to his sponsor, his and Deacon's, their benefactor whose last name when he spoke it drew guffaws of disbelief and admonishments that he not further besmirch it by speaking it again, which he was about to do when he felt on his pant leg the tug of Deacon's hand. So he sat down, but not before assuring his audience that he would report their treatment of him and the boy to the man they seemed to be looking less and less certain he had never met.

It sounded to Deacon as if the diners were murmuring the man's name all at once, over and over.

Vanderluyden.

The captain spoke to Landish. "The boy does not look healthy. There are boys in steerage who look better. He will be examined by the doctor, or else I will have to send you and the boy below decks and when we make port you will not be allowed to leave the ship."

"He's undernourished," Landish said. "That's all. That's why we're going to New York. And as for making port, I doubt that we ever will as long as *you're* the skipper. You overlook icebergs but notice little boys."

"Speak to me again like that and your first-class passage will be voided and you'll travel in steerage until we reach New York, where you'll be put on the next boat back to Newfoundland. That may happen anyway, depending on the boy. The doctor will decide."

Landish told the boy that all the passengers must be examined. "The doctor can examine us together." He spoke to the doctor, asked him not to let on to the boy that they might wind up in steerage or that they might be sent straight back across the Gulf with chalk marks on their backs to live again in some place like the attic.

The doctor examined both of them.

"The boy is healthy though his belly is as hard and hollow as a gourd. Don't provoke the captain any further. I'll mollify the passengers as best I can. Some of them, especially the ones with young children, feel sorry for the boy but not for you. They blame you for the state he's in. At any rate, I think I can get some proper clothes for both of you, which you'll wear if you have a grain of sense."

"We could take our meals in the cabin if you like," Landish said to Deacon. But the boy shook his head. Landish could see that whatever Deacon might have felt at being snubbed was overthrown by the effect on him of the spectacle that seemed to make him all but unaware of Landish in the dining room except as an obstruction of his view.

Entirely unjudgmental incredulity, amazement, wonder and delight lit up Deacon's eyes in a way that Landish had last seen on a Christmas morning when, for the first time in his life, the boy bit into a slice of watermelon.

One of the stewards who greeted passengers as they entered the dining room stood just behind Deacon's chair. The tables nearest theirs were forty feet away. "It's a very select table we've been given," Landish said.

"All the other ones are bigger," Deacon said. "How big was King Arthur's table?"

"About the size of this one," Landish said. "People were very small back then."

Snobs who think we're swabs, thought Landish, who then reminded himself that he had crossed the Gulf eight times in first class. He thought of how easily he might have made things better for the boy if he had simply made them better for himself. If he had pleased his father and skippered the *Gilbert* until the old man died. And then washed his hands of everything but the money he'd have made by then and the money he'd have made when he sold the ship. If he had somehow known of the boy before he made his choice, somehow known that the boy was not long for the Womb of Time but would soon be on his way, that they were already set by fate on paths that soon would merge.

But the boy was unforetold.

"There's a woman over there who smiles at me every night," Deacon said. "Maybe if you turn around or sit by me she'll smile at you."

Landish said nothing.

"You should sit by me so you can see. And then you won't be in my way."

Landish Druken's wide, affronting back, and wide and wild affronting head of hair, had been turned on everyone for days. He doubted they minded except that he blocked their view of the boy.

On eight crossings he had sat among them and told them he was bound for or coming back from Princeton, and told them who his father was and set out the terms of the bargain they had struck. The famed Captain Druken. The millionaire in seals. Landish had cut a finer figure then. He was better groomed, but his hair and beard, though shorter, could not quite be tamed, so he had what his shipmates seemed to fancy was the acceptably wild look of a man caught between two worlds, theirs and his father's.

He intrigued them. They listened when he spoke. He told tales of the hunt, but also spoke of Princeton, of poetry and novels that he quoted from. A writer who had a life worth writing books about. Now he fancied that the passengers to whom his back was turned had made those crossings with him years before and were bemused to see what had become of that paradoxical young man, that urbane sealer who had seemed so doubly promising.

But Landish rearranged the table and sat beside the boy. All eyes turned towards them. There was a momentary lull in conversation. Then the diners returned their attention to one another, their voices starting up as if in the wake of some awkwardly delivered toast.

Landish surveyed the room. The tables gleaming like wafers of ice. The pale, perfect clavicles of women in white pearls. The unobtrusive music of the orchestra. The bank of chandeliers that hung in unadmired splendour from the ceiling. The to-and-fro of servants. Their expressionless discretion as they made their rounds with trays upraised on white-gloved hands. The oblivious conviviality and fellowship of wealth.

He felt more jealous and nostalgic than disapproving. He would rejoin them if he could. He would re-enlist and raise the boy among them starting now so that someday he might forget what living in the attic had been like.

"Let's look at Gen of Eve," Deacon said.

Landish took the sketch from the carpet bag and displayed it on the floor.

"You can see it better here than in the attic," Deacon said.

"The room is brighter."

"Did your mother ever cross the Gulf?"

"She never left the island."

"Do you like Captain Druken's hat more than Gen of Eve?"

"No."

"If the nobleman took Gen of Eve, would you steal her back?"

"It wouldn't be stealing."

By the light of the cabin, Landish could see that the sketch was creased in places and in others had begun to fade. When they got to Vanderland, he might ask Van to frame it and cover it in glass if he could not soon afford to have it done himself.

One evening when they returned to their cabin, both beds were piled with clothes. Dinner jackets, tuxedos, shirts and trousers.

On one bed, in a tidily arranged but massive heap, were clothes for men for various occasions, and a smaller such heap of clothes for boys lay on the other bed.

Deacon's pile was full of the sort of clothes he had seen boys with long hair and dressed like girls wearing on the ship: skirts and short pants and sailor suits and hats with floppy bows.

Nothing in Landish's pile came close to fitting him. He went through all the pockets in both piles and found two dollars in coins.

"Maybe we can have one or two things altered," he said.

Landish wondered which of the men, who would soon be looking at him, had once owned the clothes he was wearing. He thought it likely that when Deacon saw other boys on the ship he'd wonder if he was wearing what until recently had been their clothes, but he was wrong. Deacon slept in his dinner jacket.

The tailor regretted that he couldn't alter shoes, so both of them had no choice but to wear ill-fitting ones when they left the cabin, Landish's feet so cramped in his that he had to scuff his way from their cabin to the dining room.

"An ill-shodden pair we are," he told the boy, whose shoes came off his feet every few steps.

A barber came by their cabin, his haircutting kit tucked beneath his arm.

"The Captain insists, sir," he said. "Not so much for the boy, but—for you." Landish, about to shout an objection, looked at Deacon.

Deacon watched. Landish sat in a chair and the barber put a sheet around him. He snipped big handfuls of hair and threw them on the floor. Landish sneezed when some fell on his face. The barber brushed his nose. Landish said Christ. His head got smaller. His hair was even all over. His throat was red when the barber shaved away the cream. "Just some cologne and we're done," the barber said. He spilled some on his hands, then put his hands on Landish's face and rubbed in a funny way until Landish said Christ again.

On the promenade deck, he put the boy on his shoulders. Some people complained that to see around or over Landish was difficult enough but impossible when the boy was on his shoulders. Landish felt the boy tighten the grip on his new, shorter hair at the first full view of Bedloe's Island.

"What is it?" Deacon asked.

"A statue like I showed you in the park."

"It's a lot bigger."

"Over a hundred feet high," Landish said. "I'm smaller than her toes."

"She has a crown of thorns. Like Jesus on the Cross. Is she Holy Mary?" Some of the passengers laughed.

"More like hollow Mary," Landish said. "You can walk around inside her. Climb up to the torch and look out across the sea. Imagine sitting on *her* shoulders."

"Who is she?"

Landish told him she was not a statue of a real person like the statues in the park in St John's. She was a symbol. She stood for something the way the plus sign stood for something. Liberty. The Statue of Liberty. That meant freedom. No one could boss you around. The passengers in steerage came from places where everyone was bossed around. The passengers in first class thought that no one in America was bossed around. The Golden Queen stood there in defiance of the sea, holding up her torch as if to say that the sea was nowhere deep enough that she would be engulfed by it, that even in its deepest part she would loom above the waves, unmatched, unsmiling, haughtily disdainful of a world whose every inch she was tall enough to see. The Golden Queen didn't want you to forget that she was there, no matter where you were or where you went.

"The Statue of Not Being Bossed Around," Landish said, and a man leaning nearby against the rail laughed. Another city had the Statue of Virtue, he said. Just like this one but with her virtue encased in a chastity belt with a lock the size of a door. Chastity meant running away when you were chased by anyone other than your husband. If you were chased but got away, you were chaste. When you ran as you were being chased, the belt made a clanking noise that brought men of virtue to your rescue. Another city had the Statue of Puberty, which depicted a boy two hundred feet tall looking astonished as he peered into his long johns.

They were coming at New York from the sea, which smelled like smoke, like St. John's did when something big burned down. Deacon wished the ship hadn't reached New York so fast. They were on their way from here to there. The name of there was not New York. They would get "there" from New York by train. Landish told him there were trains that never touched the ground, trains that went over everything—houses, streets, the people and the horses in the streets. They wound in and out like birds among the buildings. "El trains," he said, but Deacon heard Eel Trains.

"Imagine living in the attic with a train above your head, people looking down at your roof while you looked up at the ceiling, watching from your shaking bed the faces flashing by outside your window."

Landish had changed back into his own clothes and shoes, but Deacon, though he was glad to say good riddance to his shoes, had insisted on disembarking while still dressed in the manner of a diner in first class, ignoring Landish who warned him of the dirty city streets and people who assumed that the pockets of the nicely dressed were full of money.

"Here we go," Landish said as they went down the gangplank with the others. At the bottom, he lifted Deacon off his shoulders and put him on the ground. "Dry land again, Deacon," he said. "See how different it feels. It doesn't move beneath your feet. Solid land. I feel like jumping up and down, don't you?"

Deacon nodded slightly and swallowed the way he did when he was scared.

"Are you all right?" Landish said.

Deacon held out his arms and Landish picked him up and put him back on his shoulders. Deacon sagged to one side.

"Whoa, there," Landish said, looking up into his eyes. "Are you sure you're all right?"

Deacon nodded again.

"It's the excitement of a new place," Landish said.

Deacon thought of the big dot on the map that stood for New York. He felt sorry for St. John's. He wished he and Landish were still there. He couldn't understand why Landish liked New York in spite of having seen the Queen nine times. He wished Landish had never gone to Princeton-on-the-Mainland. If he hadn't, he wouldn't have met the friend he had written to, the friend who lived in not—St. John's and sent them first-class tickets to take them away to Vanderland.

It would have been an easy walk to the concourse if not for Deacon and the carpet bags. Landish had walked the route several times unencumbered, when his things had been forwarded from the ship to the train for Princeton, courtesy of Van. They were taking the Vanderluyden private train, the 630 Express it was called, after the street number of Van's house on Fifth Avenue.

Deacon clung to the collar of Landish's coat. It looked like people were on their way to Mass in a thousand churches all at once. They walked fast, as if they were late, as if worried that the doors would soon be locked. Landish and Deacon tried to hurry but everyone got in each other's way, and they didn't all make room for Landish despite his size. He had to zigzag and turn sideways, moving around so much it made Deacon giddy. Deacon couldn't help trying to look at every-thing and that made him more giddy. He closed his eyes and that made it even worse. He mustn't throw up. All the way to here on the ship and he didn't get seasick, but now—

Landish twisted his head to look back and up at Deacon. He was pale and a film of sweat covered his face. His eyes were barely open and he was crying.

"DEACON?"

"How far?" Deacon said.

The boy was vasted. Gidaddled. Colossalized.

"Not far. Nearly there. You'll feel better soon. Hang on tight."

Deacon on his shoulders, one carpet bag in each hand, Landish tried to run. They were conspicuous—the very large man with the small child on his shoulders, slipping sideways and clutching his hair—even in these streets where sights that elsewhere would catch the eye of everyone were commonplace.

Landish knew he would be helpless if someone made a grab for their luggage. He wished he had insisted that Deacon not wear his ship clothes on the street. He should have packed them while the boy was sleeping and left him with no choice but to wear the rags that matched his own. They were walking through crowds awash with men who had never seen more likely marks and would not be put off by his size or their being shod like beggars or toting luggage they would assume had been acquired in the guileless hope that it would seem unpromising to thieves. In the eyes of oncoming walkers and of men in top hats who peered at him from passing cabs, he saw only flickers of curiosity and passing looks of pity for the boy in whose fate it would never have occurred to them to intervene.

Landish stopped, put down the carpet bags and reached back to feel the boy's forehead. He was feverish.

She was onrushing, an eel with the head of a fish and the body of a snake. He dreamt of trains propelled through the waves by fin-like wings that flapped slowly like those of massive birds. He was underwater in a whale with rows of windows and chatty passengers who milled about with glasses in their hands.

Not far above the city, giant eels with wheels slid about on railway tracks while people pointed up at them and screamed.

Deacon let go of Landish's hair and wound up hanging back to back with him, Landish holding one of his feet in each hand. Deacon sometimes did this just for fun, looking upside down at whatever was behind him, holding his hat in place. Then he would swing back up into his seat, grabbing the sides of Landish's trousers and shirt.

"Hold on to your hat," Landish said, but this time Deacon didn't try to climb back up, so Landish swung him slowly round, holding Deacon by his ankles.

Deacon's hat was gone, his hair and arms hanging limply. Using his knee, Landish hoisted him up and slung him over his shoulder as he had seen women do with bawling children.

He worried that someone might demand that he identify and explain himself, accuse him of mistreating Deacon, challenge him to prove that the boy was in his rightful care, that he meant him no harm and was able to take care of him.

He needed somewhere to sit so he could let go of the carpet bags and get a good look at the boy. But he didn't want to drape a lifeless-looking child across his lap and try right there on the sidewalk to revive him, didn't want to draw more attention to them than he had already, a boy in a dinner jacket that people would assume was stolen, unless they thought the boy was kidnapped. He could only imagine how they would gape at a boy laid across the lap of a man who looked like Landish, the gentlest ministrations of whose massive hands might seem suspicious.

Van's hatred of Manhattan had never inclined Landish to hate it. He'd always fancied that he could adjust to the size and pace of the city, flourish here as he'd believed he would not in Carolina. But now he saw that no one looked as enlivened as he felt. The sheer scale of everything, the frenzied intent of it, the number of people, the traffic-jammed streets, the near-stampede of horses, the voices that were all pitched to the same excited, breathless level as if the subject of every conversation was Manhattan—it was too much for many. Something had sprung into being here that no force on earth could stand against. And he'd had no choice but to bring the boy right into the middle of it.

Landish blustered through the teeming concourse of the train station, more encumbered by luggage than the porters who ignored him. The boy began to stir, perhaps roused by the suddenly amplified sounds of footsteps, the ringing din of echoes that augured their departure to a place that wasn't home or anywhere they had ever been before.

He sat near the wall of the first-class waiting room and held the boy against his chest until he felt his heart beat as if it were his own, his hands spanning his back from shoulder to shoulder, his little finger thicker than the boy's spine, a tiny cage of cartilage so delicate that he might crush it with the slightest pressure of his palm.

Deacon woke, his ear popping when he pulled it away from Landish's chest. Men were sitting on plush chairs, which they had formed into a circle. They were drinking and smoking like the men did on the ship. The air was blue with smoke from cigars and cigarettes. Chandeliers hung above them, like on the ship. Other men strolled about, their hands behind their backs, or with arms folded like

Landish folded his when he was worried. Everyone talked low like people did in church.

Opposite Deacon, an old man, cane planted in front of his closed knees, kept adjusting a hat that had no need of adjustment.

"Where?" Deacon whispered.

"We're back in first class, Deacon," Landish said. "This is the men's waiting room. Everyone is waiting for the train. It won't be long."

Deacon said, "I fell asleep."

"That's all right. I could put you in the luggage if I had to."

Deacon looked around again. A man with a hat on his lap sitting beneath the large clock on the wall was so sound asleep that his glasses had slipped off one ear and were hanging at a slant across his nose. He saw that he was the only boy, the only child. The others must be in the women's waiting room.

Then he coughed for so long and so loudly that some of the men moved further away from him. When Landish asked him how he was, he told him he would like some lemonade. Landish thought of asking him if he could wait till they were on the train, where everything was free, but he saw the boy looking thirstily at the trays of glasses going by and pictured him trying to hold out until the train, which might be hours late, arrived. So he went to the bar and with Van's expense money bought a glass of lemonade with sugar-dusted cherries on the rim. He knew the boy would suck the sugar from the cherries while the lemonade grew warm, so he picked them off and held them in his hand.

Deacon took the glass from Landish in both hands. He wanted to wait until he couldn't stand to look forward to it anymore, but Landish told him he should drink it now because the melting frost was dripping from his fingers and the glass would soon be hard to hold. So he put his face above the glass, took the straw between his lips and began to drink. He knew that he would spoil it if he coughed, so he held his breath, drinking with his eyes closed until he had to pull away, gasping in a way that felt as good as drinking lemonade, his chest heaving like it did when he shovelled snow too fast.

He knew he might spoil it even worse if he got sick. He felt better when he burped, which he couldn't help doing in the all-at-once way that he knew was not polite. Landish moved his hand in circles on his back to coax up any more that might be there, to assure him he was undeserving of the looks he was getting from the others in the waiting room, men who were not accustomed to the presence among them of a child of seven or a man who was dressed like Landish.

"Where is the boy's mother?" asked the man beneath the clock. Landish said she was in a place where no one was so rude as to inquire where the mother of a belching boy might be.

"I should have said 'excuse me,'" Deacon said, but Landish said it was the man who should have said it before interrupting the boy's post-guzzle contemplation of the rug.

Now all the men were looking at them as if, having thought that to object to their presence wasn't worth their bother, they had changed their minds.

"You should be waiting for the train with others like yourselves," a young man said, though his tone was more instructive than otherwise. Perhaps he thought them guilty of nothing more than making a mistake.

"We have first-class tickets," Landish said. He spoke about the ship. "The clothes that I was given do not fit me, and the clothes the boy was given do not suit him." Then he said the name of the place where they were going and that of the man who wrote the letter that was in his pocket. He didn't roar the name as he had when they were on the ship, but calmly said it would have been unkind of them to refuse an invitation from a man like Padgett Vanderluyden, who had been his friend at Princeton.

"If you are going to Vanderland, Vanderluyden must be starting up a circus," said the man beneath the clock.

"May I have your name," said Landish, "so that I may tell Van that you said so?"

Deacon felt again what he had felt on board the ship when the roar that Landish let out shook the chandeliers until they made a sound like distant chimes. There was the same silence.

He drained the glass until the ice cubes rattled on the bottom and the straw made a shrieking sound. There was nothing coming up the straw but water now, the frost was gone, the straw was soggy and the outside of the glass was almost dry. Landish gave him the sugar-dusted cherries. He ate them straight from his palm, pushing them into his mouth. The man beneath the clock drew on his just-lit cigar, blew smoke in their direction, then looked away.

Deacon dozed off and dreamt that he was riding in a subsea train among whose passengers was Landish, who was sitting rows ahead of him, an unapproachable stranger.

That night, on the train, the lights of houses that Landish and the boy would never see again went flashing past. He read in the paper of an all-purpose elixir called "remedaid," and of one that would help you tell the future, called "premonaid." Obliterature. Americal. Chimerica. He knew the boy had never imagined there could be this much of anything, that anywhere could take up so much space that it could not be crossed by a man with a boy astride his shoulders, not by anything except a train whose rampage must continue unresisted to the end.

On and on they went when the sun came up, past things for which he didn't know the words or was too slow to think of. He saw it all come rushing at him, as if the earth were moving and the train were standing still, saw it sometimes from miles away, seeming to grow larger and move faster as the train approached, all things stretching out from him in descending size but at the same time drawing closer, getting larger, until they reared up at his window and were gone.

He thought of the steaming mass of the locomotive that had pulled them such a distance without breaking down or getting stuck and went even faster when it was dark and late. It sounded as if the engineer was barely in control, putting through its nightly paces the one such vehicle in all the world.

They climbed a ridge flanked by valleys that looked like once-great harbours that had shrivelled up to river-parted plains. They saw a succession of such valleys on the far sides of which were other mountains whose ridges were like wrinkled blankets overhung by haze into which the most distant of them blended with the sky.

For most of those who lived in cities, America did not exist except as they imagined it from how it was described in books or looked in photographs, as wondrous to them as to their ancestors who had never crossed the sea or even left the towns where they were born.

But then, he had never seen *his* country, and it seemed likely that he never would.

It was Deacon's first time on a train, his second boarding of a manner of conveyance that wasn't Landish.

The train went through a narrow cut and it looked on either side as if they were bearing head-on through an avalanche of rock.

Landish had marked out on the map for Deacon the route the train would take, one the boy fancied would be downslope all the way. A southward plunge on which the locomotive would slide like a wheel-borne anvil, plowing through the air, a hull on wheels, hauling a hundred cars through the vacuum that it made, funnelling in front of it a wall of wind that would be felt trackside long before those who were keeping watch could even hear the train.

Landish talked about the Mason-Dixon Line and Deacon pictured a line of Mason jars. He talked a bit about the Civil War, a state named after a pencil and one named Maryland but not after Holy Mary Mother of God but after a queen, which made Deacon think of the golden one in New York. There was Virginia and West Virginia, and Virginia came from "virgin," but again, not Holy Mary but yet another queen.

"Van's family owns this train," Landish said. "They own the waiting room and all but own the men who waited there. They own the ship, and other ships and other trains, and the tracks and all the land that you can see on either side."

Vanderland

LANDISH HAD HEARD on the train that the approach road to Vanderland was designed so that the house came into view all at once, winding through a dense but landscaped forest in which grew trees and plants not native to the continent, let alone the South.

In the back seat of a horseless carriage that met them at the Vanderluyden private railway station, Landish waited for it to loom up in front of him, the Carolina mirage that his one-time friend had said he first conceived of in a dream. Late afternoon sun slanted through the trees beside the road that alternated between light and shade in what he had no doubt were precisely calculated intervals. There was no telling what the original terrain had been. Now the road wound up and down an obviously man-made hill, then turned almost directly around as if to circle an obstacle though there was only a gully of many-coloured shrubs that could easily have been removed. The hill became so steep that Landish, who held the sleeping boy in his arms, was flattened back against the seat and saw nothing through the windshield but the sky. The car turned sharply right as the grade of the road decreased, and as it tipped forward his angle of vision increased until he saw, obscured by blue haze, what he guessed was the westernmost ridge of the Appalachians.

About three miles after it passed beneath the arch of the main gate lodge, the car turned sharply again on to a cinder driveway. The great house appeared as suddenly as if it had erupted from the earth.

Landish shook his head and tried to focus on the wrought iron–tipped spire of Vanderland's principal tower. But he could make out no single detail in the full facade of Vanderland, which, though still a mile away, towered so high it blocked the sun, casting the entire forecourt into shadow. As more of the house came into view, he saw it had the look of a French château, such as he'd seen depicted in paintings—a frieze-like jumble of triangle-topped towers, chimneys, parapets, arched doorways and dormer windows.

The car pulled up at the entrance, whose drawbridge-sized doors opened inward. Deacon in his arms, Landish stepped down from the car towards an elderly man who introduced himself as Mr. Henley. He followed the elderly butler across the marble floor of a giant vestibule in which their footsteps echoed as they had in the concourse of the station in New York.

"We can take the lift, sir," the butler said.

"He's never been in a lift," Landish said. "Nor have I. It might scare him to wake up in one."

On a wide and winding set of stone stairs, they climbed three flights. In the well of each flight hung one of the many wheels of an iron chandelier that hung from a single column fastened to the central concave of the tower, each wheel seeming to be all that held up the ones beneath it, each decorated with dozens of electric candles whose unlit "flames" were made of crystal, their "wicks" of wire filament.

Even in the as-yet-unlit tower, everything shone and gleamed, as if the great house had just that day been deemed ready to be occupied. On the third landing, the butler went right and opened for Landish the interlocking doors. He looked into what might have been a tapestry museum. Banks of wide fireplaces blazed along the walls to his right and left, all of them piled high with cedar logs, and on the walls between the fireplaces hung floor-to-ceiling tapestries that depicted scenes, some of which he recognized from Shakespeare, Goethe, Wagner and others. In front of the fireplaces were scattered large sofas and chairs upholstered in green velvet.

"Mr. Druken, sir," the butler said, pulling the doors shut as he backed out of the room.

He was just able to see the familiar top of Van's head above the back of the nearest sofa, the hair swept sleekly back towards the nape of his neck.

"Welcome to Vanderland," Van said. He didn't stand or even turn around.

Landish, the boy still in his arms, walked around the sofa. Van had a pencil-thin moustache. He was staring into the fire, his elbow on the arm of the sofa, face cupped in the palm of his hand, as if lacking all interest in their arrival, a pose deliberately chosen, Landish thought, as the best one to present on the occasion of their first meeting after many years.

"I had no idea," Landish said, standing in front of him and looking about.

Van surveyed the room as well. "No one has '*any idea*' until they come here. The house was designed by Richard Hunt, the grounds by Frederick Olmsted, whom we have to thank for Central Park, the only part of Manhattan that I can bear to visit."

At last he looked at Landish, looked him up and down, then turned his head and smiled as if at someone on the sofa beside him.

Deacon stirred but did not wake up.

"So this is the boy you rescued from the orphanage only to find that you were yourself in need of rescuing."

Landish put Deacon gently down on one of the chairs. "He's not been well on the journey and the heat inside the car made him drowsy. Why are all these fireplaces blazing on such a warm evening?"

"The spring air cools quickly at night. Anyway, the heat won't be a problem for the boy indoors. By a process I can't understand no matter how often Hunt's son explains it to me, we keep the air in many parts of Vanderland at sixty-eight degrees all year long—even cooler in rooms like this one, where I like to keep the fireplaces lit. There are no windows in the gallery. Sunlight fades the tapestries. Sit down."

Landish sat in the upholstered chair nearest Van's sofa.

"You're a sight, Landish. Good Lord. Those are the clothes you wore at Princeton. What's left of them."

"I must be one of those rare people with whom penury does not agree."

"Landish, having some marred version of you at Vanderland seemed preferable to having none at all, but that could change if I grow tired of you. It won't be like it was at Princeton. Or like I promised you it would be at Vanderland if you had come here with me years ago."

"I'm relieved to hear it. The latter part at least."

"You may not leave Vanderland for any reason without my permission, Landish. That rule applies to all the tutors, governesses, staff and servants. And to the boy. I don't want you going into Ashton and then returning to Vanderland still reeking of the place. I devised the rule for my daughter's sake. She has lived all her life at Vanderland and will not leave it, not even for a minute, until she is twenty-one, when she will go out into the world wearing Vanderland as a shield. That is my proposed arrangement. You may decline it and leave if you wish."

"I'm in no position to object to any terms."

There was no sign of the flinching, wincing expression that Van had often worn at Princeton. His hands did not shake as he lit a cigarette.

"So what about the book? Do you still immolate every word you write?"

"I have written and burned many unsatisfactory beginnings. "

"So you were wrong. You *didn't* need to live among the people that you write about. You could just as easily have burned your book here. Or maybe you'd have finished it by now. "

Deacon opened his eyes. He saw a picture of a woman on the wall, but it wasn't Gen of Eve. There were rugs on the floor. And bigger ones on the walls. Maybe they were wet and someone hung them up to dry. A lot of people could live in this place, but here you wouldn't just hear your neighbours, like at home, you would see them all the time.

"Where?" he said. "Are we in Second Class?"

"Vanderland," Landish said.

A man he hadn't noticed who was sitting on one of the green sofas laughed. He got up. He was tall and very thin. He stood with one hand in his pocket, his body bent out like a bow as, with his other hand, he held a cigarette. He tipped his head back and blew smoke towards the ceiling.

"This is the tapestry gallery," he said.

Now it all makes sense to him, Landish thought better of saying out loud: we have many fond memories of hours spent admiring our tapestries at home.

Landish sat beside Deacon on the edge of the sofa and brushed his hair back from his forehead with his hand. "This is Mr. Vanderluyden," he said.

"Hello, Deacon," Van said.

"Hello," Deacon said.

"Too tired to sit up?"

Deacon nodded.

Van smiled. "We'll have a proper meeting later, then. It will be at least a few weeks, I'm afraid. I'm off to New York in the morning. Henley will show you to the Bachelors' Wing. You *are* still a bachelor, aren't you, Deacon?"

Deacon looked at Landish, who nodded. Van smiled at him, his mouth closed in a tight line that curled up at the ends.

"Good night, Van," Landish said, lifting Deacon from the sofa.

❈

In the Bachelors' Wing Landish joined "the Blokes," as they called themselves, who tutored Van's daughter, Godwin. They would, in the same room, at the same time, also tutor Deacon, who was Godwin's age, but school was on Easter break so Landish told Deacon he would not meet Godwin for a month.

And so Godwin, as Deacon called her at first, was to be Deacon's one and only classmate.

The Blokes. There was Gough, an Englishman who wore a paunch-disguising waistcoat and frequently consulted a watch that dangled like a golden apple from his pocket. Sedgewick, also an Englishman, who was in his mid-forties, with a red, almost scarlet complexion that reminded Deacon of Nun Too Soon, and whom Landish told Deacon that first night he deemed "abhorrent" though gave him no explanation for it. Stavely, the music tutor, a small-statured man with long white hair that Deacon thought made him look like a woman. And finally, there was Palmer—the "tutor emeritutus," Landish called him—who was retired and quite deaf. He had been a tutor with the Vanderluydens for forty years, the last of his pupils having been Van. He was very pale and had liver spots on his face and throat and hands.

"What are liver spots?" Deacon asked.

"Everyone who lives is a liver," Landish said. "If you live long enough, you get liver spots."

Gough and Palmer slept in the same room, in separate, narrow beds.

"Palmer isn't just deaf and old," Landish told Deacon. "He needs help moving about and taking care of himself. His memory is very poor. He couldn't get by if not for Gough."

The Bachelors' Wing was also known as "The Blokes." All the Blokes were single, either bachelors who never planned to marry, or widowers. Women and children could not even visit, with the exception of the Bruces, a widow and her daughter, a Mrs. and a Miss. They lived somewhere in another part of Vanderland, but they cooked and cleaned for the Blokes.

They learned that the school for the children of the servants was about two hundred yards from the main house, obsured by a thick grove of poplar trees, and they were not taught by the Blokes but by governesses who also lived in the Bachelors' Wing but in a tower that shared no doors or walls with The Blokes. The women had no nickname until Landish called them the Loverlesses.

In the empty days that followed, Landish found he could at least entertain the Blokes, much as he had entertained Deacon on Dark Marsh Road. He told them of Plato's younger brother, Ditto, who followed Plato around, repeating, word for word, everything that Plato said. Socrates was exasperated with him, denouncing as unteachable by the Socratic method a student who merely repeated the questions that were put to him, and saying he would rather drink hemlock than spend another day being parroted by Ditto. He told them of an English writer who decided to call himself Charles Dickens, having previously submitted his novels under his real name, Chuck Dick. And then, one night, having still toiled for years without success, he reflected on the titles he had chosen for his books: *Great Expectorations*, a picaresque tale that followed from cradle to grave the successive owners of a brass spittoon; a book that would become *Bleak House* he had submitted to publishers as *Unbearable Abode*; *PickWick* by Chuck Dick; *The Chuck Dick Papers*; *The Twist Twins*—Olive and Oliver. Chuck Dick laboured tirelessly over a book he called *A Tale of Two Municipalities*; he considered calling his greatest novel *David Copperfield*, but changed his mind and called it *That Pennymeadow Chap*.

Some of the Blokes were pleased by their arrival. Gough gave Deacon a number of dime novels. The heroes Deacon liked were Jesse James, Doughnut Jack, the hero of *The Awful Atonement*, and Deadwood Dick, at the very mention of whose name the Blokes would start laughing.

"Perhaps if you spent your entire life on it, Landish," Sedgewick said, "you might be able to finish a chapter of a dime novel."

"The Smoker" was the largest room in the Bachelors' Wing, about the size of the attic. The rules of the Smoker were that you weren't allowed entrance without a smoking jacket—an exception was made for Deacon—and everyone was required to chip in on the brandy "pot."

Deacon sat up with the Blokes in the Smoker every night, watched them smoke and drink and listened to them talk. Sometimes he would fall asleep in his chair by the fire.

"It's as though," Landish said one evening, "I woke one morning to find myself in the middle of another life, someone else's whose past I can't recall and whose future I can't imagine."

From time to time, Palmer and Gough would communicate by an exchange of notes, which they would write while the others watched. Palmer's notebook was small and leather-bound, with a gold-coloured ribbon to mark his place. Most of the time Palmer simply sat there with the notebook on his lap and the stub of a yellow pencil tucked behind his ear.

It was on the second night that Palmer, when he noticed Deacon watching him, nodded and smiled at him and began to write very slowly in his notebook, which he then handed to Gough. Gough read aloud: "How are you this evening, young man?"

"I'm fine, Mr. Palmer. How are you?" Deacon said aloud. Gough swiftly wrote his response and handed the notebook back to Palmer, who read what Gough had written. The old man looked at Gough, then at Deacon and nodded and smiled again.

That night Landish and Deacon sat on their beds, facing each other. Landish asked Deacon what he thought of their new home. Deacon said he liked it though the attic was better because they had had it all to themselves and now they had to share most of it with the Blokes, but the Blokes were nice, so it wasn't as bad as sharing rooms with Hogan would have been. And their room was small but not as small as the bedroom in the attic and at least there were no business buckets: their bathroom was something like the bathroom on the ship, even if it was smaller.

Landish said they didn't have their own kitchen, but at least they didn't have to walk the gauntlet of kitchens to get to The Blokes and he'd rather be a tutor than shovel snow or dig a ditch. There were two windows, each of them far bigger than the porthole in the attic. There were two beds of the same size, too small for Landish and too big for Deacon. Deacon wished there was one big bed so he could still climb in with Landish.

He missed going out for their walks, when there had been things to watch and listen to. They spent time instead with the Blokes in the Pleasure Gardens with its carefully tended flowerbeds crisscrossed by pathways. The old men sat on benches and looked up at the sky while they talked. He kept asking to see the inside of the main house and Landish could only say that maybe one day he would see it. Van wasn't back from New York yet but he promised to speak to him about it when he returned. And he reminded Deacon he mustn't mention Princeton to Mr. Vanderluyden, or Captain Druken's hat, which the wealth inspector was sending to them by the mail. They were off limits, like the story of Vivvie. He just hoped that Captain Druken's hat would hurry up.

Deacon asked him how long they would be at Vanderland and Landish said he wasn't sure but it wouldn't be forever. But it startled him when Deacon asked when they were going back to Newfoundland. He got upset and said he'd told him before they left that they might never see the place again, that he'd told him they didn't have to leave but it was too late now. Deacon started to cry and Landish said he was sorry.

"We might go back," he said. "You never know."

"You never know," Deacon said.

❧

Landish thought of the other Blokes each time he retired for the night. Grown men, but none of them owned their little rooms, or even the beds they slept in. Even though he had once called an attic home, he felt hemmed in by the walls of his room and the knowledge of how nearby the others were, merely a few feet away, able to hear every sound he made as he was likewise able to hear them, the squeaking of bedsprings every time someone moved, the creaking of the floor-boards as Sedgewick paced the room in the vain hope of relieving his fear-of-God-induced insomnia. You couldn't see the sea from any-where. The woods were bigger and darker and they didn't smell the same. There was a mountain on the other side of every mountain. The mountains stretched out like ocean waves, getting smaller and fainter until they disappeared into the sky.

On Friday evenings, "darky" musicians played for the Vanderluydens and their guests in the theatre. The music could be faintly heard over all of Vanderland.

Landish told Deacon that the Vanderluydens had the run of all the other rooms at Vanderland: about three hundred rooms for three people, counting the rooms for the servants who lived on the top and bottom floors and the dozens of regular guests. He wondered how many rooms lay dark and empty every night for months, even years.

Every night, Deacon knew he would dream about the dark and empty rooms so he tried to stay awake. But he fell asleep and dreamt that when he woke up, Landish wasn't there. There was no bed next to his. He got up to look for Landish. He thought he heard the kitchen table shake like it did when Landish wrote his book, but he couldn't find the kitchen.

When Van returned from New York, Landish asked Henley the butler to ask him for permission to go farther than the Pleasure Gardens so Deacon could see the house. Stavely, the old white-haired music teacher, lispily said it was the size of more than ten basilicas. They were given permission to go only to the rear of the house. Outside, they had to stand far back beneath the trees to see it in full. Landish said the front was better and it was too bad that Deacon had been asleep the day they drove up to Vanderland in the motor car. Deacon's neck was sore from looking up, but he couldn't see the top. Landish pointed at the Bachelors' Wing—that was where they lived—but he had to admit he wasn't sure which of the many windows was theirs. A week later, Van unexpectedly sent over permission by way of the butler for them to see the front of Vanderland, which he called the east facade. You had to go halfway across the Esplanade—a long flat meadow in front of the house, with a road around it and a fountain in the middle—to see the central tower. It looked like a giant crown, infested with gargoyles and spires and dormers and parapets, towers and chimneys. Deacon stared up from the forecourt until Vanderland made him dizzy.

They walked round to the back and down the hill almost to Lake Loom, the man-made lake designed by Olmsted to reflect the house. Landish thought the west facade was not as striking except when it reflected in Lake Loom, which it did to eerie effect this day because of a freakishly late fall of snow. The house, hit by the setting sun, was the only part of Vanderland still above the shadow of the Ridge. The bright stone flickered like fire in the snow-surrounded water of the lake.

"Tell me about Newfoundland," Gough said to Deacon one night in the Smoker.

"Everything's on the hill and when we go out walking Landish puts me on his shoulders so all the men look up at me. He says it must be a nice change from dodging legs and being able to see nothing but the arse in front of me. When it's windy it's cold but on sunny days big white clouds make shadows on the water. At night in our attic you can hear the 'droning'—that's the wind. I don't mind it, but Landish does. He sits up in the kitchen, drinking grog and reading books out loud."

"What did you read, Landish?" Gough said.

Landish said that he read *The Divine Dromedary*, in which, in four-teen thousand lines, were related the adventures of Dante Alighieri and a camel named Virgil. Mr. Palmer smiled when he read what Gough wrote in the notebook.

"It's nice to have a child living at The Blokes, Deacon." Gough smiled over at him.

"Landish says you're lucky," Deacon said, "because most old people end up in the poorhouse and no one ever picks them. He says it's better to pick a baby than to have one. He says if you have a mediocre baby you're stuck with it. He says even a baby that exudes excellence might turn out to be a flop."

"Do you remember every word Landish says?" Stavely asked in his lisping fashion.

"Do you believe in Heaven?" Sedgewick asked him, leaning forward ponderously.

"The Tomb of Time," Deacon said. Sedgewick looked severely at Landish.

"You should be teaching Deacon about Heaven. He should be pray-ing every night for the souls of his parents. He should be praying for you and for himself. A time when death won't seem so funny is coming for all of us. Don't fool yourselves. Purgatory waits. Or worse."

"Sedgewick," Gough said, "I've seen you run screaming from a bumblebee, yet the certainty of burning for millions of years doesn't even spoil your appetite. Any person who really believed in Purgatory would spend every second of his life running screaming through the streets."

"We'd all know where we were going," Landish said, "if Christ had brought back to life someone with a better memory than Lazarus."

"That's blasphemous," Sedgewick said. "You're mocking a miracle."

"Lazarus the beggar," Landish said. "His family and friends were overjoyed when he came back to life. I'm sure they threw a party for him. People gave him cards: 'Congratulations on your resurrection, dear Lazarus: you're only as dead as you feel.' 'Welcome back. The people who said you were nothing but a beggar are eating crow today.' 'You're a shoo-in for a parable.' But eventually, someone must have got round to asking him questions:

"'So tell us, Lazarus, what's it like? What happens when you die?'

"'I don't remember.'

"'You don't remember? Four days dead, you come back to life and you remember nothing? Lazarus, listen. No one has ever come back from the dead. You know what no one else knows. What no one else has ever known. The answer to the ultimate question, so you really need to concentrate.'

"'I don't remember. It might come back to me, but who knows? I was only there for four days.'

"'"It might come back to me but who knows?" That's all you have to say? If Jesus was only going to raise one person from the dead, couldn't he have asked around before he did it? But no, of all the people who ever died, he picks you. He picks Lazarus the beggar instead of Aristotle. He gives Lazarus four days but overlooks Aristotle who died three hundred years ago. Can you imagine how much knowledge about the afterlife the greatest mind of all time could soak up in three hundred years? Would Aristotle ever say "it might come back to me"? Or what about Moses, who, instead of trying to remember the Ten Commandments, *wrote them down*? Well, at least you'll have the most unique headstone of all time: *Here Lies Lazarus. Again!*'"

"Absolute *blasphemy*," Sedgewick said.

"You may have noticed, Sedgewick, that Jesus didn't bring Lazarus back a second time. Jesus was no genius, but I bet you didn't have to spend a lot of time with Lazarus to know that resurrecting him was a big mistake."

"Sedgewick says I'll meet my parents when I die," Deacon said to Landish. "Do you think that's true?"

"I don't know, Deacon."

But when Landish was next alone with Sedgewick, he told him to leave the boy alone. "If you get to Heaven and I'm not there, give Shakespeare my regards and tell him that *Macbeth* could have used another draft."

The next evening, they went out for a walk and he put Deacon up on his shoulders. It was the kind of night that for some reason always brought back memories of his childhood. On this occasion, he felt a kind of nostalgia or melancholy for a time beyond remembrance, an elusive, possibly illusory time. And it brought up in him a sense of having lost or wasted something whose absence he hadn't noticed until now.

They went past the cemetery and Deacon talked about the Crosses in Mount Carmel and the Druken mausoleum. When Vanderland was first constructed, Gough had told Landish, a plot of land was set aside for a cemetery. But no one had yet died at Vanderland—the cemetery's iron gates had been opened only by landscapers since Vanderland was completed. They tended the trees, shrubbery and grass and swept the stone pathways. It might as well have been a purposeless garden in which visitors were not allowed.

Landish couldn't help thinking of the first grave, the oblong hole, the dark mound of dirt beside it. It would comprise an incongruous violation of the unmarred expanse of bright green grass.

He thought of the resting place of his parents, and of the two crosses for Deacon's parents in Mount Carmel, the one over an empty grave. With the boy on his shoulders he went back to the Bachelors' Wing.

Landish wished that Carolina was not so remindful to him of Newfoundland. Even on sunny days the wind was high. It seemed that in the mountains of North Carolina, the wind blew ceaselessly from

September to April, and Vanderland, being so elevated, took the brunt of it. It funnelled between the Great Smoky Mountains and the Blue Ridge Mountains and slammed against the windows of Vanderland, driving before it flakes of snow that pattered against the glass like the first large raindrops of a thunderstorm.

He frequently saw, from the height of their bedroom window, the front edge of a snowstorm make its way across the mountains and then—even in these last lengthening days of spring—the woods and fields of Vanderland until finally it encroached upon the rear court, where it rose up like a torrent of white water at the window and engulfed the mansion, ice pellets clicking on the other side of the glass to which his face was pressed.

Once, when a snowstorm had reached Vanderland, Landish, through sheer luck, and by way of a maze of staircases and hallways, found the Winter Garden. He knew it was off limits to him but there was no one about. In the warm, damp air, among all the fronds and flowers and shoots of bamboo, he sat in a chair and looked up through the glass dome at the sky until the dome itself was white with snow and the Winter Garden became so dark that the hanging lamps came on and the room looked like he guessed it did at midnight.

Van sent word to The Blokes that Landish and Deacon should meet him at the stables.

"Was New York as awful as you expected?" Landish said.

"It seems worse every time I go there," Van said. "But let's not talk about New York. I'm promoting you."

They were "promoted," allowed the use of a horse that Van said was suited to non-riders because she never went faster than a walk. They rode together on the horse whose name was Pageant, Deacon with his arms wrapped around Landish's belly, his face pressed against his back. Pageant was Deacon's fourth manner of conveyance, Landish said, unless you counted the cart they rode briefly in on the way to Mount Carmel cemetery, in which case she was the fifth.

Van went riding with them one day. He said he did not join the many hunting parties that set out from Vanderland. He told Landish that his father had taken him hunting deer when he was Deacon's age but that he could never bring himself to pull the trigger.

"Never had the stomach for it," he said. Whereas once his father had a gun in his hands, he seemed to see every object in creation, living or otherwise, as a challenge to his marksmanship. He shot at everything. He was affronted by anything that didn't bear the mark of a bullet from his gun.

Upon first greeting them at Vanderland, Van had given the impression that they would see little of him. But they were, inexplicably to Landish, "promoted" again. Van invited Landish and Deacon on what Landish called "firewood safaris." He said Mrs. Vanderluyden didn't want him spending time with them, but if he felt he must then better he do it outdoors than in the house where she might happen onto them.

Deacon knew there were eighty-seven fireplaces at Vanderland. Mr. Vanderluyden chose the wood for the ones that he and his family used, about thirty of them, including some that were bigger than the Druken mausoleum. When he found a tree he liked the look of, he marked an X on it with chalk, and the men following behind him, driving wooden carts, dismounted and set off from the trail with their axes and saws.

"I choose the ones that I think will burn the best," he said. "You can tell from looking at trees which ones will smell the sweetest. Poplar, beech, oak and hickory—they all smell different at different times of year."

Deacon would come to know Van's daughter as Goddie, but Gough introduced him to her as Godwin. She was named Godwin Meredith Vanderluyden and was known to almost everyone as Goddie, a nickname spoken with a mixture of irony and fondness that flourished the more her mother tried to discourage its use.

"Godwin is girl for Godfrey," Goddie told Deacon when they met in Gough's history class on their first day of school together. She was chubby with long, thick, brown, curly hair that was almost always adorned with bows of white ribbon. "Godfrey is one of my father's names. And his father's, too."

The large room in which she and Deacon were tutored was known as the Academy. It was windowless, with a bank of blackboards along one wall, and furnished with laurel wreath—crowned busts of Socrates and Aristotle and other severe-looking old men and medieval maps and globes of the world, and long, gleaming, book-littered tables, each of which was the domain of one of the tutors. Landish was to teach them writing and reading. At first Goddie was terrified of him and the volume of his normal speaking voice, which he learned to modulate while in her company.

Deacon had been at Vanderland a month but had never set eyes on her before, never so much as heard her voice.

"Mother says you take your lessons with me instead of with the servants' boys and girls because Father feels sorry for you. Because of Landish. Father used to be his friend. They went to school together. But now Landish has no money and no . . . something that begins with P."

"Prospects?"

She nodded. "And Sedgewick says he drinks too much. Mother doesn't like him. She says he failed writing so they threw him out of school, and he isn't fit to teach me. And no one else will have you. She says Landish's father, who was a filthy savage, murdered your father, who was a filthy savage too. She says it's wrong, a Vanderluyden rubbing the shoulders of the likes of you. I said I never rubbed your shoulders but she said never mind. But Father says he'll be the judge and hear no more about it. Mother says I'm to tell her everything that you and Landish do or say."

Deacon reported this to Landish.

"Be careful not to upset her, Deacon," Landish said. "Don't argue with her. Don't make fun of her. Try to ignore her when she talks like that. It's very important."

"Because Mr. Vanderluyden might get upset and give us the sack?"

"Maybe."

"Did your father murder mine?"

Landish said no, but his father took chances that he shouldn't have. He risked other men's lives. And sometimes those men died. "He *caused* your father's death and the deaths of other men. He sent him out in search of seals though he knew a storm was coming. And when the watch came back to the ship without your father, he steamed on in search of seals instead of waiting for the storm to stop, instead of searching. He told the crew that one man in a storm like that, even one who knew the ice as well as Francis Carson, didn't have a chance.

"It's called mutiny if you disobey a captain. You could be whipped or hanged. So the crew of the *Gilbert* did what they were told. But when they got back, they said they were ashamed for not defying the captain—my father."

"Were our fathers filthy savages?"

"No. Mrs. Vanderluyden values ancestry even more than Mr. Vanderluyden does. Her family name was Jandemere, and she's directly descended from the founder of the colony of New Netherland, who was also one of the founders of New York. The society magazines call her an 'American aristocrat'—something like a duchess or a baroness, or even a princess. She married beneath her, socially speaking, married a lesser name for money, thus making Van's name a better one."

"Which name is better, Druken or Carson?"

"I don't concern myself with names. But never speak in front of Mrs. Vanderluyden unless she asks you a question. Keep your answer short. Call her ma'am or Mrs. Vanderluyden. She's like Nun One, or the nobleman, or even the wealth inspector. Our fate is in her hands."

"Landish says you take after your grandfather," Deacon said to Goddie, as they waited for Sedgewick to begin geography class.

"What does 'take after' mean?"

"It means you're a lot like him."

"Grandpa was old."

"Not always."

"Father never says I take after him. Mother doesn't either."

"Landish says you look like him. He says you've your grandfather's eyes and your grandfather's forehead."

Goddie stared blankly at Deacon for several seconds, then suddenly burst into tears and ran off shouting for her mother.

"You must mind what you say to her, Deacon," Landish said when Deacon told him what had happened. "Strange forces come to play on even the most literal, unambiguous pieces of information that enter that child's mind. You and I can have our little jokes, but let's keep them to ourselves. For instance, don't mention Gen of Eve to her. I don't want her to misunderstand *that* figure of speech. And don't mention Captain Druken's hat or Princeton to her either."

"What did Goddie, I mean Godwin, tell you today?" Landish said, shaking his head when Deacon repeated a story Goddie had told in Stavely's music class called "Jack and Beans Talk" and said that in old Gough's history class she had asked how long the "Victorious Error" lasted.

"How long did the Victorious Error last, Gough?" Landish asked in the Smoker.

"The Victorious Error has lasted sixty-four years," Gough said. "A prize has been offered to anyone who corrects it."

Noah's Ark angels. Cain Unable. Lot's wife turned into a spiller of salt. Starting with Abraham, all penises were circle-sized.

Gough said that Landish was lucky. He asked him to imagine what teaching Goddie *foreign* languages was like.

Landish laughed. "She sounds almost like a little Landish."

Deacon felt sorry for her. She looked frightened when she didn't know the answer, so sometimes he pretended not to know it. The Blokes knew he was pretending, but he wasn't sure if Goddie did. He knew she wished it was like before when they didn't have him to compare her to.

She was in the habit of speaking as if she and her father managed his share of the Vanderluyden fortune in tandem. "Profits are slightly down," she announced to Landish and Deacon on their first day together for their reading and writing class, frowning as if she were speaking of a trend whose reversal would be her main task for the next few months.

Gough told Landish about the Vanderluyden fortune-founder, the "Admiral," the first Godfrey Vanderluyden. He was said to have had a written vocabulary of about three hundred words, most of which, on the rare occasions that he tried to write them, he misspelled. When he wrote words that should have had double *e*'s, he replaced the second *e* with an *a*, often to innocuous effect, such as when he wrote of going to "sea the widowe," but more famously to bizarre effect, such as when he misspelled "deed" and wrote to a man with whom he had recently agreed upon a price for a trotting horse: "Please send her dead to me to proove that she is mine."

"Father says there's no such thing as God," Goddie said. "Mother says listen to Father about everything but not God. She says it's just as well that he pays no attention to us. She says she doesn't care if he pays attention to her as long as he pays her allowance. Mother says we're not as good as God at anything. God is the best at everything. He got here first. Darkies lay on the face of the sheep. Then God said 'leather be light.' Those were the first words ever spoken. The most important words ever spoken. Everything started when God said them. It was dark so He started a fire. He sawed that which was wood. He gave us a minion over everything. Gough said minions are lesser beans. Like servants, Mother said. God is the supreme bean. The King is more like God than me. But I'm more like God than you. And you're more like God than even the smartest darky. God has no father and mother, but He's not like you. He's not an orphan. Mother says no one gave birth to him. He gave it to Himself. He sent His son to die on the cruise of fiction."

It wasn't until they'd been at Vanderland two months that Deacon met Mrs. Vanderluyden. Her name was Gertrude but Landish said he must never call her that. She came to the Academy when he and Goddie were there with Landish. Deacon thought she looked pretty and smiled at her.

"So you're the orphan who sits in my daughter's company at school," Mrs. Vanderluyden said. "What was your father's last name?"

"Druken, ma'am."

"Your *father's* last name."

Landish stepped forward. "It was Carson, Mrs. Vanderluyden."

"So Druken killed Carson. And Carson's mother. Druken made Carson an orphan. And now Carson's son is Druken's son except they share no blood. Captain Druken. No doubt the captaincy was self-conferred. The son of a murdering savage plays father to the murdered parents' son while tutoring my only child. It's not exactly an ideal arrangement for Godwin, is it?"

She covered her face with her hands and drew a deep breath, her shoulders slowly rising and falling.

Deacon looked at Landish, who ever so slightly shook his head.

"He is so small, so thin," Mrs. Vanderluyden said. He thought her voice was nicer than before. "His eyes—there's barely room inside him for his soul. He must have no idea how he came to be here. Did you have to take him three thousand miles from home to keep him from starving to death?"

"Our situation was—"

"No one's fault but yours. You let yourself be taken in by my husband. As did I. But you've no better sense than to come back to him for more."

Mrs. Vanderluyden stepped closer to Deacon. Their noses almost touched. He thought she smelled like soap. She put her hands on his shoulders. He could barely feel them. "Never harm Godwin in any way," she said. But she touched his cheek with her finger. "Mr. Druken will explain to you what I mean by harm. And what will come from disobeying me."

"Yes, ma'am."

"You're not a member of this family," Mrs. Vanderluyden said. "You have to understand that. I have no one but my daughter. You have no one but Landish Druken, such as he is. I'm sorry for that. And Landish Druken has no one but my husband, such as *he* is. You two would not be here if not for Mr. Vanderluyden. You would not be here if it were up to me. I know that sounds unkind. But there is much that you are far too young to understand. Both of you had better be on your best behaviour. And you, Deacon—I hate to be so severe with you, but you must be especially careful where my daughter is concerned. What is my daughter's name?"

"Godwin, ma'am."

"That's right. And you must never call her anything but that. If I had my way, you would call her Miss Vanderluyden, even when speaking to her."

She stood erect, stepped back and looked at Landish. "*You* must care for yours. I must care for mine. I *must*. You cannot interfere."

"I assure you I won't, even though I can't imagine how I could."

That night as he climbed into his bed, Deacon said that she was nicer than Goddie made him think she'd be. Landish too had been surprised to hear tenderness creep into her voice when she spoke to Deacon. She must not have been prepared for what she saw, a boy still disarmingly frail despite two months at Vanderland. But her undisguised contempt for her husband made him uneasy. She saw herself and Landish as kindred victims of Van, both "taken in" by him. Perhaps she was exaggerating. But she'd sounded desperate, determined to persist in a fight she knew she couldn't win.

✻

Landish confined himself to his room on Sunday afternoons to work on his book. He otherwise worked on it when, as he told the Blokes, "idleness and inspiration coincide," but he spent Sunday afternoons writing it whether he felt like it or not. He told them: "First you become an anecdotalist. Only a raconteur can certify an anecdotalist. And only a scribe can certify a raconteur. When you're allowed to write things down, you become a scribe. Then you have to choose between fiction and non-fiction. A fork in the road. Two roads that look a lot alike. But either way you're called a scribe. A scribe of fiction, first class, is not allowed to write a story, but can oversee the writing of a scene, with or without dialogue, or even a character sketch. And then you rise up through the ranks until you get your first commission and are put in charge of writing an entire work, in my case one of fiction."

Van had given him a typewriter to celebrate the three-month anniversary of their arrival at Vanderland and appointed his secretary, a Mr. Smythe, to give him rudimentary lessons in the use of the machine. That, combined with solitary practice, had resulted in his developing a technique involving only his thumbs and index fingers. His fingers were so large that he frequently struck two or more keys at once, but he had come to prefer the clatter of the typewriter to the near-silent scratching of pen on paper. The typewriter, a cast-iron Remington that, being completely unenclosed, caused Gough to describe it as being "all innards," looked like the overturned skeleton of some skinny, many-boned animal with a single rack of forty ribs.

The weather brightened through the early summer. When it was nice, the others, Deacon included, would go outside and leave The Blokes to him, but when it was wet or cold, they had no choice but to put up with the din that he made. Deacon stuck his fingers in his ears and tried to concentrate on reading. The Blokes strained to hear the gramophone. Gough told Landish that it sounded as if he was not so much using the typewriter as trying to subdue it, as if the main task of his life was not to compose a book but to exact, by means of bludgeoning it, an admission of defeat from a small creature that he kept hidden in his room. His fingers pounded the keys like hammerheads, the typewriter jumped about and thudded on his desk, which in turn knocked against the wall, while his feet kept a kind of time with his fingers, stamping on the floor with such force that the adjoining rooms shook as much as his did. The tumult went on almost ceaselessly, with pauses just long enough to suggest that he might be done for the day, and then it would resume, seemingly louder than before, as if he had asked the thing that he was doing battle with if it had had enough and been answered with some vicious, deeply personal, filth-ridden insult.

When he at last emerged from his room, his face would be scarlet red and his hair matted to his forehead, from which beads of sweat still dripped, his shirt clinging to him, so wet it was transparent and his pink back and belly showing as clearly as if, from the waist up, he was naked.

"You look as though you've got a fever," Gough said one day. "How many pages did you write?"

"Ten," Landish said. "But I used the letter X a lot. A lot more than any other letter."

"Why?" Deacon said.

"Because every word in his book contains the letter X," Sedgewick said.

"Because, Deacon," Landish said, "it's the best letter to type over other letters with. It's the best way to cross out things that look worse on paper than they sounded in your head. Sentences you can't believe you wrote and pray you don't remember. Sentences that, in other circumstances, it would amuse you to know that *anyone* could write."

"And you'll tell no one what the book's about?" Gough said.

"I'm afraid that I'll stop writing if I talk too much about it."

"Or maybe you're afraid you'll start," Sedgewick said.

"You're too hard on yourself, Landish, that's all," Stavely said, curling a strand of his long white hair round his finger. "Sedgewick may be right. Why don't you let someone else see what you write before you cross it out?"

"Too late for what I wrote today," Landish said.

"What do you mean?" Gough said.

"I crossed out everything. Every last word. And then I burned the pages."

"Good God, Landish," Sedgewick said, his voice so high-pitched it made Landish wince. "What a waste. For us, I mean. We could have all had some peace and quiet this afternoon."

"How much have you kept since you started, if you don't mind my asking?" Gough said.

"Nothing. I may be in the process of writing, and will one day be trying to find a publisher for, the first entirely expurgated book."

That evening, Landish was the last to leave the Smoker. Deacon, alone in their room, heard him holding forth as he used to in the attic. About the dots, he hoped, or even Sedgewick—Landish kept telling him he "sensed" the man could not be trusted—but he was almost certain he was upset about Captain Druken's hat, which was long overdue. Two days before, he'd said he wished Captain Druken's hat would hurry up. He had many times written to the wealth inspector but received no replies. In his letters, he always referred to the hat as "the item that you promised you would send to me." He couldn't call it a hat, he told Deacon, because the letters might wind up in the wrong hands.

He listened to Landish for what seemed like hours, his tone rising and falling. The other Blokes shouted from their rooms for him to go to sleep.

"I was reading aloud something that I wrote," he told Deacon when at last he came to bed.

"I'm sure the wealth inspector will keep his promise," Deacon said.

Landish said that he was sure too, in a way—at least that he'd keep his promise if he was still able to. "Who knows what may have happened since we left?"

"What may have happened?"

Landish said someone might have found out where the inspector was hiding the hat.

"The nobleman?"

"Maybe. Or someone else. Almost anyone. I was a fool to leave without it. The wealth inspector might be in trouble because of me. How could I have left my father's hat in someone else's hands and then gone off three thousand miles away?"

"What kind of trouble?" Deacon said.

"The man might be in jail for all I know. A wife and three children left with no one to support them. Or he may not be as honest as we think. A man who is paid to withhold vouchers from the poor. He may have made some sort of deal to sell the hat."

Deacon shook his head.

"You might be right. Maybe he sent it when he was supposed to and it went astray on the way from there to here. Things go astray. Between there and here, someone might have stolen it. Opened the crate and stolen the box. Things get sent and don't arrive. It happens. That's why I should have found some other way."

Deacon asked Landish what he would do with the hat if it arrived. Landish said he would show it to the Blokes, and Van too. But even so, Deacon must not talk to anyone about the nobleman or how Landish got the hat back. And he'd make up some story about why it took the hat longer than it took them to get to Vanderland. He smiled reassuringly at him, undressed and got into bed. But he tossed and turned. He couldn't bear to think why the wealth inspector hadn't replied. If he'd washed his hands of the hat and of him and the boy, he wouldn't blame him. There might be someone at the mail depot who was telling the nobleman that the wealth inspector was getting letters from America, where Landish Druken went.

In the morning, when they woke, he got up and sat on the edge of his bed, facing Deacon. He said he thought he knew what had happened to the hat. The wealth inspector *had* sent it—it had arrived in a crate at Vanderland, delivered to that part of the house where freight from the train was received. And in spite of its having been addressed to Landish Druken, Van had opened the crate and taken the hat, which was now hidden somewhere in one of the hundreds of rooms at Vanderland.

"How would Mr. Vanderluyden know the hat was in the crate?"

Landish said he wouldn't have known anything about the hat, he had probably just opened the crate out of curiosity—who would tell him not to?—and found it and decided he must have it for no reason but that it belonged to Landish.

"Because of Princeton?" Deacon asked.

Landish said he wasn't sure, but he was certain he was right that Van had the hat even though he had no proof.

"But he picked us," Deacon said. "To help us. He didn't know about the hat."

Landish said he picked them because he felt guilty for what he did at Princeton, but that didn't mean he wouldn't hurt his friend again if he got the chance.

Deacon wasn't sure Mr. Vanderluyden had done what Landish said. You couldn't find a hat in such a house. "What will you do?" he asked. "Vanderland's so big. You can't sneak about from room to room, people will see you." Landish said they had to pretend they didn't know Van had stolen the hat—after all they couldn't afford to accuse him, couldn't demand he give them back the hat. They had to pretend they didn't know he'd stolen the hat. "At least I know it's here," he added. "At least I know it's nearby. That's something, I suppose."

"I suppose," Deacon said.

But Deacon knew Landish would think about the hat almost all the time until it was found or arrived from Newfoundland or until he couldn't stand it anymore. He wasn't sure what would happen then. But he was glad Landish was happy about one thing: at Landish's request, one of Vanderland's carpenters had framed Gen of Eve in black wood and covered her in glass. Landish considered hanging it in his and Deacon's room, on the wall opposite their beds, but Deacon said he wouldn't want someone, not even Gen of Eve, looking at him all night long. So he hung it in the Smoker, and the Blokes—all but Sedgewick—complimented his mother on both her draftsmanship and her attractiveness.

"She's almost smiling," Gough said. "But she looks tired or care-worn or something. Perhaps she sensed that her time was short."

"It's not the *Mona Lisa*," Sedgewick said. "It's merely a crude pencil sketch. Who knows what effect she was aiming for?"

At noon, Goddie would go off for lunch in the Lesser Banquet Hall and Deacon would go back to The Blokes to have lunch with Landish and the others. Mrs. Vanderluyden did not eat lunch, declaring it to be a "vulgar, rustic custom," but Mr. Vanderluyden insisted that it made sense to eat when the body most had need of nourishment. It was, he said, part of the "new way" at Vanderland. Goddie would come back from lunch and her post-lunch nap with a glazed, sated, drowsy look about her. It was for some reason always after lunch that she was espe-cially resentful of being paired with Deacon in the Academy.

"Did you enjoy your lunch, Deacon?"

"Yes, thank you."

"What did you have?"

"A slice of sausage and a piece of bread. And an apple. A five-point apple."

She smiled. "I didn't ask you what you fed your horse. What did you really have?"

Deacon didn't answer.

"I had the most delightful lunch. Veal chops and roasted potatoes. And strawberries and chocolate ice cream for dessert."

Deacon pictured a large plate bearing two veal chops encircled by large, fat-basted roasted potatoes, all of it covered in gravy.

Goddie slumped in her chair, lazily kicking her feet, which didn't reach the floor, staring at Deacon, her hands clasped on her blue-velvet-dress-covered belly that rose and fell as if she was slightly out of breath.

"You're not my brother, you know. You're not even my eleventh cousin times three. You're only here because Father likes Landish. He doesn't like you."

Often she would fall asleep shortly after the first lesson of the after-noon began. As they were on orders from Mrs. Vanderluyden that Goddie must never be touched, the Blokes woke her by loudly clapping their hands or stamping their feet. Goddie would wake in such alarm that she would gasp or scream or cry out for her mother. Once, she slid straight off the chair and onto the floor and, beginning to cry, would not budge from where she sat until her mother was brought to help her up.

"She has a much fuller day than the boy does," Mrs. Vanderluyden said. "That's why she doesn't do as well in some things. The poor thing is exhausted. You men should focus less attention on the boy and more on Godwin. I don't care how clever you think the boy is. I know he's your pet, but you're being paid to educate *my* child, not someone else's."

Landish said that Goddie would set records. Before she left Vanderland, she would be the richest person never to have set foot on a ship or train. Never to have seen a town, let alone a city. Never to have seen a thing her father didn't own. Never to have set foot in or on something she wouldn't own someday.

Goddie was also instructed daily by a number of governesses who taught her posture, comportment, etiquette, manners, costume. Mrs. Vanderluyden said that their collective task was to stifle her Vanderluyden half and cultivate her Jandemere half, to rid her of whatever "coarseness of nature and ill-refinement she may have inherited from my husband's side of the family."

It was in the after-lunch periods that Goddie would look at Deacon with an expression of intense concentration before holding forth:

"Landish is a Druken, so there's no telling what he might do to you someday. He might murder you. Finish the job. Finish the Carson family. You're just a bother to him anyway. Landish has a woman in Ashton. But she won't marry him as long as he has you. He would have finished his book long ago, but he has to spend his time and money taking care of you. You can't get into Heaven unless you have a grave. God can't take your father's soul until he finds his body. Your mother's in Heaven all by herself. So even in Heaven she's unhappy. Mother says your mother lost her mind when she heard about your father. She didn't get her mind back when she went to Heaven. *If* she went to Heaven, because Mother says that if an apple like you fell from her, who knows what kind of tree she was."

But the next time she saw Deacon, she would be penitent to the point of bursting into tears, hiding her face in her hands. "I'm sorry I said those things, Deacon. None of them are true. Sometimes I'm so hateful and so mean. I don't know why. It comes into my head and I say it. I know it's wrong, but I can't help it. You don't say bad things to me. You don't say *anything* to me. Maybe I wouldn't say things if I was smart like you. I know I'm not smart. I heard Father say to Mother I can't hold a candle. That's a smilie. He hurts my feelings sometimes. If you tell me you hate me, I'll be very sad, but I won't tell Mother."

"I don't hate you, Goddie."

"I hope I never say bad things to you again. You're very nice. I'd be so lonely and unhappy if you went away. Like I was before you came here."

Deacon tried without success to imagine what it meant that his mother had "lost" her mind, so he told Landish what Goddie had said.

"There's no *woman* in Ashton, Deacon. I've never been to Ashton. As you know, I'm not allowed to leave Vanderland. The book—I may never start it, let alone finish it, but it won't be your fault either way. My book is in Just Mist and might just stay there forever."

Deacon told him that one second Goddie was nice and the next she was mean. Landish said that was called "turning" on someone. Deacon said that eating food, even just talking about food, made her turn on him. "Gustatory nastiness," Landish said, but didn't tell him what it meant. Deacon said she made fun of his lunch.

"Tell her you had prime rib for lunch." Then he said he was joking and Deacon mustn't joke with Goddie. Landish said Goddie and her mother were "Daughter Fickle and Mrs. Snide."

Deacon felt sorry for Goddie when Goddie was sad. And when Goddie felt sorry for *him*. And for Mrs. Vanderluyden who didn't *sound* mean when she said mean things. She said "son of a savage" but then she fixed his collar and said, "Off you go, out of my sight."

Deacon thought Goddie smelled nice. She was the first girl he had ever met unless he had met one in the Murk. She looked soft. And she was always pink like Deacon was after tub time. Everything she wore looked new. She wore one dress in the morning and another after lunch. She was bigger than him, but her hands were smaller. She told Deacon after lunch one day that her mother said that Deacon would never grow. He would always "be the runt of the little." But her father said he would grow when he was good and ready.

"If they must be tutored together," Mrs. Vanderluyden said to Landish, "then I want him properly dressed. I don't want Godwin spending her days in the company of a boy who looks and smells like the child of a scullery maid."

Landish asked Mrs. Vanderluyden if she meant to model Deacon on the boys his age who came to visit Goddie from New York. "I don't want to look like them," Deacon told Landish. Landish agreed with him that they looked like girls, their long hair done up in curls and flounces and in some cases even ribbons. They wore sailor suits and hats, short pants or skirts, gleaming, black-buckled shoes and white knee-high socks. They wore Buster Brown suits with large floppy silk bows at the neck. They looked like the boys on the ship.

"I will dress him as I see fit," said Mrs. Vanderluyden. "Don't worry. There's no point in trying to make him look like his betters. The result would be absurd. There's no disguising what he *is*. Near presentability is the most I'm hoping for, for Godwin's sake."

Overseeing a tailor, a barber and a governess, from whom she said she was not expecting miracles, Mrs. Vanderluyden had Deacon made over into something that she said would have to do. His hair was cut short and slicked back and flat with sweet pomade. He was measured for clothes of which three identical sets were made: a brown jacket with near-shoulder-width lapels that narrowed to nothing at the waist; a white shirt with a buttoned-down collar; a brown bow tie; a paisley-patterned velvet vest; brown shorts that came down to his knees; brown, silver-buckled shoes; and white mid-shin-length stockings.

"Ma'am says you should give him a good scrubbing every morning," one of the maids told Landish. "Scrub out his ears and clean beneath his fingernails and between his toes."

After lessons, Deacon changed back into his white shirt and trousers with suspenders as quickly as he could.

"There you go—Goddie-ready, Goddie-worthy," Landish would say every morning as he applied the final flourish of pomade.

Deacon was glad to have been spared the indignity of some sort of indoor, beribboned hat such as Goddie's New York friends were made to wear, but otherwise felt as absurd and uncomfortable as, judging by the expressions of the Blokes, they thought he looked.

"Well, well, aren't you something now, all dressed up like that?" Gough said, unable to keep from smiling the way he did when he was pretending not to notice something.

"Goddie seems oblivious to his being a less onerous affront to her than he was before," Landish told the Blokes.

But one day, at the end of the last lesson, she said, "You look nice."

Deacon smiled.

Bursting into tears, she ran off as if she had never been so hurtfully insulted.

They were "promoted" again. Van said that he was going to give them a full tour of Vanderland no matter how long it took. They should start early.

In the vestibule, through the stained glass windows of which the sun shone on the marble floor, he told them about the early days when they were building Vanderland, and showed them photographs. You couldn't tell from the grounds of Vanderland what Carolina was like, he said—every tree and plant and grain of sand came from somewhere else. Landish asked him if he would have taken the marsh from Dark Marsh Road if Frederick Olmsted, the landscape architect, had told him he needed it for Vanderland. Of course, said Van.

Deacon listened as Van told them how Vanderland began.

No one could remember what things were like before. They dammed streams, they made some run in different ways. They used up a lot of horses and mules ripping trees out by their roots. If there was a hill where they didn't want one, they got rid of it and put it where they did want one. They blew up rocks they didn't like and brought in nicer ones from Mexico. It took thousands of men eight years to get the place just right. They made Lake Loom where no lake used to be, and for the house they dug a hole deeper than a dried-up lake. They took a picture from the bottom, of two men looking down into the hole.

The walls were made of stone that masons cut up into blocks that looked like squares of fudge. A good granite block was thrown away unless it fit just right. The wood for the floors and walls came from places that were famous for trees. They plowed with something called a tractor instead of an ox because you didn't have to shoot a tractor that had broken down. Some men gave their lives. They were hit by lightning. Or dynamite went off too soon. Things fell and not all of them got out. The roof was slick on rainy days. Some men who worked when no one knew how sick they were gave up the ghost on summer days when it was hot. They sacrificed themselves for something that wasn't finished yet. He wished they could have seen it—but there might be a monument someday.

Landish began to sing:

Good King Vanderland looked out
On the Feast of Stephen,
When the poor lay round about,
Deep and crisp and even.

"The same old Landish. Half-baked satire. You wouldn't know what to do with money if you had any," Van told him.

Van showed them the guest wing, long corridors like those in hotels, rooms on both sides. Men strolled arm in arm with women, nodding or saying hello to Van, then moving on. Sometimes a butler walked beside a wheelchair, pointing out to its stupefied-looking occupant the main features of the house.

"You see how lucky you are, Deacon?" Van said. "Not everyone gets a guided tour from me."

Deacon was too short to see over most things. Take your time, Van told him. Look first, then walk. Landish said the house was an obstacle course of the priceless and the precious. Everything you thought was glass was crystal. Nothing had a hole in it. Nothing was dirty or wrinkled. There were no hobnail marks or other kinds of scuffs on the wooden floor. There were little white statues on small tables with bent and skinny legs. Walk slowly, Landish said, because you never knew when something priceless might be just around the corner or behind a chair. Every room was full of paintings you could spoil just by touching them. One of a boy with a big orange. He looked as if he didn't know what it was for or that you had to peel it first.

Landish said there was one painting you could spoil just by looking at it. You could only admire the box that it was in. Even Mr. Vanderluyden had never seen it. He took the word of the person he bought it from that it was in the box. Landish said that the older something was, the more it was worth. You couldn't put a price on something that was so old it would fall to pieces if you sneezed. If something was made and no one could be bothered making another one of it, it was worth more than almost anything. The only existing copy of the most boring book of all time was a bargain at any price. Things that belonged to famous people were priceless no matter how mean the people had been. The bidding would be fierce for an authenticated pair of Herod's socks.

Van said Landish was a philistine.

He showed them the small, gravity-driven master clock, inconspicuously located above the entrance to the stables, which drove, by an electrical connection, all the other clocks in the house, the "slave clocks" as they were called, some of which were fifty times the size of the master clock, which looked like a dinner plate. He said he was like the master clock. If not for him, Vanderland would wind down to nothing. Everything would stop. The generators, boilers, refrigerators. The lights would all go out, the fires. Everyone would leave and the rooms would lie empty. The people of Ashton would scale the wall, smash the windows. He asked them to imagine Vanderland open to the wind and rain, lived in by animals, scavenger birds gliding about among the chandeliers.

"The point of living is to be remembered, Deacon. Remembered for *doing* something. There is no afterlife but that one. One instant you're alive and the next—nothing. As suddenly as if your head had been chopped off."

"Surely a tour of Vanderland is possible that includes no mention of decapitation," Landish said.

"The world was not made. God did not make Vanderland. I did. I did not once consult with or meet by chance with God."

"What about the Tomb of Time?" Deacon said. "Landish says no one knows what it's like because no one's ever been there and come back. Except Lazarus and Jesus and——"

"The gibberish he's filled your mind with," Van said, glancing at Landish.

"Van thinks God resigned," Landish said. "Because of declining health and a desire to spend more time with his family."

On day three of the tour, as they were partway through the middle floors with their massive living halls, Landish remarked that Deacon was looking especially tired. "Would you like to ride in a wheelchair, Deacon?" Van asked. "We'll be walking a long way. I'm afraid those little legs of yours may not be up to it. I'll push you and Landish can walk beside us."

"There's no need for that," Landish said, but Deacon nodded. The chairs were parked in a large closet just inside the main vestibule for those guests who, though able to walk, were elderly or infirm.

Van had a servant bring them a wheelchair. The servant pushed it across the marble foyer. It was enormous, its handles a foot above Deacon's head. The wheelchair had an upholstered back, four wooden wheels with spokes, two large wheels on the side and two smaller ones in front, flanking a cushioned footrest. The armrests of the chair were too high for Deacon to use, so he sat with his hands in his lap as if he lacked even the use of his arms. Landish lifted him into it and Van wrapped a tartan blanket around him, tucking it in behind his shoulders and his feet so that nothing but his head showed.

They resumed their tour. People Deacon didn't know looked at him, then at the chair and smiled. He wondered if they thought he couldn't walk or was so sick he might die soon. When he smiled back, they smiled even more and nodded to him. The chair glided along soundlessly on the smooth floor. When he arched his head it looked as if the ceiling was moving backwards.

Landish appraised him. He looked like a spoiled but sickly child monarch being wheeled about a palace that no one expected him to live long enough to inherit.

They encountered Mrs. Vanderluyden in one of the living halls. "A most unusual entourage today, Van," she said, as she came towards them, her long, blue dress swishing with each step. "This is ridiculous. You look like the boy's attendant, pushing him about while Mr. Druken walks unoccupied beside you with his hands behind his back. If only you paid as much attention to our guests." She spoke while walking and did not stop to wait for a reply from Van, but made for the nearest door and slammed it behind her.

Van said, "We have so many guests—people come and go like hotel guests. Many leave without ever having met me, without my ever having set eyes on them. That's fine with me. Gertrude manages the guest list. I leave it to her to make sure that no one feels snubbed."

"I can think of no one better suited for the task," Landish said.

"Well, I'm not one of the sights of Vanderland, I won't be gawked at by guests and visitors as if I'm a feature of a Hunt and Olmsted house. I built Vanderland. I am its creator. I'll show myself to whomever I please."

Van took them to the Greater Banquet Hall, which reminded Deacon of the churches he and Landish had gone to on winter Sunday mornings to get warm. Dust motes swarmed like mosquitoes in a shaft of sunlight that brightened half the floor. He liked churches best when they were almost empty, just a few people in the pews, nobody saying a word or looking around, only statues on the altar, the ruby-red and light blue votive candles lit, but that was all.

Looking down from the walls were the mounted heads of moose, caribou, deer and elk. "You have a lot of trophies for someone who hunts nothing but firewood," Landish said.

"They're in keeping with the frieze above the fireplaces," Van said. "It's a scene from Wagner. Above each of the mounted heads is hung

the flag of one of America's original thirteen colonies. That one—with
the single star surrounded by the golden scroll—is North Carolina."

On the floor opposite each other, on either side of the Greater
Banquet Hall, were two Grizzly bear skins, flattened to their maxi-
mum length and width as if by a steamroller, arms and legs out-
stretched, open-mouthed. Between the almost horizontally stretched
hind legs of each bear was the tuft of a tail.

The snapping of logs in all three of the massive fireplaces echoed
in the hall.

"The dining table seats eighty," Van said. "The room is very different during formal occasions."

"Cozier, no doubt," Landish said.

"Deacon, when you see a room with deep reds and dark wood,
you'll know that it is one of my favourite rooms."

They went slowly round the great table, starting from the bank of
fireplaces, proceeding clockwise towards the organ loft and another
bank of fireplaces at the far end. Two rows of forty upholstered scarlet-
red chairs faced each other across the table, as if assembled for a ceremonial inspection, each chair staring unswervingly at its fellow across
the way. "Throne" chairs, one for Van, one for Gertrude, stood at the
head and foot of the table. The table was not set nor covered with a
cloth. Reflected in the gleaming expanse of wood were two golden
candlesticks, which stood on either side of two golden water jugs, as
well as two wheel-shaped chandeliers that hung high above, like those
in the well shaft of the principal tower. Landish could just make out,
far above the chandeliers, the curved beams of the ceiling, arching
wooden buttresses that formed a perfect dome above the room.

"What do you think, Deacon?" Van said.

"It's nice," Deacon replied. "Really nice," he said when he saw that
Van looked disappointd.

Deacon bore the same colossalized look as when he first set eyes
on the Golden Queen guarding the access to New York.

"Deacon is getting tired." Landish watched the boy, who was trying to tilt his head back far enough to see the ceiling.

"Nearly done," Van said.

He brought them to the library, which he said was the centrepiece of the house, even more so than the Greater Banquet Hall. He said that the library's frescoed ceiling was brought over from Italy in one piece and laid atop the library as one might put the lid on a teapot. The library contained twenty-five thousand leather-bound books.

"A lot of unburned words," Van said, smiling at Landish, then at Deacon.

A circular wrought-iron staircase led to a catwalk that ran all round the library, interrupted only by the chimney of an enormous fireplace. Behind the fireplace was a hidden elevator by which guests who forswore the staircase could rise up to the second floor, or go up further still to the observatory from which, through a telescope, Gertrude and her guests peered up at the stars.

Van took them to the largest of the living halls. It looked to Deacon like the waiting room at the station in New York.

There was a gaming table and chess set that, Van said, once belonged to Napoleon.

"The motto of Vanderland is 'There is a world elsewhere.' It's taken from Shakespeare's *Coriolanus*."

"It seems an ironic motto," Landish said, "given that it's the complaint of everyone at Vanderland that the entire world *is* elsewhere."

"As much of the world as anyone needs lies within the walls of this estate," Van said.

He showed them the tapestry gallery where they had first met. "I go to Europe every summer to find treasures like these."

"Does Gertrude travel with you?" Landish asked.

"No. She goes to New York when I go to Europe. Or else she stays at Vanderland."

"Too tired to go on, Deacon?" Landish asked. Deacon shook his head.

They went from floor to floor by the stairs instead of the elevators, whose walls were ornately decorated and carved and might, Van said he feared, be scratched by the wheelchair. Servants carried the wheelchair up and down the stairs. Deacon walked between them, holding hands with both of them, and climbed back into the chair whenever they reached the next floor.

Van said that many newspaper and magazine articles had lavished praise on Vanderland, but none of them had shown a true understanding of the place. So he wrote a piece himself under the byline of a famous columnist whose silence he bought by threatening to have him fired and make sure he never worked again.

"It must have made for a nice change," Landish said. "Fixing someone else's name to something you wrote."

Van ignored him. "'Vanderland is American in the sense that it belongs to all Americans.' That's part of what I wrote. What I wanted to say. I didn't silence all of Vanderland's critics. The simpleton barbarians. Come. I'll show you."

In his study, the only room with a lived-in appearance that he'd shown them, he took a leather folder from a writing desk, opened it and read aloud: "*Imagine coming upon a sixteenth-century French château while on safari through the jungles of the Amazon and you will get a sense of how laughable a sight is this Carolina Castle of the Vanderluydens.* This—this thing was one of a series of pieces in the *New York Herald* called 'Such Are the Rich.'" He continued reading, his voice rising in volume: "*He thinks so little of the world in which the rest of us must live that he has built an alternative one, a counter-world called Vanderland. Vanderland should be called Wonderland. Just when one thinks one has witnessed the absolute height of extravagance, there is still more of it to come.*'"

He threw the folder up in the air, scattering above their heads pieces of newsprint that fluttered to the floor. "The fools!" He shouted so loudly that Landish put his hands on Deacon's shoulders from behind. "Vanderland is *not* a country estate. It is where we *live*. Not in

New York. We *live* at Vanderland. That is what is new. I neither follow fashion nor seek to create it. I do not hope for imitators, do not hope to set a trend or have it said of me that I began a fad."

"I think Vanderland is unlikely to start a fad," Landish said.

Van smoothed back his hair with both hands and loudly exhaled.

"So that's what *I've* done since Princeton," he said. "I think it measures up quite well against the accomplishments of others."

"Hear, hear," Landish said.

"So ends your tour." Van clasped his hands behind his back. "Perhaps I should have confined it to the swimming pool and bowling alley in the basement."

Van called for the butler, who escorted Landish and Deacon back to The Blokes.

Deacon asked Landish to tell him a bedtime story about Vanderland.

Deacon lived in the Fortress of the Forest. If he left, even for one hour, his punishment would be banishment. He could not come back and he had nowhere else to go.

The Fortress wasn't his. It belonged to Good King Padgett. Deacon lived in the chicken wing, for men who were afraid of women. It was better than his former lodgings, an attic with a ceiling two feet high where it peaked in the middle.

Until he left the attic, Deacon had never stood up indoors. That was why he was so much shorter than Princess Godwin.

His job was to guard Princess Godwin, who was also not allowed to leave. Her punishment was vanishment. She would simply disappear the moment she set foot on unroyal soil.

Deacon longed to go back where he'd come from, the island of Atlastica, but he didn't know the way. And he was paid in Vanderbills that you could only spend in the Fortress.

Queen Gertrude could not leave the forest under pain of diminishment. She would become a commoner the second she set foot on unroyal soil. She would never again set eyes on the Princess.

The King slept in the Red Bed from which all others were forbidden.

Each person at the Fortress was assigned some form of punishment that they would suffer if they left: banishment, vanquishment, vanishment, relinquishment, ravishment.

They were the Prishoners of the King.

"That one's too scary," Deacon said. "Tell me a better one."

"It's not scary," Landish said. "It's just made up. I'll tell you a different kind tomorrow night."

Landish, alone in the Smoker, held forth so loudly about the Vanderluydens that Gough, Sedgewick and Stavely came out of their rooms to try to coax him into his.

"For God's sake, Landish," Gough said, "keep your voice down or we'll all be sacked. And you'll wake Deacon again."

"There's not a drop of brandy left," Sedgewick complained.

"Thank God the house is so big," Stavely whispered. "And thank God the Vanderluydens sleep on the other side of it." He thrust his hands crossly into the pockets of his dressing gown.

"Yes," Landish said. "In God's house, there are many rooms.

'Padgy's room is painted red
And Trudy's room is yellow
Trudy's has a nice big bed
But Padgy's not her fellow.'"

"Christ, Landish, shut up," Gough said. "It's not as if that woman thinks highly of you as it is."

Deacon came out of his room and Landish fell silent.

"Please, Landish," Deacon said. "Please do what Gough says or we'll all be sacked."

But Landish was not to be stopped. He moved about as if dancing with a woman while he sang.

"Padgy's has a big bed too
Big enough for four of him
But Trudy says they never screw
'Cause even Padgy's dick is slim.
One thing about him's very fat—
I'm speaking of the poor man's chance
Of ever doing more than chat
And getting into Trudy's pants.
Each one wears a kind of mask
They say she dallies with some churl
Prompting everyone to ask
Is Goddie really Daddy's girl?"

"STOP IT," Gough shouted.

"I have it on good authority that what I sing is true," Landish said. "Hell hath no fury like a husband horned."

"So now you know what everyone at Vanderland has known for years. Please do as the rest of us have done and say no more about it."

"Pipe down, Landish," Sedgewick hissed. "Mrs. Vanderluyden thinks quite highly of *me*."

"That's because you give Goddie higher grades than you give Deacon. Show her a map based on Goddie's knowledge of geography. She won't think so highly of you then."

The next day, a sheepish Landish took Deacon aside. "Pay no attention to anything I say, to you or to anyone else, while I've been drinking."

"You said Mr. Vanderluyden is not Goddie's father. Did he make a contribution?"

"No. He didn't. Not to Gertrude, anyway, it seems. We're done for if you say a word of this to Goddie."

"Who laidith Lady Gertrude?" he said the next evening in the Smoker after Deacon had gone to bed.

"One of the inner circle. At one time second only to Hunt. The engineer/architect named Thorpe," Gough said. "He lives in New York. Mr. Vanderluyden banished him from Vanderland. Pretended it was because of insubordination. Gertrude sees him while she's there."

"I don't know what she's thinking," Stavely lisped. "She'll be penniless if he divorces her."

"Perhaps she's in love with Thorpe," said Landish. "I expect Van doesn't know what to do about her. The always flummoxed Van of Princeton wouldn't have had a clue."

"You sound as if you're reveling in the man's misfortune," Sedgewick said. "Just as you did last night when you were drunk. You've no excuse this time."

"I need none to speak my mind."

Gough said Gertrude travelled to New York on the Vanderluyden Express whenever her husband's travels and art collection tours took him somewhere else. He would no sooner leave for St. Louis, Chicago, London or Paris than she would start preparing for New York. There were intervals of weeks—and sometimes even months, he was told— when neither of Goddie's parents was at Vanderland, when she was overseen by her chief governess, Miss Esse.

"I hate it when they're gone," she said to Deacon. "The longer they're gone, the more I think they won't come back. But I hate it almost as much when they come back, because they quarrel terribly and shout at me as if I've done something wrong."

"Gertrude was once more charming than she is today," Van told Landish in the master living hall one night. He had asked Landish to leave Deacon with the Blokes.

"You're not much impressed with Vanderland, are you Landish?"

Van said. "You're no more impressed with me than you ever were. All those smart remarks and rhymes you made. In front of Deacon. You think me the same as I was when we were schoolmates. Friends. I hope you haven't taken your promotions to be a signal that I wish to renew our friendship. They are mere courtesies for old time's sake."

"I haven't taken them to be a signal of anything," Landish said. "But why do you care what I think of you?"

Van said that, again, "just for old times' sake," he wished to tell Landish a story that might change his opinion of him.

He said that Gertrude was very young when they married, and saw no reason that a good match should preclude romantic love. She did not, until their wedding night, speak of love. Nor did he.

"But then she told me that she loved me and asked if I loved her. Perhaps I should have gone along with it, the whole pretence—but I didn't. I couldn't. I was very fond of her, but I was not in love with her."

Gertrude said she wanted more than to be thought of fondly by her husband. She said she wanted to be loved. When Van said nothing, she became upset and began to cry. Not until he told her with what she called "unmistakable sincerity" that he loved her would she let him near her, she said.

So he told her that he loved her, but she said she knew he didn't mean it.

This went on for sixteen months. She wouldn't even let him hold her hand. "I don't know why I let it go on for so long. Perhaps I should have sought an annulment. But it is always assumed, in cases of non-consummation, that the husband is to blame. That is, it would have been assumed that I didn't because I couldn't. Or didn't want to. And there would have been much humiliating speculation.

"Well, one must make choices. I did what I thought and still think was right. If I was wrong, I was wrong. I never did fall in love with her. I had never hoped to fall in love. I wasn't looking for love. I have never hoped for love."

Gertrude told him she couldn't stand a loveless life. As a prelude for asking him to end the marriage, he assumed. But then she told him of the matter in New York.

"Yes, it was from her that I first heard of it. Don't feign surprise. I know that you know about it, Landish, everyone does. I was enraged. Two years of playing coy with me, her husband—well, you can imagine how it was."

Over the course of months, he tried to convince her of the folly of what she was doing. But she said that she would not languish at Vanderland while he gadded about the world.

"So I have brought matters to their just conclusion. We argued a few nights ago, worse than ever. But by that time I had already done what needed to be done. Unknown to her."

"What have you done?" Landish said.

"Mr. Henley will show you to the library at eight this evening," Van said, "but don't come inside. Wait in the tapestry gallery. Don't make a sound. Gertrude always comes and goes by the elevator. She won't see you. She won't know you're there."

"You're asking me to eavesdrop?"

"I'm telling you to."

"Is there a penalty for non-compliance?" Landish said, laughing. Van turned his back and walked away from him

Landish wondered what Van would do if he defied him and simply stayed at The Blokes instead of going to the library. He pictured himself eavesdropping on the Vanderluydens, dutifully skulking in the shadows of the tapestry gallery. Until shortly before eight, he kept telling himself he wouldn't do it. But then he left The Blokes and arrived at the gallery just in time. He stood to one side of the library doors. He heard the whirring of the elevator and the clanking of the doors as Gertrude opened them. For a long time the room was so silent Landish wondered if Van had yet arrived. But then he heard Van say: "No sooner am I out the door. What must the servants think?"

"I never think about what servants think," Gertrude said.

The modulations of her voice suggested she was walking back and forth.

"A little discretion—"Van said. "Everyone *knows*."

"Everyone *always* knows."

"You talk as if it's something that all couples do. But I've never done it."

"No. You've never done it. You've never done *it*. With anyone. Were you thinking of having me as your virgin bride forever?"

"I've stayed away from you because of you, not because of me."

"You stayed away from me because of *him*. It was bad enough when all you did was talk about him, but now that you've *brought* him here—"

She means me, Landish thought, and was barely able to resist the urge to stride into the room. He felt certain it wasn't the first time she had made the accusation. And Van had wanted him to hear them argue.

"That's absurd," Van said. "You're as likely to repeat a rumour as be the subject of one."

"I am in love. I have been for years."

"Gertrude, there is no need for you to end your affair. *I* have ended it."

"What do you mean?"

"Would you like to know what his price was? Or should I say what yours was? The man whose undying love you think you have is at this moment on his way to England. He has been well compensated for the inconvenience of such a sudden and permanent relocation. And he has, with unmistakable sincerity, assured me that you and he will never meet or correspond again. So, Gertrude, keep yourself involved in your betterment projects from now on, and while you're at it, make such a project of yourself. I won't be fitted for a new set of horns every few years."

"What if I tell the truth, make it known that Godwin is not your child but his? Would you like to be thought of as the Vanderluyden who finds men more—inspiring?"

"I would simply deny that our marriage was unconsummated. Who would take your word for anything at this point? I would divorce you and keep Godwin. You'd be lucky if you set eyes on her again."

Landish raised his hand, intending to wipe the sweat from his forehead, and struck the underside of a lamp that was fastened to the wall. Van and Gertrude stopped talking. Landish turned to hurry away but realized that Gertrude would reach the doorway of the library in time to see him, to recognize him as, his back to her, he made an inglorious, ridiculous bid to escape. He was unable to think of any facial expression he could assume that was appropriate to the occasion of being caught by Gertrude Vanderluyden in the act of eavesdropping on her and her husband.

"Is there someone out there?" Gertrude said. "What are you up to, Van? What would you stoop to?"

"That's what people will soon be saying of me instead of what they're saying now. Padgett Godfrey Vanderluyden will stop at nothing."

There was the sound of Gertrude's hurrying footsteps. One of the library doors opened inward and Gertrude stood half hidden by it, looking out, surveying the gallery. Landish thought the door might be blocking her view of him but she let go of the door and slowly walked towards him. She shook her head and covered her mouth with her hand to suppress what he took to be a laugh until he saw that her eyes had welled up with tears that would have spilled out had she blinked.

"I wouldn't have thought that even you would be capable of this," she whispered.

"I'm sorry," Landish said. "I—"

"It will be something worse next time, Mr. Druken. And something still worse after that. He can't have you here and not know the limits of your affection for him. Your fear of him."

She struck him hard on the chest with the heel of her fist and pointed back into the library behind her.

"Four years I've spent in this place. Shackled to him for my daughter's sake. You have been here just over a year and already you're creeping about in the dark eavesdropping on me because he told you to."

Landish made to step away but she put herself in front of him.

"The mere fact of your being here under his roof emboldens him. He brought you and the boy here for a reason. He may not even know yet what it is. I don't. Do you?"

Landish shook his head.

"Yet here you are, you and the boy, brought here by a man who does nothing but think of ways to *improve* this house. He loved you. Perhaps he still does, or will again."

"We were merely friends."

"No. Something more. To *his* mind at least. Look, Mr. Druken. I have not always been as I am. Of the woman I was, however, there is only enough left for Godwin. Until just now there was enough for her and her real father. His abandonment of me was inevitable, don't you think?"

"I'm sorry to have made it that much worse."

"You know, I would not speak of you and the boy as I do if I did not sense that your being here will somehow destroy us all. I see that you think I'm being melodramatic. Perhaps I am. I hardly sleep, can't bring myself to eat. From now on, I will be under what amounts to house arrest. My undoing has begun. One thing will never change. I spoke of your limits. I have none where the good of my daughter is concerned. None. So if my husband sets you a task that in any way concerns her, tell him no."

She brushed past him and walked off into the darkness of the tapestry gallery, from which he soon heard the opening and closing of a door.

"Come in, Landish," Van shouted.

Landish went into the library, where Van was seated before the fire, smoking a cigarette.

"You gave the game away," Van said, chuckling.

"I feel sorry for her," Landish said. "Why did you want me to hear all that?"

Van motioned with his hand to the chair beside him, but Landish shook his head.

"This is not the sort of thing that a gentleman should gloat about. But I got them *both*, by God, I got them *both*. She will confine herself to Vanderland from now on. She will leave it only when accompanied by me."

Landish looked at Van until Van could no longer meet his gaze and looked away.

"She has a different explanation than you do for why your marriage has not been consummated."

"You know that I am not like that. I have not done all this for *you*. She exaggerates. It's true that I spoke almost constantly of you. But not for the reason she implied. I missed the way things were at Princeton. I was never happier. Nor were you, I believe. We could have brought that happiness to Vanderland. I often told her so. But I did not mean *that*."

"So why *did* you want me to hear the two of you?" Landish said.

"I told you. So that you would see that I am far from being the boy that I was at Princeton. I have been nothing like that boy for quite some time. It's only fair that you know whom you're dealing with."

"Dealing with?"

"Good night, Landish."

Landish went back to The Blokes, to the empty Smoker with its dying fire. He poured himself a glass of brandy. He could not stop thinking of how Gertrude had sounded when she spoke of him to Van. Jealous. Exasperated. Humiliated. As if she had not grown used to the notion that Van had never loved her and never would—and all, she seemed to think, because of Landish. And what to make of the new Van? Not so new, given what he had done at Princeton. But that had been for other reasons. For love? Perhaps. Yet now he saw himself as someone whom Landish was "dealing" with. He knew now that he and Deacon should leave. But how would they make a go of it? Landish thought that *he* might somehow get by, but Deacon . . .

He felt sorry for Gertrude, but even more so for Goddie. One day she would find out everything. Who her father was. Where he was and how he came to be there. How Van had dealt with him. With them. The day would come when Gertrude would have to tell her lest she find out some other way.

He wondered how Thorpe really felt about Gertrude. Landish suspected that the alternative to accepting the money and leaving the country would not have been a pleasant one.

But now Mrs. Vanderluyden stopped going to New York on the 630 Express or elsewhere alone. Landish heard from Gough that there was talk among the servants that Mr. Vanderluyden must at last have taken her in hand, and of her long-overdue "comeuppance."

She made it clear that she still longed for Manhattan, her family, her social peers, the place of her childhood, the excitement of the ever-growing, ever-changing city of New York about which several letters written by what she called her "never-to-be-exiled friends" arrived each day. Goddie showed Landish and Deacon the newly finished portrait of her mother painted by Giovanni Boldini, hanging beside a newly finished portrait of her darkly ascetic-looking father by J.A.M. Whistler. Against a dark background, she wore a black hat the size and shape of an umbrella, a floor-length black dress from which protruded the dagger-sharp toes of black leather shoes, a shroud-like sash of white silk entwined about the dress that she held in place, one hand at her throat, the other at her waist, her arms sheathed to above the elbows in beige silk gloves. Goddie looked convinced that the very process of being depicted had transformed her mother, transported her into some realm from which Goddie would forever be excluded.

"I don't like it," she wailed. "I wouldn't let that Joe van Boldi paint my picture. Mother is sweet. Not mean and selfish like the woman in that picture."

❋

In spite of what they were fed by Mrs. Bruce, Landish maintained the massive, heavily muscled physique of the Drukens. He would not, his father used to say, have looked out of place fastened to the prow of a sealing ship.

"I'm a Druken," he said, looking at his large-knuckled hands. "There's nothing I can do about it. It is a fact that no amount of sitting on my backside reading and writing books can change."

Whereas Deacon, despite being descended from what Landish called "the tough stock of the Carsons," seemed fated to be thin and puny-looking and forever ravenous, no matter what his diet. Landish would give him half of what the Bruces put in front of him, and all the Blokes but Sedgewick would give him something from their plates. Deacon ate everything but neither gained an ounce nor lost the sickly, pallid complexion at every sight of which Gough would shake his head and try to disguise a look of startled dismay.

"He looks like he's been eating nothing but gruel since he was born," Sedgewick said. "I doubt that a bite of my dinner is all that stands between him and his Maker."

Landish was more concerned about Deacon's remaining so short and thin than he let on to him. It seemed the boy was even hungrier than before, *feeling* hungry even after some special-occasion dinner with his belly full of food. On Palmer's birthday, he ate not only his dinner but half of Palmer's birthday cake, stopping at half only because Landish said that if he ate any more he would get sick.

"It's not what the Vanderluydens are having for dinner tonight, is it, Deacon?" Landish said. And Deacon couldn't help but think of Goddie sitting at the table he had once got a glimpse of when he made a wrong turn on his way to the Academy—a round table in the Lesser Banquet Hall lit by candelabras and spread with gleaming crystal, china, silverware, huge tureens of steaming soup and stew, lavish platters of roast beef, a servant standing discreetly behind Goddie who, but for Miss Esse, was eating alone. The servant was silently and unobtrusively refilling a glass with ice water, removing a plate after each course and replacing it with another.

Deacon dreamt that all the Blokes, Gough, Palmer, Sedgewick, Stavely and Landish, were gathered round his bed to witness his last breath. "He's paler than Palmer," he heard Gough say sadly.

At last Landish decided he must beg another favour of Van. "Please have Deacon examined by your doctor. I wouldn't ask if not for the boy."

Van replied, "Begging favours rather becomes you."

"If you never do another thing for me, do this," Landish said. "Don't punish Deacon just because of how things are between you and me."

But the doctor pronounced that he could find nothing wrong with Deacon "per se."

That night Van sent notice that he would be coming to the Smoker to visit Landish, and that he expected Deacon to join them. The Blokes, uncertain of what they were meant to do, gathered in the Smoker, nervously silent before and throughout the visit except when, upon his arrival, they stood to say hello and shake his hand. Deacon had dressed in his school clothes.

"Van," Landish said, nodding to Van who, saying "Landish," nodded back. As always, they did not shake hands. Landish remained standing in spite of Van's suggestion that he pull up a chair beside his.

Van had Deacon stand in front of him. He put his hands on his slight shoulders. "Even in clothes that fit, he looks so thin," he said, flexing Deacon's shoulders with his hands. "Nothing much but skin and bone. Like me, but worse."

"He says he doesn't *feel* sick or tired," Landish said. "Just hungry all the time."

"I dare say he's always felt the way he feels. He probably doesn't know what feeling well is like. Mark my words, any child who looks like this is sick."

"I took him to a puniatrist in St. John's," Landish said. "That's a doctor who specializes in making boys less puny. No improvement. So we took him to a cheerupodist, who has been of some help. He's terribly expensive, but Deacon has been smiling more."

Van ignored him. "How would you like to have a proper lunch every evening, Deacon? Lunch is the proper name for what Godwin has in the evening before she goes to bed."

Deacon turned to Landish, who nodded slightly. "What do you mean, sir? A *proper* lunch?"

"The sort of lunch Godwin has. In fact, one exactly like she has, every evening. You could eat as much as you like. We could call it dinner."

Deacon looked again at Landish, who this time raised his eyebrows to indicate that the choice was Deacon's.

"I suppose that would be nice, sir," he said.

Van laughed. "Of course it would. You'll be Godwin's guest, her dinnermate. And have dinner with her friends when they come to visit. As it is now, when Mrs. Vanderluyden and I have visitors, Godwin has to have dinner with a lot of grown-ups, or with a governess. I always take dinner in my room unless we are entertaining guests. Godwin enjoys your company very much. She says that if not for you, school would be unbearably dreary. No offence, gentlemen." The Blokes laughed.

"Where would we have dinner?" Deacon said.

"In the Lesser Banquet Hall. You'll like it very much."

"Not here? Not with Landish and the Blokes?"

Van smiled. "The Bachelors' Wing is no place for a girl. So it's settled then? At six-thirty tomorrow, someone will come for you to take you to the banquet hall. Tomorrow, it will be just you and Godwin."

Deacon looked to Landish and back at Van. "All right, sir," he said.

"Good lad. Godwin will be glad to hear it."

He stood and, saying a single good night, made his way from The Blokes before Landish had a chance to speak.

"A proper dinner," Sedgewick said. "Right in front of us, he as good as says that we lot can go on making do with improper dinners."

"I thought he meant I'd be eating here," Deacon said. "I thought just the dinner would be different."

"It looks like you've been picked again," Landish said, but Deacon shook his head and coming back to his side hugged him around the leg.

"That's all right," Landish said. "You'll still have lunch and breakfast with us."

Deacon turned to Sedgewick. "I'll bring you back some proper food," he said.

"No, thank you. I won't be fed proper scraps off some boy's plate night after night."

Later, pretending to be asleep in the Smoker, Deacon listened to the Blokes.

"I should have told Van I would talk it over with Deacon and get back to him about it." Landish's voice was raised. "Instead of just standing there like a fence post."

"You call him Van"—that was Sedgewick—"but when he says hop to it, you hop to it just like the rest of us."

"You did the right thing," Gough said. "Sometimes even boys like Deacon aren't the best judge of what's best for them. He should be twice the weight he is and six inches taller. A common cold could mean the end of him."

Deacon's first dinner with Goddie was delayed. Mrs. Vanderluyden said that, as she had no intention of letting her daughter witness the table manners of the ill-bred, nor of teaching Deacon table manners, and was doubtful that Landish's knowledge of them exceeded the boy's, he would be instructed by Godwin's governess, Miss Esse, who would decide when he was "ready."

Deacon learned table etiquette as quickly as he did most things and was declared "ready" by Miss Esse in two days. The next day, a butler arrived at The Blokes at six-thirty and escorted Deacon, scrubbed and pomaded, to the Lesser Banquet Hall. Goddie was sitting at a large round table, facing the door.

"Hello, Deacon," she said. "Isn't this nice?"

Miss Esse sat at the table, several chairs away from Goddie.

Deacon looked around the room, whose walls, though brown, weren't made of wood but what he thought was leather. There were portraits of women in large hats and long dresses who all looked rather like Goddie's mother. The table was draped in a white cloth that reached the floor. The chairs weren't red but something like orange, which meant that Mr. Vanderluyden didn't consider this to be one of *his* rooms. Deacon sat down nervously on one of them, certain he would stain the tablecloth or break one of the dishes that were red and gold around the rims. Beams of sunlight slanted through the windows whose shapes were traced out on the floor beyond the table, the dust mote–swarming light passing just above their heads in a shaft that Deacon thought of interrupting with his hand. But he kept still.

He recalled what the Greater Banquet Hall was like and tried to think of the lesser one as being inferior to it. But the table in the lesser one was round and had thirty chairs. The ceiling was so high that everything echoed, voices, footsteps, silverware. They sat at opposite poles of the circle, twenty feet apart. All the empty chairs and all the empty space between the table and the walls reminded Deacon of the days when he and Landish went to church but almost no one else did because it was so stormy. The late sun shone through the windows, red and blue and green depending on the colour of the glass.

"Mother says Father pushed you round the house in the wheelchair," Goddie said when Deacon was seated. "She says you're so lazy you find it too much of a bother to lift a knife and fork."

Deacon decided that the faster he ate, the less time he would have to spend with Goddie and the sooner he could go back to The Blokes. It also occurred to him that the faster he gained weight, the sooner he'd be back having dinner with the Blokes. He ate three of every course and was still ready for the next course when Goddie was. He was able to speak only between courses, his mouth otherwise so stuffed with food, his cheeks bulging so that it looked like he was holding his breath.

"Don't choke yourself, Deacon," Miss Esse said.

But though he ate each course as quickly as he could, he realized that the length of dinnertime would depend on how fast Goddie ate, which was very slowly. She deliberated over every forkful, staring at it as she paused with it raised halfway to her mouth as if she thought there was something in it that shouldn't be there. And when she noticed his stuffed cheeks she laughed so much at the sight that she left her food untouched.

"Eat something, Godwin," Miss Esse said.

Goddie rolled her eyes. "If only you could see yourself," she said. "You look like a giant chipmunk!" But soon she seemed sad. She looked at him, tears in her eyes, biting her lower lip.

"You don't like having dinner with me, do you?" she said.

"Yes, I do," Deacon tried to say, his mouth stuffed with roasted potatoes that scorched his tongue.

"I wish you really did," she said. "I don't have any friends. Those New York boys and girls are not my friends."

By the time Deacon left for The Blokes with the butler, he felt that if he opened his mouth while looking in the mirror he would see at the back of his throat the last few bites of his third helping of peaches, vanilla cake and cream. He followed the butler through the house, feeling light-headed, his stomach painfully distended, so much sweat running down his forehead that his eyes stung and he could barely stand to keep them open. He stared at the butler's back. The butler never turned his back on Mr. Vanderluyden. That was why he walked out backwards through the doors. When he spoke to Mr. Vanderluyden or listened to instructions from him, he looked up as if Mr. Vanderluyden were on the ceiling.

Deacon was determined not to faint or be sick on one of Mr. Vanderluyden's rugs. If he got sick, the Vanderluydens would think he didn't
like their food, or didn't like Goddie. Mr. Vanderluyden would think that
no amount of good food could make Deacon grow or fix what was wrong
with him. So he would give him and Landish the sack. He wondered if
he was going to die in his boyhood no matter who did what for him.

Hearing a knock, Landish opened the door of The Blokes. The
butler bowed slightly and waved Deacon inside with an exaggerated
and, Landish thought, faintly ironic flourish of his hand. He might have
been regretfully and gravely commending to his doom some recently
deposed monarch.

"Good God, Deacon," he said. "What's happened? Are you all right?"

As the butler closed the door, Deacon looked up at Landish and the
room began to spin. He was dimly aware of falling forward.

When he opened his eyes, he was lying on his back on the floor, all
the Blokes on their knees around him, even Sedgewick. It reminded
him of his dream in which all the Blokes had gathered round his bed.
They unbuttoned his collar and trousers, removed his shoes. He felt
Landish's hand on his forehead.

"I think I ate too much," Deacon said.

"Maybe you should make yourself be sick," Landish said, but Deacon
shook his head. He believed he had made progress towards his goal of
being reunited with the Blokes and was determined not to put back
on to his sentence one minute of the time that he had served in exile,
or to rid his body of one ounce of the food that, in everyone's opinion,
he so badly needed.

"Let's put him on the sofa in the Smoker where we can keep an eye
on him," Gough said.

"If I get sick, will we be sacked?" Deacon asked.

Landish shook his head. "I just hope that you can digest as much
as you can ingest. You can't go from puny to robust in just one meal,
you know."

The Blokes laid Deacon on the sofa and folded his hands on his stomach. "The flatter the better," Gough said, removing all the pillows so that Deacon's head and feet were on the same level. Deacon was soon drowsing, almost asleep but able to hear himself snoring slightly.

The Blokes returned to their brandy.

"Methinks the urge to purge has passed," Landish said.

"As has, alas, a gust of wind," said Gough.

"Another urge may soon emerge," said Stavely.

"It's shameful," Sedgewick said. "The boy made a pig of himself."

"Yes," Gough said. "And then he ate it."

"To eat with such relish and yet feel so hellish," Stavely lisped happily.

"To start with gestation and end with prostration," said Landish.

"For he on runny stew hath fed / And drunk the swill of Vanderland," added Gough.

"I'm surprised he left the butler uneaten," Stavely said. "I wonder if what will prove to be a fruitless search for Goddie might not even now be under way."

Deacon drifted in and out of sleep, in and out of dreams and half dreams in which the only voices were those of the Blokes.

"The Kid is Fed. Long Live the Kid."

Landish: "The Vanderland pantries empty lie / While he whom they were emptied by / But half-full lies and—you may laugh—thinks only of his empty half."

"Dining with the Vanderluydens," Sedgewick said. "And to think we shared our meals with him."

"We?" Gough said. "I don't recall you parting with so much as a pea."

From then on, each evening, Mr. Henley would arrive at The Blokes to escort Deacon to the Lesser Banquet Hall. "I believe your man has arrived," Landish would say when, at precisely six-thirty, there was a knock on the door of The Blokes. Deacon soon knew the way, but the butler still escorted him to ensure that he didn't stray from the hallways into any of the rooms and didn't touch or knock into anything.

The butler, standing exaggeratedly erect and staring unswervingly forward in a trancelike way that, after the first few times, Deacon couldn't help but mimic, walked a few yards in front of him, his arms never moving. They walked in solemn silence as though, Landish told him, he was being led to a formal "installation," as if the butler should have been bearing the Royal Mace on his shoulder as they made their way to Deacon's throne.

Deacon followed the butler down the stone staircase of the Bachelors' Wing, through the breezeway that led to the main house, along dimly lit, portrait-hung hallways that emerged into a succession of brightly lit, enormous rooms, empty living halls, the long, narrow tapestry gallery, past the entrance to the library and across the Winter Garden's marble floor, encountering servants who seemed not to see them, nor even to hear their footsteps. When they encountered a closed door, the butler opened it, preceded Deacon through and held it open for him with his left hand without turning to see where he was. Deacon decided he didn't need to look at anything to "see" it. And each evening after dinner the ceremonial march of butler and boy was repeated through the labyrinth of Vanderland back to The Blokes.

"Thank you, Henley old chap," Goddie said to the butler when Deacon arrived. She looked at Deacon and laughed.

Goddie said it was much more fun to have dinner with Deacon than with a governess who never spoke to her except to correct her posture or criticize her table manners. "I like Miss Esse," she said, smiling at Miss Esse, "but not the others, so I do things wrong on purpose just to get them to speak to me and to make sure they don't fall asleep. It's dreadful when the one person you're having dinner with falls asleep."

But then Goddie the Bad would start, staring at Deacon as if she had caught him stealing from the Vanderluydens.

"Mother says it's proper while dining to speak in low tones to the servants, so she thinks it would be appropriate if you did not speak to them at all. Mother says that you're like a pig that we're preparing for the slaughter, except that no amount of food can fatten you up. She says that, in spite of all that you consume, you will *be* consumed. By CONSUMPTION!"

Moments later, Goddie the Good's lip would tremble and she would cover her face and begin to cry.

"Father says that most of the time I am Goddie the Good. He says I must try to always be Goddie the Good. But sometimes, he says, I am God-awful, ungodly Goddie, and then look out. He says I must not let Goddie the Bad get the best of me or else I'll always be unhappy and unloved. I couldn't bear to be unhappy and unloved. You love me, don't you, Deacon? I love you. Really. You should just pretend that you can't hear God-awful Goddie. She's not me. I don't mean what she says, all right? Pretend. Promise?"

But he discovered that to ignore God-awful Goddie was not so easy as to promise to ignore her, especially when her New York friends joined them for dinner.

"Deacon has no parents, you know. He came here with a dreadful man named Landish who bought him in some place where they sell boys. You can't even buy a darky anymore, but you can buy a Deacon. Can you imagine being bought instead of born? He lives with the tutors. The Blokes, they're called, because they're English and they're old. Lowborn highbrows, Mother calls them. Landish is one of my tutors. He went to Princeton with my father. Even the best schools make mistakes, Mother says. Deacon dines with me because he's not long for this world, Father says, and it would be a pity if even his *last* days were a misery. No, better he make a misery of my daughter's days, says Mother. They're ever so funny when they talk about Deacon."

Goddie fell silent. Deacon looked at her and saw that her lower lip was quivering, which meant that Goddie the Good was back. He knew she didn't want to burst out crying in front of what Landish called her Cronies, so he burped loudly and everyone, including Goddie, laughed.

She wiped her eyes with her handkerchief.

"Deacon can be so funny," she said. "He's not so bad, really. No one else can tease him, only me. That's the rule, agreed?"

The Cronies nodded.

Goddie had different visiting "friends" every weekend. Most of them went a year or more between visits. Some came with their parents, some with governesses. She told Deacon she couldn't remember most of them from one visit to the next. They showed up at Vanderland and she took her mother's word for it that they had visited before and that she had enjoyed their company.

"But I don't know who they are mostly," she confided in Deacon one mealtime. "I heard Mother tell Father many children visit once and never come back because their parents can't coax them. She says staying at Vanderland is worse than visiting the seven neighbours of Hercules."

Gough told Landish that her parents more or less recruited visitors for her—conscripted boys and girls whose parents dared not decline an invitation from the Vanderluydens.

"The Patterson girl is coming this weekend—you remember her, don't you?" Mrs. Vanderluyden would say to Goddie, who would tell Deacon that she'd pretended to her mother that she remembered the Patterson girl. Sometimes, when there were five or six visiting at once, Deacon heard her call them by the wrong names, even when Mrs. Vanderluyden would tell her the names in advance and have Goddie say them back to her. She might quiz her at any time. "Who's coming to visit this weekend, Godwin?" she'd say, and Goddie would struggle to remember, sometimes succeeding but more often saying the name of someone who had visited the week before, or even the name of a character from one of the reading books assigned by Landish. "There are so many names, Deacon!" she said one day, lying miserably face down on the large velvet sofa in their clasroom.

"You tell me the names and I'll remember them for you," Deacon said.

So that weekend, Goddie told him all the names as soon as her mother told her and he repeated them back to her. "Tell me the names again," she said, and Deacon told her and she nodded and smiled at him.

"The poor girl," Gough said. "What an odd childhood. She will grow up in this oddball, misplaced mansion. She will feel as though she spent her childhood in a barricaded village of three hundred people."

"They say *their* friends are scared they'll be next," Goddie said. "Isn't that so mean? They say it's not their fault Father makes me live in Darkyland. They talk about you too, Deacon, though nobody remembers your name either. They say Father treats a savage better than he treats his only child. They say people call me Oddie Goddie. They make jokes about how Father keeps me locked up all the time because I'm crazy. 'Now your daughter is the laughingstock of New York,' Mother says. 'Well, that should tell you all you need to know about New York,' he says. 'Oddie Goddie,' Mother says, 'and she's only seven years old. She'll have such a reputation by the time she's twenty-one there'll be no point in her ever leaving Vanderland.'"

One weekend, a batch of Goddie's Cronies came to visit from New York and among them was a boy a few years older than Deacon. At dinner the first night, Deacon boasted, "My father's writing a book."

"Idiot," Goddie said. "He isn't writing a book, he's just pretending. And he's not your father." She looked severely at the boy Deacon had been trying to impress. "You mustn't listen to anything Deacon says. He's not a Vanderluyden. He mixes everything up. He doesn't know how anything at Vanderland works. Father is writing a book. He says that Deacon's father who isn't his father is only writing *in* a book. Then he burns it."

"What kind of book is your father writing?" Deacon asked Goddie.

"One with pages that are blank until he fills them in. Father says your father wants to write the Great American Novel but he failed and Father says that if not for him, you and Landish would be living in the

Great American Hovel. He says anyone can write *in* a book but not just anyone can write a book."

"She said Van is writing a book?" Landish said that evening. "She said 'a book'?"

Deacon nodded.

"Van is spreading the notion that I've spent years in a failed attempt to write a novel and am now merely pretending to write. Perhaps I am. But his ambition is born of a desire to succeed where I cannot. He's chosen writing only because it was *my* choice. He'd have chosen to be a sculptor if I had tried and failed to be one."

Van, who liked to spend time in the library before he went to bed, began to summon Landish and Deacon to join him there, he and Landish drinking glasses of cognac and staring into the massive fireplace, "ruminating," Van said. He said there was a little room, a hidden one, just off the library, which he used as his writing room. "You should call it the Rume," Landish said. Van looked at him blankly. "R-U-M-E. In fact, this whole library is a Rume."

Deacon lay curled up in a chair, sleeping or watching the two men who stared into the fire and spoke of things he guessed they knew he couldn't understand. He liked to listen to them, though, and follow the play of their expressions. Above the mantelpiece there was a painting of some people wearing sheets and helmets. There was a woman carved in dark brown wood on each side of the painting. Van's voice—"I brought the ceiling over in one piece from a palace in Venice. The owners of the palace could no longer afford to maintain it. There are parts of it all over Vanderland. The ceiling is a fresco by Pellegrini."

The three of them craned their heads back to look up.

"Godwin says you're writing a book?"

"Yes. I don't burn what I write."

"Perhaps you should try it."

"Imagine coming here, to Carolina I mean, and facing as your first task building a house before it gets so cold you freeze to death. Imagine your main ambition being not to perish any sooner than you have to."

"I'm from Newfoundland," Landish said, "but I'll *try* to imagine it."

Sometimes, just as the butler was ushering them into the library, Landish and Deacon heard him talking to someone conversationally, though there seemed to be no other voice.

"Whom are you talking to, Van?" Landish asked.

"The chimney witch," he said.

"I don't believe in witches," Deacon said.

"She only comes out when there's no one here but me. You two scared her away."

"What does she look like?"

"At first she looks like smoke. She comes out from the fireplace and hangs there in mid-air. Then the smoke becomes a woman, an ugly old woman who sits right there in the chair that you're in now, Deacon. When she heard you, she went back up the chimney."

Deacon looked into the cavernous fireplace. It was large enough for someone to hide in behind the half-burned stumps of wood still left over from the clearing of the land that years ago made way for Vanderland. He half dreaded and half hoped that some smoke would come wafting out and turn into the chimney witch.

"That's enough about chimney witches," Landish said.

"The chimney witch is worse than any creature in a dream because she comes out of the chimney when I'm still awake. And because she's real."

"I said that's enough," Landish said.

"You shouldn't come here by yourself," Deacon said in a low, fearful voice. "I wouldn't come here by myself."

"Even if you did, you wouldn't see the witch. She only comes out when there's no one here but me."

"Then we'll always come here when you do," Deacon said. "And then you'll never see her either. We'll protect you from her."

"I don't think Landish is concerned with protecting me."

It got so that Deacon couldn't sleep in his own room for fear that Mr. Vanderluyden was in the library talking to the witch. Sometimes he fell asleep in the library on Landish's lap or in the witch's chair, which he thought smelled more like smoke than the others did. He began to have what Landish thought were chimney witch–inspired dreams about his parents.

The sentence Landish always used to describe what happened to Deacon's father was "He was lost at the seal hunt." Deacon began to think of him as still being "lost," forever trying to find his way home, taking wrong turn after wrong turn, confused, afraid, alone, but never giving up.

He dreamt of his father walking through the snow to what he thought was his house, only to find when he reached it that it wasn't his but one lived in by strangers, a mother and a boy whom he could see through the window, some other man's wife and son. He dreamt of him going endlessly from house to house. He would wake from these dreams drenched in sweat, shouting. The air itself seemed black and thick and wrapped like arms around him. Sobbing, eyes closed against the darkness, he sometimes got up and, mistaking the location of the door, started pounding on the walls with his fists. Landish would pick him up and walk him round the room until he fell asleep.

Deacon had no idea what "the ice floes" looked like. He heard the phrase, whenever Landish said it, as a complete sentence. The ice flows. It never stops. He thought of bits of ice he had seen bobbing along in a cold, dark brook in winter like the ones that fed Lake Loom. He dreamt of his parents, unable to find each other, forever apart, each of them "lost," his father lost at sea, his mother having "lost" her mind as if she had misplaced it, lost from each other as he was lost from them, and sometimes he dreamt that it was he who was lost at sea, he who lost sight of the others and couldn't find his way back to the *Gilbert*. And then he would find himself back at the brook, kneeling, staring at the water, his face just inches from it and what he thought was his reflection until he saw the man lying on his back at the bottom of the brook, open-eyed, staring up through the water at the sky. Whenever Landish said "the sea," it was Lake Loom that Deacon pictured. "Lake Gloom" was how he heard it, how he said it. "A body of water," Landish called it. And so it seemed to Deacon that his father's body was "of water."

My father is a body of water, he told Landish.

Landish told Deacon that Vanderluyden engineers had made Lake Loom, but he couldn't think how a lake could be made. And his father was of a body of water much larger than Lake Loom. He was "of" all bodies of water. One morning in late spring, Deacon looked down from the rear court at the frozen, snow-covered surface of Lake Loom and pictured the *Gilbert* hemmed in by ice. His father jumped over the gunnels first, followed by his watch of men, all of them trudging round the point until they passed from sight. And then he pictured the watch returning to the ship without his father, the last of the leaderless, slump-shouldered men pausing to look back, trudging on. Landish would lie awake or lightly asleep, waiting to hear the boy struggle to wake from one of his dreams, talking to himself in the other bed. When he screamed, Landish would hurry to wake him. Often, by the time he got there, Deacon had thrown himself on the floor, where he lay tangled in blankets.

If Landish had had a lot to drink, Gough got to Deacon first. He would lift Deacon under the arms and take him out to the hall, where the light was always on. "There you go," Gough would say as Stavely, wearing his dressing gown, his long white hair in tangles, tried to assure him that "it" had only been a dream. Sometimes Gough would sit on the floor beside Deacon's bed, take him in his arms, press his small head against his chest and rock him slowly back and forth as Stavely, in the doorway, his white hair adrift, stood and watched as Landish went on sleeping.

If Landish woke, he would take Deacon from Gough, who would give him a look that made him wince.

"I've never known a child to have such dreams," Gough said.

"You should know better than to say some things out loud in front of him," Landish said.

"There is much that I could say out loud in front of him," Gough said, "but I don't think you'd like it if I did."

"Such as?"

"You have another work-in-progress in your life," Gough said. "Your book may still be a tabula rasa, but what's written now on that other slate can never be erased. Ten years from now, you won't be able to revise his past to make it better."

"So you're saying I should give up on the book?" Landish demanded.

"Don't be an idiot," Gough said. "Better you merely cut back on some other things. He models himself after you."

"And I'm an unsuitable model?"

"Yes. As are we all. As will be everyone he ever meets."

"You and Palmer—you fill notebook after notebook with a short-hand language you invented and I can't even fill one page with English. Sunday after Sunday goes by and I write nothing worthwhile. I see them stretching out in front of me, an endless succession of afternoons of Sabbatical futility."

"Don't worry," Deacon said.

"I'm sorry," Landish said. "I'm sorry I didn't wake up when I should have, Deacon."

One night as they lay in their beds, Landish told him they could leave Vanderland if they wanted to.

"Where would we go?"

Landish said he wasn't sure. He felt sure of almost nothing. He wasn't sure that Vanderland was causing Deacon's dreams. The boy might have such dreams no matter where he lived. Or it might be that one year could make that much difference in the working of a boy's mind. He wondered if Deacon was having bad dreams because he doubted that Landish would be there to comfort him when he woke from them.

"We'll stay a while longer, all right?" Landish said. "We'll see how things go. They might get better."

"We can't leave without the hat," Deacon said. "We can't leave before the hat gets here. If we're gone when it gets here——"

"Let's forget about the hat."

"I think the wealth inspector hasn't sent it yet," Deacon said.

"What's he waiting for? He hasn't answered even one of my letters."

"Maybe if we had the hat, I wouldn't have bad dreams."

"What makes you say that?"

"I don't know. I never had bad dreams before."

"If anyone should have bad dreams about that thing, it should be me. But I've never dreamt about it. Not even when I had the fever in the attic."

"Maybe you did but don't remember."

The school days were done till the fall. Summer lay ahead. Gertrude had come to the Academy to collect Goddie. Deacon had gone back to The Blokes. There were just the two of them, Landish and the governess who was called Miss Esse, who taught the drawing class.

She had been encouraging Goddie to paint a portrait of herself using her reflection in a free-standing mirror as her model.

"You can't stay still *and* paint your reflection," Goddie had said repeatedly. "And I don't like staring at myself. I'll stay still and *you* paint *me*."

As Goddie and Deacon left, Miss Esse sat side on to one of the tables and rubbed her forehead with her fingers. "It's meant to be an exercise in self-awareness," she said, sighing and laughing. "Perhaps you should have her *write* about herself, Mr. Druken."

Except to say hello or goodbye, they had never really spoken to each other.

Landish gathered his lesson books from another table. "That would be unfair," he said. "I can't write about myself. Why should she have to?"

"You burn it all," Esse said. "As a person, at the end of a day, might burn the memory of that day. No clemency as yet for a single moment or a single word. You sentence your sentences to death the instant they're born."

"I'm more of a startist than an artist. I was once a starving artist but am now a raving startist."

Esse smiled. "Why do you burn your book?"

"Because it all too closely resembles me," Landish said.

"By that reasoning," Esse said, "you should set your*self* on fire."

Landish drew a chair to the side of her table, laid down his books and sat facing her, their knees a foot apart. Her eyes were dark blue, her face pale and faintly freckled.

"Who's been telling you about my writing?" he asked.

"Everyone knows about it. Why do you do it? Given the brief lives of your mistakes, you'll never learn from them."

"I have to forget what I've written. If I didn't, I'd be too discouraged to continue."

"So many burned beginnings. It seems sad. I can't help picturing whole books, never read, going up in flames. If you're not generally compelled to destroy what you create, why not try something else?"

Landish stood and picked up his books.

"I'm sorry," Esse said. "I spoke out of nervousness. Please, sit down."

Landish sat, hoping he didn't look as sulky as he felt.

"Why Esse?" he said. "What does it stand for?"

"Siobhan." She spelled it for him before he could tell her that he knew the name, so familiar in Newfoundland, its origin and meaning.

"It's often mispronounced and misspelled, especially by children. Mrs. Vanderluyden suggested that Godwin call me Miss Esse. It caught on. Even informally. All my friends here call me Esse. The governesses, the Blokes. I've been here since Godwin was born. I can see myself doddering round Vanderland when I'm eighty. A family fixture. Good old Esse." She smiled, averted her eyes from his and wound a lock of her hair around her finger. "Regarded as if I predate Creation."

Esse removed her bonnet. Hair of a shade of red Landish had seen before, but not in Newfoundland.

He saw that she was wearing a hairnet.

She began to remove the net slowly from the front, peeling it back and wincing when it became caught in her hair.

"I only wear it out of necessity," she said, her words broken by little sighs of pain.

As if she had freed it from the last obstacle, the net snapped back and Landish was startled to see a mass of near-shoulder-length hair come tumbling out.

Her eyes looked as if, though she had taken his measure in a second and already knew him better than he ever would, she might forever keep that knowledge to herself.

"I would like to have met your father," she said.

"No one who met him ever said afterwards that they were glad they did."

"And your mother."

Her collarbone was so prominent yet fragile-looking that he fancied if he pressed her shoulders together, it would fold perfectly in half.

He wondered what she would do if he reached out and took her hands.

"I've kept a journal for years," she said.

"Then you're a real writer," he said.

"I've never thought that way about writing, as something I could make a career of or satisfy my ambition with. It seems that all I ever do is put things into words. I'm trying to make a record of a largely uneventful life."

"Whereas I am burning the record of a *very* eventful life."

"You know," she said, "sometimes, when I look at a person, it is as if I am not with them but remembering being with them, remembering from a time so far removed that the memory seems to have no context and I see the person as they are, free of all connection with time and place and circumstance. Have you ever felt that way?"

The hair on the back of his neck stood on end. And he was suddenly looking back at both of them from a time when not only this moment, but all the moments of their lives, had passed. She looked at him. He was filled with a piteous tenderness and love for the soul he saw, knowing that this might be as clear a glimpse of it as he would ever have. His eyes welled up with tears. He reached out, pushed her hair back behind her ear and drew the tips of his fingers across her cheek. She edged forward in her chair, took his face in both her hands and kissed him.

Gaelic. "God is gracious."

"Sedgewick told Mother you're having nightmares," Goddie said.

Deacon nodded. He glanced at Miss Esse, who seemed lost in thought.

"So am I."

"No, you're not," Deacon said.

"Everyone has nightmares, not just you."

Deacon shrugged.

"Have you ever seen a dead person?"

"No. Have you?"

"No. What about your parents?"

"I know where my mother is. Her remains."

"Mother says it's just as well she's gone, poor thing. She says she was probably more dead than alive."

"You don't even know what that means."

Goddie began to cry. "I know. I'm sorry. Mother says Father's the reason I can't help saying things. I get mean when I'm afraid or when I'm sad. I don't know why. I'm sorry you're so sad."

"Does your mother ever say nice things?"

Goddie opened her mouth as if she might scream.

"Mother is nicer than anyone. She sits with me when I can't sleep. Or she lets me sleep with her. And she gives me hugs and kisses all the time and calls me her one and only darling child. She lets me brush her hair and she brushes mine and she says that we're best friends and that she doesn't love anyone as much as she loves me. I'd rather have her than Landish. Mother says there's not a drop of his blood in your veins so Mother says almost anyone could mean as much to Landish as you do. She says one day Landish will just up and leave. You'll wake up in the morning and he won't be there and that's the last you'll see of Landish Druken."

Miss Esse slapped the table. "Goddie! You really mustn't say such things!"

Deacon began to cry. Goddie pushed back her chair, stared at him, then ran to him and put her arms around his neck and her cheek against his head. "Please forgive me, Deacon," she said. "Please, please, please. I wish you had good dreams." She kissed him repeatedly on top of his head, which soon felt wet. Then she let him go and ran, still streaming tears, from the dining room, barely dodging a servant who was entering, tray-encumbered, from the other side.

Van had told him that two famous writers had been guests at Vanderland for the past few months and were soon to leave. In the Smoker that evening, Landish, standing and staring into the leaping fire, hoped that Deacon and the Blokes didn't notice his flushed complexion or the trembling of his hands, in which he held a glass of brandy and a cigar.

"Henry James and Edith Wharton," he said. "I've never heard of Edith Wharton."

"*Henry James?*" Gough said, looking about at the others. "Can you imagine, gentlemen? To think that we are sleeping under the same roof as such a great writer. Large though the roof might be."

"In fact, Van has invited me to meet both Mr. James and Mrs. Wharton in the salon after dinner tomorrow evening. Deacon is invited as well."

Gough's face broke into a wide smile.

"I take it that the rest of us are not invited," Sedgewick said. "What's the point of inviting the boy? I dare say I've read more Henry James than he has."

"Henry James is perhaps the greatest living writer, Deacon," Gough said. "Some think perhaps the greatest novelist who ever lived. How lucky, Landish. The first fellow writer you meet will be Henry James."

"We're fellow bi-peds," Landish said. "That's about as much as we have in common. Perhaps as much as we'll ever have in common."

"We'll have to wear our best clothes, Deacon." Landish grinned at him. But Deacon, sitting on the sofa, did not look particularly happy, especially since Landish by this time most nights was decks awash.

Landish took Deacon's hand as the butler led them from The Blokes to the salon. Deacon stood as straight as the butler and tried to walk like him but Landish pulled his hand to make him stop.

The two house guests were seated flanking the fire, Gertrude on Edith Wharton's left and Van to the right of Henry James who was sitting with one foot, its shoe removed and wearing what looked to be several heavy socks, resting on a cushioned stool beside the fire.

"A bout of gout," Henry James said, glancing at them over his upraised glass of brandy. Deacon was surprised to see Goddie sitting beside her mother. She smiled at him as if to promise she would later share a joke with him about the foolishness of the evening.

"Mr. Landish Druken," Van said. "And his charge, Deacon Carson Druken. Mrs. Edith Wharton and Mr. Henry James." Edith Wharton, who wore a dress of such dark blue that Landish at first took it to be black and her to be a widow, gave him her hand when he extended his with a quick half bow that he was certain looked ridiculous, and said that he was pleased to meet her. "I'm very pleased to meet *you*, Mr. Druken," she said. Henry James kept both hands closed about his glass.

"It's an honour to meet you both," Landish said, awkwardly aware of his bulk.

The first thing Deacon noticed about Mr. Henry James was that he had a bushy beard that was all of one piece with long, wide sideburns. Then Edith Wharton, her dress rustling, rose and crouched down to his height, taking both his hands. "Hello, Deacon Carson Druken," she said, and Deacon suppressed an urge to throw his arms around her neck. "Come sit by me"—standing up, she guided him towards the fire, her hand on his back—"Mr. Vanderluyden tells me that you're a very, very bright boy."

"I suppose he has derived *some* benefit from his proximity to Godwin," said Mrs. Vanderluyden.

"You read a lot don't you, Deacon?" Mrs. Wharton said.

"I'm going to read every book in the library."

"All twenty-five thousand of them?" She laughed and cupped his face with both her hands. Deacon nodded. "I still read a lot," she said, "but oddly I don't enjoy it quite as much as I did before I became a writer."

"Godwin reads voraciously," said Mrs. Vanderluyden.

"So you tutor Godwin?" Henry James addressed Landish.

"I am one of several who do." Landish took a brandy from a tray extended to him by the servant.

"Landish is an aspiring writer," Van said.

"One either is or is not a writer," Henry James said. "You can aspire until you expire, it won't make any difference. Tutors should toot and writers should write. I had many tutors as a child. Torturers I called them. But I managed to endure them. And succeed in spite of them. As did my dear friend, Mrs. Wharton. I had so many I can't remember most of them. My family travelled a lot—London, Paris, Geneva, Bonn—as did yours, Edith. You too have been everywhere. Were you tutored, Mr. Druken?"

"No," Landish said. "Not in the way that you mean."

James gave him such a frankly appraising look that Landish felt himself blush. He remembered Van's dream at Princeton of inviting world-famous writers to his great house among whom Landish, he had promised, would hold court.

"You're a man of few words, Mr. Druken. In every sense of the expression it would seem."

Van laughed and turned to Landish. "I told Henry that you burn everything you write."

"Yes, it's true. I've so far burned every word of the book I'm writing."

"In London," Van said, "Henry was invited to dinner at a different house every night for a year. His reputation preceded him."

"I find that I get invited to dinner parties more often when my reputation has not preceded me," Landish said.

"Interesting. Among whom do you believe yourself to have a reputation?" James asked.

Deacon saw a drop of sweat run down Landish's face and into his beard. "Mr. James," Landish said. "Do you mind my asking if you're working on a new book?"

"A book of mine which I've called *The Turn of the Screw* was recently published. There are characters in it who resemble Godwin and this boy of yours."

"Henry, you're *wicked*," Mrs. Wharton said.

He prodded his gouty foot with the cane. "I didn't burn a word of it. The *New York Times* said of it, and I quote: 'It is a deliberate, powerful and horribly successful study of the magic of evil. The manner is always graceful and scrupulously polite.'"

Edith Wharton was holding Deacon's hand. "What you need is a wife, Henry," she said. "You have too much free time. *None* of us can keep up with you."

James threw back his head and laughed loudly, waving his hand at her as if to ward her off. "I am not merely a confirmed bachelor, Mr. Druken. I am a professed celibate. A virgin, in fact."

"What's a virgin?" Goddie's high voice piped up. She jumped about on her chair to face her mother.

"A paradox," Landish said. "Someone who on the one hand has never had any and on the other keeps it all to himself."

"How vulgar," Gertrude said.

James ignored her. "But one can know women without having known a woman. I am a virgin who writes frequently about women."

Landish said, "My apologies. I merely spoke in a spirit of repartee."

"Indeed you did," said Edith Wharton, patting Deacon's back as if the witticism had been his.

"Mrs. Wharton is working on what I am sure will be a wonderful book called *The House of Mirth*," Van interposed.

"I grew up in a house in which there was a dearth of mirth," Landish said.

"As there is in Lily Bart's home too," she replied. "I hope you will read my book. I'm not sure when it will be finished and published, but when it is I will send you a copy. And sign it for you."

"Thank you." Landish's voice quavered, so grateful was he for her kindness.

"Mr. Druken," James said, "has inspired me to write a book called *The House of Girth*."

Edith Wharton exclaimed, "I declare a ceasefire."

"Van," James said. "I have to tell you this house is an absurdity. It is like some immense, gorgeous practical joke. What in God's name are your family and it doing out here in this irretrievable, niggery wilderness?"

It was impossible for anyone in the room to ignore the look of devastation on Van's face as Gertrude laughed.

"That is a question that I have often asked my husband."

"The whole place is based on a fundamental ignorance of comfort. And such gaudy desolation, Van. Really, what is the *point*? Edith has a wonderful estate, one she also designed herself and caused to be built. The Mount. I've stayed there many times. I very much prefer it to here."

"Don't be concerned, Van," Edith Wharton spoke up quickly. "That's just the gout talking. Please, don't look so distressed. Deacon, my friend's leg pains him a great deal, which is why he must keep it on that little stool—it's called a gout stool."

"Do you plan to marry, Mr. Druken?" James said.

"I don't—no, I suppose not."

"Just as well. You would be twice encumbered with a wife."

"Deacon is not an encumbrance."

"Don't you have any other advice for Landish, Henry?" Van asked. "Writing advice?"

"I would be grateful," Landish said.

James sighed and adjusted his foot, wrapped in its many socks, on the chair, grimacing slightly. "All right then. Even assuming that you do have talent, you must travel. You must meet people unlike yourself. You must learn other languages if you wish to be a master of your own. Am I to take it that you only speak whatever language it is that you're attempting now?"

"Henry!" Edith Wharton exclaimed, as Gertrude laughed.

"Well, Edith, you said yourself that you can never say you've read the Russians or the French if you've only read them in translation. Which means I have not yet read the Russians, I suppose. The best advice I can give any writer is have the good sense to be born rich."

"I declined my inheritance," Landish said.

"Why on earth did you do that?"

"Certain conditions were attached to it. My father wanted me to succeed him."

"As what?"

"As him. He wanted to leave me his life so that I could go on living it after he was dead."

"What *was* your father?"

"He was a ship's captain. A sealing skipper. The men who served under him harvested one million seals. They caused to be built his reputation as the greatest sealer who ever lived."

"Well. *His* memoirs might have been interesting."

"Yes, they might have been. Though I'm sure that he would have stipulated that they not be published until after his death, owing to his eccentric disinclination to be hanged."

"An estimable brute, I'm sure."

"Worth writing about," Landish said.

"Yet you have turned your back on the very people you knew best. No wonder you burn what you write. What would young Joseph Conrad write about if he had never gone to sea? Ship's captains. First mates. Sealers. Fishermen. Have you been any of those things?"

"A sealer, I suppose, but only briefly."

"So then."

"I write about things I *am*. A writer. A boy. A man. A son. A friend. A student. A boy's guardian. And about where I come from. Newfoundland."

"You write about no one but yourself." James eased his foot on the stool, grimacing with pain. "The only way for everyone to be equal is for everyone to fail. Therefore some *must* fail. There is no point in gracelessly blaming others for your fate."

"You're being cruel, Henry." Mrs. Wharton frowned at him.

"When it comes to books, there is not the great divide between the classes that you seem to imagine. My father's sealers would while away the time between eighteen-hour watches reading your books.

As they went over the gunnels in a snowstorm, all the talk was of Roderick Hudson and what might become of him among the upper classes of Europe."

James pointed at Deacon, who was sitting rigidly in his chair. "One can't help thinking what this child, in other circumstances, might accomplish."

Landish stood. "In other circumstances," he said, "Deacon would not be Deacon. He blames no one, gracelessly or otherwise, for what he is. Nor do I." He crouched, and took Deacon in his arms. Deacon burrowed his face into the crook of Landish's arm.

Deacon woke in his bed to the sound of Landish's voice in the Smoker.

"Mr. Henry Virgin James thinks I should have been a sealer."

"You didn't cause a scene, did you, Landish?" Gough said.

"I merely told him I preferred the works of *Jesse* James."

"You didn't."

"No. I would have. But I didn't think of it until now."

"What happened, Landish?"

"I can just hear Van. 'You must meet my daughter's amusing tutor, Landish, who believes himself to be a writer.' The Wilhelm Meister of Vanderland. And his thrice-named encumbrance. The celebrated celibate spoke of my encumbrances. The things I would have to rid myself of if I wanted to become a writer. My many encumbrances. He has none, you see. None of the encumbrances of life. Overgrown, erudite brat. He and Van. Little Lords Fondled Not. The Portrait of a Laddy. Yet to woo. Never will. Pronounced me unsuitable. Ineligible. Henry will go away and live to write another day. Whereas I, I am not a writer, Gough. I should write or admit that I can't. I am holding Deacon back by pretending. Mr. James pointedly wondered what Deacon might accomplish in other circumstances."

"I'm sure he meant if he'd been higher born."

"No. More like if I'd been never born."

"Oh, shut up, Landish. You're merely feeling sorry for yourself. Recognize a master when you see him and curb your self-indulgence."

"You think me self-indulgent."

"If *you're* not, the word should be stricken from the dictionary."

Servants wheeled Deacon and Goddie about in wheelchairs, side by side. Goddie said she bet it was more fun than a bicycle. Together, they saw parts of Vanderland she had never seen before, the Ramble, the orchards, the vineyards.

Deacon joined her on Sundays when someone from the stables took her for drives throughout the estate in a carriage. He knew that he was pale by comparison with the soil-tilling blacks and the Southern-born whites. As always, Deacon tried to hide from Goddie his astonishment at the sight of the blacks, not telling her that, before taking the train south from New York, he had never seen a black person in his life. The gardeners stopped their work to watch the two children bowling along in the open carriage, stared at his frail paleness, and, in low tones lest someone hear and report them to Mr. or Mrs. Vanderluyden, called him Goddie's Ghost. Goddie would laugh. She would exhort him to join her in waving at them. She would call out to the ones whose names she knew. "Hi, Billy. Hi, Mary." They might simply have been playing different parts in a game devised as much for their sake as for hers.

They sat before the fire in the Rume, Landish smoking a cigar that Van had pressed upon him.

"It was something, wasn't t?" Van said. "Henry James. He's been my friend for years."

"And is he still your friend?" Landish said. Van ignored him.

"There are times when I cannot believe that I caused such a place as Vanderland to be built," Van said.

"I am looking forward to the day when I will be born rich," Landish said.

"Mrs. Wharton was right. It was the gout talking. But enough about the other evening. How are you managing your confinement to Vanderland?"

"It's better than confinement to an attic."

"But there are things you can't do here. No worthwhile things but—you are a man who chases after certain kinds of women."

"And you are one who overestimates their desire to escape."

"Yet you can never bring yourself to say you are his father. I have never heard you say it. You might aspire less and write more if you lived alone. If you were free to travel."

"I am free to travel. It's travelling that isn't free."

"Perhaps you ought to have been the sealing captain your father wanted you to be. It is a wise man who knows his place."

"And an unwise one who presumes to tell me mine. I've had enough for one night, Van."

"Running away again?"

"You are right not to have made the beast with two backs even once, not even to see what it was like," Landish said. "It's a scary, hairy, howling, bellowing beast, Van. Much better to make the beast with one back, four fingers and a thumb."

"What a crass and vulgar fellow you can be I have known since we met, but there was never such bitterness before in that wit of yours."

"There is nothing new in my striking out when provoked. And I am as well able as ever to tell when someone is provoking me. As for my wit, it is the same as the one you so often passed off as your own."

"Virginity has placed no limits on Henry's genius. Quite the contrary, he believes. Mrs. Wharton's father was George Frederic Jones.

Are you familiar with the expression 'keeping up with the Joneses,' Landish? It refers to the family of Mrs. Wharton's father. Her mother was Lucretia Stevens Rhinelander."

"My mother was Gennie Druken, Newfoundlander," Landish said.

"I think highly of Deacon. He is not the beggar boy I imagined when you first wrote to me about him."

"Why did you invite me to the Rume tonight?"

"I no longer equivocate," Van said. "I see, exactly and instantly, what must be done. I issue orders in my accustomed manner, and others, in the manner of men accustomed to following orders, carry them out."

"You were not so sure of yourself at Princeton. Or when you were spending time with Henry James."

Van looked into the fire, his expression like that of someone brooding over a grievance that could never be repaid. He threw his brandy glass into the fireplace where it smashed into pieces.

"What are you trying to convince me of?" Landish said.

"I want you to know that I am someone who does things, not merely someone who causes them to be done. I am not the self-loathing fellow I once was. One day, perhaps, I will be able to put my last ghost to rest."

"Your last ghost?"

"Something you can help me with. I'll have more to say about it soon."

Though Deacon told himself there was no such thing as a chimney witch, he thought of her making her way from chimney to chimney through catacombs that connected all the chimneys at Vanderland. He went to sleep face down but woke up on his back and heard a sound like the swishing of a dress across the floor. The scream that would chase the chimney witch away before someone wide awake could see her grew louder in his mind, but the hand of something held his breath long past the point where he could bear it until finally his voice came bursting from the dream and he threw himself from bed as if to dodge a slab of stone that had fallen from the ceiling. Gough was again the first to reach him.

So that he could be with Esse, Landish began to accompany the junior members of Van's engineering team—the ones who lived at Vanderland and maintained the inner workings of the house—and the governesses on their Sunday afternoon summer hikes through the Ramble. The governesses held parasols to shield them from the fierce Carolina sun. The sight of them picking their way through the Ramble as if they had never been outdoors until today made him feel absurdly out of place, unaccountably *there* among people who would not have thought him much more foreign had he been Chinese.

He wished that he could take her hand in his and speak as he would have if they were walking through the Ramble by themselves.

The other men walked with their hands clasped behind their backs, Landish with his arms swinging at his sides. Landish and Esse did their best to be last in line during their walks through the Ramble so that they could talk at least somewhat openly to one another. They became known as the stragglers, the slowpokes. The others would stop to let them catch up. The young engineers teased Landish for walking so slowly, telling him he had no land legs.

Sometimes Landish would lag just behind Esse. He touched the small of her back. It was damp with sweat. She pushed his hand away and coughed in protest. Sweat trickled from the hair at her temples and down the back of her neck. He traced the wet furrow of her neck with his index finger. She made as if to shoo away a fly and coughed again. She looked back for an instant. She mouthed "Stop," tried to look cross with him but smiled. Her face was flushed.

"There are three hundred rooms in this house," he whispered. "There must be one where we'd be safe."

"There isn't a room in the world where I'd trust myself with you," she said.

In bits and pieces, in stolen moments, he told her everything about himself except Captain Druken's hat. He didn't want to admit to her that he had stolen it, broken into someone's house at night like a common thief.

He slipped a note into one of her books: *My Dearest Esse, I am in love with you. Someday, when the circumstances are right for all of us, will you marry me?* She wrote back: *I too am in love with you. I won't burn your note. I'll hide it. You do the same with mine. I now possess the heart, and the collected unburned works, of Landish Druken.*

When the circumstances are right. He couldn't imagine them ever being right, yet felt certain that, somehow, they would be. A governess could not marry. They—all three of them—would have to leave Vanderland, a prospect that would not have daunted him if he'd been able to imagine any "situation" he could find that would allow him to properly support Deacon and Esse.

She had never seen an ocean nor any body of water so large you couldn't see the other side. "They should have called *me* Landish," she said. "When I was a child in Virginia my friends pronounced my name, Siobhan, 'Shove on.' I shoved on as far as Vanderland in Carolina. More than eight years ago I came to Vanderland and I haven't left the grounds since. Here I can read constantly—I doubt you could name a place that I don't know more about than you do, yet I have been nowhere. A train ride from Virginia to Carolina. The greatest adventure of my life so far. Little Deacon has travelled more than I have. I know the story of the world by heart. I teach it to others. But I'm not in it yet."

Landish lived in a near-constant state of elation. The mere sight of her rendered ludicrous the notion that the universe was in any way, anywhere, deficient.

He decided that, for now at least, Deacon mustn't know. This secret would be harder for him to keep than that of Captain Druken's hat. Deacon might give it away in the Academy just by looking back and forth between Landish and Esse, smiling, as he always did at the sight of the happiness of others. And there was the chance that he would be upset by the intrusion of Esse into their lives, her intrusion into Landish's affections.

"If you're not happy with your situation, then you should find another one," Goddie remarked primly to Landish in the Academy as they were about to start, in late summer, one of the extra lessons that Gertrude had reluctantly admitted Goddie needed. Deacon had been more or less conscripted to join her.

He turned in surprise. "Who told you that I'm not happy with my situation?"

"Sedgewick told me in our Geography lesson. He said you do nothing but complain. He said you go into Ashton and get drunk with fairy ladies and then come back and make fun of the Vanderluydens if not for whom you would starve to death."

"Sedgewick said that?"

"He said you think you're as good as Father and you should be rich like him."

Deacon glared at her from his seat at the table next to hers. "Landish didn't say that."

"He said you drank so much last night you might still be drunk."

"Godwin, you must have misunderstood Mr. Sedgewick," Landish said. "I've never been to Ashton. Imprisonment is a condition of my employment, as it is of your existence. I'm quite happy to get by on a twig from the family forest. Quite content with and grateful for my twiglet. What man who is paid a twiglet a year would begrudge his employer ten million trees?"

"We weren't just *given* our fortune, you know. " Goddie twirled a globe of the world on her desk. "My great-grandfather the Admiral built all the ships and railroads in America."

Landish strode back and forth, his hands in the pockets of his trousers, certain that he should say no more and certain that he would.

"Indeed he did, Goddie. With his bare hands. All by himself. That's why he was called a great grandfather and not just a passable one. They say you never saw such a man when it came to rustling up a ship or a railroad with spare parts. He would take what less resourceful people threw out in the trash and quick as a wink work it up into a steamship or a locomotive."

"You don't have what it takes to get rich." Goddie swept the globe off the table and onto the floor with both hands. It broke quite neatly in half. Her mouth quivered. "You made me do that. You're full of mediocre blood. Father says that all the time. That's why you're poor. That's why you drink so much. Father says weak men drink too much because they feel sorry for themselves."

"Or maybe they feel sorry for themselves because they're weak and drink too much. It's a tricky thing, cause and effect."

"You know I could have you dismissed." She pouted, her pretty mouth turning down. "If I told Father how you speak to us, the kind of things you say about him and Grandfather and the Admiral."

"Please don't tell your father, Goddie," Deacon said. He was seated at the table next to hers.

"Deacon, I don't need your help with Van," Landish shouted.

"I'm telling Mother you called me Goddie!" She covered her face with her hands but peeked through her fingers at Deacon.

"Please stop, Landish," Deacon said. "Stop making her cry. She's right. I can smell it when you're decks awash."

"Goddie and the Holy Guest," Landish said. He left the Academy even though the class had not yet begun.

Deacon thought about Esse. He'd seen Landish take her hand and seen that she didn't pull away. Seen her smile and blush and squeeze his fingers. Landish's voice sounded different when he talked to her. And she was quiet when he was in the room. She pretended not to notice when he was nearby but Deacon knew she noticed. But Landish didn't know he knew about her. He picked her and she picked him. She sounded different now, even when she talked to Deacon. Nicer. She sounded like she'd picked him too, but he wasn't sure. No one had ever picked Landish. Not really. Landish might make a contribution. They would have a baby that was theirs, not someone else's. Not the baby of someone who was in the Tomb of Time. It wouldn't be the same anymore.

Landish and Deacon were again invited to the Rume. Deacon refused to hold Landish's hand as they followed Henley through the maze of Vanderland.

"Still mad at me?" Landish said.

Deacon nodded.

The butler opened one of the large doors to the Rume but walked away without announcing their arrival. They heard from inside the murmur of a voice.

"Is he talking to the chimney witch?" Deacon asked.

The Rume was dark but for the flickering of firelight. Off to their left, out of sight, was the fireplace that was the size of the Druken mausoleum. Deacon knew that if the lights were on he would have been able to see Napoleon's chess set and the big white bowl from China like the one that Mr. Vanderluyden once told him Goddie broke.

She had said it didn't matter because her mother said it was probably just "some Chinaman's shitpot."

"Van?" Landish said.

"Come in." His voice was so low that Deacon barely heard it above the snapping of the logs in the fireplace.

"I can't see," Deacon said, and he felt Landish's hands on his shoulders, guiding him forward.

They went inside. Van was kneeling in front of what Deacon took to be a piece of furniture, perhaps a kind of bench, that lay crossways before the fire, more than spanning the width of the fireplace. It looked like a long narrow coffin, but its top was covered in red velvet and there were no handles on the sides. His hands were resting palms down on the velvet.

"It's a trunk of sorts," he said. "The exterior was carved by the man who carved the mantelpiece. It's quite ornate, isn't it, like a sarcophagus. Appropriate. Please, sit down."

He did not look up as the two of them sat down behind him, Deacon keeping his distance from Landish, holding a pillow tight against his chest.

"I was fourteen when my sister, Vivvie, was born, Deacon," he said.

"Deacon knows about Vivvie," Landish said. Van, still staring ahead into the fire, shook his head.

"You know what I told you, Landish," Van said. "It was not the whole truth."

"Then tell me the whole truth, for once," Landish said. "But make no mention of a chimney witch."

"For fourteen years, I had been the youngest child, the youngest of four boys. My mother was forty-one. No one told me that she was expecting. I'm sure my brothers spoke of it among themselves but not to me. My father, well—it was only rarely that he spoke to me at all. The five of them, as well as other relatives, and my tutors, governesses, the servants—no one bothered to invent a reason for my mother's lying in. She stayed in the guest wing of our house on Fifth Avenue.

"I was as discreet as my elders tacitly instructed me to be. But I was mortified. Forever aware of the near proximity of a woman who was not only pregnant but was my mother. I blushed in the company of others, especially women. I couldn't imagine how things would ever again be as they had been, for the end of all this secrecy would be the impossible-not-to-acknowledge fact and sight of a newborn child.

"My brothers and I were taken to the nursery to see her a few days after she was born. They regarded her with fond amusement, this red and wrinkled little thing. I don't know how long it was before they set eyes on her again—months, probably—but I went to the nursery as often and for as long as I was allowed to.

"I was not, as I had expected I would be, embarrassed at the sight of her. I was . . . smitten. There ought to be a special, particular word for it, the love of a gawky, adolescent boy for his infant sister. I had never seen a newborn. I suppose I thought—if I had ever considered this or any other matter regarding infants—that they were the size of babies one saw being pushed in prams by their nurses. I had not taken much notice of babies of any age or size before. What I couldn't converse with didn't exist. I had defined the word *sibling* as 'brother.'

"But here was this shrivelled, all but blind, completely helpless, completely dependent tiny *thing* known as my *sister* who looked, I was assured, much as I had looked at her age. Vivvie.

"Strange though it may seem to you, and sometimes seems even to me now, I formed the notion that only if constantly looked over, constantly watched, could she continue to exist. It was not that I feared that, while no one was attending her, while she was lying there alone in her crib, she would suffer some mishap—smother in, be strangled by, her blankets. I believed—though I couldn't have put it into words at the time—that she was too new, too small and fragile to persist while unobserved, that someone older had to supply her with the self-consciousness, the self-awareness that she lacked and without which her *self* would vanish.

"So I sat for hours by her crib, staring at her, fretting every time she made a sound, ignoring Nurse's reassurance that babies were much stronger than they looked. She cried and gargled as if her lungs were stuck in her throat, let loose earsplitting screeches and squeals for which I could think of no explanation but that she was in agony. 'She does it because it's the one thing she *can* do,' Nurse said. Perhaps she was right. How else could she assert the fact of her existence?

"I spent a lot of time in the nursery, far more than anyone thought was proper, let alone normal, for a boy. My brothers coined the term 'abnormale' to describe me. Nurse felt put out at first. She saw me as some sort of odd, meddlesome nuisance, even rival, and an interloper in whose company none of the women who came and went felt comfortable or free to converse or comport themselves as usual. I necessitated the invention of many euphemisms. I was sent from the room when the wet nurse arrived and when Vivvie needed to be changed.

"But Nurse was won over by how much I doted on Vivvie. She taught me how to hold her, how to support her head and shield the soft spot, how to coax from that fragile cage of skin and bones a belch as loud as you would hear in any tavern. It got so that, often, she would stop crying or go to sleep for no one but me. Nurse would send for me, and to the scorn of my father and brothers, I would ask Mother's permission to be excused from the dinner table or the living halls. In the nursery, I would slump on a sofa, lay Vivvie on my squeezed-together legs, and rock her back and forth while Nurse watched and shook her head in wonder at how quickly Vivvie would fall quiet as she stared at me and chuckled as if something about the look of me amused her.

"'What are you doing, boy, apprenticing to be a nurse?' Father said. 'It's not what your brothers were doing at fourteen. I doubt that there's even a fourteen-year-old *girl* of our set who spends her time as you spend yours. You dote on that child more than your mother does. In fact, it would be unseemly for your mother to spend one-tenth as much time in the nursery as you do. Minding babies is women's work, women of a station in life far below yours. It was not so that his grandsons could spend their time in the pale of wage-earning women that my father built up a fortune from the money his mother staked him for a single Hudson River taxi dory. You have no business in that nursery. A young Vanderluyden man does not accompany a pram-pushing nurse through streets lined by the houses of our friends and other near equals. It's not just you who's the laughing-stock of the neighbourhood, it's also me, the man who allows his sissified son to be the escort of his infant sister's nurse. You're acting like some giddy, moonstruck, knackered little rooster who doesn't know what hens are for, let alone which ones are meant for him. It's unnatural, this infatuation with your sister.'

"But my mother took my side, saying that I was just going through a phase that I would soon grow out of, a phase, she said, that many girls and women of our set told her they found quite sweet and charming. She said that my passions were sorting themselves out and would find their proper objects in good time. 'Sweet and charming,' my father said, and told us how men thought of by women as sweet and charming were looked upon by other men.

"He more or less gave up on me. 'Baby girl and maybe boy,' they called Vivvie and me.

"I walked about the nursery with a towel on my shoulder in case Vivvie spit up. When Nurse and the governesses spoke of me to one another, they called me 'young Mr. Vanderluyden' as if there were a second, silent adjective in front of 'young.'

"I would have slept with her cot beside my bed if Mother had allowed it. I couldn't sleep, thinking of Vivvie in the nursery, lying in her cot at night, her crying ignored by Nurse, who said it was good for her lungs and a sign that she was strong and healthy. My room was far from the nursery but I was certain I could hear her. Nurse said I would spoil her if I picked her up every time she cried. She said I was making her job harder because Vivvie preferred me to her and wouldn't sleep when I wasn't close by. 'She knows it when you come and go,' she said. 'She knows your voice.'

"In spite of my mother's prediction, my passions didn't sort themselves out and find their proper objects. I mean nothing sinister by that. But I remember the feeling of Vivvie's little body in my arms, a chest half the size of my hand going up and down against my own, her breath warm and her little mouth wet against my cheek. Vulnerable, trusting, absolute blamelessness. There was nothing like it in life as I had known it until then.

"'You can't devote your whole life to hovering over Vivvie,' my mother said. 'Think of how difficult it will be for her when you go off to Princeton. If only for her sake, you should leave her to Nurse and the nannies from now on.' I tried for her sake, as my mother put it. I lasted one day and one night. I worried that she would think that I'd abandoned her. I found it unbearable to think that she would, even for an instant, think herself betrayed by me.

"I went to the nursery and at the sight of me she shook the bars of her crib. Things were soon exactly as they had been.

"'Enough,' Father said. 'This has been going on for over a year. I wish I could send you off to Princeton tomorrow.'

"I'm never going to Princeton," I said. "What do I need Princeton for? My brothers didn't go. You merely want to correct a family deficiency by having a son who went to Princeton. I can't learn anything there that I can't be better taught by my tutors.

"It was only a few nights later that Vivvie choked to death on a button from a man's shirt. From one of mine, Nurse said."

"Wait," Landish interrupted. "You told me at Princeton that your sister drowned. I told Deacon——"

"Now I am telling you the truth," Van said. "I couldn't bear to do it at Princeton."

"The account you gave me of your sister's drowning was far too elaborate and detailed to be a lie, Van."

"It wasn't a *lie*. It was a necessary, sustaining fiction. Let me finish telling you the truth and perhaps you'll understand."

"Either you are out of your mind now, or you were when we met." Landish couldn't bring himself to add that the original version of Vivvie's death, the telling of which had brought him to tears and left him in need of a prolonged, consoling hug from Van, had been a self-serving story in which Van made himself out to be an unappreciated, unacknowledged hero who had been accused of causing the very death he had risked his own life to prevent. Van had chosen from the infinite number of alternatives a vainglorious fable.

Van put up his hand to silence him. "A button from one of *my* shirts, Nurse said. Though I found none of my shirts to be missing a button, this became the story in the household, assumed by my family, the staff and the servants to be true—a button proved I must somehow be to blame. There formed the vague notion that her death had proceeded from some disordering of the natural way of things. What except trouble or even tragedy could one expect when a young man stepped as far out of his rightful place as I had? Whatever chance I had had to live down my reputation for oddness vanished with Vivvie's death. I was no longer Padgett Godfrey Vanderluyden. I was the young man whose single shirt button caused the freakish death of the infant sister with whom he had been so freakishly infatuated. How apt. I felt all eyes on me whenever I appeared in public, at gatherings, in church . . .

"After first hearing of her death, I gathered all the shirts in my closet, and sought out the ones being laundered, and laid them all out on the floor of my room. I went slowly through every shirt, counting the buttons, feeling for them, frantic when, for an instant, I thought that one was missing. There were thirty-seven shirts, twelve buttons to each shirt. Four hundred and forty-four buttons. None were missing. I put every shirt in this trunk, which I locked and hid beneath my bed. But I was so preoccupied with grief that the shirts became, bizarrely, my intimate connection to Vivvie. I wanted no one else to touch them. So I told the others I had burned every one of them. I was a boy of fourteen. I didn't know that would make them more supicious of me. 'But there, you see,' my father said. 'That's as good as a confession. The closest we'll ever get to one from *him*.'"

Van patted the trunk that lay on the floor in front of him. "Every night I opened the trunk and checked the shirts for missing buttons. I took the trunk with me to Princeton and checked the shirts every night in my room, Landish, while you were sleeping."

"Mr. Vanderluyden, if you know there's no buttons missing, why do you count them?" Deacon asked.

"The trunk has been with me since she died. I never lock it because I know that every night I will search the same shirts for what I know I will never find. I can't help it.

"Nurse should have found the button. She checked the crib whenever she put Vivvie down for the night. Or at least she was supposed to check it. Nurse should have heard her. She was sleeping in the same room. How could she not have heard her? I would have. Everything in that house was managed to perfection. The whole thing is so unbearably absurd. The child of the richest man in the world. The button from a shirt.

"And as for Father and my older brothers—all four of them said they hadn't seen her, hadn't been in the nursery, for weeks before she died. The official cause of death, and the one that those of our set pretended to accept, was given as 'sudden fever.' But I was the one struck down by her death as if by the worst sort of illness. I couldn't eat or sleep, didn't leave my bed for months. There was some sort of service for Vivvie that I doubt my father would have let me attend even had I been able to. I had been tutored, not rigorously, in religion. I had never given God much thought. Now I gave him none. I could put no credence in a God who merely looked on while the most innocent and blameless of his children choked to death while lying alone in the darkness.

"The housekeeper came to my defence when Nurse said that it was my button that she choked on. She said that shirt buttons were constantly being lost and replaced. She said that if any of us lost a button, it might have been replaced before we noticed it was missing. But you know me, Landish. I was as fastidious about my clothes back then as I was at Princeton. If a button was missing, I'm sure I would have noticed. I'm sure of it. Don't you think I would have?"

"I'm sure you would have." Landish placed his hand on Van's shoulder, where he crouched before the fire and the trunk. "You mustn't blame yourself. I only wish you had told me this at Princeton."

"But that's who I was, you see. It's who I was the day we met, the day I sat beside you on the bench. The Vanderluyden who, by an unmentionable accident, caused the death of his sister on whom he had doted to the point of becoming a family embarrassment. Everyone knew. Yet no one said a word to you? I was sure that someday you'd confront me with the truth. I dreaded it. But I couldn't bear to tell you."

"No one said a word. The measure of their fear of your family, I suspect. They might call us sodomites but even our worst enemies dared not cross that line."

"I think of Vivvie many times every day. I still speculate about the true source of the button. Nurse might have been mending someone's shirt. Father or one of my brothers might have paid Vivvie a rare visit. I wonder if they checked *their* shirts as I checked mine, still wonder if one of my brothers is harbouring a dreadful secret.

"I remember Vivvie as I saw her last, standing and holding the rails of her crib, laughing as I poked her belly with my finger."

Van turned and looked at Deacon, who was staring at him wide eyed, his eyes welling up with tears.

"Padgy Porgie, pudding and pie/Killed the girl who made him cry/ When the Iron baron had his say/Padgy Porgie went away."

"Even if it *was* a button from your shirt—" Landish began, but stopped when Van stood.

"I have many times tried to convince myself to burn those shirts in this fire, burn them one by one as you burn the pages of your book, and burn the trunk as well. Four hundred and forty-four buttons. Some nights I have counted them a hundred times over. I have knelt here with a shirt in my hand, bunched it up and reared back to throw it, only to lose my nerve and replace it in the trunk."

"Shall we help you burn them, Mr. Vanderluyden?" Deacon's small face was whiter than ever.

"Come here, Deacon," Landish said, but Deacon stayed put, his eyes shining with tears in the firelight and glued on the man in front of him.

"I'm going to do it tonight," Van said. "But not now while the two of you are watching. Go back to The Blokes."

"Make sure you burn them," Deacon said. "Don't listen to the chimney witch."

Van reached into the inside pocket of his housecoat and brought forth something wrapped in white paper that Deacon thought at first was a gift for him or Landish.

"I also plan to rid myself of this."

"What is it?" Landish said.

"It's the button. It popped out of Vivvie's throat when Nurse clapped her on the back. It was too late by then. Nurse gave the button to my father. He gave it to me in a little box tied with ribbon on my sixteenth birthday. I had no idea what it was. I opened it at dinner in front of everyone. My mother left the table, but my father and my brothers just sat there and stared at me. Inside the cloth covering, the button is made of metal that might not burn in the fireplace. I would probably search for it among the ashes. So I plan to throw it into the deepest part of Lake Loom."

"Can I see it?" Deacon said.

"No," Landish said, standing up and, taking Deacon by the hand, all but dragging him from the chair. "It's time to leave Mr. Vanderluyden alone."

"Landish is right," Van said, and turned back to the velvet-covered trunk.

At The Blokes, they sat on Landish's bed, Landish pressing Deacon, who was still crying, to his chest.

"Why does he count the buttons when he already knows how many there are?"

"Because he can't help it."

"He should put a lock on the trunk. Then he'd know for sure that none were missing."

"He knows. He'd unlock the trunk and count the buttons."

"Why?"

"I told you. He can't help it."

"Vivvie's mother must have been sad. And her father."

"I'm sure they were."

"And the nurse. Do you think she dropped the button?"

"It was an accident, whatever happened. It was no one's fault."

"He counts the buttons."

"He can't help it, he said."

"He thinks the button might have been his. Because of what the nurse said."

"Maybe. A small, cloth-covered button the same colour as a bed-sheet. I suppose she might have missed it. It might already have been in Vivvie's mouth when the nurse put her down for the night."

"Where is Vivvie buried?"

"I don't know for sure, but I think New York. Near her parents probably."

"Mr. Vanderluyden doesn't like New York."

"I don't blame him. Not now."

"Because of Vivvie?"

"She puts some things in a different light."

"Mr. Vanderluyden."

"Maybe."

"He made Vivvie sound nice. *He* sounded nice when he talked about her. Most of the time. He sounded happy."

"Almost happy."

"He remembers her. She was in the Murk, but he wasn't. Maybe, in the Tomb of Time, she remembers *him*."

"Maybe she does."

Landish thought about Van alone in his room at night, pulling out from beneath his bed the trunk that was filled with shirts, counting their buttons over and over again. He thought of how he must have felt when his young wife told him she was pregnant. It would have been painful enough to hear even if he'd never had a sister. But he must have thought instantly of Vivvie, hearing of this child that wasn't his.

He felt sick with guilt just thinking of how it would have been had he found Deacon one morning as the nurse had found Vivvie. He couldn't imagine bearing such a burden for the balance of his life. And though he knew that such suffering was not justification for making others suffer, he wasn't sure that he could have resisted revenging himself on the blameless just as Van had done when he betrayed him.

He doubted that Van had burned or would ever burn the shirts, or throw the button in Lake Loom. But he wondered why he had told him the truth about Vivvie, after all this time.

❈

Deacon counted the buttons on his shirt, rolling them between his fingers. He couldn't imagine ever having been so small that he could choke on a button. She had to hold the bars of her crib to keep from falling down. Deacon wasn't even in the Murk when his father died. He was still in the Womb of Time. He wasn't as old as Vivvie when his mother died.

He had been like her when he was still at Cluding Deacon. Not knowing one word. Trying to crawl. He couldn't remember it. She would be older than him now. Older than Goddie. Grown up. Maybe she would have looked a bit like Mr. Vanderluyden. She might have lived at Vanderland with him. Vanderland would be different. Mr. Vanderluyden might not be so unhappy. Deacon and Landish might still be in Newfoundland, in some place nicer than the attic. Goddie's aunt, sort of. Aunt Vivvie. He wondered if Goddie knew about her. He didn't think so. Choking on a button was something she would talk about. But it was all Just Mist. It wasn't real. Vivvie went to the place from which no one knows the way back home. Even babies had to go there by themselves. He knew that if he fell asleep he would dream about the button and the chimney witch, so he stayed awake all night.

Landish brought the sketch of Gen of Eve to the Academy, ostensibly to show as an example of a self-portrait for Goddie's drawing class, but really so that Esse could see it.

Gertrude was leading Goddie from the Academy just as Landish entered.

"What do you have there?" she said.

"A self-portrait by my mother. A pencil sketch she drew many years ago."

"I want to see it," Goddie said.

"There's no time," Gertrude said, leading Goddie away, who looked back longingly over her shoulder at Landish and the sketch beneath his arm.

"Gen of Eve and Landish. So she was expecting when she drew this," Esse said. "Expecting you. How lovely. And clever. A wonderful keepsake, Landish. I can't imagine a sweeter one."

"I remember her drawing other sketches, staring at the part she was working on through a magnifying glass. A magnifying glass in one hand, a pencil in the other. She would squint, frown, sigh. She said her work was hideous."

"Then I'll bet it's best admired through a magnifying glass." Esse took one from the drawer of her table and began to pore over the sketch. "Oh, it's marvellous, Landish," she said. "Every detail is just right. She must have spent weeks, months at it."

The sight of Esse smiling as she looked at Gen of Eve brought to his eyes a sudden rush of tears.

The Rume was almost dark.

Mr. Henley had come to fetch him, saying that Mr. Vanderluyden wanted to see him to show him something special. They had walked together through the chandelier-lit house with its deep shadows, but now he was alone. There was a note pinned to Mr. Vanderluyden's red chair: "Deacon, I've gone upstairs in the elevator. I'll just be a minute."

The lamps were not lit in here, not even the two blue ones with the white globes on top that Landish said had cost a fortune. There was a golden tree of candles beside the iron staircase, but none of the candles were lit. Neither were the candles on the catwalk overhead, so Deacon couldn't even see the books. There was an old globe as high as Deacon on one side of the fireplace. He spun it and stopped it when it came to Newfoundland. A relief globe, it was called. The land was raised. You could feel the mountains with your fingers. The fire was so low you couldn't smell the smoke.

The trunk that looked like a long narrow coffin lay in front of the fire. He saw now that the red velvet–covered top was divided into squares. He wrote his name in the velvet with his finger, then moved his finger back the other way and wiped it out. The trunk was uneven, a bit higher at one end than the other so it wobbled when Deacon sat on it. He got up, knelt on it and pressed down with both hands. It was still uneven, and he wondered if Mr. Vanderluyden would think that he had broken it.

He heard a sound on the catwalk and looked up to see him standing at the top of the circular stairs, leaning his arms on the little balcony from which you could oversee the Rume without being seen—or give a speech if you wanted to.

"Do you want to see inside the trunk? All you have to do is raise the lid. I'll show you." He walked down the narrow, winding stairs, one hand on the rail, the other in the pocket of what looked like a bathrobe, though it wasn't white but red. "Satin" was the word for cloth that shone like that.

"Come kneel by the trunk," Mr. Vanderluyden said. They knelt side by side, before the trunk, before the fire. Mr. Vanderluyden raised the red velvet lid. "There are hinges on the other side. It doesn't have a lock. It's meant for storing clothes. I could stretch out full length inside it with my arms above my head. If I stood it on one end, I could step inside and close the door behind me."

"What's in it?" Deacon said. The lid was blocking what little light came from the fireplace.

"Shirts," said Mr. Vanderluyden. "The ones I told you and Landish about."

"You said you were going to burn them."

"I decided not to."

"Did you throw the button into Lake Loom?"

Mr. Vanderluyden got up and lit the red candles on the candle tree.

Almost everything in the library that wasn't made of wood was red. The wood was dark, and it was carved into shapes like the statues in the park. It shone like it was polished every day. There was a painting on the ceiling of clouds and angels with red dresses and white wings, and babies who were chubbier than Goddie and held their hands up in the air like they were falling.

The shirts, though yellowed with age, were buttoned and neatly folded, arranged in two even piles in the far left corner of the trunk, which otherwise was empty. There was enough room in the trunk for ten times as many shirts.

"Thirty-seven shirts. Twelve buttons to each shirt. Four hundred and forty-four buttons," said Mr. Vanderluyden. He reached into the trunk and removed a shirt from the top of one of the piles. Its collar and cuffs were almost brown and frayed to the point that soon they might separate from the shirt altogether. He handed it to Deacon.

"Count the buttons," Mr. Vanderluyden said.

Deacon carefully unfolded the shirt. It felt much lighter than the ones he wore. He could almost see through it. There were holes in the tails as if Mr. Vanderluyden had poked his fingers through them. Deacon counted out loud. There were two buttons on each cuff. "One, two, three, four." One on either side where the collar closed. "Five, six." He counted the buttons down the middle. "Seven, eight, nine, ten, eleven." He looked up at Mr. Vanderluyden. "Eleven?" he said.

He counted them again and got eleven. "Why is one missing?"

Mr. Vanderluyden took the shirt from Deacon, folded it carefully, replaced it in the trunk and slowly closed the red lid. He stood.

"Let's take the elevator up to the roof," he said.

"I've never been in an elevator," Deacon said.

"Not many people have," said Mr. Vanderluyden. "Don't worry. It just goes up and down." He took Deacon's hand and led him around the column of the chimney. He slid open a wooden door, a panel in the wall, then did likewise with the elevator's iron door, which Deacon was relieved to see was made of crisscrossed bars that he could see through. They stepped inside and Mr. Vanderluyden pulled the iron door back into place. He pushed a button and the floor began to rise beneath their feet like the floors had done on the boat.

"Pulleys, cables, wheels, weights and counterweights," said Mr. Vanderluyden. "That's all. Powered by the generators in the basement." The elevator slowed, stopped. Mr. Vanderluyden opened the iron door and a wooden one. He took Deacon by the hand again and led him out onto the walkway of the parapet, which ran round the upper walls of Vanderland like an elevated road. The air was cool. Deacon felt relieved to be outdoors, no longer in the little room that rose up as if by magic.

There wasn't a cloud. "The moon is almost full tonight," Mr. Vanderluyden said. "If it wasn't for the moon, we could see more stars."

"What happened to the twelfth button?" Deacon said.

"I should have noticed when I lost it."

"Everybody loses buttons."

"I suppose. When Nurse gave my father the button that Vivvie choked on, he told me to take my shirt off and hand it to him. I was left standing there in front of everyone, wearing nothing but an undershirt. He counted the buttons. When he found that one was missing, he threw the shirt back in my face."

"You were sad when Vivvie died."

"Very sad. But I thought like the others. They blamed me. I blamed myself."

"But you said none of the buttons were missing."

"I told you what I wished was true. It's hard not to—when you meet someone who doesn't know the truth, who doesn't know anything about you, it's hard not to tell them what you wish was true. It's as though what people don't know about you never happened. You can start again. New. Go back to before everything was spoiled. But other people's ignorance does not undo or change the past. And so you never feel absolved. You never feel better."

"It's not your fault. Landish knows that too."

"I've changed my story twice now. He might not believe a word I say."

"I'll tell him you sounded sadder than before."

"I should burn the shirts, shouldn't I?"

"Like Landish burns the pages?"

"No, not like that. He will never run out of pages to burn."

Deacon imagined Mr. Vanderluyden feeding the shirts into the fire one by one, saving the one with the missing button until last, watching it burn the way Landish watched the last page burn. Landish did it every night. Gough said it was a ritual, but Sedgewick said that made it sound too grand.

Mr. Vanderluyden leaned on the edge of the parapet.

"Isn't it something, Deacon? No matter which way you face, it looks the same. Vanderland is in the very middle of the mountains."

There wasn't a sound. It was as if the clamour of Vanderland had been carried off by the wind, the place scoured of sound by the wind, which had since died down. How strange the silence seemed in the wake of such an uproar. The actors had withdrawn from the stage just before the curtains rose, but something of their recent presence still hung in the air, like the first moment that followed the passing on to elsewhere of the soul of Vivvie.

The moon was low and bigger than the sun. It lit up the mountains. But the Smokies weren't smoky and the Blue Ridge was more black than blue. They didn't blend together like they did on sunny days. He saw the upper treeline of each ridge and the spaces in between the trees. The mountains would be dark when the moon went down.

"I can't see over the wall," Deacon said.

"Here, I'll lift you up." Van took Deacon beneath the arms and lifted him until his feet were even with the ledge. "Stand on the ledge, Deacon. I won't let you go." Deacon put his feet on the ledge. This was the highest up he had ever been. A motor car came up one side of the Esplanade. Its lights reflected in the fountain and spread out across the grass.

"Isn't it something?" Mr. Vanderluyden said. "You can walk all the way around Vanderland on this pathway. I own everything you can see from it except the mountains and the sky. Sometimes it feels like even they are mine."

There were people far down below on the steps, guests who had come out to meet the car.

"We can see them, but they can't see us. They can't even hear us, but the sound of their voices carries up. It would be nice if I could run the entire place myself, have it all to myself, day and night."

"You'd be lonely."

"I suppose. If there was another Vanderland just like this one next door, a replica that no one lived in, I could go over there from time to time."

Deacon imagined another, empty Vanderland and wondered if its Rume would have a chimney witch.

Mr. Vanderluyden lifted him down.

"Were you afraid up there?"

Deacon shook his head.

"Don't tell Landish that I stood you on the ledge."

As he walked into the library, Landish glanced up automatically, as he always did, at the beautiful domed ceiling with its fresco of white-winged angels. Van was waiting for him, his tall, thin figure leaning against the black granite mantle of the fireplace, the wooden frieze rising behind him. Landish stopped in the middle of the room.

"I cried on your shoulder when you told me of your failure to save your sister from drowning. So misunderstood but so heroic. Now I'm trying hard for your sake to try to understand why you had to not only invent that tale but then another consisting of only part of the truth about the missing button. Yet you then told Deacon the whole truth. You shouldn't have told Deacon."

"Confessing to Deacon has lightened my spirits somewhat."

"You don't look or sound like it. By the way, it hasn't lightened *his* spirits. He's been waking from God knows what sort of dreams."

"He's most often woken in the arms of Gough, you being absent from The Blokes or too drunk to notice a boy crying in the bed beside your own."

"Said Sedgewick."

"What would you say to the idea of Deacon being raised at Vanderland?" Van said.

"He *is* being raised here. For as long as you care for me to tutor Godwin."

"I have a proposal to make concerning Deacon. Come, sit down."

"Is there someone else who needs company while having dinner?" Landish heard his voice quaver. He felt as though he had fallen into a trap that he should have known had long ago been set for him.

Van smiled. "I know it was never your intention to remain at Vanderland. What if, when you left, Deacon stayed behind? To become a part of the family, I mean. A Vanderluyden. He would be the other man of the house."

"As you once wanted me to be. Deacon and I are a family. Van, nothing can make up for Vivvie's death."

"You can't bring yourself to say you are his father."

"I didn't think it would be fair to his first father, Carson of the *Gilbert*, a man I will never come close to equalling."

"Have you thought about his future, Landish? Really thought about it?"

"You sound as though you're offering to take him off my hands. Adoption is a strange form of philanthropy."

"If you left here with the boy, what would you live on? If you found even the lowest form of a 'situation,' I could make it vanish in a instant."

"But why *would* you?"

"I'm quite fond of Deacon. As is Goddie. You can't imagine what a blow it will be to her if Deacon leaves. There are many parents in this country who would give up their only son if I offered to make him my heir. You will by no means leave Vanderland penniless if you decide as I hope you will."

"I'll never give up Deacon."

"You would if you had no choice. You would if your life and his depended on it."

"Why would you make such a threat?"

"Give it some thought." Van stood. Landish felt himself dismissed. "Good night, Landish."

Landish all but crawled down the stone staircase, looking down through the rings of the iron chandeliers to the vestibule, where a man he took to be the butler stood, staring up at him.

"Henley, did I wake you?" he said. "Or do butlers never sleep?"

"Please don't go any farther, Mr. Druken. By the way, I am not a butler. You and I met some years ago. My name is Mr. Trull."

"Trull? Good old pistol-packing Trull from Princeton? Are you still packing those pistols? Is he still paying you to keep an eye on me?"

Mr. Trull drew a pistol from his coat pocket and pointed it at Landish. "A hole between your eyes is what you need," he said.

Landish turned and crawled back up the stairs. He pounded on all the doors.

"Awake, awake," he roared. "Treason is afoot."

Doors opened. Gough, Stavely, Palmer and Sedgewick came out in their dressing gowns. Deacon came out, but Gough guided him back to his bed, then motioned the others into the Smoker and closed the door behind Landish as he stumbled through.

"Three sheets to the wind and decks awash," he shouted.

"Obviously," Gough said. He stood with his back to the door barring escape.

"No more roaming for me tonight, is that it?"

"Nor brandy," Gough said. "And lower your voice."

Landish sat heavily on the sofa, facing Gough.

"He offered me a bribe for Deacon," he muttered. "I will by no means leave Vanderland penniless if I leave without Deacon. Well, I bought him from Cluding Deacon for fifty dollars and he's not much bigger now, so he might fetch eighty at the most."

"I curse the day you two set foot in The Blokes," Sedgewick said.

"What's happened, Landish?" Gough asked.

"He wants to buy the boy from me. He wants to be his father. Godwin and Deacon Vanderluyden. Deacon the new heir of Vanderland. Gertrude, who adores him so, would be his mother. It will truly endear him to Gertrude if her husband tells her of his plans to leave to Deacon everything that would otherwise have gone to Goddie."

"Give him the boy," Sedgewick snapped. "And good riddance to both of you."

Landish rose, threw an errant punch at him, and fell down. Sedgewick turned his back on him and left the Smoker, slamming the door, while Gough and Stavely helped Landish to his feet.

"I can't get my bloody bearings."

"You could have hurt Sedgewick," Gough said.

"He threatened me. And Deacon. He said I'd give him Deacon if my life and the boy's depended on it."

"He *said* that?"

Landish nodded.

"But nothing *more*? You must have misunderstood his meaning, Landish."

"Perhaps," Landish said. "Perhaps I did." But he was thinking that he could not remember when Deacon had last hugged his leg or reached between their beds to hold his hand.

※

Deacon wondered what Goddie's room was like. She said it was bigger than The Blokes' rooms put together. He thought about waking up in the dark in a room that was so much bigger than his and Landish's. Every morning, Goddie saw her nurse, maid and governess before she saw her mother. They got her ready to see her mother. All day she felt like he did when they were having dinner. She didn't have to lift a finger. She went everywhere in a wheelchair now whether he went with her or not. She said it was her chariot.

Lying in bed, looking at Landish who was asleep, Deacon thought about the night before. Deacon had heard Landish tell the Blokes that Mr. Vanderluyden wanted Deacon to live with him. "Surely," Gough had said to Landish, "the only question you should concern yourself with is does Deacon want to live at Vanderland." Mr. Vanderluyden had Goddie but he'd never made a contribution. He wanted a boy but he still didn't like Mrs. Vanderluyden enough to make a contribution. Landish—though decks awash—had told the Blokes that Deacon might like to have the run of Vanderland—he could play in the whole house. He would still have dinner with Goddie but he wouldn't go back to The Blokes when they were done. He would have his own big room. They were penniless on Dark Marsh Road. How would he like to go back to the world of business buckets, noblemen and wealth inspectors? No banquet halls. Baths in wooden tubs so small your head got stuck between your knees. Landish said he'd be set for life, to say the least. He said wealth wasn't the worst thing you could abandon someone to. Or for. He said maybe Deacon would be all right if he went his merry way. Landish seemed to be still decks awash when he came to bed, but he'd said nothing to Deacon.

Deacon began to cry. He wondered if Landish had been speaking with Esse. Maybe she'd told him Landish would be better off without him.

Deacon felt like he did when Landish had been feverish, when his eyes were open but he didn't know anyone was there and couldn't hear him when he said his name, so it was like he was the one who wasn't there. He remembered looking at Landish and trying not to think about the Tomb of Time.

He thought about Vivvie, and his parents, and all the people in the Tomb of Time who were never coming back. If Landish left him, they'd each have their own path in Just Mist. They wouldn't walk the same path anymore. He didn't want Landish to go his merry way, but he didn't want him to stay if he didn't want to.

He got out of bed and shook Landish until he woke up. He told him he didn't want him to go and Landish hugged him so hard that Deacon's back sounded like when Landish cracked his fingers. Deacon wasn't sure if the hug meant Landish wouldn't leave him after all or was going to but didn't want to say so.

"You should tell Mr. Vanderluyden that you picked me first," Deacon said to him, his arms around Landish's neck. Landish made a face as if he had said something silly.

"I picked you, too," he said.

"Did you?" Landish said.

Deacon nodded.

"Now that Mr. Vanderluyden has spoken to you about you leaving, I'm terrified."

"Yes," he said. "So am I."

"I can't imagine that the two of you will ever be apart."

"I try not to imagine it."

She had said that when she first heard him speak she thought he was from Ireland. He had smiled. It made him feel better not only just to look at her but to listen to *her* voice, in which there was still some of the drawl of Virginia.

"Have you been too worried about Deacon to write?"

He shook his head. But he told her that the thought of losing Deacon had somehow led him to wonder if he would burn what he wrote no matter how good he thought it was. She looked perplexed. "I've been thinking lately," he said, "that the burning might be the most important part. Maybe I write only to keep myself supplied with pieces of my life that I can burn."

Perhaps, he said, his book would be finished when it was literally "finished." Done when it was gone. Perhaps he was slowly ridding himself of the urge to write.

She said it sounded like a gradual form of self-destruction. He thought about it. When he burned the pages, he felt frustrated, angry, but ultimately—he couldn't find a word for it.

She had a friend among the governesses whom she was certain she could trust, she said. Her room, and all the other rooms in the wing, were empty in the middle of the afternoon.

"There's a daybed by the window," she said. "We can sit on that and talk and still keep watch on the outside steps."

But the curtains were closed when he got there. At first, the window was the only thing other than her that he was able to make out in the gloom. She was sitting on the daybed, at an angle to him. He sat beside her.

He looked at her lips. It would have been necessary to bend forward no more than a foot to press his own against them.

She looked as if she was not wearing a corset. Her dress had shifted to one side and he could just make out a measure of bare skin beneath her hair. As he drew her towards him, she rose so that she wound up sideways on his lap. She put her arms around his neck and rested her head on his shoulder, her forehead against his cheek.

As she nestled against him, he brought one hand up and brushed her hair back from her face, her mouth and neck. He inclined his head with the intention of kissing her, expecting her to raise her mouth to his, but she remained as she was except that she held him tighter and pressed even harder against him, then pulled away so that, for an instant, he thought she meant to get up.

Her hair was not red. It was orange. The colour of a blasted tree. Thick tangled strands of it hung down across her cheeks and some of it was wet and matted to her forehead.

He was startled by how warm and soft her shoulder felt beneath his hand. He thought of how bereft he had been for so long of something so nourishing.

"Tug on my dress," she said, staring at his throat. "Just tug and it will slide down off my shoulders." He did as she said and she pulled her arms out of the sleeves until the dress, beneath which she was wearing nothing, was bunched around her waist. She held out her arms and he pulled her to his chest.

It was fall now, coming on to winter. Van had not spoken to Landish in months about his proposal. Landish hoped—and knew his hope to be in vain—that he never would again. Van was waiting, perhaps trying to wear down Landish.

It was almost a week since the night in the Rume when Van proposed that he leave Deacon with him. Landish had found himself staring at Deacon whenever he could without the boy noticing. And he saw him undefined by his relation to anyone or anything, a nameless, timeless child who existed in a kind of pure present, ever-ongoing, never-changing. The soul, unless you believed it was a register of sin, would be like that, wholly without context, inviolate, unaltered by a journey that ended in the Tomb of Time.

He remembered the look in Deacon's eyes when they lived in the attic and he had told him he was going out but would soon be back. And no matter how many times he broke his promise that he would never get decks awash again, Deacon believed him when he crossed his heart and hoped to die. Each betrayal hit, surprised and hurt

Deacon like the first one. Nothing but another promise that Landish knew he wouldn't keep could console him.

But Landish doubted that he could manage without the boy. Not even the company and love of Esse would sufficiently bolster his spirit to make up for the loss of Deacon. On the other hand, he wasn't sure he could manage *with* the boy, even without Van's threat to scuttle his every endeavour hanging over them. He didn't want the boy to end up as the mass of people did, spending their lives at work from which they earned just enough to keep their bodies strong enough to do more work. He could think of no future that he was confident Deacon would even survive into adulthood, let alone enjoy, if he left Vanderland.

Sometimes, lately, at twilight, he would walk for an hour or so searching for clarity in his thoughts. He would stop on a height of land and survey the great house, the hundreds of columns of blue smoke rising straight up from the chimneys when the evening wind died down. And there would sweep over him the certainty that he was but a fleeting incongruity that would leave no sign in this place of ever having been here.

They went out walking on the Deer Park bridle path. Landish said he wasn't decks awash, but he was groggy from the brandy in the Smoker that evening. Landish put him on his shoulders. He hadn't done that for a while, so it felt special. There was snow along the edges and the trail was wet and muddy in the middle. Deacon grabbed Landish by the hair so he could lean back and look up at the sky. The snow had fallen straight down like it almost never did in Newfoundland, large flakes of the kind they used to get just before it rained. But large ones didn't turn to rain when there wasn't any wind, and the evening was very still.

He bet the first stars were out between the Blue Ridge and the Smokies.

"How much day is left?" he asked.

Landish said you couldn't get lost on a path this wide or trip on one this flat so it wouldn't matter how late it was when they turned back.

Landish said he might go away.

Deacon knew what he meant, but he said, "Where will we go?"

Landish said he wasn't sure but he might have to go away for a while by himself. Not to go away for ever, like Mr. Vanderluyden had said, but just for a little while. And Deacon would be fine and well looked after, and play with the Blokes and Goddie. Then he'd come back to see him.

His voice was like it was the night he went out by himself to steal the hat. When he told him what to do if he wasn't back by the time the sun came up. Or when he went out to visit one of the Fair Ladies and pretended he was looking for food to eat. Deacon's heart beat fast and he thought he might be sick.

"How long?" he said. Landish said that sometimes you could never tell. It all depended on things you couldn't know until after you were gone.

He said the two of them should leave tomorrow, pack up everything, say goodbye to everyone, and ask Mr. Vanderluyden to give them tickets like before so they could take the train to somewhere else this time, go back the same way but get off at one of the places that looked nice when they didn't know where they were going.

Landish asked how they would get by. You couldn't make a go of it if you had no money, no food, nowhere to stay. He said he'd never last in any kind of job that he could get and even if he did, how would he take care of Deacon? He said Deacon deserved better than a life of barely getting by or worse. Deacon said they would find another wealth inspector who would give them vouchers and they would walk around looking for odd jobs like they did before.

Landish said Deacon was too young to understand. You couldn't spend your whole life in an attic.

Deacon said he could.

He told Landish to put him down, but Landish took hold of his legs and said no because he might run off, get lost in the woods and freeze to death. Landish said he would be better off without him. Landish sounded like he was crying.

Deacon said it wasn't his fault that Landish stole Captain Druken's stupid hat back from the man he gave it to. He said he bet Landish had to leave because of Captain Druken's hat. They had to leave the attic because Landish stole the hat. They had to leave Newfoundland and come all the way to Vanderland just because Landish wouldn't let the nobleman keep the hat even though he gave it to him. And now Landish was leaving again, and maybe the hat already arrived and Mr. Vanderluyden had it and he'd steal the hat again from Mr. Vanderluyden. Nothing mattered to him but the hat.

Landish stopped walking. Deacon pulled his hair with one hand and drummed on his head with the other. Landish pulled him off his shoulders and carried him in his arms so tight he couldn't move. He tried to get away but Landish wouldn't let him.

Landish said nothing was decided yet, nothing was decided. Deacon cried and Landish told him not to. Don't cry, Deacon, don't cry. I won't leave. I changed my mind. I promise.

Deacon squirmed until he faced away from Landish. He threw back his head and hit him in the face. Landish dropped him.

Deacon landed on his feet and ran from the path into the woods where it was darker. "Stop, Deacon," Landish shouted. "Don't run too far, I'll never find you." Deacon kept running. He was lower than the lowest branches. He didn't have to duck. There was light enough for him to see the trees.

He heard Landish cursing. Deacon hoped he was bumping headfirst into everything, getting scratches on his face. Soon he couldn't hear him. He must have stopped so he could listen for him. Deacon stopped. He counted to a hundred twice until he was sure Landish had gone back to the bridle path.

Deacon wasn't sure which way to go. He ran until he couldn't see the trees in the deepening darkness. Then he walked with his hands in front of his face. He came out on the slope that led down to the stream that ran into Lake Loom. Olmsted's stream. It was easy to find. The water was silver because of the moon.

He could walk around Lake Loom and then keep going straight until he reached the wall. Goddie said the road was just outside the wall. He wasn't sure how far it was. Maybe farther than the Crosses. It was so cold and the moon was so bright he could see his breath. Palmer said that if you knew the sky well enough it became a kind of map that you could use to get where you were going, especially at sea but even in the woods if you went high enough above the trees to see the stars.

The lake was frozen and covered in snow except where it was broken by the stream that went beneath the ice about six feet from shore. He might make it to the wall if he could walk across the lake, but he didn't think he would if he had to walk around it. There wasn't a path. There'd be no moonlight in the woods. There might be other, deeper streams that he couldn't cross or that he might drown in like Landish almost did when they lived on Dark Marsh Road.

Landish said he weighed so little that if he walked on water it would only come up to his ankles.

Deacon stamped on the ice with one foot. It cracked and water bubbled up. The ice was not much thicker than glass. He bet that in the daytime you could see right through it. He wished he could skate across. Goddie had skates but Landish had never bought him skates. It wouldn't take long to skate across if you knew how.

He looked up at the moon. It wasn't in the same place as before. It would get orange and bigger as it sank below the Ridge. Then there would be nothing but the stars. He looked behind him at Vanderland, high up on the hill. More than half the lights were on. He wondered what the Blokes were doing and where Landish was. He wished he was in the Smoker listening to Landish making fun of Sedgewick. But then he thought about what Landish told him on the bridle path and he knew he was lying and was going away for ever. He looked up at the sky and shouted "Landish!" It felt as if he was shouting at the stars.

Having alerted a blacksmith that Deacon was missing, Landish ran towards the lake. He blew on his hands to keep them warm and wondered why he hadn't thought to wear his gloves. He imagined that the last of those who had ventured out to take the air were heading back to Vanderland and thinking of the fires they would soon be seated by. He trailed Deacon's footprints down the slope to Olmsted's stream, then followed the stream to Lake Loom, to the very edge of which the footprints led.

On the lakeshore, there were prints pointing every which way and trampled on by other prints, as if Deacon had turned round repeatedly, hoping for a clue from his surroundings as to what he should do next.

There was a small, dark patch of ice about a foot from shore, a faint concavity from which the new snow had been melted by water that had seeped up through the cracks. He thought Deacon had likely tested the ice with his boot to see if it would hold him. There were no other dark patches, just the open channel where the current of Olmsted's stream carried out into the lake.

A line of footprints led away from the trampled patch of snow to where the shoreline was broken by the stream. There were no footprints on the other side. Deacon's prints led to the water's edge. They ended there.

He wondered if the boy had slipped and fallen while trying to cross the stream, slipped and struck his head on one of the large rocks that rose up from the surface. The current looked strong, but he doubted that the water was much past Deacon's knees. But there was no telling how abruptly the water deepened where the current met the lake.

Given what the boy weighed, he would only need to fall forward a few feet, perhaps while trying to get his balance, to have wound up in water deep and fast enough to carry him out into the lake. He might have gone in just minutes, or even seconds.

Landish couldn't make out the end of the channel. It was possible that the boy had stayed afloat long enough to bring up against the ice, possible that he was still there, soon to go under and out into Lake Loom, but still alive, his face and hands pressed to the underside of the ice.

He took off his coat and boots and waded into the channel. He was soon waist-deep in water so cold that when he tried to shout the boy's name he couldn't make a sound. He'd be over his head before he reached the ice. He looked around. A side current might have carried Deacon under the ice closer to shore, under the ice on either side of Landish. It would be too dark under the ice to do anything but blindly try to find him with his hands. He could smash the ice to pieces with his fists for all the good it would do the boy. He tried to shout again but barely managed to croak out Deacon's name.

The boy might not be in the lake. But he could not otherwise account for the disappearance of his footprints from the snow. He looked across the ice at the far, moonlit shore.

It would be wholly his fault if the boy was gone. He would hear the accusations of many in his dreams, but the loudest of them all would be the boy's. There could be no pardon for losing Deacon to his father's fate, for losing the son entrusted to him by the widow of Carson of the *Gilbert*. He would not be able to go on if the boy was gone. He would not have been able to if he were wholly blameless, but most of what the boy had said on the bridle path was true. He thought of Deacon running downhill to the lake in the darkness. As alone in his last moments as his father must have been. Running because, having been betrayed, he could think of nothing else to do. Everyone must go alone to the place from which no one knows the way back home. No exceptions, not even for children. Not even for a

boy who was half the size of other boys his age. He wished that he had
never said such things.

"LANDISH."

At first he thought his name came from far out on the lake, perhaps
even from the other side of it. He heard it twice more and realized
that it was a diminishing echo.

He turned slowly, chest deep in water, trying to keep his footing
on the slick rocks of Lake Loom.

Deacon thought he could run back into the woods and get lost on
purpose for a while. Landish had told him what to do if he got lost in
the winter at night. He'd made him memorize the rules. Number one
was don't get lost. Number two was don't pretend you're not lost
when you know you are. Number three was stay put but don't stay
still. Mark off a room-sized space and never leave or lie down in that
room. Start a fire if you can, sing songs and picture what your room
will look like when the sun came up.

He was at the water's edge. If he went in, he would feel it soaking
through his clothes. They might never find him, never know for certain
that he died. Forever lost like his father, Carson of the *Gilbert*. Another
cross without a grave. Just a marker like his father's in the cemetery
on the windy hill below Mount Carmel. He would see what Landish
saw when he went through the ice. Like a pie crust from inside the pie,
Landish said. But he'd rammed his way up through the ice head first,
emerging like someone who had climbed up from the bottom of the
river on a flight of stairs. But Deacon knew he wasn't strong enough
for that. He wasn't strong enough for anything.

Deacon saw himself in the lake. All but for his head and arms.
Hanging on, clinging to the wet and slippery ice, head tilted back as
he tried to shout while he was gasping from the cold. Landish would
blame himself.

It was cold, but he didn't feel cold. His heart beat like a bird's. He was so warm he was sweating. His clothes were wet and sticking to him like they did when it was hot. He pulled his pants away from his skinny, good-for-nothing legs and his shirt away from his belly and chest. He bet that he was red all over. Moonlit mist rose from the open channel in the lake made by Olmsted's stream. Even in Carolina, nothing looked colder and darker than open water in winter.

Landish had picked him but didn't want him anymore. Landish had picked Esse. Landish and Esse, without the nuisance of a puny runt like him. Landish asked Mr. Vanderluyden to take him off his hands. He'd said in the attic that Captain Druken's hat was something called his inspiration, and it didn't matter where it was, or whose it was or even *if* it was, as long as he remembered it. Landish and Esse would take Gen of Eve away into Just Mist and Deacon would never see the three of them again.

He would walk up the stream, in the stream so Landish would see his footprints in the snow, leading to the stream. There'd be no hole where he went through, so they would think he had walked down the stream into the channel like Goddie walked down the steps into the swimming pool in the basement of Vanderland. Landish would think he had done it, walked into the lake and disappeared beneath the ice. He stepped into the stream. The water was shallow, but it was so cold it made his shins and ankles ache. He kept going until trees closed in above the stream from both banks. He couldn't see a thing when he looked upstream or at the sky.

But when he turned around, he saw the lake, moonlit, bright. It made him wish he hadn't tried to make it look like he went in. He decided to go back and climb up the hill to Vanderland and The Blokes. Landish might be there. He waded towards the lake, trying to go fast but having to drag his feet through the water because he couldn't lift his legs high enough to clear the surface. He heard from far up on the slope what Mr. Vanderluyden called his wolf pack. But they were just dogs. He wasn't afraid of them. Even if you walked right through a pack of them all they did was sniff the ground. No one went out hunting after dark, not even when the sky was clear and the moon was full, but the dogs sounded like they did when they had the scent of something. He heard a gunshot and the voice of someone he thought must be shouting at the dogs that were getting closer to him. Through the bare branches that blocked his view of Vanderland, he saw torches coming down the hill. "Dea . . . con," someone shouted, dragging out his name as if they thought he was a thousand miles away. It echoed round the lake. He tried to call out, but he couldn't. He tried to wade faster but the water was deeper.

Emerging from behind the branches, he saw Landish coming at him from the lake. Landish walking out of Lake Loom the way he walked out of the river.

Deacon began to run towards him, stubbed his foot on a rock and all but dove into the channel where the running water met the lake. His head went under. He breathed water through his nose and mouth. He got to his hands and knees, coughing and snorting. The back of his nose and throat burned like they did when he woke up in the night-time with a cold. Dick and the happy couple hurt so much he grabbed them with both hands.

He slipped and went under again. This time he couldn't find the bottom with his hands or feet.

Landish saw nothing but the snow-covered lakeshore and an upstream grove of cedars. He didn't know who had shouted to him, but it had sounded like someone older than the boy, though perhaps that was owing to the sound of the rushing stream.

"DEACON."

It came from high up on the hill behind the house. He saw the lights of torches and heard the excited barking of Van's harriers. He

chested shoreward, against the current, barely making headway. He
lost his footing, fell backwards and went under. He was soon standing again, spitting, wiping his face, pushing his dripping hair aside,
lips quivering.

Through a film of water, he saw Deacon emerge from the darkness
where the branches of the cedars closed above the stream, stagger-
ing as though on his last legs, arms pumping though he was barely
moving, wading almost silently with hardly a ripple in front of him
or a wake behind.

"Jesus, Deacon," Landish cried just as Deacon toppled face first
into the stream and went under.

Landish plucked him from the water by his hair with one hand. He
took him in his arms and thrashed his way to shore.

A horse with Van astride it stopped just short of them.

"Give him to me," Van said, but Landish shook his head. Van dismounted and tried to take Deacon from him, but Landish pushed him
away so hard that Van fell onto his back, skidding in the snow. The
horseman just behind Van pointed a pistol at Landish. It was Mr. Trull.

"For Christ's sake, Trull, *don't*," Van said. "You'll hit the boy.
Landish—take the horse."

Landish put Deacon on Van's horse and climbed on behind him.
They rode along the shore, taking shortcuts along the lake, the horse
galloping through the ice and water and snow spraying up around
them. Mr. Vanderluyden's best horse. The best one at Vanderland. He
held Deacon's small body hard against him with one arm. The speed
of the horse uphill made it feel as if the wind were blowing through
them and he tried to shield the boy from the cold. His clothes were
glazed with ice, and so were Landish's, though not frozen solid yet,
like they were after he fell through. The harriers followed them barking in mad pursuit. They went past men holding torches aloft, and
Deacon opening his eyes for a moment thought he was looking at the
Golden Queen in New York.

The horse went instinctively where horses weren't allowed. She followed a trail through the orchard that Landish hadn't known was there, tore through the Ramble, raced across the rear court where Goddie had played croquet in summer with her Cronies from New York. Landish thought she would gallop straight across the Esplanade, but she turned sharply at the corner of the house and stopped in front of the steps that led up to the tree-high doors of Vanderland.

Van's version of what happened was the talk of Vanderland. They talked of Deacon Carson Druken who had bolted while walking on the bridle path with Landish, run off into the underbrush because of something Landish did or said. Landish, who gave chase but couldn't catch him, ran back to the stables where he found the blacksmith still at work to announce that with a cold night for which he was ill dressed coming on the boy was missing and would freeze to death if not soon found. A search party comprising every man at Vanderland, including Mr. Vanderluyden, spread out in all directions from the house, on foot, on horseback, wielding torches, shouting Deacon's name. Mr. Vanderluyden found him, it was said, fished him by the hair from the waters of Lake Loom just as he was going under. A blacksmith saw the boy dive into the lake at the mouth of Olmsted's stream. Another second and he would have disappeared beneath the ice, dead by his own hand though he was but a child. Landish hit Mr. Vanderluyden and would have hit him again if not for Mr. Trull. Mr. Vanderluyden rushed Deacon back on horseback to the house where the boy was administered to by the Vanderland doctor, who put him in a metal tub of near-boiling, mentholated water by which the boy was revived from the torpor induced by his immersion in the frigid lake.

"I'm sorry," Deacon told Landish. "I ran up the stream so you'd think I'd drowned. But then I changed my mind."

Landish understood that the boy hadn't really known how much he would frighten him. He didn't know, and hopefully would never know, how it felt to bear the blame for someone's death. Captain Druken was to blame for the death of the boy's parents, and Landish almost to blame for the death of their son. And maybe Van was to blame for Vivvie. Deacon couldn't know that he would recall the sorrow and dread of this night no differently than if Deacon really had been lost and his remains recovered in the morning from the waters of Lake Loom. And it seemed to Landish that the boy's belief in him was likewise lost, not since a few hours ago but since some moment whose passing neither one of them had noticed, perhaps as long ago as Newfoundland.

Deacon said he hadn't even meant to get wet above the knees. He said it was mean of him to make it look as if he had drowned himself. He said his teeth were going like a typewriter when they put him in the tub.

"Mine, too," Landish said.

"But it wasn't as bad as falling in the river, was it?"

Landish shook his head.

They didn't talk about the argument they had on the bridle path.

"Did you think I was a goner?" Deacon said.

"I wasn't sure."

"What would I do if I had a fever?" Deacon said.

"You'd look right through me," Landish said, "as if I wasn't there. You'd make accusations against the furniture and try to start a fight between the bedposts. You might remember something from the Murk."

"What?"

"Your mother maybe. But you'd forget her when the fever went away."

"Why did my father stay with the men of the *Gilbert* if they were goners anyway?"

"I think it would have been hard just to leave them there, knowing they were watching as you walked away."

They tried to make jokes but they didn't laugh. Deacon said they don't have winter here. Landish said that winter here was like October in St. John's. Three months of October. Nothing here would grow as high as Deacon if you planted it in Newfoundland. The sound of the wind would keep the Vanderluydens awake for weeks. Landish said the ice on Lake Loom was covered with tiny footprints that led to tiny holes where foolhardy mice had fallen through. Deacon said Goddie laughed and held her belly when he told her that after one storm, there was nothing left above the snow on Dark Marsh Road but chimneys.

Deacon and Landish were quiet. Deacon knew they were stuck for words. He lay down on his bed, his hand in Landish's, and said, "Tell me a story."

"All right," Landish said.

Deacon sailed from Atlastica on the S.S. *Carson* with a wizard named Landish. They crossed the Antic Ocean to the coast of Wonderland where, in a storm, the *Carson* sank. Deacon was borne ashore on the back of Landish. They went to Wonderland, to the Fortress of the Forest, and stayed with Good King Padgett, who was once Landish's best friend but was a very sad man now. His queen offered a reward of a million Vanderbills to anyone who could break the spell cast on the king by Landish. Landish was in love with the Mistress of the Fortress of the Forest. He told her and Deacon that one day all three of them would return to Atlastica and they would never leave again. But no one, not even Landish, knew the way back to Atlastica, for its location was ever changing. Deacon and Landish didn't even know how much they liked Atlastica until they left and saw the way things were in Wonderland—

"Esse is the Mistress of the Fortress of the Forest, isn't she? The one Landish is in love with."

"Yes, she is."

"Did you make a contribution?"

"No. Well——"

"You love her more than me."

"I love you, Deacon. Not more not less. I love you."

"I've been with you a hundred times as long as her."

"That's true."

"Will you get married?"

"Someday, I hope."

"You're going away without me."

"No."

"Yes you are." He withdrew his hand. "I'm going to sleep now."

At six-thirty, Mr. Henley came to The Blokes to take Deacon to dinner. Deacon followed him down the stone steps of the grand stairway, through the breezeway and the Winter Garden.

The butler went the wrong way, the way he went when he was taking him to the Rume to visit Mr. Vanderluyden. Deacon thought about telling him Goddie was waiting for him in the Lesser Banquet Hall but he knew he wouldn't listen. He stared up at the butler's back as they went past the tapestries. He saw the closed doors of the Rume ahead. Light from the fireplace that was bigger than the Druken mausoleum flickered through the crack between the doors. The butler, without even slowing down, took the handle of each door and pushed them open. He did what Landish said was called standing at attention as Deacon walked past him. Inside, Mr. Vanderluyden was sitting in front of the fire.

"Hello, Deacon," he said.

"Hello, sir," Deacon said. "Goddie's waiting for me for dinner."

"You're having it here tonight. Goddie's having dinner with her mother, so you'll be having it with me."

A table with one chair facing Mr. Vanderluyden was set before the fire. The butler took the handles of the doors again and walked backwards from the room, pulling them to as he went.

"Actually, I won't be eating, but I'll sit with you," Mr. Vanderluyden said. "I've never had what people call a healthy appetite for food. I eat enough to keep from getting sick, but food doesn't really interest me. But I'm sure *you're* hungry. You always are. I don't know where you put it all, do you?"

"No, sir."

"Are you feeling well after your adventure in Lake Loom? No chills?"

"No, sir. It was an accident."

"It wasn't an accident that you were down by the lake alone on a cold winter night. You must have been very upset about something."

Deacon was silent.

"Well, sit down."

Deacon took the silver covers off the bowls and plates. There was soup and bread and lamb chops with mint jelly and potatoes with specks of parsley that Deacon tried to scrape off with his fork but couldn't. He ate quickly, licking the last crumbs of butterscotch cake from the back of his spoon.

"There," said Mr. Vanderluyden, "all done?"

Deacon nodded.

"Come sit in the chair beside mine. Don't worry about the chimney witch. You know she won't show herself unless I'm here alone."

Deacon sat in the chair and watched the leaping flames around the huge logs. The fireplace was the biggest one in all of Vanderland.

"Mrs. Vanderluyden will soon be staying in New York. She likes it more than Vanderland. Goddie will be staying here. Don't tell anyone until I say you can."

"Landish and I were in New York," Deacon said. "I didn't like it. Landish didn't mind the big Golden Queen and the Eel Train, but I did."

"The El Train," said Mr. Vanderluyden. "We built it. The Vanderluydens."

"I'm sorry I didn't like it. I had a dream about it."

"Well, that's all right. I don't like New York either. It's all dust and mud and horse manure and streams of human vermin in the streets."

A log snapped loudly and sent out a shower of sparks.

"Deacon, what do you think Landish would rather be, your father or a writer? If he had to pick one."

"I don't know."

"Why do you think Landish can't write and burns all his words?"

"He can't put people into words."

"Why not?"

"I don't know."

"Maybe it's because of you. I don't mean that it's your fault, really. It's not his either. He tries to take care of you because your mother told him to. Because he feels he's to blame for what his father did. But Landish didn't take away your parents. His father did."

Deacon nodded.

"Landish can't take care of you. He admitted it to me. That's why he gets drunk at night and leaves you to the Blokes. And carries on with a governess."

Deacon began to cry. He turned his head away from Mr. Vanderluyden.

"I'm sorry," Mr. Vanderluyden said. "I know that you like Landish and he likes you. But what if you'd both be better off without each other? It would let him write so he didn't have to burn the pages every day. That's why Mrs. Vanderluyden is going to New York, because we make each other unhappy. It's the same with you and Landish."

Deacon didn't answer. It was hard to stop crying once you really got going.

"I would like you to stay here with Goddie and me. You could live here in this house, not just in The Blokes but in the whole house. All of Vanderland would be as much yours as mine. As would the name of Vanderluyden. Deacon Vanderluyden. And someday, when I'm gone, it would *all* be yours. Goddie's a girl, so you would be my heir. Your parents would be very proud of you, and very happy that you were living in a castle and not in an attic. Think of your mother, Deacon."

"Can she see me from the Tomb of Time?"

"Of course she can. Well. It's getting late. You should go back to The Blokes or Gough will worry. Think about what I've said. What it would be like to have the run of Vanderland, to play here and live here, *and* make Landish happy. And remember, don't repeat a word of it to anyone. It's our secret."

"All right."

"Just let Landish think you had dinner as usual with Goddie and don't mention we met here in the Rume."

Landish had adopted him and now Mr. Vanderluyden wanted to adopt him. Deacon Vanderluyden. Because Goddie was a disappointment.

He wouldn't want to stay with Landish if Landish didn't want him, if Landish would be better off and happier without him. "Go, Landish," he imagined himself saying. "Go away. I'll be all right. I'm sorry I made you so unhappy."

Landish accepted Van's invitation to ride with him on Sunday afternoon on the trail around Lake Loom. As a stablehand was tacking up Van's horse, Landish walked about, waiting for him, wondering what he was up to now.

"Am I being taken off into the woods to be done away with?" Landish said, as Van walked up to him.

"I told you that if your life and Deacon's depended on it, you would let me have Deacon. I said nothing about doing away with anyone."

Van mounted swiftly and easily. He cantered along the paddock fence while a stablehand led Landish's horse across the yard and another boosted him into the saddle by making a stirrup with his hands. The horse was much bigger than the one he was used to. She was old with not a gallop left in her according to the stablehand, but his usual horse had been chosen earlier by a guest who had left early in the morning with a hunting party that would not return until after dark.

"She's a plodder," Landish said to Van, as he came up alongside him.

"She was once our finest horse," Van said. "She's not often chosen anymore. No one picks her anymore, as Deacon would say. I thought she would enjoy getting out. This might be her last time around the lake."

They set off in the dappled shade of a canopy of leaves towards Lake Loom.

"How is your book progressing?" Van said.

"You've brought me out here to talk about my book?"

Van shrugged.

"It's not progressing. On the contrary. It's as though the typewriter removes letters from the pages, pecks them off and eats them."

"How many pages would you say you've written?"

"Thousands."

"And all of them burned." Van laughed. "Some of what you wrote at Princeton was very good. Do you still have that mad play, *Nutstewyou?*"

"I still have it in my head. Every word."

"Yes, I expect a lot of people do. Your victims. I've given up on the book I told you about."

"Why?"

"I feel especially absurd when, while I am writing, I look up from my page at the thousands of volumes that surround and tower over me, and that make the single sentence I am trying to construct seem so inadequate by comparison with the millions in those books that have been judged worthy of eternal preservation. But I have many consolations. What's one unfinished book compared to Vanderland? But you have nothing *but* your book."

Van urged his horse into a trot. "I'm going to ride ahead a bit," he shouted over his shoulder. "I'll come back to meet you. I won't be long."

Landish tried in vain to goad his old horse along. But moments later he saw Van riding back towards him at a canter. Slowing his horse to a trot and drawing back lightly on the reins with one hand, he stopped in front of Landish. In his other hand, he held Captain Druken's hat box balanced between him and the saddle horn.

The wood and the silver clasps gleamed as they never had before, not even when the hat was in his father's care. He hadn't really seen the hat the night he stole it. It had been too dark in the nobleman's house, and he had carried it away in a sack that he had handed over to the wealth inspector waiting in the shadows for him at the end of Dark Marsh Road. There had been no time to linger over the exchange of the hat, let alone inspect the hat itself. Now the precious laurel wreath of sealers gleamed in the Carolina sunlight as it rested on the saddle of a horse in the otherworldly woods of Vanderland, in the possession of the young man who had once befriended him at Princeton.

"Surprised, Landish? I told my people to work on it as if it were going to be displayed in one of the galleries. I've had it for the last month. You went to a lot of trouble for a mere hat, Landish."

"So, it seems, did you. What do you want, Van? I see old Trull hovering as usual, with his pistols no doubt."

"Exactly what you want, I think. For Deacon to be happy."

"I don't care about that hat."

"Yet you had it shipped here from thousands of miles away. I bought it from a Mr. Nobleman who wrote to me, telling me that it had been stolen from him and would soon arrive at Vanderland. His intent in contacting me was mercenary from the start. So he dropped his claims easily for a certain sum.

"There is a man—I understand he is a social welfare inspector— whom Mr. Nobleman referred to as your accomplice. He's still inspecting, still living with his wife and children. I had some inspecting done up there in your home town myself, Landish, in these last few months. In such a place it was not hard it seems for Mr. Nobleman to get wind of the many letters your accomplice was receiving from Vanderland. With some of these in hand, he confronted him and he confessed.

"So I have a proposition for you. I can have you sent back to Newfoundland, where you and he will both stand trial. Or you can simply leave without the boy.

"I'd hoped it wouldn't come to this. I'd hoped you'd see the sense of leaving Deacon here with me. But I don't think you ever will. I'd hoped to cause the least unpleasantness, for Deacon's sake.

"You had only to let Mr. Nobleman keep the hat. Much would be different then. I would have no way to take Deacon from you. The two of you could have simply walked away from Vanderland. To what, God only knows, but whatever your fate, it would have been one that you freely chose. But you, *you* could not renounce the hat. You could have come to Vanderland free and clear of your past, which is more than I was able to do. Deacon is fortunate to have been picked by you, Landish. Other men would have said good riddance to the hat and made Deacon the primary motive of their lives. In which case, he would never have risen above the drab, ill-fated mass into which, by mischance, he was born."

"What now, Van?"

"You can meet with Deacon and say a proper goodbye. Or you can cause Deacon great anguish by forcing Mr. Trull to escort you back to Newfoundland where you and your accomplice will be tried and found guilty and go to jail."

"I know now whom I'm dealing with."

"I am very fond of Deacon, even more so than I am of Goddie who, as you know, is not my daughter."

"Deacon is not your son."

"Nor yours. He will soon get over you. Sooner than I did. If you do the sensible thing. We'll go back to the house by the vineyard and inside by the cellar door." He tipped his hat to Mr. Trull. "Keep your eye on him. He looks like he has a mind to make a fuss."

In the Smoker, Deacon sat with the Blokes. At dinner, Goddie had been the same as always. She was Goddie the Bad for a while. She told him he'd be a Bloke when he grew up, but not at Vanderland because there'd be no need for Blokes when she was gone. All the Blokes would be turned out and wind up God knows where. They wouldn't just stay in The Blokes until they died, like Palmer would. Then she started crying and said she felt sorry for the Blokes. Deacon wondered if Mr. Vanderluyden would let the Blokes stay in The Blokes when there was no one left for them to tutor. He might if Deacon was still there and asked him to.

The others had left the Smoker and gone to bed. Landish sat in a chair before the fire. He looked around. Three windowless rooms. He couldn't hear a sound from outdoors, nor any from inside the house except those of Gough preparing for the night, whose shadow he could see beneath the door.

He was trapped, now, with no choice but to leave Vanderland without Deacon. He tried to convince himself that it was for the best. He thought about the attic and the privations that Deacon had assumed were commonplace. He thought of how it would be for Deacon if his having a roof over his head ever again depended on a man as small-souled as the nobleman, or someone even worse. He prayed that never again in his life would Deacon have to curry favour with or be polite to a man like Hogan.

At Vanderland, all that he couldn't do for Deacon, or protect him from, would fall away. What the boy had so far suffered and endured would sink into the Murk.

But it might take less than Landish going to prison to make Deacon fret himself to death. Whatever assurances Landish gave him, Deacon would think it was his fault. There would be no convincing him that Landish would not be poor and perish like a dog that no one could afford to feed, that he would not be lonely in the nighttime when the wind came up and it sounded as if the walls were caving in, that he would not be sad when he remembered Deacon. Unless he could give him a lifetime of reassurance in the few minutes or hours that Van might let them have to say goodbye, the boy would fret and mope and pine until the knobs of his backbone were poking through his belly.

Van had sent him two bottles of cognac. He swore to the Blokes that he would only have a taste. He drank both bottles.

"I've thought it all through," Landish told Van the next night, after being summoned to the Rume. "You're right. I'm leaving Vanderland without Deacon, so better that I do so in the way that least upsets him."

"It's for the best." Van smiled. "You'll think so, years from now."

Van extended his hand but Landish ignored it.

"There is another matter, another person involved."

"Another person without whom you'd hate to leave."

"Yes."

"Yes. And I thought Gertrude's was the worst-kept secret at Vanderland. A governess. A governess of all things. Sedgewick and others have told me. You have apparently done a poor job of hiding your infatuation with this girl. You and your governess will soon leave in the Packard. A good thing I taught you how to drive it."

"I'd like a few days. I want to say a proper goodbye, not just to Deacon but the Blokes and Goddie—and your wife."

"You'll leave three days from now." Van handed him an envelope. "Money. A lot. Enough to take you and Godwin's governess far from here. Be careful that it isn't stolen from you."

Landish nodded. "Take good care of Deacon."

"I've changed, Landish. I've come to realize the true worth of the lofty sentiments of novelists and poets and artists of all kinds. Such sentiments are merely the means by which we fool ourselves into thinking that we're as noble in life as we portray ourselves to be in books. But when that nobility is tested, it will not stand. You, a sealer's son, must know that. You are hardly a Romantic."

"Perhaps I've changed."

"I think you'll be glad to hear I'm divorcing Gertrude. On the grounds of adultery. I'll never cease to be the laughingstock of Vanderland and New York until I do. Deacon's becoming my son will mean the rebirth of Vanderland.

"So the main reason is that I don't want her to have anything to do with Deacon's upbringing. I'm sure you don't, either. I don't want her interfering or telling Goddie things that she'll repeat to him.

"I won't leave her destitute either. I won't destroy her. I'll find something modest for her in New York, support her in some fashion. I'd rather not be embarrassed by the ongoing spectacle of Gertrude Vanderluyden's decline.

"Goddie will stay here, of course. She isn't mine by blood, but she is in every other way. I hope it's not too late to remove the mark of Gertrude from her.

"It is my hope that Goddie and Deacon will become brother and sister—and great friends. It will do each of them a world of good to have the other as a sibling. It will take some time for Goddie to get used to Gertrude being gone. But she and Deacon can learn much from each other. You know, Landish, I feel more hopeful than I have since I first met you. I believe that most of us will look back fondly on the coming days, however difficult things may be at first."

Landish lay down on the sofa in the Smoker and hoped for sleep to come until, certain that it never would, he got up and tried first to write and then to read, but could manage neither. He sat all night in a chair beside the window, staring out into the darkness until the blue of morning began to show above the Ridge. He went out and walked downslope to the shoreline of Lake Loom. He loved the volatility of the sky in North Carolina. Clouds were always racing in some direction, even on sunny days, as if they were in a panic, all clearing out to somewhere else while they still could.

He looked up at the house. *The premises of my nemesis.*

When the sun was fully up, he went back to the house.

Mr. Vanderluyden told Deacon about bitterness and failure and strong young men who died of broken hearts when they were older because they never had a chance to live out their dreams. He said that Landish had agreed to leave, even though he would miss Deacon and Deacon would miss him, so Deacon could live out his dreams.

Deacon pictured Landish watching as the footman put his carpet bag and typewriter and Captain Druken's hat into the boot of his new motor car—a present from Mr. Vanderluyden. He pictured Landish sitting with Esse in the front seat of the motor car as they drove away from Vanderland. They would go down the winding hill beneath the branches of the trees, between the bare stalks of flowers that grew higher than a man, past the gatepost, through the archway of the main gate lodge, then down the last hill to the bumpy road that led to Ashton.

※

Landish read, yet again, the letter that Deacon had left on his pillow.

Dear Landish:

You picked me. I didnt pick you. A baby cant decide who picks it.
You picked me because my mother made you pick me. But now Im
old enough so Im picking Mr. Vanderluyden. He picked me too.
He says Ill never want anything. Id rather be the ear of
Vanderland than perish of neglect. Youre funnier than him but
youre not too funny when your decks awash. Thats why Gough
gets mad with you. You dont care if someone gets the sack because
of you. Peple are afraid of you because youre big your voice is
loud and you get mad a lot. Youre ten times as big as Goddie and
you made her cry. So I think you should go away and write your
book and take care of Esse and Gen of Eve and your fathers hat.
Be on your merry way. Im glad you told me about the murk and
the Womb of Time.
    Thats all
    Yours truly
    Deacon

Alone in the Smoker, Landish stood in front of the portrait of Gen of
Eve. Gen of Eve and Landish. He looked at his mother's hint of a smile,
her dark eyes.

His mother had left him when he was about the same age as Deacon.
Except that Gen of Eve was not to blame, whereas he would not now
be leaving Deacon if he hadn't stolen Captain Druken's hat, if he had
found some alternative to writing to Van, asking him to help them.

Landish had been left with a man who might well have been
deranged. Now he had no choice but to do the same with Deacon. Even
if he, Deacon and Esse somehow managed to escape from the estate,

they would be indigent fugitives trying to outrun a Vanderluyden. What a futile, harrowing interval of freedom they would have. One from which Deacon might never recover and that might end with Esse standing trial as the accomplice of a thief.

He wondered what Gen of Eve would do, what advice she would give him.

He remembered when there had been just him and his mother in his father's house. Gough had said that she looked tired or something in the portrait. She was pregnant so that might be it. She might have been feeling apprehensive about the sort of life her child would have with Captain Druken as its father—boy or girl, it would have been born a Druken and a Druken forever be. Gen of Eve, she had called herself, a child of Eve, as, in a sense, all men and women were, a child of the first woman who had had no last name, just as her husband, Adam, had none. But she had signed the portrait "Gen of Eve Marcot"—not her married name. "Landish" she had called him. It was an unusual name. More of a last name than a first name. She said she didn't want him to have to share his name with anyone. She could have made up any name but yet she made up that one. Perhaps the woman who coined "Gen of Eve" had had a reason?

He sat at one of the end tables, took a pen and a piece of paper from his pocket and wrote "Landish" on the paper. He tried its anagrams. His land. Island if not for the "H." Maybe she thought "Landish" would incline him to do Landish things and stay away from the sea. He made up anagrams of "Landish Druken" and came up with nothing that made sense. He tried "Landish" with his mother's maiden name, "Marcot." His mother had signed "Gen of Eve Marcot." He had never been certain for what reason. In defiance of the infamous Captain Druken who left her alone so many days and nights, spurned their house and their bed in favour of the *Gilbert*?

Landish Marcot. Then he remembered that she had given him a middle initial. 'B.' Landish B. Marcot.

In no time he unscrambled the letters. He didn't even need to write them down.

"Not Abram's Child," he said out loud, looking at the sketch of Gen of Eve. "It's been in my name all along, waiting to be found."

His father had known. Captain Druken, the man who "brought back" a million seals, had known that he could not bring forward from his wife a single child. He had known that another man had fathered Landish, the boy whom others had taken to be his son and whom he raised as if he *was* his son. Though the last part might not be true. He might not have sent to Princeton a young man he knew to be a Druken, might not have allowed him to renounce the *Gilbert* and refuse to follow in his father's footsteps. He might have forced him to captain the *Gilbert*, or tried to. But knowing that Landish was not his son, he knew what no one else still living knew, that the Druken line had ended, that the apparent line of succession was a sham. And so he had renounced Landish in spirit, perhaps, long before he had done so in practice . . . And had given to Landish a token whose ironic meaning he assumed he would never know, never decipher, the bitterly jestful last vestige of the Drukens, the cuckold's hat, emblem of a dynasty defunct and of the marriage of two who remained "unmarried" and alone until the end.

He walked around the room, went back to the portrait. His very name was a refutation of the Drukens, of the man in whose footsteps it was assumed by all that he would follow, the man whose nature, whose family's nature, he feared he had inherited. He wondered if his mother would have told him when he was old enough to understand.

Gen of Eve. The meaning of the sketch and of her signing it Gen of Eve was that Landish was not Captain Druken's or the other man's son but hers and hers alone. Wholly hers. As if he had no father. Gen of Eve's. *Mother, I have lost him. I have been a vain and vengeful fool. Abram's blood may as well be mine, though yours runs in my veins.*

*The blood of a woman who would have been a fitting wife for Carson of the
Gilbert. You are in me, as I was in you when you drew this likeness of yourself. In my circumstances, what would you do? Not even the half of me that
is composed of you can find an answer. I have lost him, the little boy whose
life has so changed mine, a life I accepted into my care just as you brought
me into yours.*

"I have a present for you," Goddie said, grunting as she dragged out
from beneath the dinner table a large box wrapped in blue paper and
tied with white ribbon. Deacon wondered if it was Captain Druken's
hat, but it seemed much too large for a hat.

"A present?"

"It's for your birthday. Don't you know when your birthday is?"

"Not really. No one knows for sure."

"Well, Mother told me it's your birthday on Sunday when we don't
have dinner together, so I'm giving you your present now. You're not
to open it until you get back to The Blokes. Do you think they'll have
a party for you at The Blokes?"

"They might."

"So here's my present for you. Mother's not as mean as you think
she is, is she?"

"No. What's in the box?"

Goddie shook her head. "Mother says she knows I can't keep surprises. But I hope you like it."

"I'm sure I will. Thank you, Goddie." He pulled the box to his side
of the table.

"I was going to wait until you'd finished dinner, but I don't think
you're ever going to finish it. Henley will carry the box back to The
Blokes for you."

"I'm not very hungry."

"Deacon Carson Druken isn't hungry? You're not sick, are you?"

Deacon shook his head.

He looked at the ribbon-wrapped box. There was a card attached that said "To Deacon from Godwin." Mrs. Vanderluyden's handwriting. It scared him that Mrs. Vanderluyden had given it to Goddie to give to him.

"Maybe we can have a party for you, Deacon. I'll ask Mother."

Deacon nodded.

"You'll be lonely on your birthday unless we have a party." Her eyes filled with tears. "I'm sorry I'm mean to you sometimes. "

He wasn't sure if he was soon to be her brother, but knew he wasn't supposed to say that. He got up, walked around the table, put his hand on her shoulder and kissed her on the cheek. She threw her arms around his waist and pressed her head against his stomach.

The butler carried the box. He went the wrong way again. He didn't make a beeline for The Blokes. He didn't make one for the Rume.

They went down long hallways until they came to a closed door. "This is the convalescent suite," the butler said, putting the box down. "Stay put until someone comes out for you." He quickly went away.

The first words Deacon ever heard him say. It was like hearing Palmer suddenly piping up.

The door opened and a man came out. They were indoors, but his hat was on. His coat was buttoned even though the house was warm. He looked like a constable but he didn't have a badge or a billy club. He had a big moustache like an upside-down horseshoe.

"You go ahead of me," he said, and picked up the box. He nudged the door open with his shoulder just wide enough that Deacon could slide through.

❈

The butler had that morning brought word to Landish that Van was not feeling well and wished to meet him and Miss Esse in the convalescent suite later.

"I will return for both of you at seven," he said formally.

With Landish and Esse behind him, the butler tapped on the door. Gertrude opened it and motioned them inside. Landish noticed Deacon first—sitting, upright, looking white, forsaken, confused— beside a large blue box, and then a man he had never seen before. Then Van sitting wide-eyed on the side of a bed, his arms bound behind his back, his mouth gagged, his feet tied with rope. The stranger was standing with a pistol in one hand, the other hand behind his back.

"Oh my God," Esse exclaimed behind him.

Deacon came across the room to Landish in a rush. Hugging his leg began to cry.

"Captain Druken's hat box," Gertrude said. "As well as what you call Gen of Eve. Packed so that the glass won't break. And also the ring box that Van's father gave to him that contains the missing button from Van's shirt. Presents for all of you. From Van."

"Don't leave me, Landish," Deacon wailed into his trouser leg. "I won't be a constant runt. I'll be nice to Esse. I'm sorry I'm a curse. I liked it more than you did when we lived on Dark Marsh Road. If you *have* to leave me, it's all right. You can live here when I'm big enough to be in charge. I won't be a nuisance then. Mr. Vanderluyden said I'd have lots of money and I can send you money in between—"

"Could someone please keep the child quiet?" the man said.

Esse knelt and took him in her arms. "Shhhh," she said.

Gertrude began to remove the gag tied around Van's mouth.

"Aren't you afraid that he'll shout and be overheard?" Landish asked.

"The convalescent suite is all but soundproofed. I told the servants that I would myself attend to my husband during his illness, which I assured them wasn't serious. Consequently, there is no one within two hundred feet of the suite. This section of the house has been sealed off, all of its doors closed and locked."

"What about Trull?"

"He's at the main gate lodge. As always. Keeping an eye out for you. My husband told him, Mr. Druken, that you and Esse would be leaving in a couple of days, alone. But it seems that Mr. Trull trusts you less than Van does."

"How stupid," Van said, shaking his head free of the gag. "All four of you will hang for this. And then I will have Godwin and Deacon and be rid of you, Gertrude, and you, Landish, just as I'd planned."

"I had nothing to do with whatever *this* is," Landish said.

"We won't be caught," Gertrude said. "I've told Godwin that we're leaving Vanderland. She's delighted. You don't want her. You want merely to deprive me of her. Just as you want to deprive Mr. Druken of the boy."

"In my own house," Van shouted. "Landish, you're involved in this!"

"I came to the convalescent suite because I was told you asked me to. I have no idea what's happening. I only know that that gentleman's gun would work as well on me as it would on you."

"I have no plans to harm my husband," Gertrude said. "I mean only to prevent him from taking Godwin from me and the boy from you. He will soon be the sole permanent resident of Vanderland. He will be miserably alone. That is how it should be."

"Don't be a fool, Landish," Van said. "The police do the bidding of the Vanderluydens."

"LANDISH," Deacon wailed again. He tasted the tears in his mouth and began to cough. He clung to Landish's leg as Landish dragged him farther away from Van.

"You have to be quiet, Deacon," Landish said. "We'll be leaving Vanderland soon."

"Don't worry, Deacon," Miss Esse said. "This man and Mrs. Vanderluyden are helping us."

"Are they taking you against your will, Deacon?" Sweat ran down Van's forehead. "He's too young to understand, Landish. Imagine what he'll think of you ten years from now when he realizes what he might have been, what he might have had, if not for you. And Vanderland is ruined, *ruined*. I should have shored it up completely, plugged up every crack and crevice. Everything that I despise and have all my life opposed has seeped into Vanderland. It slithered in with Gertrude. You and the boy tracked it in on your boots. It was smuggled in and left here by this traitor who holds me at pistol point. Thorpe. Yes, Landish, this is Thorpe, Godwin's father. Landish, help me!"

Thorpe. Landish wondered if the moustache was a disguise. Richard Hunt's second-in-command was back at Vanderland, back from wherever he'd been banished by Van. "Van, I am, like you, being held at gunpoint."

"I have all my life been betrayed by those who were closest to me. My every act of generosity has been answered with contempt. And you, Thorpe, you don't have the nerve to look me in the eye. He once worked for me, Landish. He betrayed me with my wife. In this very house. Gertrude, you're going to run off with a scoundrel who has only come back to you because he has spent the bribe—"

"Sir, we have been in constant correspondence—" Thorpe began, but stopped when Gertrude raised her hand.

"Why bother to argue with him?" Gertrude said. "It's not as if we need his blessing or approval." Thorpe was red-faced but he held the gun firmly. Landish couldn't account for Gertrude's demeanour, her complacent certainty that she and Thorpe and Goddie would somehow evade the Vanderluydens for the balance of their lives. Landish couldn't imagine either of the threesomes living inconspicuously enough to do so no matter where on earth they went.

"With a pair of fools for parents," Van said, "what else but a fool could Goddie be?"

Gertrude smacked Van across the face so hard that he fell back onto the bed.

"Don't," Deacon said and began to cry again.

"Thank you, Deacon," Van said, his voice barely audible as he struggled upright again despite his bound hands and feet.

"Are you and Goddie going to New York?" Deacon said to Mrs. Vanderluyden.

"We're going somewhere. Mr. Druken, the Packard is waiting for you three on the road beside the servants' school. We have to be going. We'll take the service elevator to the basement. You'll leave the way the darkies come and go. That's as far as I'll take you."

"Deacon, stay here," Van said. "You're like your father, Carson of the *Gilbert*, who stayed with his men even though he thought they were done for. So that he could do what? Hold their hands? They had each other's hands to hold."

"Stop it," Landish said.

"What a *waste*. All you had to do at Princeton was accept my invitation. How different things would have been for both of us."

"That's Just Mist," Deacon said.

"Yes," Van said. "Just Mist. Soon your very lives will be Just Mist. Except yours, Deacon. Where are the dead, Deacon? You told me once."

"The Tomb of Time."

"That's right. Gertrude and Thorpe and Landish and Esse will soon be in the Tomb of Time. And you will be brought back to live with Goddie and me at Vanderland. Not everything is lost. Something can be salvaged from the wretched Mist. Gertrude—"

"I mean to leave you with nothing but what you had the day we met."

"It won't be hard for me to find you, Gertrude. You must know that. How fast can you travel? What ship or train will you take? The Vanderluydens own them all. How far can you go? You've destroyed yourself. In no time Goddie will be back at Vanderland. You'll never set eyes on her again."

"Goodbye, Van," Landish said.

Van averted his face. "That day I sat beside you on the bench, I thought I would forever remember it as one of the great days of my life."

"You still can if you choose to," Landish said.

"Go away, Landish. Leave me as you did before."

"Goodbye, Van," Landish said. "Come, Deacon, Esse."

Deacon turned to look at Mr. Vanderluyden as Landish took his hand.

"Don't listen to the chimney witch, Mr. Vanderluyden," he said. "Sometimes you're nice, you picked us from the attic. You should have made a contribution."

"Watch him carefully," Gertrude said to Thorpe. "I'll be back soon. Landish, take the box."

They made their way through parts of Vanderland that no guests and few Vanderluydens had ever seen—narrow, dim, musty hallways with low ceilings, doors just a few feet apart that reminded Deacon of the stable doors, row after row of them, none of them lit. Now and then he heard the sound of snoring or coughing or the murmuring of the voices of domestic staff from inside a room. The floor was made of loosely interlocking stones, some of which wobbled noisily beneath their feet. *The way the darkies come and go.* It was a tunnel that had no ceiling and no floor, just loose planks above your head and a narrow footway made of stones. Drops of water trickled from the whitewashed walls.

There was no one around, as if word had silently spread through the tunnels and hallways of the servants. Esse took Deacon's hand now and said they had to hurry. Landish carried the box containing Captain Druken's hat, Gen of Eve and the ring box in both hands. It was still partly wrapped in blue paper. "Don't say a word or make a noise until we get outside," he said. Light bulbs that were far apart hung from bits of string. Deacon saw a rat, but Landish said that was the least of their worries.

The hallway narrowed. They made their way single file, Mrs. Vanderluyden first, then Landish. Deacon kept a grip on the hem of Landish's coat and Esse kept one hand on Deacon's shoulder.

There were no more rooms. The tunnel came to an end at a wooden door.

"Esse, take the boy outside and wait for Mr. Druken," Mrs. Vanderluyden said.

"It's all right, Deacon," Landish said. "Go outside with Esse."

"It's dark outside," Deacon said. "And you said we had to hurry."

"I'll be out soon," Landish said.

Esse pushed open the door and she and Deacon went outside. Gertrude took hold of Landish's arm, restraining him, and pulled the door shut. She stepped closer to him, close enough that, even in the near darkness, he could see the fear and desperation in her eyes.

"Van is right," Landish said. "Sooner or later we'll all be caught. Why did you involve the three of us in this? Why didn't you just leave with Godwin and Thorpe?"

"Because, you see, there's been a dreadful accident. Mr. Vanderluyden had a pistol in his coat in case he needed to protect himself from you. I will confirm that he always carried a pistol when he went to visit you—a man your size of whose loyalty he had always been unsure. He was not accustomed to firearms. It discharged while he was in the suite with you and me. I am a witness to how, while Van was bending over to retrieve a piece of paper from the floor, the gun went off. A bullet from close range, straight through the heart."

"Thorpe. You won't be believed."

"Perhaps not. But Godwin will be rid of the man she will otherwise always think of as her father. And I have had the help of someone who is not known to be in this country, let alone in Carolina or at Vanderland, so I don't care if I am believed by every person at Vanderland, every person in America, to have murdered my husband, as long as no one can prove my guilt."

"I still don't understand—"

"I included you in case something went amiss. Should Van somehow survive this or, despite his death, should his brothers get wind of his affection and plans for the boy . . . well, he or they could still lay claim to him, and Godwin could still be cheated out of what is rightfully hers. So the boy must go, as must the person in the world I can rely on to do his best to make sure he *stays* away from Vanderland. You are not a guarantee of anything, Mr. Druken. But you are all I have by way of insurance."

"In part, I think you're doing this for Deacon. Almost as much as for Godwin."

"He is a child, but like no other I have known." A tenderness that he'd heard before when she first spoke to Deacon but that still surprised Landish crept into her voice. "However, I love my daughter no less for that."

"But this is murder, Mrs. Vanderluyden."

"Yes." She drew a deep breath, standing to her full height. "Such as he is rumoured to have committed when *he* was but a child. And might well commit again."

"Have you considered what the terms of Van's will might be?"

"I believe I have considered everything, Mr. Druken. I know that Van has named one of his brothers as trustee of Godwin's estate until she comes of age. The will stipulates that she live on at Vanderland until then or else forfeit her inheritance."

"So you will have to live out the balance of your sentence at Vanderland after all."

"I have long thought that I could not bear to spend twelve more years in this living grave, Mr. Druken. But I will stay because I must and it will be bearable without Van. With Goddie and Mr. Thorpe. I have a fantasy. I know it to be no more than that, but it sustains me. Mr. Thorpe knows the inner workings of Vanderland as well as Mr. Hunt's son and far better than my husband. And I have for a long time been thinking of a way by which this prison of a house might be destroyed. A near lake of gasoline for the engines that power the house is stored in the basement. There are boilers the size of locomotives. Thousands of tons of coal and wood. An armoury full of gunpowder and dynamite. It would be something, Mr. Druken, don't you think, Vanderland wrecked, plowed under as Carthage was plowed under by the Romans.

"So much for what I wish could happen. The rest is not a fantasy. I will, after a respectable period of mourning, marry Mr. Thorpe. And I will one day buy or build in New York a house that suits *me*. I am a Vanderluyden by name, by marriage, and all of New York society knows it had better pretend to believe that Godwin is one by blood."

"I can't help wondering what you were like when you married Van," Landish said. "The idealistic, romantic young woman who wouldn't let him near her until he told her that he loved her and sounded like he meant it. Until he said 'I love you' with 'unmistakable sincerity.'"

"I have my daughter. Godwin will be upset when she finds out that Van is gone. But she will get over it. She is young and strong. You didn't think, did you, Mr. Druken, that I'd be content to merely frustrate my husband's plans to take her from me and make the boy his heir? If there'd been no other way, I'd have shot him dead in front of witnesses.

"I have never *been* with any man but Mr. Thorpe whose love for me does not have about it an unmistakable sincerity. Nor does mine for him. But he will do. Now I must be getting back. And you must be on your way. It won't be long before the alarm is sounded. You had better put as much distance between yourself and Vanderland as possible."

She reached inside the sleeve of her dress and withdrew an envelope that she handed to him. "Some money," she said, "to go with what my husband gave you. And I never want to set eyes on you again." She turned and walked away from him.

Landish thought of Van lying dead on the floor in the convalescent suite, a windowless soundproofed room somewhere deep inside the house. Van was once a boy who, rightly or wrongly, had been accused of murdering his sister. He had conceived of and built Vanderland, the

monumental asylum where no eyes dared meet his, and the prospect
from all the windows was of the never-changing mountains of the South,
by whose perfect exclusion of him he must have been affronted. Landish
could think of no life but Van's that had been so entirely Just Mist.

Deacon couldn't see at first because he still had the lightbulbs in his eyes.
But then he saw the motor car beneath the trees beside the school, and
they went quickly towards it. "Let's wait for Landish before we get in,"
Esse said. "He won't be much longer." He took her hand.

The night air was warm. The snow and ice from a week before had
melted.

Landish came out and ran over to them. He put the box containing
Captain Druken's hat and Gen of Eve in the back of the Packard.

"Get in," he said. "Be quick about it."

Esse got in the front. Deacon reached the back door handle but he
couldn't make it work. Landish came around and opened the door, picked
him up and put him in. "Get down on the floor when I tell you to," he said.

Deacon watched in exctiment as Landish turned a crank at the
front of the Packard like you did to bring up water from a well. The
Packard shook, then made a noise and the shaking almost stopped as
Landish leapt into the front seat. The Packard moved a bit, then
stopped, then moved again. Landish cursed and prayed and turned
the wheel a lot. He said he went faster with Deacon on his shoulders
than this contraption ever would. But Deacon heard the crackle of the
tires on the cinder path. Landish said, "Hold on." They made it to the
Esplanade, swerved and almost hit the hedge. "Dear God," Esse said.
Landish said it was bad luck to look back but he and Deacon and Esse
looked back.

"We never said goodbye to the Blokes," Deacon said. He tried to find
The Blokes but he couldn't tell one part of Vanderland from another.

"We'll write to them," Landish said.

They were heading down the driveway now. Landish told Deacon and Esse to duck down at the main gate lodge. No lights were on inside. The bar with the black and white stripes was up. Landish thought he could just make out Mr. Trull at the window of the lodge, staring as he had the day they met at Princeton.

"Not much farther," Landish said. "We'll get rid of this thing as soon as we can buy a horse and carriage."

Deacon looked back and saw some men with rifles running after them.

"They're chasing us, Landish," he shouted over the noise of the car.

The lights of the main gate lodge came on all at once. The black and white striped barrier dropped like a felled tree onto the hood of the Packard. The headlights and windshield of the motor car exploded. Too late, Landish shielded his face with his arm. Esse ducked down onto his lap and he covered her face with his hand.

"Deacon!" Landish said.

"I'm all right. The glass didn't get me," Deacon said.

Landish felt the muzzle of a gun against his temple. He was blinded by the lights of the lodge, but he recognized Mr. Trull's voice. "Get out, all three of you."

"There's glass everywhere," Landish said.

"Then hope for the best while you're getting out," said Mr. Trull.

Landish considered grabbing the barrel of the gun and yanking the rifle from Trull's hands. But smoke was rising from the front of the Packard, and Deacon had seen more than just one man chasing them.

"Be careful getting out," he told Esse. "Deacon, stay put. I'll come get you." Landish shook the shards of glass from the front of his clothes and climbed gingerly from the Packard. He stood face to gun with Trull, who aimed the double barrel at his head.

"I'm going to take the boy from the car," he said. Trull nodded and retreated two steps. Landish opened the rear door and took hold of Deacon who was on his hands and knees in the back seat.

"Your forehead is cut," Deacon said as Landish took him under the armpits and lifted him from the car.

"I'm all right," Landish said. He set Deacon on his feet and took his hand.

Everything within a hundred feet of the lodge was brightly lit. More than a dozen men stood at the edge of the light in a semi-circle, guns pointed at Landish. Two of the men parted to make way for Van, who was breathing heavily. He doubled over, his hands on his knees.

"You stupid murdering fool, Landish," he said. "I gave you yet another chance and yet again you wasted it. You'll hang for this."

"I did only what I was told to do while being held at gunpoint."

"I assure you no judge or jury will agree with you. Miss Esse will also get what she deserves, and Deacon will stay here with me, Godwin and Gertrude, who will contradict your version of what happened. Thorpe will soon be on his way to a place from which not even Gertrude can entice him back to Vanderland.

"They meant to murder me, Landish. She told me so. An accident, she meant to make it seem. And all of Vanderland would have passed to a child, a girl who is not even mine. They would have killed me if not for Mr. Trull, who forced his way to the convalescent suite when he heard from the servants that I was ill. I will not send Gertrude to New York. Not now. She will stay here with me and her daughter in the greatest of the great houses of the world. She will die here."

Deacon pulled his hand from Landish's. He walked to Van, who now was standing erect. He looked up at him. "You can still have me if you let Landish and Miss Esse go," he said.

Van tried to smile. He crouched down to Deacon's height.

"But they've done bad things and must be punished," he said.

"All Landish did was steal a hat someone stole from him. The nobleman can have the hat. Landish doesn't want it anymore. I'll be unhappy if you don't let Landish go. I'll wonder if he's in the Tomb of

Time. I won't be what you bargained for. The chimney witch won't go away. I love Landish. Landish loves Miss Esse."

"And who loves *me*, Deacon? You do, don't you?"

"Vivvie loves you. She'll be glad to see you when you get there. She knows you didn't put the button in her mouth."

"I'll never see Vivvie again. I don't miss her anymore. I loved her, but I was just a boy. I have loved no one since, except Landish. What did loving Vivvie get me? A lifetime of being regarded as a freak whose supposedly unnatural affection for his sister was somehow transformed into a murderous hatred of her.

"As to what loving Landish got me"—he stood, threw open his arms and looked around—"it got me *this*. Near murder at the hands of my own wife and her lover. We have come to this, Landish: you, captured, on my orders, by a posse of men with guns, and me holding forth about love and murder to a child in the middle of the night."

Deacon glanced back at Landish who had his arm around Miss Esse. Deacon turned back to Mr. Vanderluyden and gave him a leg hug. He wrapped his arms around his leg and pressed his head against him. Mr. Vanderluyden didn't put his hand on Deacon's head or run his fingers through his hair like Landish did when Deacon hugged his leg. He tried hard not to cry. Mr. Vanderluyden tried to pull away from Deacon but Deacon held on to his leg.

"I don't want to stay here, but I will. I'm sorry I don't like it here. You didn't pick me first. Landish did. So I won't be yours even if you keep me. But I'll stay here if you let Landish go. He picked Miss Esse—"

"Enough, Deacon. Please," said Mr. Vanderluyden.

Deacon cried harder.

"Van," Landish said, "it is autumn in the heyday of the Drukens and the Vanderluydens. Our winter will be here before most have even noticed the start of our decline."

"Landish used to lug me back and forth on his foot in the attic when we lived on Dark Marsh Road," Deacon said.

Van tried to pry Deacon's fingers from his leg. "Let go," he said. "I won't have you clinging to me like an animal."

"Vivvie would have loved you if she grew up all the way," Deacon said.

Mr. Trull stepped forward, gun in one hand, and tried to pull Deacon away. Together, he and Van pried Deacon's arms and hands from Van's leg.

"Go to Landish," Van said. He fell to his knees and sat back on the heels of his shoes, his hands on his thighs. And so he recounted the last version of the story that Deacon, Landish and Esse would ever hear.

The nurse found the baby just after its bedtime. The whole house was still awake. Van was still wearing the shirt he had shown Deacon which his father had checked for a missing button. There was never any doubt about whose shirt the button came from. The bottom button of the front set, one of two that are worn tucked inside the trousers, one of two that, had they come loose by accident, could not have found their way into the crib. The only question was how the button got inside the baby's mouth.

"I loved Vivvie. I have loved no one since—not even you, Landish, not even you, Deacon—as I loved her."

Delicate, bookish, brooding, weak-willed, easily brought to tears, Van was entirely lacking in the Vanderluyden mettle and robustness that his dory-rowing grandfather and his father so admired. His father, when he was angry with him, often declared that he would leave to Van no more than a father with several sons would be expected to leave to one of his daughters, if indeed he left him anything.

Van's father doted on the baby girl as much as Van did. Unmistakably a Vanderluyden, Van's father said, an object lesson to Van by the age of one, even though a girl, because she grew faster than any of his sons had. Van's father would sing her praises to family and friends, repeating in public that he would leave his money to her and give Van a girl's portion. When he did so in Van's presence, the boy would run from the room in tears. When she died and Van's father discovered that a button was missing from the very shirt Van was wearing, he openly accused him of putting the button in the child's mouth. He might have done Van physical harm had Van's mother not called for her older sons and the servants to hold him back.

"You can't imagine what life in that house was like from then on. I suffered a breakdown. My mother was never able to convince my father that Vivvie's death was an accident, but she pleaded with him not to leave to me less than my fair share of the estate. But there was much talk and speculation about what I might have done. The rumours persist to this day. I've no doubt they were rampant at Princeton."

"I never heard a word of them," Landish said. He shook his head in bewilderment. "Will you never be truthful with me? One way or another, we will likely never meet again. Are you going to leave me forever wondering what I mean or meant to you or what you might or might not have done?"

"Everything that I told you I felt for Vivvie I did feel. But I was terrified that my father would make good on his threats to disown me. I was still a child but I had heard of young men far better equipped than me to make their own way in the world come to misery and ruin when their fathers cut them loose—one who took his life and another who went insane and was committed to some dreadful place and there forgotten.

"I went to the nursery without having decided I would do it, let alone how. It had to seem to be an accident. I couldn't be suspected. But I loved her, so I couldn't bear to touch her, place a pillow on her face, fight her, subdue her perhaps. I knew I could never see that through.

"It occurred to me that the odds of survival would be in her favour if I simply put a button in her mouth. And the idea of letting someone or something else, some other agency, decide my sister's fate appealed to me. I fancied I would not wholly be to blame if she died. If the button did her no harm, if she simply swallowed it, no one would know. If she began to choke and was saved, revived, and the button was found and discovered to be mine, I would at most be accused of carelessness. As I would be if she died.

"So I removed the thread that attached the button to my shirt. I took the button between my thumb and forefinger, held it over her mouth and, when she yawned, simply dropped it in. I didn't have to force it in, didn't have to touch her. She closed her mouth but didn't cough. She never made a sound. She merely looked at me as she always did. I kissed her on the forehead and hurried to my room. I lay, fully clothed, on my bed. I waited, not favouring one outcome over the others. I didn't think or feel afraid. My mind was blank until I heard Nurse screaming."

"Poor Vivvie," Deacon said. He began to cry. "Oh God," Esse whispered and Deacon took her hand.

"There is nothing at my core but guilt. There is otherwise no *being* at the innermost of me. I have nightmares that I was, am, the origin of nothing. Nothing began when I was born and the world will in no way be diminished by my death. I thought I would exist forever, in the minds of those who will one day admire this house and wonder about the man who built it. But I know that other greater men deserve that honour. I only bought their minds. And for me, it is ruined now. All of it. But I once thought that if nothing else you, Landish, were the kind of man who would remain my friend no matter what, no matter if you knew the truth."

"Then why didn't you tell me the truth?"

"I would have if you'd come to Vanderland when I first asked you to. I fancied that if I told you of my secret crime, my guilt would be halved, and that we would share a bond of friendship that no force on earth could break."

He stood up and brushed the dust from the knees of his trousers.

"There is a peculiar kind of loneliness that can settle on you in a place like this at night. Perhaps you've felt it. The darkness. The silence. Or its opposite, the roaring of that awful mountain wind. This is not the sort of place where it pays to live alone."

"Van, I do know what you speak of, that darkness. I left you to die at the hands of your wife. If not for Trull, you would be dead now, and I would be as guilty as your wife."

"My dear Landish. Goodbye. We'll resume our own paths through Just Mist. I'll often wonder what became of you, but I'll never seek you out again. Go. You can read about me and mine and Vanderland in the papers. Take Deacon and Miss Esse with you. And Captain Druken's hat. But give me back the ring box that my father gave me. I'll store the button somewhere in the Rume."

He gave them a carriage drawn by a pair of horses. Deacon and Miss Esse sat up front with Landish who held the reins. They found the road that went to Ashton but they turned the other way. Landish said they would go north all night if they could. He wasn't sure if they were fugitives. They would shadow the train for a while. They would wind their way along the rivers, through the valleys, between the mountains you could never reach no matter if you drove for days. Mountains, he told Deacon, were the opposite of people. They came out of the Womb of Time as big as they would ever be. The mountains in the west were young and strong. They had snow that never melted. The mountains of the east were in Just Mist. They were little more than hills they were starting to forget.

The Blue Ridge and the Smokies. The Appalachians. And all the other names they never knew and never would because there was only one place where they knew the names of everything—and they were going back there now. They were headed home to Newfoundland and Landish thought for the first time that they might just make it.

Landish felt the past, the present, the history, the yearning of a nation that, like Newfoundland, would never have a heyday, passing by them in the dark.

Boswell had said that you should write a biography as if you were taking revenge for a friend. Landish had been doing something like that in his novel, had been adding his voice to that of the many who had condemned the Drukens. Yet he understood the Drukens better than he did the people whose lives they had destroyed. This was what caused his distaste for his own words, drove him to rid himself of them as if he were scraping dirt from long-neglected fingernails. It was pointless for him to assay a depiction of the Drukens in a novel as if he were a literary vigilante. His writer's voice, if it was but one more of accusation, was superfluous.

He thought of the pair of wooden crosses on the hill below Mount Carmel, the unattended grave of Deacon's mother, the unattended plot of Deacon's father. He thought of Carson who stayed behind so that the men and boys would think, long past the point of hopelessness, that there might still be hope. He thought about Captain Druken. He should have gone to see him, forced his way into the old man's house, anything rather than let the oath of disownment be the final words that passed between them.

He wondered if, one day, unable to bear life at Vanderland, Gertrude would make good on her fantasy. He imagined the whole house and grounds ablaze, along with the Pleasure Gardens and the many-coloured grasses of the Ramble, the apple orchards and the forest from which Van chose the trees that would smell the best when he burned them in the Rume. The Rume, the twenty-five thousand books it held, the chess set by which Napoleon whiled away his exile, the survivor of the pair of Ming Dynasty bowls, the gallery of tapestries, the paintings by Renoir and Manet, the sculpture-cluttered living halls, the hanging lanterns and the buttressed dome of the Winter Garden, the principal tower and its stairwell-spanning series of iron chandeliers, the dormers and the windows as high as schooner sails, the colonnades festooned with gargoyles and figureheads, the many terraces, the main conservatory, the master clock above the entrance to the stables, the Greater Banquet Hall, the yellow bedroom and the red one next door that Van forsook in favour of the Rume, the never-seen-by-Landish kitchens, the bachelors' wing, The Blokes—the fall of Vanderland would be reflected upside down in the surface of Lake Loom.

Landish hoped that it would never come to that, hoped that, as Van had said, something could be salvaged. Long after Van had left it, long after his reasons for building it had been forgotten, the great house and its treasury of art would still endure, a commemoration of a dream that would live on oblivious to the circumstances of its birth, to such temptations as those by which Van had been overthrown. It sorrowed Landish to think that, in that parallel, unlived life of Just Mist, the day that Van had sought him out when they were students was, would always be, the first day of a friendship that neither he nor Van would ever spoil, the very meeting of two souls which Van, at least, had guessed was the way to his salvation.

As they made their way home, Landish wrote the first of many words that he left unburned. After reading them aloud to Esse as Deacon slept, he stored them in the box with Gen of Eve and Captain Druken's hat.

Author's Endnote

GEORGE VANDERBILT died unexpectedly while recuperating from an appendectomy in March of 1914 at the age of fifty-two, his personal fortune exhausted but for Biltmore. Cornelia was married in 1924 at Biltmore, the near-exclusive home of her first twenty-one years. She was divorced in 1934 at the age of thirty-four and did not remarry. After George's death, Edith married Peter Goelet Gerry, senator of Rhode Island.

Acknowledgements

DIANE MARTIN, erstwhile and much-missed publisher at Knopf Canada, saw me through the writing of much of this book, and most of my other books. She has been a true friend these past twenty years. She often said she had the best job in the world, and she would still have it if not for an unforgiving illness. Canadian literature has lost a great champion. Diane and her husband, David, now live in their most loved place on earth: Woody Point, Newfoundland. They are Newfoundlanders. Louise Dennys, executive publisher at Random House of Canada, is now my editor. Her graceful and gracious brilliance has helped sustain me over the past year. My book and I owe her a debt that cannot be expressed. Many thanks and much affection to associate editor Amanda Lewis, whose keen eye and wonderful sense of humour were such a boon to me. Sharon Klein, my publicist— what can I say but that you somehow keep on getting both better and younger. Hats off and a cigar to my agent Robert Lescher. Love and thanks to my brothers and sisters, Ken, Craig, Brian, Cynthia and Stephanie. We saw Mom and Dad and each other through it. The six of us together saw them home. A final word of love to Rose, Rose of all my days.

WAYNE JOHNSTON was born and raised in the St. John's area of Newfoundland. His nationally bestselling novels include *The Custodian of Paradise*, which was nominated for the Scotiabank Giller Prize, *The Navigator of New York*, which was a finalist for the Giller Prize and the Governor General's Literary Award for Fiction, and won the Atlantic Independent Booksellers' Choice Award, and *The Colony of Unrequited Dreams*, which was an international bestseller, won the CAA Award for Fiction and the Thomas Raddall Atlantic Fiction Award, was a finalist for Canada Reads, the Giller Prize and the Governor General's Literary Award for Fiction, and will be made into a film. Johnston is also the author of the bestselling memoir *Baltimore's Mansion*, which won the Charles Taylor Prize for Literary Non-Fiction and the UBC Medal for Canadian Biography. He lives in Toronto.

www.waynejohnston.ca

A NOTE ABOUT THE TYPE

The body of *A World Elsewhere* has been set in Perpetua, a typeface designed by the English artist Eric Gill, and cut by the Monotype Corporation between 1928 and 1930. Perpetua (together with its italic partner Felicity) constitutes a contemporary face of original design, without historical antecedents. The shapes of the roman characters are derived from the techniques of stonecutting. Originally intended as a book face, Perpetua is unique amongst its peers in that its larger display characters retain the elegance and form so characteristic of its book sizes.